I'm almost at the door when I hear a rattling sound and realize that something unfamiliar is *in* the clutch. I open it and peer inside—it's a locket I've never seen before. Silver and shiny, but there's something old-looking about it. I take it out and feel a jolt of energy run through me. A memory, a feeling, flashes in my head: this locket is mine.

There is a tiny piece of paper inside the clutch, too. I unfold it. Written in handwriting I do not recognize is one word:

Remember

www.totallyrandombooks.co.uk

MYSTIC
CITY

THEO LAWRENCE

CORGI BOOKS

MYSTIC CITY
A CORGI BOOK 978 0 552 56764 0

Published in Great Britain by Corgi Books,
an imprint of Random House Children's Publishers UK
A Random House Group Company

This edition published 2012

1 3 5 7 9 10 8 6 4 2

The Random House Group Limited supports the Forest Stewardship Council (FSC®), the leading international forest certification organization. Our books carrying the FSC label are printed on FSC®-certified paper. FSC is the only forest certification scheme endorsed by the leading environmental organizations, including Greenpeace. Our paper procurement policy can be found at www.randomhouse.co.uk/environment.

Set in Griffo

Corgi Books are published by Random House Children's Publishers UK,
61–63 Uxbridge Road, London W5 5SA

www.randomhousechildrens.co.uk
www.**totallyrandombooks**.co.uk
www.**randomhouse**.co.uk

Addresses for companies within The Random House Group Limited
can be found at: www.randomhouse.co.uk/offices.htm

THE RANDOM HOUSE GROUP Limited Reg. No. 954009

A CIP catalogue record for this book is available from the British Library.

Printed and bound in Great Britain by CPI Bookmarque, Croydon, CR0 4TD

For my grandmother,
Eileen Honigman

and

In loving memory of my uncle,
Mark Honigman,
who inspired me with his vast knowledge
of literature and his love of learning,
and who is missed by all

· PROLOGUE ·

So little time is left.

"Take this." He folds the locket into my hand. It throbs as if it has a pulse, giving off a faint white glow. "I'm sorry for putting you in danger."

"I would do it all again," I tell him. "A thousand times."

He kisses me, softly at first, and then so fiercely I can hardly breathe. Rain falls everywhere, soaking us, splashing into the canals that twist through the hot, dark city. His chest heaves against mine. The sound of sirens—and gunshots—reverberates between the crumbling, waterlogged buildings.

My family is drawing closer.

"Go, Aria," he pleads. "Before they get here."

But footsteps are behind me now. Voices fill my ears. Fingers dig into my arms, tearing me away.

"I love you," he says gently.

And then they take him. I scream in defiance, but it is too late.

My father emerges from the shadows. He aims the wicked barrel of his pistol at my head.

Inside me, something bursts.

I always knew this story would break my heart.

PART ONE

But he that dare not grasp the thorn
Should never crave the rose.

—Anne Brontë

· I ·

The party has begun without me.

Slowly, I descend the main staircase of our apartment, which curves dramatically into the reception lounge, currently packed with important guests. Tall ceramic vases line the room, overflowing with roses of every variety: white albas from Africa, pink centifolias from the Netherlands, pale yellow tea roses from China, and roses altered with mystic dye right here in Manhattan to produce colors so electric they hardly seem real. Everywhere I turn there are roses, roses, roses—more roses than people.

I reach behind me for assurance. My friend Kiki gives my hand a squeeze, and together we slip into the crowd. I scan the room for Thomas. Where is he?

"I hope your mom doesn't notice we're late," Kiki says, careful not to trample on her dress. Gold, but not garish, her gown falls to the floor in luxurious waves. Her black curls flow past her shoulders in delicate dark loops; both eyelids are dusted with a shimmery pink that makes her brown eyes sparkle.

"She's too busy schmoozing to care," I say. "You look mag, by the way."

"So do you! Shame you're already taken." Kiki eyes the room. "Otherwise, I'd marry you myself."

Practically all the members of the New York State Senate and Assembly are here, as well as our most prominent judges. Not to mention the businessmen and society folk who are indebted to my father, Johnny Rose, or his former political rival, George Foster, for their own success. But tonight isn't about them. Tonight, the spotlight is on me.

"Aria!"

I quickly find the speaker. "Hello, Judge Dismond," I say, nodding to a large woman whose blond hair is swept up into a tornado funnel.

She smiles at me. "Congratulations!"

"Thank you," I say. Since the wedding announcement, the entire city has been celebrating the end of the war between Thomas's and my families, or so I'm told. The *Times* is going to do a profile on me as a political darling and a champion of bipartisan unity—Kiki's been mocking me about it ever since I told her. *My best friend, the darling,* she says in her best phony newscaster voice. I have to cross my eyes and smack her just to get her to stop.

Kiki at my side, I continue my meet-and-greet duties, floating through the party as if I'm on autopilot. "Thank you for coming," I say to Mayor Greenlorn and our state senators, Trick Jellyton and Marishka Reynolds, and their families.

"Quite an engagement party," Senator Jellyton says, raising his glass. "But then, you're quite a girl!"

"You're too kind," I say.

"We were all surprised to hear about you and Thomas Foster," Greenlorn says.

"I am just *full* of surprises!" I laugh, as though I've said something funny. And they all obligingly laugh with me.

I've been groomed for this since I was born—practicing the art of small talk, remembering names, graciously inviting senators' daughters to sleepovers and birthday parties and smiling even when their horrible, zit-faced brothers pretend to bump into me so they can cop a feel. I sigh. Such is the life of a political darling, as Kiki would remind me.

We make our way along the edge of the party, dodging guests and waiters dressed in white who weave through the room carrying trays of hors d'oeuvres and never-ending champagne. I search for Thomas but don't see him.

"Are you excited?" Kiki asks, plucking a miniature lamb burger off one of the trays and popping it into her mouth. "To see Thomas?"

"If by 'excited' you mean 'about to vomit,' then, well, yes."

Kiki laughs, but I'm being serious—I am full of nervous jitters. I haven't seen my fiancé since I woke up in the hospital two weeks ago with partial memory loss. After my accident.

From a distance, the guests seem happy, Rose family cronies mixing easily with Foster devotees. When I look more closely, though, I can see that nearly everyone is shooting nervous, shifty glances around the room, as if the social niceties will be cast aside any second and the families will go back to treating each other as they always have.

As enemies.

My family has despised the Fosters since before my father's father's father was born. Hating them and their supporters is part of what it means to be a Rose.

Or rather, part of what it *meant* to be a Rose.

"Aria?" A young girl rushes up to me. She's around thirteen, with frizzy red hair and a burst of freckles across her forehead. "I just want to say that it's *so* upper about you and Thomas."

"Oh, um . . . thanks?"

She closes in. "How'd you pull off so many secret rendezvous? Is it true that he's moving to the West Side? Do you—"

"Thaaat's enough." Kiki takes over, pushing the girl to the side of the room. "You've got more questions than you do freckles, and that's saying something."

"Who was that?" I ask Kiki once the girl is gone.

"Dunno." Kiki huffs. "Boy, but do they make 'em *small* these days. And round. She was like a little potato. Definitely a Foster supporter."

I frown, curling my fingers into frustrated fists. People I've never even met seem to know every detail of my torrid affair with Thomas Foster, when I can't even remember *meeting* him, let alone falling in love.

When I was released from the hospital and arrived home, I was told of our engagement. I asked my mother why Thomas wasn't at the apartment, why he hadn't visited me in the hospital. "You'll see him soon enough at your engagement party," she said. "The doctors say your memory might still return—perhaps when you see Thomas, it will all come flooding back."

And so here I am. Waiting. Watching for Thomas, so that I can remember.

Kiki must sense that I'm struggling. "Just give it some time, Aria. You loved Thomas enough to defy everything for him—for now, just trust in that."

I nod at her good advice. But *time* is the one thing I don't have. Our wedding is planned for the end of the summer. And it's already almost July.

Guests move all around me, the women swathed in bright colors, parading their jewelry, tattoos, and mystic decals. The men are mostly tall and wide, with rough-looking faces and slicked-back hair.

A distinguished gentleman I don't recognize approaches and extends his hand. His fingers are rough, calloused. "Art Sackroni," he says.

Nod, smile. "Aria Rose."

He is older, with a handsome, weathered face and the black vines of a tattoo creeping up his neck. The Foster family crest—a five-pointed star—is inked in navy blue above his left eye. "I hope you and Thomas will be very happy together, Aria."

"Me too," I say, half meaning it. Two incredibly large men—one black, one white—stand behind him with puffed-out chests, their bow ties looking ready to burst from around their throats. They, too, have tattoos that snake from under their collars.

"It's not every day a young princess finds her prince," Sackroni says.

It sounds corny when he says it like that, but I'm hoping he's right—that once I see Thomas, it will all come rushing back to me and I'll be thrilled to be marrying him instead of terrified.

I think back to when I overdosed on Stic, an illegal drug made of distilled mystic energy. People take it to feel what it is to be a mystic, to experience super speed, incredible strength, a greater harmony with the world, for a fleeting few moments.

I was told that my parents found me unconscious on my bedroom floor, vibrating as if my body were filled with a thousand bees. I can't imagine how I even got hold of the pills. None of my friends use. But I must have gotten them somehow, and leave it to me to screw things up. It's so *embarrassing*. Rich people in the Aeries do Stic all the time. I can't believe I was so stupid—and so unlucky—that the *first* time I tried it I ruined everything.

I remember almost everything else, like what I ate for lunch one day last month (oysters, flown in by my dad from the West Coast) and how it affected me the next morning (two hours hugging the toilet and tossing them all up). So why can't I recall anything about Thomas?

Thankfully, there wasn't any bad publicity. No one outside my immediate family, the Fosters, Kiki, and a handful of doctors and nurses know what happened. Apparently, while I was in the hospital, Thomas came to my parents and confessed that we'd been dating secretly for months. That we wanted to get married.

Now here I am. I should be happy. Overjoyed. But mostly I'm just . . . bewildered, especially about how well my parents took the news.

"There you are," my father says, guiding me toward where my

mother is talking to Kiki. "Claudia, dear," she is saying, "you look gorgeous. Truly ravishing."

"Thank you, Mrs. Rose," Kiki says. "You look stunning, as always."

My mother gives a small, tight smile. Her hair is sculpted into a French twist, her normally blond locks now a mystic-infused scarlet so radiant I nearly have to close my eyes. Her face is slathered in makeup, designed to attract attention and inspire awe.

I look tame compared to her: my makeup is all neutral tones, my brown hair blown out and tucked simply behind my ears.

"You look good, Aria," my father tells me. "Respectable."

I glance down at my dress, the cream-colored silk, the neckline detailed with tiny blue and pink roses, exposing my collarbone and plunging toward my waist in the back. *Of course I look respectable,* I want to say. *I'm a Rose.* But others are watching, so I thank him politely. He nods but doesn't smile. My father never smiles.

My mother's eyes flash around the room, darting over the grand piano and the series of blue period Picassos, past the windows, whose curtains are drawn back to reveal a moonlit city. Then her face lights up and she sings, "Thomas! Over here."

My *fiancé.*

Thomas happens to be gorgeous, with clear tan skin and short brown hair parted on the side. His eyes are dark, like mine, his lips full and inviting. I recognize him immediately from posts on e-columns and pap shots and whatnot, but he's far more striking in person than on any TouchMe screen. He has a magnetic energy. Any girl in all of the Aeries would be thrilled to marry him. He's worth billions, and one day he might even run the city.

My stomach begins to flutter. For a second something tickles the back of my mind: My hand in another person's hand. A pair of lips brushing against mine. A feeling of . . . warmth.

Then it's gone.

Thomas winks at me confidently. Staring at him now, I imagine how I *could* be attracted to him, how I should still *be* attracted to him, even though my memory gives me nothing. And so I pretend: I smile as my parents do, as Thomas does, as our guests do. Because this boy *must* be what I wanted—I defied my family for him, after all.

"Mr. and Mrs. Rose." Thomas shakes my father's hand, lightly kisses my mother's cheek.

It's incredibly disconcerting. When I was little, if I even *said* the name Foster, I was chastised and sent to my room. And now . . .

I exhale a long breath. It's all happening so fast.

"Aria," Thomas says warmly, pecking me on the lips. "How do you feel?"

"Great!" I say, squeezing my clutch and shifting my hands behind my back. They're shaking, and I don't want him to take them in his. "You?"

He narrows his eyes. "Fine. But I wasn't the one who—"

"Overdosed," I reply. "I know."

This is it? Where are all the memories? I was supposed to remember meeting him, falling in love, and . . . Damn. I'm still a blank slate when it comes to Thomas.

My parents exchange a curious glance, no doubt wondering what I'm thinking, but then things get even stranger: Thomas's parents appear.

"Erica! George!" my father says, as though they are his dearest friends. He draws Thomas's father into a masculine hug.

"Everything looks *beautiful,*" Thomas's mother says to mine. Erica Foster's dress is an emerald green that matches the dozen or so delicate circles tattooed along her neck. "Absolutely breathtaking."

"Thank you," my mother says with a forced grin.

My father takes a champagne flute from one of the waiters and raises it. "Everyone! Your attention, please."

When my father speaks, people listen. Guests stop talking and turn in our direction. The string quartet stops playing. Thomas slips his arm around my waist, and I am reminded of how oddly we are on display. It's a show for all the most important people in the city, but also—maybe especially—for me.

"It is no secret that George and I have had our differences, and so have our families for generations," Dad says. "But that's all about to change. For the better." There's a quick burst of applause—people know what's coming. "Melinda and I are proud to announce the engagement of our daughter, Aria, to young Thomas Foster. A couple has never been more in love than these two."

There is loud and sustained applause—it goes on just long enough that my father has to fan his right hand to silence everyone. This, too, feels staged. I can feel Thomas's hand on my bare arm. He rubs his thumb along the back of my elbow and my pulse begins to race.

"I'm sure most of you were surprised to hear of the engagement. Initially, Aria and Thomas hid their affair from all of us. But admitting the truth had a positive effect: it forced our two families to . . . rethink our rivalry.

"We decided to bury the hatchet. No more will we fight among ourselves. Aria and Thomas have brought us all together using the oldest power in the book: true love. So, Thomas, thank you. And Aria, my dearest darling daughter, thank you, too." My father kisses me on the forehead. I'm dizzy with the attention.

The applause this time goes on even longer, and it's so strong it pounds against me and Thomas like crashing waves. We link our hands and raise them, inciting the crowd to even louder clapping. Thomas's palm is sweaty.

My father's speech has surprised me. He is a con man and a blackmailer, a leader of thugs. Head of a political party that controls half of Manhattan. To him, love is something you use to manipulate the weak.

But now he is saying that true love trumps all. Ha.

"Which brings me to my next point," my father continues, the applause dying away. "There are enemies out there bigger than either of our families, and the only way to confront them is to follow the lead of these two lovers—to stand united! A radical mystic named Violet Brooks has been gaining power. The poor nonmystic families in the Depths mistakenly think she can offer them higher-paying jobs, and the registered mystics support her for obvious reasons: she's one of them. This woman threatens to destroy everything we've built here in the Aeries. As you know, there hasn't been a third-party mayoral candidate since the Conflagration.

"So tonight, in addition to this engagement, George Foster and

I are announcing our political union. In times of danger and mystic threat, we must all come together. Now that Mayor Greenlorn's term is approaching its end, George and I will both be endorsing *one* candidate in the upcoming election: Garland Foster."

Garland, Thomas's older brother, appears next to us and gives a confident wave. He looks like a more mature version of Thomas, only with blond hair and a thinner and slightly more sinister face. At twenty-eight, Garland is ten years older than Thomas, but he's still quite young for politics. His wisp of a wife, Francesca, stands slightly behind him, a delicate hand on his shoulder.

"So please," my father finishes, "raise your glass and let us drink to the beginning of a new era: for my family, for the Fosters, and for this glorious city!"

The string quartet begins playing again, and my father whirls my mother into the middle of the room, which has been cleared of furniture for the party. George and Erica Foster follow.

My father's words echo in my head: *mystic threat*.

Once lauded for helping to enhance and strengthen our city, mystics are now feared. Uncontrolled, a powerful mystic's touch can kill an ordinary human.

Personally, I don't understand what all the fuss is about. These days, nearly two decades after the Mother's Day Conflagration, the mystic-organized explosion that took so many innocent lives, all mystics are required by law to be drained of their powers twice a year, rendering them harmless. Most live far away from us, among the poor, in the lower level of the city, known as the Depths—a place too terrible and too dangerous for anyone from the Aeries to even visit. The mystics in the Aeries are servants or waiters or government workers who don't care about revolution or power. All they care about is earning enough to survive.

But not all mystics are harmless, I know. There are those who went into hiding, who refused to register with the government and be drained of their magic. Who are lurking in the Depths. Waiting. Hiding. Plotting.

Thomas's arm drops from my waist. "I haven't seen Kyle yet," he says.

"Neither have I." My brother, Kyle, despises the spotlight. Parties are *not* his thing. He's probably holed up somewhere with his girlfriend, Bennie.

"Would you like to dance?" Thomas asks. He looks like he really does want to dance, and too many people are watching for me to say no. I hand my clutch to Kiki and step into the middle of the room.

Thomas's hands are slightly clumsy, as though they're unfamiliar with my body. I suddenly wonder whether we've seen each other naked, and feel my cheeks warm.

"I was really worried about you," he says, rocking us gently back and forth. His cologne smells of cedar and the slightest hint of vanilla. The quartet is playing something beautiful and slow by Górecki. "You hurt yourself so badly."

"Other than some headaches, I feel completely fine." *Except for the fact that you're practically a stranger.* I push that thought away, letting the music fill me. Maybe if I dance long enough, I'll remember what it felt like to dance with Thomas for the first time. Surely we've danced together before? My skin tingles with a feeling I can only call anticipation. Thomas is eligible, handsome, and clearly attracted to me. If I'm as in love with him as everyone says, then I'm quite lucky.

"How did we meet?" I whisper so that no one else can hear.

He pulls back slightly. "You really can't remember anything?"

I shake my head.

Ever since I was a little girl, I have wanted to fall in love. The love you see on TV or read about in books, where you find your missing half—the person you were meant to be with forever—and suddenly you're complete. That's the sort of love my parents say I share with Thomas. Why, then, when he touches me, does it merely feel like a touch?

I thought true love would sear me.

My mother appears, slipping her hand between us. "Aria, I need to borrow your fiancé for a moment. Governor Boch wants to speak with him."

Thomas chastely kisses my forehead. "I'll be back."

I watch them go. Is this what my future with Thomas will be—business, meetings, and our parents? My chest suddenly feels constricted, like my gown is too tight.

I need to get out of here.

I scurry along the far wall and press the panel by the balcony. It reads my biometrics and the door disappears, then reappears behind me. Outside, it's blazing hot. My arms and neck and legs are immediately damp with sweat.

The heat, they say, is because of the global climate crisis, the melting of snow and ice around the world and the rising sea level that swallowed Antarctica and all of Oceania. Global warming is also to blame for the canals that line the Depths, filling what used to be low avenues and streets with seawater. Soon, the scientists say, the rising waters will overtake the entire island.

No one knows exactly how soon *soon* is.

I walk forward to the edge of the balcony. Before me is all of the Aeries, so high above the surrounding water it sometimes feels like a city afloat, not even tethered to the earth. A few dozen stories below me are the light-rails; sleek white cars blink in and out of stations, bright blurs between the shadows of the skyscrapers. The skyline is jagged and spectacular, illuminated by the city's mystic light posts: super-tall glass spires full of the mystic energy that fuels all of Manhattan—the only useful thing about those freaks, my father always says.

The spires pulse and glow; there seems to be a rhythm to the way they brighten and fade, a kind of visual music. They almost look alive—more alive, anyway, than the guests here tonight.

I carefully roll up the hem of my dress, step on the iron railing, and then swing myself over. I've done this before, a dozen times when I was younger. It relaxes me. The wind tosses my hair and I can barely see, my hands tight on the railing behind me. Slowly, I lean out, the canals thin ribbons of silver in the darkness below me, the hot wind buffeting me until I am reminded: I fought for true love, and I won.

Now I just have to remember it.

I picture Thomas grabbing my hand, Thomas catching me as I run into his arms, Thomas kissing me in dark corners or in light-filled solariums, but it just doesn't compute. I glance back at the party. From here, it's just a jostle of dark suits and bright dresses, barely visible through the condensation on the glass doors.

Behind me, the updraft catches my skirt, and I laugh as the material billows around me. Enough. Time to climb back onto the balcony, where it's safe.

This is when I see him—a face in the corner that startles me.

I can't tell who he is; the light from the wall sconces barely reaches him. "Hello?" I call. "Who's there?"

I've started to bring my leg back over the railing when my other foot slips.

And just like that, I'm falling.

There is the sharp pain of my knee cracking against the ledge, my chin hitting the railing, my body slipping heavily backward. At last I catch a railing with one hand and clutch it tightly.

My body slams against the building's side and I almost let go, but no: I am suspended over the city. I squeeze tighter. Only my five fingers clenched around an iron bar are saving me from plunging thousands of feet to my death.

I feel sweat slicking my palms, my grip loosening. My heart pumps ferociously and I pray silently, *Please don't let me die. Please don't let me die.*

Then the boy is there. I am crying and my vision is blurry, and it's as if he is there but also not there, like a ghost.

"Grab my hand," he says, lowering his arm.

"I can't! I'll fall."

"I won't let you," he tells me. I blink away my tears but I still can't see his face. I hear the sound of his breath, his exasperation, his fear. "You have to trust me."

With one hand still around the iron bar, I swing the other toward the mysterious boy. He catches it and pulls me up, but my legs still dangle below the ledge. His touch feels incredibly warm, like his fingertips are going to scorch my skin.

"Good," he says. "Now the other."

"I don't think I can," I say. My whole body is aching.

"You're stronger than you think," he says.

I will myself not to look down. I take a deep breath and shift my right hand from the railing into his grip, noticing a starburst tattoo on the inside of his wrist. Then I am up, up, and over.

My feet touch the balcony, and I begin to sob—tears that have been welling in me all night. "Shhh, you're safe. You're okay," he says, and even though it's a billion degrees outside and I've probably ruined my most gorgeous dress, I believe him.

Finally, I feel the pressure of his grasp lighten, and I hear him stepping away. Who is this boy who just saved my life?

I whip my head around, searching for him, but he's gone, as if by magic. I have no clue what he looks like. I never even learned his name.

Just then, a familiar voice calls out. "Aria? Is that you?" It's Kiki.

"What are you doing out here?" she asks, approaching me. "I'm burning up."

I decide to keep what just happened to myself for now. "I was just thinking," I say.

"Well, stop thinking and start dancing! Thomas is looking for you. He says they're playing your song."

"We have a song?" I ask stupidly.

"Apparently. Come on," Kiki says, handing me back my clutch.

I'm almost at the door when I hear a rattling sound and realize that something unfamiliar is *in* the clutch. I open it and peer inside—it's a locket I've never seen before. Silver and shiny, but there's something old-looking about it. I take it out and feel a jolt of energy run through me. A memory, a feeling, flashes in my head: this locket is mine.

There is a tiny piece of paper inside the clutch, too. I unfold it. Written in handwriting I do not recognize is one word:

Remember

· II ·

The next morning I wake before Davida comes to help me bathe and dress. My chin is sore from last night's fall, and my knees are bruised, but otherwise, I'm fine. More than fine, actually—I'm elated to feel something besides a crippling sense of memory loss.

Thomas.

I've been taught my entire life to despise him, but he actually seems . . . nice. Concerned. Sensitive. Maybe if my memory *doesn't* return, I could learn to love him all over again.

I roll out of bed and splash water on my face in the bathroom. Luckily, I've been endowed with my mother's dewy skin and my father's big brown eyes. As I purse my lips in the mirror, I have to admit I look pretty good for a girl who almost died.

I find my clutch and shake out the locket, turning it over in my hands. Nothing about it seems extraordinary. It is smooth, for the most part, with tiny grooves in a sort of swirling pattern. No clasp. It's completely solid.

Maybe it's not a locket at all, just a seamed heart.

I take out the note. Stare at it for a moment. Then I drop the locket and the note back into my clutch, closing them away in my armoire. *Remember. . . .*

Then I sit down with my TouchMe. My parents took it away after my overdose but gave it back to me last night before the party.

I scroll through the various applications to my email. I search for "locket," but nothing comes up. Then I search the messages by date, starting with the most recent ones. A few congratulatory notes regarding graduation and the engagement, but that's it—nothing from Thomas or Kiki or any of the other girls at Florence Academy who graduated with me about two months ago. And there are no texts whatsoever—the memory is almost completely blank.

There's a knock on my door. Davida. I cross the room, my feet sinking into the soft gray carpet, and press the touchpad.

"May I come in?" she asks as the door retracts.

"Of course," I say, and put my TouchMe down. Davida is, as usual, in her uniform of all black: long-sleeved blouse with a dramatic collar, tapered pants tucked into well-polished shoes with no heels, thin black gloves.

The gloves are her personal touch. She has always worn them—since she was eleven, anyway. That was when she suffered a tragic cooking accident at the orphanage where she grew up. I've never seen her hands, but Kyle gave me nightmares when I was younger by imagining what they must look like: *scar tissue halfway to her elbows, the skin marbled and stiff and shiny, like the hands of a movie monster.*

"You're up early," Davida says. Her dark hair is pulled back into an impeccable bun. At seventeen, exactly my age, Davida has the kind of face girls dream of having—wide hazel eyes, high cheekbones, lips that dominate the lower half of her face. Unlike most people in the Aeries, my parents refuse to employ mystics; Davida and the others in our household are all members of the nonmystic lower class. "Magdalena has started a pot of coffee if you'd like some."

Magdalena mostly serves my mother, and she brews the darkest coffee of any of our help—too dark for me. "No thank you, Davida."

I watch as Davida goes to make my bed. She leans down and picks up the end of the comforter with one hand, straightening it with her gloved fingers. "How are you feeling?"

I've heard that question so many times lately that it makes me want to scream. Coming from Davida, though, it's a relief. Technically, she's my servant, but we've never had a formal relationship. Being the same age, we grew close quickly. We're friends. My parents haven't minded that we get along or that we spend time together, as long as she does her work and knows her role in the household. "I'm not sure. I *feel* fine physically, but, well . . . I'm a bit jumbled up."

Davida squints at me. "What happened to your chin?"

I'm about to tell her about my fall when I notice that the glove of her right hand has left sooty prints on my comforter. She sees them, too, and tries to slap the soot away.

Odd. Davida is never anything but pristine. There's something she's not telling me, and soot like that can only come from one place. "Davida, were you in the Depths?"

Just then, my mother strolls in. "Good morning, Aria," she says. "Davida."

Davida straightens. "Good morning, Mrs. Rose."

"Is it?" my mother asks. Her voice is particularly grating today. "Aria, I'm so disappointed in you. We're lucky the Fosters had too much champagne to notice your behavior last night."

"Me? What did I do?"

"You went outside on the balcony and ignored people."

"Only for a few minutes—"

"This was your engagement party! Acting distant only makes people think you don't want to get married."

"I thought I was acting nice," I tell her, "but if I was acting distant . . . maybe it is because I still don't remember Thomas. I've told you this. You can understand why I might be a little shy."

My mother perches on the edge of my bed and stares at me intently. I'm tired of constantly having to prove my worth, my devotion to the family and to our political ambitions. I always come up short.

"How am I supposed to marry Thomas if I don't even know him?"

My mother waves her hand in the air. "Nonsense, Aria. You *love* him. You snuck around with him in the Depths, betrayed everything our family stood for, and risked your father's anger—and our downfall. It's a shame your own poor decisions have confused what you were obviously once so passionate about."

I'm immediately ashamed. My love for Thomas *must* have been strong. The Depths are a wild, dark place. Going there is dangerous. I wouldn't have risked my life for just anyone.

"Really, though, what's the harm in pushing back the wedding—even just another month?" I ask tentatively. "Maybe my memory will return by then."

My mother's lips tighten, and she says her next words slowly. "Your father and I have done everything possible to help you regain your memory—consulted specialists, procured off-the-market pharmaceuticals. I know it's only been two weeks, but we're trying, and there is more than just your feelings at stake."

Two weeks is not a long time, I want to say, but it doesn't matter. The message is clear: it doesn't matter that I don't remember. I'm marrying Thomas no matter what—and it feels like a death sentence.

"Maybe if I just talk to Thomas, have some time alone with him . . ."

"You *had* time with him, Aria," my mother says. "Last night."

"We weren't alone! That was a *huge* party." If I snuck around in the Depths with him, and they've accepted that, why can't I see him alone now?

"Once you're *married* . . . you can spend as much time with Thomas as you like. Until then, focus on getting better." My mother claps her hands together, and her scowl is replaced by a sunny smile. "You have a doctor's appointment tomorrow, darling," she says, and she sounds like a warmer mother. "We'll be sure to tell him that your memory loss has yet to improve. We all want you to remember Thomas."

She kisses me on the forehead and leaves.

I try not to cry. I *will* remember.

Davida rests a hand on my shoulder. "Come," she says. "Let's get you dressed."

Kiki arrives a few hours later to take me out to lunch. We're meeting up with my brother's girlfriend, Bennie Badino, then attending a plummet party.

"Can I tag along?" Kyle asks, splayed out across a couch in the living room.

"Absolutely not," says Kiki, who is standing impatiently in the kitchen, a Slagger purse dangling from her elbow. She's wearing a knee-length skirt the color of ripe tangerines; her sleeveless beige top is tight across her chest, with a low V-neck. "It's a girls' lunch. If you came with us, it would be . . . a girls' lunch plus a boy."

"I can be a girl," Kyle says. "I'll just pretend to have no common sense and cry all the time for no reason."

"I don't mind if he comes," I tell her, smoothing out my skirt. Kyle and I haven't spent a lot of time together recently—at twenty, he lives at the university during the year, and is only home for the summer.

Kiki throws her arms up. "Doesn't anyone care about the sanctity of feminine bonding over expensive salads?" She stamps her foot. "I refuse!"

"Fine, fine." Kyle gets up from the sofa and runs a hand through his hair. Unlike mine, his complexion is fair; he has light green eyes, blond hair, pale skin. Almost every girl at Florence Academy has had a crush on him at some point. "I'll ring up Danny and ask him to eat with me. And then when you try to come over and hang out with us, we won't let you. Boys only. See how you like it."

"We'll like it just fine," Kiki says, then turns to me. "Now come on. We're going to be late meeting Bennie if we don't leave *now.*" She rushes over to Kyle, kissing him once on each cheek. "It's what they do in Europe," she says. "My mother just got back from Italy. All they do there is kiss on each cheek and eat spaghetti. Anyway, ciao!"

We exit the building and cross the arched bridge that links our skyscraper with the next, then another bridge to the nearest light-rail station. There are stations throughout the Aeries. They're all oversized rectangular buildings made of reflective glass to help block heat from the sun.

Kiki and I step inside—unlike the air outside, it's ice cold in here.

"Come on, Aria. Keep up!"

The station entrance opens into a large waiting area, where people are milling about, meeting friends on incoming cars or simply seeking respite from the heat. On either side of the station is a wall of terminals—one for cars heading uptown, another for cars heading downtown—and lines of people. The lines can get quite long, but the light-rail moves so quickly that you never have to wait more than a few moments.

"Waiting," Kiki says as we're in line and the light above Terminal Four lights up, indicating it's available, "is never as fun as *not* waiting."

A shuttle blinks in almost immediately.

We walk forward and Kiki presses her hand against the scanner.

flashes on a screen overhead. The doors retract, letting her into the car.

"I do love seeing my name in lights," she says over her shoulder.

The doors remain open as I complete my own scan.

ARIA ROSE

flashes overhead as I enter the car.

"The Circle," Kiki announces to the car's autopilot. She plops down on one of the cushioned seats. I sit, too. Even though the rail is incredibly smooth—it barely feels like we're moving at all—I've sometimes gotten nauseated when I look outside the glass and see the city flashing by.

A few minutes later, the doors open at the Circle, the complex of stores and restaurants around Fifty-Ninth Street on the West Side, which we love to frequent. Everything is enclosed in a large glass dome to keep out the hot air, the buildings connected by tiny bridges with mystic slidewalks that move beneath your feet.

When we were younger, Kyle and I would come to the Circle and just stand still, letting the pavement shuffle us all around the inside of the dome. We would look at the shops and smell the food, content simply to watch. These days all we do is see each other on the way in and out of the apartment, if that. We barely even text.

Now, Kiki and I bypass all the stores and head straight to the American, which is the perfect venue for a plummet party. Made entirely of glass, the circular dining room provides a panoramic view of Manhattan, and when you're there in the evening, all you see is blackened sky.

Just as we're about to enter, I turn to Kiki. "Did you happen to notice if one of the guests at the party last night had a starburst tattoo?"

"Hmmm?" Kiki says, half listening and fixing her hair.

"A boy . . . well, someone our age. Who might've had a tattoo on his wrist. Did you see anyone like that?"

"No," Kiki says, shaking her head. "But I wish I had. Sounds hot."

Inside, we're greeted immediately and taken to the front of the line.

"Ah, Ms. Rose," says the host, a young man with spiky black hair. "So good to see you again."

"You too, Robert."

"You must come more often. Congratulations on the engagement." He beams at me. "May I see it?"

"See what?" Kiki asks.

"The ring, of course," Robert says.

I glance at my hands, which are completely bare. Engagement ring. I can't remember ever having one, and yet . . . this seems like such an important detail. I'm surprised my mother didn't make an issue of my not wearing one last night.

"Is our table ready?" Kiki asks, thankfully changing the subject.

"Follow me," Robert says with a bow. "Your other guest is already seated."

I hear Bennie before I see her. "Ladies! You look gorgeous!" Bennie is tall, with legs that go on forever. She has black, shoulder-length hair and skin the color of the caramels I used to eat when I was younger. She's three years older than me—Kyle's age—and while she's not conventionally beautiful, she has a certain spark that draws people. A brazen confidence, a sense of adventure. Plus, she shares my taste in music: bands with boys who sing about broken hearts. Of all the girls my brother has dated, I like her the most.

"Thank you, darling," Kiki says. We exchange a round of kisses and sit down. "I feel more plucked than a chicken," she continues. "I went to the dermatologist this morning and got a pore zap."

Immediately, two waiters—servants from the Depths—fill our water glasses. Etiquette dictates that we not speak to them. As a child, I used to feel guilty about letting Depthshods serve us. I remember once when I was ten, thanking a waiter—both of us were slapped by my mother as a result. I haven't risked it since.

"A pore zap?" Bennie asks skeptically. "I've never heard of that."

"Me either," I say.

"I'm not surprised." Kiki looks around the room as though she suspects someone of eavesdropping. "They're very experimental. I could have dropped dead then and there." She smacks the table. "That's the price we pay for beauty, girls!"

"But what *is* it?" Bennie asks, leaning forward.

Kiki shakes her head. "Sorry, Bennie. Love ya, but you've got butter lips. Can't keep a secret. Once I tell you what a pore zap is, the entire Aeries will know, and then everyone will look as good as I do and I'll have no chance of getting a boyfriend, which defeats the whole purpose of getting a pore zap in the first place."

"Hey!" Bennie says. "I resent that. I do not have . . . butter lips."

"They're so buttery I could rub a piece of bread on them and I'd have myself a meal," Kiki says.

Bennie gasps. "You're so full of—"

"Ladies," I interject, "what is everyone going to eat?" I glance down; each table setting has a menuscreen to touchpad your order. I quickly choose a chicken salad and change the subject, asking Kiki what on earth happened to my engagement ring while Bennie ponders the menu.

"It's being engraved," she says. "Thomas mentioned it last night. Didn't anyone tell you?"

"Oh. No, but that makes sense." I feel relieved. A simple answer.

"If I'd actually known you were even dating, I could have told you that a while ago," Kiki says. "But you're the lady with the secrets." Her voice is tinged with disappointment. She's mad at me for keeping my relationship with Thomas from her, and I understand her frustration.

"I'm sorry, Kiks. If I could remember *why* I didn't tell you, well . . . I'd tell you. But I don't. Don't be mad, please?"

She sighs, scrolling through the touchpad and ordering her lunch. "Fine, whatever. I'm hungry. Should I get the squid? Is squid good?" She presses down with her thumb. "I guess I'll find out!"

Hearing about my engagement ring leads me to think about another piece of jewelry: the locket. Perhaps Kiki knows something about that as well. I catch her gaze. "Did Thomas ever buy me a locket?"

"What's with you and all the questions today? I don't know. Maybe."

"Think," I say. "Bennie, do you remember seeing me with a locket? An older-looking thing shaped like a heart? Vintage?"

Bennie shakes her head.

"Thomas has bought you a ton of presents, I'm sure," Kiki says. "What do you care about some old locket?"

I don't know what to say without revealing too much. The mysterious locket, the cryptic note—surely they are pieces of a puzzle, but I have no clue how to put them together.

"Never mind," I reply. "Just wondering."

The food comes quickly, and the three of us do what we do best: eat and gossip. Bennie wants to know more about the party, since she spent most of it upstairs in Kyle's arms. She's in her third year with Kyle at West University, where all the Rose supporters go. Kiki and I have both been accepted to West, too. Typically, after graduating from high school, people from the Aeries take a year to travel and see the world before entering college.

I'm going to be a wife.

Despite that realization, I find the conversation comfortable, familiar, just as it always was before the overdose, and I'm grateful for it.

And then it's time.

We push aside our plates and stand with everyone else, then are directed to the opposite side of the dining area, which has been roped off. Servers hand out glasses of champagne as people take their spots before the windows.

The plummet party is about to begin.

Because of global warming and the seawater that fills Manhattan's depths, the foundations of the city are eroding. Every year, certain buildings are deemed unsafe because of water damage belowground—to the cement, the soil, to whatever it is skyscrapers rest on. The condemned buildings are abandoned, and a team of demolition experts guides the wreckage straight down so that no one is hurt. At first, these occurrences were feared by those in the Aeries; now, however, they're celebrated.

Really, they're almost beautiful to watch: the corner of a skyscraper suddenly sinks and the building contorts with a low shriek of metal, windows shattering as the stresses reshape the walls and floors. Then the upper floors accordion down to the waters below.

By the time a plummet begins, everyone in the building has already fled to safety—but not always. Sometimes a sinking comes on suddenly, and then workers rush in and try to support the building while rescuers empty the floors.

They don't always arrive in time.

The building we're losing today has been around for over a century, a tall black skyscraper with a mirrored front.

"What do you think happens when the building actually sinks?" I ask.

Kiki rolls her eyes. "It goes into the ocean, silly."

"That's not what I mean." I glance around the restaurant. People are chatting idly, waiting for the party to begin. What must it be like to witness a plummet from below, to live in a world where it rains granite and glass?

"Well, then what?" Bennie asks.

I think for a second. "Everything happens so smoothly from way up here. I wonder what it's like in the Depths. If things get . . . messy."

"Who cares?" Kiki says, shrugging as a trio of girls move past us. "Hey, isn't that Gretchen Monasty?"

"What is she doing here?" Bennie hisses. "She should stay on her own side."

I blink. Gretchen Monasty—her family is a huge supporter of the Fosters. She's pretty, I suppose, with sleek brown hair, almond-shaped eyes, and a nose that scoops to a pointed tip. I've seen her picture on tons of gossip blogs; she's quite the socialite. I'm surprised she's here, but since Thomas and I are getting married, I suppose the decades-old boundaries that divide Manhattan into East and West sides no longer matter.

"Calm down," I say. "It's no big deal."

Even though it sort of is.

A bell rings. Everyone quiets, and Kiki and Bennie and the rest of the crowd gaze out the window at the building that's about to fall. I, however, can't stop staring at Gretchen. I remember my mother's words this morning, and I know what a Rose daughter should do.

"Excuse me"—I lean past Kiki and hold out my hand—"we haven't met, but I thought I would say hello. These are my friends—Bennie Badino and Kiki Shoby." I smile as genuinely as possible. "I'm Aria Rose."

One of the girls standing next to Gretchen—with stringy hair and milky eyes—leans forward. "We know who you are," she says.

Then Gretchen's other friend finishes her sentence: "And frankly, we're not impressed. Don't you think some things should remain how they were—separate? My parents don't like yours for a reason."

The bell rings again and the top part of the building folds in on itself like it's made of soggy paper. Even from inside the restaurant, the noise is tremendous—a harsh shrieking of metal and stone, bending and scraping, the vibrating booms of the floors falling atop one another like heavy rocks banging underwater.

My smile fades. "Excuse me?"

Before us is a cloud of atomized rubble, a dusty billowing where the building used to be. Once the smoke clears, nothing is there anymore. Just a hole in the skyline, like a missing tooth.

I expect Gretchen to apologize for her friend's inexcusable behavior. Instead, she stares at me with disgust. "Thomas was right about you."

Gretchen has hit me right where it hurts: the fiancé I can't remember.

Kiki pipes up, her face beet-red. "I. Have. Never," she says, "witnessed such rudeness from such hideous girls in my entire seventeen years on this spinning planet. You have some nerve." She wags a finger in Gretchen's face and says, "Some nerve." Then she turns to me and says, "Let's go, Aria."

Bennie, who has remained silent this entire time, follows Kiki as she pushes past the rows of people. I trail behind them, focused on Gretchen's mouth, which is wide open. Meanwhile, the building is gone. Everyone around me is applauding wildly, overjoyed by how quickly something can disappear. Am I the only one who wishes things would come *back*?

Later that evening, I stare out the windows in my bedroom. It's dark, and the city lights sparkle like jewels. The sky is midnight blue and streaked with smoky wisps of clouds. The hint of a moon reflects off the silvery webs of the nearby bridges and terminals.

I know I won't be able to sleep. I can't get Gretchen Monasty out of my head, the snotty tone of her voice: *Thomas was right about you.*

Right about what? Was she talking about the overdose or something else?

The locket. The note. Maybe Thomas knows something that can help me, something he hasn't been able to tell me in front of my parents, or his.

I should ask him. I grab my TouchMe, about to call him, when I realize I don't have his number. Odd. Unless I was worried about my parents finding it, so I never put it in there to begin with. I think for a minute. It's not like any of my friends would have his number. Plus—like me and my parents—I'm sure he's unlisted.

I want to pull out my hair or scream in frustration. But neither of those things will solve my problems or bring my memory back.

On the surface, my story is a simple one. I fell in love. I took a drug. I had a bad reaction, and I'm suffering some temporary memory loss as a result.

But if I really think about it . . . there are so many things that don't make sense, questions that beg to be asked and answered—most of which involve Thomas.

I listen quietly, hearing nothing in my apartment. It's just after ten-thirty at night; my parents must be asleep, the servants turned in. I glance back outside, at the starless sky. On the East Side, across the city, my fiancé is probably in his bedroom—and he may very well have a clue to help unlock my past.

The answer, I realize, is simple: I must go to him.

· III ·

Escape is not easy.

A simple fact: every fingertouch scanner that operates every door in all of the Aeries is hooked up to an electronic security grid. The west side of that grid is overseen by my father's security entourage. A system monitors the location of every individual, and the central operators are alerted when certain people of high status—myself included—make a move.

Because the Grid is watched so closely, I'm able to travel around the Aeries without bodyguards. I had them when I was little, but when I turned sixteen, my father granted me my freedom. Or at least, as much freedom as you can have when you're constantly being monitored.

"A true Rose can fend for herself," he told me. Though I'm sure he regretted those words when I started sneaking around with Thomas. Whenever that was.

Just before my accident, Kyle let it slip that the back elevator in our kitchen operates without a fingertouch—it just requires a passcode, which he gave me—and that it goes directly to the sub-entry level of the building. My father and his associates use it when they want their illicit activity to remain off the Grid.

Which is exactly how I want my activity to remain tonight.

Wearing the cloak Davida gave me for my birthday last year, I move slowly down the stairs, across the main floor of our apartment, and into the back elevator. I hold my breath as the door closes.

When it opens, I'm in an eerily bright room—the service entrance. The floor is pristine silver save for a black path that leads outside. I tread softly, hoping there aren't any invisible sensors or hidden cameras. I wait for an alarm to sound, or the security guards to burst in and stop me.

Nobody does.

Outside, I start sweating before I've even crossed the narrow bridge that connects our building to its neighbor. I keep to the shadows as I hurry past the light-rail station, its glass roof shining brightly against the black-blue sky. I can't use the rail. It tracks passengers. Instead, I must take the long way to the East Side to ensure that my father isn't notified of my whereabouts.

A few blocks down is a Point of Descent. While light-rails operate solely in the Aeries, PODs are like elevators to the Depths. Nobody we know uses PODs, only the Depthshod and the mystics who work in the Aeries. Why would anyone ever want to go down to the canal levels unless they absolutely *had* to?

But that snobbery is something I can use to my advantage: PODs run an oldware version of fingertouch—slow, outmoded technology that doesn't interface well with the new software in the Aeries. So it's less likely anyone will be able to track me.

I place my hand on the scanner and am cleared.

The inside of the POD is much dirtier than I imagined. Fortunately, I don't have much time to inspect it closely before we descend.

Despite having lived in Manhattan my entire life, I have only been to the Depths once before, on a closely monitored field trip with the Florence Academy. I remember the awful stench, the people with no homes to call their own and no food to fill their bellies. Everything and everyone was dirty and undesirable. We were told that the Depths were full of people who'd murder us for whatever we had in our pockets.

Leaving the POD, I realize that the Depths are exactly how I remember them: sticky-hot, loud, dangerous. Water gently laps at the foundations of the buildings, a constant sound track as I walk along the raised sidewalks. I move past a row of crumbling brownstones and shops, their windows caked with so much grime I can't even see a hint of my reflection. Everything is darker down here. I don't know where I'm going, but I try my best to not look suspicious. Swarms of people move past, their faces hidden by mist rising from the warm canal water that fills the streets.

I can practically taste the salt water in the suffocating air. Folks pass me by, chatting in loud voices, oblivious to my presence. There's something undeniably exciting about it all—being somewhere I'm not supposed to be late at night, seeing real people live their lives without them noticing me.

Blending in feels good.

A hunchbacked woman with frazzled hair approaches me.

"Spare a few pennies, miss?" I take out some change and drop it into her creased palm.

It feels odd to have real money. Everything in the Aeries is paid for by finger scan, billed directly to the bank. Luckily, I've come prepared, taking a stash of coins I've collected over the years.

I come upon a slight hill, where the old street rises out of the waters and is walkable. I step over a black garbage bag onto the pavement, then cross to the water's edge, where gondoliers sit patiently in their boats, smoking and waiting for customers.

Years ago, the government installed motorized gondolas in the canals. They're operated by gondoliers; this is how most people get around in the Depths. Once I'm on the East Side, I'll ascend via POD and then find a way into Thomas's residence. I may not know his phone number, but the Fosters' home address is common knowledge.

The only real problem is what to say once I'm there. "Why did you talk about me with Gretchen?" is too accusatory, while "Tell me everything you know about what happened to me" is too . . . demanding. I have to play this just right.

But if Thomas knows something, and he loves me, why *wouldn't* he want to help?

A few girls my own age rush past, laughing and calling out. They wear simple dresses of gray and dirty white and washed-out navy. I can tell by their healthy coloring that they're not mystics—rather, they're members of the lower class who live in the Depths. New York City's poor and downtrodden, a population of millions whose votes my parents have never cared about before and now, thanks to Violet Brooks, are terrified of losing.

"How much?" one asks a gondolier.

"Where ya going?"

"East," the girl says. "To Park." The gondolier holds up his hand and flashes all five fingers. The girls hop aboard.

I motion for a gondolier, then gingerly navigate the broken pavement. Careful not to fall into the water, I climb into one of the boats and sit. My skin feels like it might boil, it's so hot; I want to remove my cloak entirely, but I'm too afraid I'll be recognized and reported.

"Where to, miss?" The gondolier looks young—not much older than me—with a sweet face and messy red hair.

"East," I say, just like the girl. "Seventy-Seventh and Park."

He nods and starts up the gondola. There are no oars or paddles, only a tiny electronic wheel. It takes a few moments for us to clear the gondolas ahead, but then we're moving swiftly along the canals and twisting through the Depths. I peer over the side and watch the murky water. It looks far from refreshing: dirty greenish-brown, with a sour smell that turns my stomach.

Noise carries over the canals as we motor along—laughter, music, yelling that alarms me at first but that I gradually realize is coming from a game between two young boys on the street.

"Kids," the gondolier says with a chuckle. "Never a quiet moment."

I can barely hear him over the motorized hum. The gondolier seems nice—young.

We round a corner, and the water-filled canyons between the

buildings suddenly open out into a wide expanse of blue-black sky. The Magnificent Block, I remember from that long-ago field trip. This is the area where the registered mystics are forced to live. In truth, the Block is far from magnificent—dark and dreary, with flimsy-looking tenements one on top of another like stacks of playing cards, peeking out from behind a stone enclosure.

Years ago, this place was called Central Park. I've seen tons of pictures of when it was lush and green and filled with trees. People would come here from every corner of Manhattan to play and picnic and escape the city. But that was before global warming, before the seas rose and hid the park under thirty feet of dirty water. Before it was designated a reservation for mystics and walled off. The parts that remain above water are spectacularly dingy but pretty much invisible to the rest of the city, thanks to the high stone walls and rusty-looking gates that seal off the area.

The divide is quite clear: mystics inside the Block, everyone else outside.

Once we're past the Block, the buildings rise again, and after we cross a few more streets, the gondolier pulls up alongside a raised sidewalk. He loops a rope over a post and draws the boat in so that it gently scrapes the walkway.

"Here, miss," he says. I hand him some coins and he helps me from my seat.

The night air is darker now, save for a soft twilight glow from the numerous mystic spires in the city. I stay to the shadows, where my face will be difficult to see. Those in the Depths hate the Roses *and* the Fosters. Many of them would love to see me dead.

Here on the Foster side of the city, people use strange sidewalks that were built up over the years into steep banks as the waters rose. But the construction was done by citizens, not the city, and the sidewalks are shabby things that are hard to walk on.

I reach Park Avenue and discover that the POD terminal is actually on the other side of the canal. But a short block away there is a footbridge, easy enough to cross. I look up and see the bright towers: the Foster residence. I'm just about to climb the steps of the bridge when I am cut off by a group of wild teens.

There are four boys—all broad-shouldered and thick, dressed in grays and blacks—and two girls standing off to the side, nearly invisible in the shadows of a crumbling abandoned building. Their faces have a pale, hollowed-out look, all sunken cheeks and waxy skin, as if they haven't eaten for days.

The faded awning over their heads reads BROWERS. A storefront of some kind, though judging from the spiderwebs of shattered glass that were the shop windows, this store hasn't been open for years.

The tallest boy, who has rust-colored hair and dull eyes, sneers, "What are ye looking at?" He steps closer, and the other boys close in behind me. The girls just stare.

"You mute?" another boy asks. They all start to laugh. I think again about how people in the Depths would be happy to see me and my family dead, and my hands shake.

"I'd like to pass by, please," I say, trying to sound polite. I realize immediately that *polite* is wrong. *Polite* marks me as someone from the Aeries.

"'Pass by'?" the tall boy repeats in a high-pitched voice. He guffaws. "What are ye here for? Stic?" He pulls out a vial filled with electric green pills. "Good stuff. Promise. Fifty for two."

Stic. Part of me is curious about the pills. I want to see what one looks like up close; maybe it will help revive my memory. But I don't trust these boys.

"No," I reply. Screw polite. I need to sound tough. "Now let me by."

One of the boys moves to the right. In my rush to pass them, the hood of my cloak falls away just as a nearby spire pulsates with energy. The light illuminates my face, and the two girls let out gasps.

"Aria Rose!" one of them says.

"This is so upper," the other one whispers. "No freaking way."

"No, you're mistaken," I say, pulling my hood back up.

"I'd recognize you anywhere." She calls to one of the boys. "Darko!"

I hurry up the stairs, but it's too late: someone rushes up behind me. My cloak is yanked off and the boys surround me.

"Look what we got here," the little one called Darko says. He nudges the tall one with his elbow, then grins. "Isn't it past your bedtime, sweetheart? Does Daddy know you're down below?"

I reach for my cloak, but he tosses it to one of the girls, who squeals and drapes it around her shoulders. "Oh, look at me," she says to the other one, "I'm Aria Rose. Aren't I glamorous with all my fancy threads?"

"Let me," the other girl says, ripping the cloak from her friend. "Ooh la la! I'm Aria Rose. So pretty. So important. Blah blah barf."

They all laugh. I try to stay cool, but everything inside me is screaming that something awful is about to happen. "Very funny," I say. "Now will you let me through? I'm late. Someone . . . People are waiting for me. They'll come looking for me soon."

" 'People'?" Darko asks, baring his teeth. "Like your fiancé? Do you know what a rat he is? What animals they *all* are?"

The tall boy grabs my wrist. "Your families are the reason my parents don't have money. Why we barely have food." He takes something long and silver from within his shirt. "Ever hurt because you're so hungry? Know how painful that is?"

I try to whip away, but two of the other boys hold me still. Slowly, the tall boy turns over my arm. He skims the jagged piece of metal over the pink skin that runs from my elbow to my wrist, letting the edge hover over one of my veins. I am trembling now.

"Please," I say.

He licks his lips with his thick, wet tongue. "Please what?"

"Please don't hurt me."

He tilts his head, looking almost puzzled. Then he plunges the metal deep into my arm.

I cry out, watching as my blood spills down my arm, pooling red in my palm.

He yanks out the metal and holds it up to the light. My blood is black along its edge. "Oops," the boy says, laughing. "Must have slipped."

I close my eyes, willing the pain to stop. I am going to die here. I am going to die for my stupidity.

A rush of wind hits my cheeks.

I open my eyes, and everything before me is different.

The tall boy who shivved me drops to the ground, and the pressure that was on my arms is gone. A ray of green light whizzes by me, nearly two feet long and as narrow as one of my fingertips. The light cleaves the air with a whoosh, and a high-pitched ting fills my ears.

Then I see a second ray of light, identical to the first. It connects forcefully with the neck of one of the other boys, the one with rust-colored eyes, who blows back and falls to the pavement.

This is when I realize that the rays of light are attached to a boy. They must be some sort of mystic energy—which means this is a rebel mystic. Someone who has not registered with the government, who has illegally retained his powers.

The girls back away and turn; I can hear their shoes clobber the pavement as they run. Then I hear the zip of the mystic's rays, so green they're nearly blinding. The mystic whips around me, shielding me from Darko, who has picked up the fallen shiv and is waving it aimlessly through the air.

"Fight like a man, not a freak!" Darko yells.

The mystic just laughs and thrusts his arms into the air. The rays channel into the sky, braiding together from each finger into two thicker beams, one from each hand, like swords of light, wider at the base and sharp at the tip. The pulsing color ignites the sky, casting a greenish glow on Darko and the remaining boy and the lifeless audience of buildings around us.

I am spellbound. I nearly forget that my arm is bleeding. The scene is so magnificent that even Darko stops his slashing and looks up.

This is when the mystic strikes.

In an instant, he cuts the beams from the sky to the ground. The sound they make reminds me of when Kyle and I were younger and used to catch fireflies on the roof, cupping them in our hands and holding them up to our ears. The buzzing is so loud it seems to fill the Depths.

Darko is blasted in the chest. He's tossed nearly ten feet into the air, his arms and legs moving wildly. Then he falls, and I hear the sickening crack of bones.

The remaining boy has a look of horror on his face. He starts to run, but the mystic strikes him in the back—there's a thunderous clap when the green beam finds its target, and the boy flops onto the street.

It's only then that I realize I've been holding my breath. I exhale deeply, filling my lungs, and cast my gaze on the mystic, whose rays have retracted and who is standing in the middle of the street with his hands tucked casually in his pockets.

As if he were anyone. As if he were normal.

Rebel mystics are outlaws. They're dangerous and are to be reported immediately. I know this from a thousand public service announcements I've seen all my life. But . . .

This mystic saved my life.

After a moment, he looks at me and says, "Are you all right?" His voice is deep and smooth as syrup.

I'm shocked by how handsome he is. Clear blue eyes—not as dark as the ocean, but deeper than the sky. Hair that looks touched by the sun, with hints of darker streaks. Thick eyebrows. A straight nose. A square, solid jaw.

"I'm hurt," I manage to say, suddenly feeling woozy.

"Let me see," he says. "Hold out your arm."

He takes my hand in his. A kind of intoxicating warmth spreads through me.

"Hold still." He touches his fingers to the injury. His hand glows from within, like the inner deep burn of a log pulled from a fire. Its radiance throws everything else into shadow—his bones, his skin, his clothing. For a moment he seems to be made of light.

My skin feels sizzling hot. When he lifts his fingers, I see that the cut has healed. Even the blood is gone.

"I—I—"

He smiles at me. It's a beautiful, soothing smile.

"You're welcome," he says. He brushes some of his hair away from his eyes and wipes sweat from his forehead. Then I hear sirens, and a worried look crosses his face. The bodies strewn on the pavement begin to stir. "We need to get out of here before they wake up. Come with me." He wraps a strong arm around my waist and pulls me to him.

So I do what any girl would do when a gorgeous boy saves her life in the seedy Depths of Manhattan: I let him take me away.

· IV ·

"Large cup. Black."

The waitress nods at the boy, then looks at me. There are no menus here in this tiny shop. It is the kind of place I might have walked right by—inconspicuous and dark on the outside, the words JAVA RIVER pressed into the awning.

Inside, though, it is full of light and sound. A handful of plush blue booths are filled with all kinds of people. Mostly families, but there are a few solos eating pastries and drinking coffee. The walls are a creamy color, covered with framed photographs of mountain ranges.

"The same," I say. The waitress—a blob of a girl with curly black hair and a pierced nostril—nods and ambles away.

I give my attention back to the mystic boy who saved me. "Thank you," I say. "For . . . carrying me."

His face is blank, which makes me feel like an idiot. I haven't been carried by anyone since I was a baby. Certainly not a boy my own age. And certainly not a mystic.

But when he took me in his arms and led me away from that

terrible scene, I had no fight left in me. I simply closed my eyes, rested my head on his shoulder, and relaxed. It felt good to be able to trust someone—if only for the length of a few city avenues.

The mystic is still expressionless. His hood is up, covering his hair, making him look like he's trying to travel incognito. He's not perfect. I can see this now. His nose is slightly crooked, as though he was in a fight and never had a doctor set it properly; an inch-long scar runs just above his left eyebrow. His cheeks are light with stubble. He is rugged-looking, the exact opposite of Thomas, whose hair is always combed, his skin smooth. This mystic boy is something else entirely.

He has the kind of face that takes you by surprise. Earlier, on the street, I thought it was one thing—handsome in a conventional way, like porcelain or the colored diamonds my mother keeps in the Rose family vault. But now I see it is quite the opposite, a face too hard to be pretty, too mysterious. It is the kind of face that sucks you in, makes you want to surrender all that you know, all that you are, just to capture its attention.

It is dangerous, this face, this boy. And not simply because he's a mystic, though that is danger enough.

He already has a hold on me. I'm not sure if it's attraction or fear. Or both.

The mystic looks calm. If I didn't know better, I would never guess that he's just been in a fight. He's wearing a red T-shirt and a pair of jeans, and a blue jacket made out of sweatshirt material. He radiates health—and because of that, he stands out here, among other mystics who have had their powers drained.

Typically, those who've had their energy removed have a sickly look about them that I've noted in pictures and learned about in school, and occasionally seen in person. They're drained, of course, to protect us against another revolt like the Mother's Day Conflagration. Without their energy, they can't hurt anyone, and the people who live in the Aeries are safe.

"Where are we?" I ask.

"Java River," he says, pointing to the wall where the name is painted.

"I know *that,*" I say, longing for my lost cloak. I'd hide myself in its folds. No one seems to be paying me much attention, but I feel as though all eyes are on me. On us. Maybe I'm just paranoid. "But where *are* we?" I motion to the window. To what is outside.

He leans back. "Oh. We're near the Magnificent Block," he says casually.

I feel my eyes widen. "We're near the Block?"

"Yeah," he says. "Near. Not *in*. Don't worry, you're safe." He looks at me strangely. "Where did you think we were?"

I can't answer his question, though I certainly didn't think we were so close to the Block. I expected the surrounding area to be a little more . . . run-down, and surprisingly, it's not. The people here look a lot like me. They look—well, *normal.*

"This is one of the few joints we're allowed in outside the Block," he says. "It's not legal per se . . . but the owners here are pretty decent. All the other restaurants and stores have checkpoint scanners when you enter to keep out the mystics."

"Even the drained ones?"

He nods.

"Is that why you brought me here?"

"Sure. Also, I like the coffee."

I look around. Java River's customers seem to come from every walk of life: there are girls and boys my own age who don't seem evil in the least. A group of sandy-haired young men in the window are laughing and playing cards. And at the far end of the long room are a half-dozen oldsters, sipping coffee and watching TV and arguing with each other about what they see there.

Yes, their complexions are wan; their skin is paper-thin. They look weak, fundamentally tired as a result of the drainings. But these people aren't the menacing individuals I've been warned about my entire life—the deviants and drained mystics who supposedly line every street in the Magnificent Block. That is what we were taught at Florence Academy. What I was taught by my parents.

It doesn't seem fair—if they're drained, why can't they go anywhere they want?

The boy seems to be reading my mind. "Not what you expected?"

"No, not exactly."

The waitress comes with our coffee and sets the mugs down in front of us. The boy immediately takes a sip, but I stir mine with a spoon, waiting for it to cool.

We sit like this for a few minutes. I should be going. It's late, and I still need to find Thomas. And yet, something about this mystic is compelling me to stay here.

I clear my throat. "Thank you for saving me. And for . . . my arm."

The unspoken words are: for using your power to heal me.

I don't say them out loud, for fear of who might be listening. Rebel mystics are illegal. These are the people my father hunts down on a daily basis. If he knew I was in the Depths, sitting directly across from a fully empowered mystic . . .

"You're welcome."

He leans forward. His irises are speckled with lighter shades of blue around the edges. He sips his coffee.

"My name is Aria," I say to break the silence.

"Like from an opera." His voice is so soft I can barely hear it.

"Well, yes, actually. My mother's a big fan."

"Any one in particular?"

I squint. "Why, do you know opera?"

"You assume I don't?"

"Well, it's just that—"

"I'm a mystic, so obviously it's impossible for me to have even an *ounce* of culture." His voice is tired, tinged with bitterness. "What do they teach you up there?" He points at the ceiling, but I know he means the Aeries.

"Listen, that was rude of me. I'm sure you're cultured, of course you are. I've just had a bad couple of weeks, and now a really strange night. I'm sorry." I take a big gulp of coffee. "So, um, which is your favorite?"

He stares right at me, and I can see him soften a little. Then the right corner of his mouth twitches just a little, and he breaks into an enormous grin. "I was just teasing you, mostly. I hate opera." He puts his hand over his heart. "I've got more of a rocker's soul."

He laughs as though he's really enjoying himself, and his entire face lights up. I start laughing, too—in fact, I can't stop. It feels so *good*. I can't remember the last time I laughed like this.

"A rocker, huh?" I repeat with a bit of an eye roll, but he knows he's got me. I can see it in his eyes. "So . . . what do you play?"

He gives a quick nod. "Guitar."

"I love music," I say, trying to focus on anything—the floor, the table, my coffee—except how he smells, like smoke and sweat and salt from the canals. "My parents gave me tons of lessons when I was a kid—piano, flute, oboe—but I was never any good."

The mystic raises an eyebrow and looks amused. "I find that hard to believe."

"Oh?"

He looks me up and down, and I feel practically naked; the intensity of his gaze is so strong I can actually feel my stomach churn.

"I'd imagine you're the kind of girl who is good at everything you do."

I know he means it as a compliment, but it makes me think of the overdose. Of failing so completely. Losing my memories to Stic and disappointing my family and Thomas. The scene with Gretchen at the plummet party and the upcoming election.

I shake my head. "Not everything."

"Don't worry about it. I'm bad at tons of things." He offers me a smile while tracing the edge of his coffee mug with a fingertip. It's strange to see his fingers looking so normal when I know what they can do.

"Like what?"

"School," he says. "I was never good at math. Or science. Or anything, really. That's why I dropped out."

I gasp instinctively. "You dropped out of school?"

He chuckles. "There are more important things, you know. At least to some people."

"I suppose," I say tentatively. "So what's important to you, then?"

The boy looks thoughtful for a moment. "Friends. Family."

"That's good," I say, then immediately wonder why it matters to me that we share the same values. It's not like I'll ever see him again.

"And equality," he says, then picks up his mug and takes a long sip. I wonder if that was supposed to be a stab at me. Surely he knows who I am, who my parents are? There's no way a rebel mystic—or anyone from the Depths—could possibly support the Roses and the Fosters. We've been despised by mystics in the Depths for ages—not that we ever really minded, as long as things stayed the same.

I avert my eyes. He must find me despicable, with my wealth and good fortune. Which is disappointing because . . . because why? I glance back at him and I can hear my own heartbeat. Deep down, I know why. I just don't want to admit it.

I like him.

My throat feels dry and scratchy. I'm engaged. I can't like him. I don't even know his name. Thomas's face flashes before me: the richness of his eyes, the honey color of his skin. What am I doing here?

"Aria?"

I look up. "Yeah?"

"Are you okay?"

No! I want to yell, but it's not his fault this conversation is the most comfortable one I've had in ages, that simply looking at him relaxes me. "Are you going to tell me your name?"

He scratches his head, confused, as though he'd been expecting a much more intense question. "Sure. It's Hunter."

I expect him to say more, but he doesn't. "So . . . what else do I need to know about you? We're practically strangers."

Something about the question strikes a chord in him. The muscles around his mouth tense; his posture becomes rigid. The boy I've been talking to suddenly morphs into something harder, colder. He takes out his wallet, removing a few bills and placing them on the table. "No offense," Hunter says, "but it's best if things remain that way."

Then he takes out his phone and punches a few buttons, texting someone.

"Seriously?" I'm confused by the sudden change in tone—one moment we're laughing, the next he's distant, leaving? "I was just attacked. You saved my life. We don't have to be friends or anything, but you don't have to be so . . . so . . ."

"Rude?" He looks up, the pure blue of his eyes still startling. "Look, Aria. You seem like a nice girl, but as long as you're safe, my work is done. My friend Turk is coming to pick you up and take you home. Wait for him here." He narrows his eyes. "Don't come back here, okay? You're safer in the Aeries. Where your sort belongs."

He stands. Simply looking at him makes my heart beat faster. I want him to stay, but there is nothing that ties him to me. We really are strangers. The thought makes my insides ache.

"Goodbye, Aria," he says, and though he's determined, I can tell he's pained.

I sit still, frozen with sadness. Even though he's telling me goodbye, the way he says my name feels like the warmest hello I've ever received.

It's only as he's leaving that I see a tiny tattoo in the center of his left wrist.

In the shape of a starburst.

"Wait!" I slide out of the booth too quickly and fall onto the floor—and now everyone is looking right at me.

"Miss?" someone asks. "Are you okay?"

I get up, shake myself off, and hurry outside. I look around frantically but the streets are practically empty. How did I let him go *again*?

I try to calm my breathing. I wasn't hallucinating—there *was* a boy on my balcony last night, and it wasn't someone who'd been invited to the party.

It was Hunter. He's saved me twice in two nights.

I stand for a few moments underneath the JAVA RIVER awning, hoping he'll return. Then I feel silly for waiting. I'm Aria Rose. I live in the Aeries, and I'm engaged.

Thomas. He's the one I'm supposed to see tonight, and I haven't thought of him once since I saw Hunter.

When I realize Hunter's not returning, I go back inside—my table hasn't been cleared. Behind the cash register, an old woman with grayish skin harrumphs at me, her hair knotted into a bird's nest on top of her head. I sit down to wait for Turk.

Why did Hunter save me in the first place if he didn't want anything to do with me? Without thinking, I stare into my coffee mug and down the scalding liquid in one gulp. I wince. My throat, and my heart, are on fire.

• V •

With a name like Turk, I'm not sure what to expect. This is what I get:

A boy with copper skin and egg-shaped eyes, hair fashioned into a Mohawk, the sides sheared close to his scalp, the top ablaze with color, morphing from black at the roots to bright platinum near the tips. Silver piercings run through his earlobes and his right eyebrow. His clothes are tight and black, long pants and a sleeveless shirt exposing hills and heaps of muscle. His arms are colored from wrist to armpit with tattoos: fire-breathing dragons and dangerous-looking swords, nearly naked women and strange mythological creatures.

He has the same healthy coloring as Hunter—another rebel. His legs straddle a white motorcycle with chrome wheels and black accents on the seat. I've only seen a motorcycle on the Internet and never would have guessed how *big* they are. He spots me through the window and beckons me outside.

On the street, the hot summer air makes me feel like I'm in a sauna. Turk holds out a sleek silver helmet and cocks his head. "You gonna get on?"

He must be kidding. "Absolutely not."

"So you're just gonna hang out here?"

Good point. I have to get back to the Aeries, and I can't afford a gondola—the rest of my money was hidden in my cloak.

Turk extends the helmet a second time. "You seem like a reasonable girl, Aria. Let me get you home in one piece. I'd say you're a bit out of your league."

"How does this thing work?" I ask skeptically, eyeing the cycle. The engine is nearly twice the size of my head, the exhaust pipes polished to a shine. "It looks too big for most of the streets."

Turk laughs. "Let's just say this sucker is . . . enhanced." He winks. "For your riding pleasure."

"Okay," I say, grabbing the helmet and slipping it on. I go to climb on the cycle but there's only one seat—and he's on it.

Turk slaps one of his thighs. "Step on up, sweetheart."

I raise my eyebrows. Turk matches my expression.

I groan. "Don't do anything funny."

"Nope," Turk says, offering me his hand. "Nothing funny about this at all."

He hoists me up and I settle between his legs. He presses a button and a sleek pair of handlebars extend from a slot in the front of the bike.

Turk leans forward, his arms wrapping around me when he grabs the bars. "Ready?" he asks, lips close to my ear, his breath warm and sweet.

"Sure," I say.

"Just tell me where to go," he says.

I whisper my directions as Turk pushes a tiny button and we erupt in flames.

Turk's bike really *is* enhanced. Magical, even.

We tip forward on the narrow streets, so drastically I have no idea how gravity is functioning, so fast there's no time to be sick, veering left, then right, skipping over broken concrete and garbage and shattered bottles, building after building bleeding into each other as we pass.

We whirl and zoom past a fleet of gondolas tied up for the night, sleeping in the black water, their prows knotted to posts along the sidewalks. The cycle is narrow enough to creep over a stone bridge, nimble enough to take hairpin turns in alleyways.

Our only exchange is the way our bodies move with the bike, how Turk's arms are snug around me. I close my eyes and imagine he is someone else.

And then we stop.

The handlebars retract and Turk leaps off the motorcycle, landing with both feet firmly on the ground. I slide less gracefully off the side and remove my helmet—my hair is wet, matted to my forehead. I scrape my fingers through it as Turk watches me.

"What?" I say.

"Nothing. Nice to meet you, Aria."

He's about to remount when I stop him. "Wait," I say, my hand on his arm. "I need to ask you something."

"About?"

"Hunter." He smiles knowingly, and the look on his face tells me he's been expecting this. "I know you two are friends," I say, "and . . ."

"You don't know anything about him?"

"Exactly."

"There's not much to know."

"What's that supposed to mean?"

Turk shrugs. "Hunter's a mysterious guy. If he wants to tell you something, he'll tell you. If he doesn't, he won't." Turk cradles the helmet he lent me under one of his arms. "But do yourself a favor. Just let things be. Forget about him."

Forget. Something I am quite good at, apparently.

"Well, I appreciate the ride, at least," I say softly.

"The pleasure was all mine," Turk says. He straddles the motorcycle, places the helmet in his lap so he can use both hands, and starts the engine. "Be careful. You know what you're doing?"

I glance at the POD a few steps away. His question makes it clear that he knows I gave him directions to Thomas's apartment building and not my own. Granted, we live on opposite sides of the city, so it wouldn't take a brain surgeon to figure out I'm heading in the wrong direction. But at least Turk isn't trying to stop me from going.

"I'm fine. Thanks." I point to the helmet. "Aren't you going to wear that?" I yell over the roar of the cycle.

Turk only smirks. "Of course not." He points to his Mohawk, which has somehow remained unharmed despite our travels. "I don't want to mess up my hair."

Then he's gone, leaving behind a cloud of fast-fading sparks.

Thomas is surprised to see me. Which kind of figures, since it *is* around midnight.

"Aria?" He shoots an irritated glance at the manservant who ushered me in.

"They announced Ms. Rose on the intercom, sir. I assumed you had arranged to meet her." He reminds me of my father's man, Bartholomew—same white hair, same bland features.

"I did no such thing, Devlin," Thomas says. His hair is messy tonight, without any gel. I like it more this way. "You should know better."

"I'm sorry, sir," Devlin says, bowing his head.

Thomas is far from properly dressed—he's wearing a pair of linen pajama pants. His shirt is unbuttoned, and he hides his chest by crossing his arms. It's not the kind of chest that should be hidden: broad shoulders and sculpted pectorals lightly dusted with hair. His stomach is tight and flat. Thomas is more muscular than I imagined, more athletic.

I must be staring, because he reaches over, lifting my chin with his fingers so I'm looking at his face instead of his abdomen.

"What are you doing here, Aria?" He sounds almost unhappy.

"I—I wanted to see you." Which is partly true, but not for the reasons I'm implying. I'm thankful for the cool air in his apartment after being outside in the deadly heat, but my pants and shirt are wet with sweat, and now I'm beginning to shiver.

Thomas purses his lips. "Do your parents know you're here?"

"Of course not." I reach out and touch his bicep. "Why does it matter? We didn't care about them before, did we?" My voice has gotten louder, but I can't help it. "We need to talk, Thomas." I look at Devlin. "Alone. It's important."

Thomas is silent, his face unreadable. Then Devlin says, "Shall I frisk her, sir?"

I step back. "You're kidding, right? Why would I carry anything dangerous?"

"Not harm me," Thomas says. "Harm *you*."

It takes a second, but then I get it. He's worried I have Stic on me.

I'm left with no choice. Devlin pats me down, pressing his hands against my arms and torso and legs. Then he runs a handheld scanner over every inch of my body. Its insistent beeping makes me want to smack someone. I've never felt so humiliated in my life. Thomas doesn't even have the decency to frisk me himself.

Finally, Devlin announces, "Clean."

"I could have told you that," I say with a snarl.

"It's protocol, Aria. Not personal," Thomas says. "Devlin, please take Aria to my bedroom. I'll be there momentarily." He turns to me. "My parents are at a charity function. I need to call them and check when they'll be home so they won't find you here. I don't want you to get into any trouble."

Devlin bows a second time and motions down the hallway. "Please, miss, follow me." Once we are far enough away, he whispers, "Sorry about the scanner, miss."

The Fosters' home is sleeker than ours: simple, clean lines, modern-looking furniture. There is no carpet anywhere; no hardwood floors, either. Instead, each room is tiled in shiny colors. For the first time in my life, I miss my mother's antique end tables, tubular vases, and thick drapes.

Mystic paintings in sleek black frames are spaced throughout the apartment; the colors swirl together as though the paint is alive, moving just enough so that the images never stay exactly the same for more than a few seconds.

I stop for a moment and study one—an oil painting of the city skyline—and watch as the sky darkens from gray to blue to black, then back to gray again. It's stunning, really.

I could stare for hours, but I move on.

Thomas's room is nearly bare—a large bed on a black platform against the far wall. A desk with his TouchMe and a chair that looks more impressive than comfortable. Two framed movie posters—Charlie Chaplin's *A King in New York* and *Cat on a Hot Tin Roof* with Paul Newman—and three long windows overlooking the East Side skyline. The walls are white; the floor is black. A gray lamp with a metal body sits on a nightstand.

Devlin leaves me alone in the room. After a minute or two, I start to snoop.

I press the touchpad next to his closet and sift through his clothes—dozens of pants and shirts and suits and ties, unadventurous in terms of color and style. More appropriate for men our fathers' age than for a seventeen-year-old who just graduated from prep school.

Then to his bathroom, where I search through the cabinets. Nothing odd to report, except for a bottle of mystic headache reliever like the one Kiki carries with her. I leave the bathroom and glance at his nightstand: an aMuseMe and a pair of headphones, and a glass of water. Thomas is neat. Clean. Seems to be hiding nothing.

I'm not sure what I'm looking for exactly—my room has been wiped clean, but surely there must be some proof of our love that he's held on to.

Then I hear hushed voices approaching. Devlin and Thomas. I face the doorway, trying my best to look innocent.

Thomas steps inside and presses a panel on the wall; the door closes with Devlin still outside. Thomas wordlessly slips on a checkered flannel bathrobe from his closet, wrapping the ties around his waist. He hasn't shaved today, and he seems tougher than he did at the party last night. More natural. More dangerous.

I wait for him to continue scolding me. Instead, he sighs and collapses on his bed. He pats the empty spot next to him. "Hi," he says softly.

"Hi," I say back, sitting next to him.

"I'm sorry about before. You just caught me off guard."

"I don't deserve to be treated like that, Thomas. I didn't do anything wrong."

He puffs out a breath. "Oh no? You only took Stic without telling me."

"I'm sorry," I say. "Honestly. I don't remember *why* I did it, but there must have been a reason. But that's not me. You know it's not . . . don't you?"

He scooches closer. "Maybe you were upset about something. I'm just sorry you didn't feel like you could share that with me. I need to be a part of your life, Aria. We're going to be married. We can't keep secrets from each other." He pulls me to him. It feels awkward.

"Are you friends with Gretchen Monasty?"

I can feel Thomas's body tense. "Why?"

"I saw her today," I say, "at a plummet. And she mentioned you, and . . . well, she said that you spoke to her about me, and I'm just wondering what you said. Did you tell her about the overdose?"

Thomas looks offended. "I would never. My parents and I agreed to keep that private, for everyone's sake."

"Would you have said anything else?"

"Absolutely not," Thomas says. "I barely know the girl."

I think back to this afternoon, to what Gretchen suggested. Why would she lie? Then I look at Thomas. Why would *he*?

"Were you anywhere near my clutch? The bag I carried last night?"

Thomas widens his eyes, pressing his hand to my shoulder. "Aria, are you okay?"

"I think so," I say. I can tell he's wary of me now, suspicious of my mental health. I need a different tactic.

I reach for his chest, where his heart is, and feel its steady beat. His breathing is jagged, short. His eyes are wide open.

"Touch me," I say suddenly.

He coughs. "What?"

"Touch my heart."

His right hand moves slowly, as though it's been dipped in molasses, fingers spread so that I can see the spaces between them. Ever so lightly, he presses just underneath my collarbone.

"Lower," I tell him, loosing my shirt and moving his hand inside. His fingers edge over the top of my breast. We both tremble, and I am sure: we have never done anything like this before.

"There," I say. "Can you feel that? My heartbeat?"

He gulps, staring at me. "Yes."

"Tell me a story," I say, closing my eyes again.

"What do you mean?" Thomas asks.

"Tell me about us. Something romantic. Please." Even if I can't remember our relationship, maybe for my parents' sake, for Thomas's sake, and for the love of the Aeries, I can learn to love him.

I try to picture Thomas in my mind, in my memory. His hand is deliciously hot against my body, and mine against his. His chest rises and falls beneath my touch.

Eventually, he speaks:

"Right. Let me see. The first time we ever kissed was in a gondola, at night. Not night, exactly—nearly night. Dusk. You were wearing, um, a short red dress that showed off your legs. We met at our usual place near the Magnificent Block, and then we took a gondola around the city. I stepped in first to help you, but the boat was rocking, and you almost fell right into the water. I caught you, though, and you sort of . . . melted right into me. I leaned down and kissed you. It was like how it is in the movies—sort of slow at first, but wonderful. We were both a little sweaty, and the gondolier was giving us weird looks, but we just laughed at him. We didn't care. We were just happy to be together. I never wanted to stop kissing you, Aria. Never."

I'm about to tell him that I don't remember this when a memory pops into my brain and I go silent. Images from his story begin to color the blackness in my head until the moment comes alive: I am waiting underneath a building with a broken awning near the Block. I remember running to meet someone—Thomas?—and falling into the gondola, just like he said.

The images unfold out of nowhere, but they are so vivid it's like I'm seeing them in Technicolor. It's dazzling. Then my memory of Thomas goes blurry. His features go liquid and rearrange themselves, his nose lengthening, eyes broadening and tightening, lips stretching into a scary grin. When he moves, there is a delay, the rest of his body microseconds behind his head.

I shake my head hard, and everything fizzles out.

Gray.

White.

My mind is a blur, and then it is blank.

I open my eyes and I am back in Thomas's room, on his bed. We are still touching, only his hand feels heavy now. My palm is sweaty and I lift it from his chest. "Weird."

"What's wrong?" he asks, looking concerned. "Are you okay?"

"Not really," I say. "Something just happened to me. Something—"

The sound of shattering glass interrupts me. There in the door are my parents, standing with shocked expressions on their faces. My father is in a dark suit, his dress shirt open at the neck, the knot of his yellow and blue tie loosened. A water glass is in pieces on the floor. I must have knocked it over.

"Aria, you're leaving. Now," my father says, letting out a growl.

Thomas sits up and distances himself from me on the bed.

I turn back to Thomas. "You called my *parents*?"

In a flash, my father is there beside the bed, grabbing my shoulder. His fingers dig into my flesh; I yelp, then stifle my scream. There is no use in fighting—I've been caught. I glare at Thomas, boring a hole into him with my eyes.

I feel incredibly betrayed.

My father drags me down the hallway and out of the apartment.

I don't question it when we descend into the Depths instead of taking the light-rail across the Aeries. Stiggson and Klartino, two of my father's men, walk behind me; I follow my parents down a tiny, trash-strewn street to a broad canal—Lexington Avenue—lined with docks where gondoliers wait for fares. They glance at us, curious, clearly struck by the oddity of our presence.

My father finally speaks to me. "Did one of them take you across?"

I study the men. "No." I'm not sure why he's asking. It can't be for a good reason.

We walk along the canal. Spot another group of gondoliers. None of them looks familiar.

"Johnny, what is the point of this?" my mother asks.

"Be quiet." He turns to me, lips pulled back into a snarl. "Any of these men?"

I shake my head.

We travel across a handful of streets, closer and closer to the Magnificent Block, stopping whenever we see gondoliers. Sweat drips from every part of me; the night is sweltering. My shoes pinch my toes. All I want is to go home.

Finally, we come across a lone gondolier waiting near the side of the canal. My father stops, Klartino and Stiggson at either side. "Is this him?"

I study the man. His hair is dirty and his cheeks are speckled with pockmarks. It is not the red-haired boy whose gondola I rode in, but he might as well get the dressing-down my father intends to give the boy. It won't matter one way or another to a gondolier, and my father's anger will only worsen the longer we keep walking.

"Sure," I say, exhausted.

The gondolier looks bewildered. "Sir, what do you want? I don't got no money."

My father laughs, happy for the first time all evening. Klartino and Stiggson follow with menacing chuckles. Dad looks at me and says, "Listen to me and listen carefully, Aria. I don't know what you were playing at tonight, but the fun is over. You are not to do anything to jeopardize this marriage. *Anything*. Do you hear me?"

His voice is grating and scary, his face full of anger.

"Yes," I manage to get out. "I hear you. I'm sorry."

Dad's body relaxes at my apology. "Good girl," he says. "That's settled, then."

I sigh in relief.

"Oh, and Aria?" my father says. His thick eyebrows are raised, the lines of his forehead thin and dark.

"Yes?"

He reaches into his waistband, removes a silver pistol, and—before I have time to blink—shoots the gondolier in the head. It's deafeningly loud. I exhale a sharp cry.

The man crumples like a puppet and tumbles backward,

splashing into the canal and floating on the water. Without being directed, my father's bodyguards pick up an oar and drag the man in. They'll dispose of his body later, I know.

My father hands the gun to one of his men, dusts off his hands, and calmly says to me, "Never sneak out of the apartment again."

· VI ·

When they've finished filling six vials with my blood, it's time to move to another room.

"Come with me," says one of the nurses, a blimplike woman in a tight white coat, her wheat-colored hair pulled back into a severe ponytail.

I follow her into a larger room with an enormous rectangular machine. Everything is white and sterile. I feel dirty in comparison. I am in a teal hospital gown tied loosely in the back. My feet are bare.

It is the day after I watched my father kill a man, and we have still not spoken. My mother refuses to discuss it, and my father went straight to bed when we arrived home last night. He was already gone when I woke up this morning.

"The doctor will be ready in a moment," the nurse says, closing the door behind her, leaving me alone.

With my thoughts.

I have always known that my father is dangerous. You don't get to be the head of a family that controls half of Manhattan without spilling a little blood. But until now, he has always been careful to keep me as ignorant as possible of his dirty deeds. Every time I close my eyes, I see that gondolier tumble backward. That poor man! He'd done nothing wrong, but he lost his life because I was tired and sweaty, because I said he'd done something he didn't do.

I keep seeing the man's face over and over in my head. I am responsible, and it feels horrible. I know my father is capable of killing again, and I refuse to be the cause. From now on I'll do anything to keep him from hurting others—even if it means submitting to his will.

"Good to see you, Aria."

I look up. Dr. May has entered the room. He walks past me, the nurse trailing behind him like a pet dog. My mother is just inside the door, watching anxiously.

Dr. May opens a drawer filled with latex gloves and pulls on a pair. Then he removes a pair of wire-rimmed glasses from the pocket of his lab coat. Glasses are rare these days—most people have surgery to correct their vision as early as possible. But he is old-fashioned and, well, old. Like the examination room, everything about him is white: the thin strands of hair that sit atop his head, the chalky pallor of his skin, his mustache and, of course, his clothes.

"Aria," he says. "How do you feel?"

There are so many ways I could answer that question. "Okay."

Dr. May snaps his fingers and the nurse darts up to him with a folder, avoiding eye contact. "Your mother tells me you are still suffering from minor memory loss."

"It's not minor." The hospital gown is stiff against my skin. "It's very serious," I say, wondering if Dr. May can erase the image of my father's face as he pulled the trigger. I shake my head and steel my nerves.

"Indeed. The brain works in mysterious ways. But there are some things that can help make it less mysterious." He motions to the massive machine at the far end of the room. It's long and thin, like a coffin, with one open end. A long silver table extends from it, and he motions for me to lie down. I do, and he prepares a syringe, clear liquid spurting out the needle tip as he tests it.

Behind him is an entire wall of medical instruments, displayed like trophies: scalpels of varying lengths; syringes, some as thick as my wrist, others so thin as to nearly be invisible. There are instruments I could not even begin to name, metal curves and hooks and things that grip and expand, contract, sew—a terrifying collection.

"What's the needle for?" I ask.

"Relax," Dr. May says, taking my arm. His glove feels powdery against my skin. "So many questions."

"I can't ask questions?"

He looks at me and laughs. At least, I think he laughs—the sound is forced and screechy. Unnatural. "Of course you can," he says. "I just don't have to answer them."

Then he jabs the needle into one of the veins inside my elbow.

When he is done, Dr. May discards the needle, smooths his mustache with two fingers, and scribbles notes in a thick manila file.

After, he swiftly prepares another needle, this time with a blue liquid, and pricks me again. Then another. And another. They grow increasingly painful.

"These injections will help speed your recovery," the doctor says. "Now, Aria, we're going to slide you in here to get some clear pictures of your brain. We did this after your overdose, but now that your system has had time to clear the Stic from your body, perhaps we'll get different results. How does that sound?"

"Okay." Maybe the test will explain what's going on inside my head. "Oh, and Doctor?"

"Yes?" he asks.

"Yesterday, I think I felt a memory of Thomas returning . . . but it was strange."

"Strange how?"

I look at him to gauge his reaction. "I was remembering something Thomas and I did together, but all the parts of the memory—the way he looked, the sounds, the smells—were just . . . off. Like they'd happened to someone else. Or were part of a bad video."

Dr. May looks puzzled. He exchanges a quick glance with my mother. "I'm glad you told me." His nervousness bothers me. If he truly wanted my memory to come back, he would be excited that I remembered Thomas. Wouldn't he? Instead, he looks . . . worried. Frightened, even.

The question is, *why?*

Then he goes back to his table and prepares one more shot. It takes him a moment to find a place to jab me; my entire right arm is beginning to bruise.

After the injection, Dr. May hands the nurse the empty syringe. "Now, Patricia here will operate the machine. Once you're done, she'll escort you to my office, where we can discuss the next steps in your recovery. Just lie back, Aria, and relax."

Relax. As if it were that easy.

There is a whirring at first once I'm slid inside, then a rhythmic banging, like someone is taking a hammer to the side of the machine.

Bang bang bang. Dr. May exchanging glances with my mother. *Bang bang bang.* My father shoots a man in the head. *Bang bang bang.* Thomas, his heart beneath my hand. *Bang bang bang.* I am getting sleepy. *Bang bang bang.* Turk's motorcycle. *Bang bang bang.* Hunter's touch healing the gash in my arm. *Bang bang bang.* What is wrong with me? What has happened to my life? Will I ever have any control?

Bang bang bang.

Bang bang bang.

Bang bang bang.

"That wasn't too bad, was it?" Patricia asks once she wheels me out of the machine and I can see the light again. I am still for a moment; then I swing my legs over the side of the table.

I grunt. What does *she* know about bad. "How long was I asleep for?"

She looks at the clock on the wall. "About three hours."

I shake my head. Three hours?

"Don't worry," she says, "it's a long procedure."

What could they possibly have done to me that took three hours? The whole thing feels wrong, but I know fighting my father and anyone on his payroll right now is dangerous. I feel so alone. I watch as Patricia shuts down the machine.

"Come on," she says, motioning for me to follow. "I'll bring you to the doctor."

We stroll down a long corridor, passing another examination room every few feet. I stare at the white carpet as we walk.

Dr. May's office has a rectangular plaque—

DR. SALVADOR MAY

—on the door. Patricia points, then starts back down the corridor. I knock softly, but there's no response. So I press my ear to the opaque glass; surprisingly, I can hear voices on the other side. I brace my hand against the wall and listen.

"Really, Melinda, I wouldn't be so worried—"

"How can you say that," my mother says, "when the last time was such a failure?"

"This time will be different," Dr. May says, "this time will be—"

Suddenly, the door retracts and I fall into the office. I must have pressed a touchpad accidentally. I land with my hands and knees on the carpeted floor. Then I pick myself up and brush off the hospital gown.

Dr. May and my mother stare at me like I'm deranged. I shrug and say, "Sorry."

"Aria!" my mother says, her face aghast. "Haven't you heard of knocking? It's not as though you were raised by a pack of wolves."

"Please, sit down." Dr. May motions to an empty chair. His

desk is cluttered with family photographs and a stack of files that teeters dangerously near the edge.

"The results of the exam are uploaded instantly into my TouchMe," he says, scrolling the screen with his finger. "And from what I can tell, you have a beautiful brain." He smiles without showing his teeth. I think it's an attempt to be comforting.

What am I supposed to say to that? "Great. Beautiful brain," I repeat.

"I'm confident that your amnesia will fade in time," Dr. May continues. "The effects of Stic are still not completely understood, as the energy from every mystic is as unique as a fingerprint. Did you know that mystics have different-colored hearts?"

I did, but only now do I imagine the oddness of, say, a yellow heart. But aren't we all just a multitude of colors inside—red arteries and blue veins and pink muscle? Perhaps a yellow heart isn't so odd after all.

"Stic is nothing more than distilled mystic energy. Depending on who it comes from, the effects will vary," says Dr. May. "It's impossible for us to know exactly what you ingested. Luckily, there seems to have been no lasting damage." He shuts off the screen and folds his hands on top of his desk. I stare at him and rub the inside of my arm, which aches from the shots. "I know it's been difficult for you, Aria, but I *am* hopeful that you will be feeling better in no time. The injections today will help."

"Thank you, Dr. May," my mother says, seeming satisfied. I'm not convinced, though.

Suddenly, I hold out my open palm, hoping she'll find it with hers. Even though she hasn't held my hand in years. Even though we are not close like that.

Instead, she stands and kisses Dr. May softly on the cheek, careful not to leave behind any trace of her lipstick. "That is quite a relief," she says. "Isn't it, Aria?"

I close my waiting fingers into a fist, nod, and say, "Yes. *Quite.*"

That evening, I search my closet for the perfect dress. I've never thought much about all the clothes I own, but after yesterday, I can't stop thinking about the Depths and how, in comparison, everything in my apartment is so . . . expensive.

I select a peach-colored minidress with a high waist and beaded fringe around the hem. Why does my family have so much money? It's never made much sense to me—my mother doesn't work, and sure, my father collects bribes from city officials, but that can't account for the insane amount of wealth the Roses have amassed over the years. Can it? I don't think I've ever bothered to ask about any of the details.

I glance in the mirror and fix my hair. I'm being forced to go on a date with Thomas. And a chaperone. It seems that despite the fact that Thomas called my parents and let his servant frisk me last night, and despite the mind-numbing guilt I feel over the man my father shot, I'm expected to be seen with my fiancé for the sake of the election. Expected to be happy. The best I can hope for is that last night was a fluke. That Thomas was, as he said, caught off guard by my visit and wasn't acting like himself. That we can still fall in love. Again.

I feel like my body has been taken over by puppeteers. I'm so tired, and even as I dress, I feel the strings above my head being pulled—by Dr. May, by my mother and father, by Thomas. No one gets close enough to touch me; they maneuver me from above.

"Make sure to smile," my mother says as I'm about to leave the apartment with Klartino. "You never know when someone is going to take your picture, Aria."

"I will." I clench my teeth and smile so widely that my face hurts. My mother rolls her eyes and walks away, down the hall that leads to my father's study. I haven't had a bodyguard in over a year, and Klartino isn't exactly my first choice for a chaperone. He has thick, nubby hands and a sour-looking face; the entire right side of his neck is covered in a green-ink tattoo of a tiger clenching a rose in its teeth. Nice.

But I guess after the stunt I pulled last night, I'm not exactly my parents' favorite person at the moment. And Klartino *is* pretty intimidating. I wonder how he and Stiggson disposed of the gondolier's body. If he cared at all that a man died right in front of him.

Probably not.

We're eating at the Purple Pussycat, a throwback to the speakeasies of the 1920s. The restaurant is owned by Thomas's family and sits atop a spiral building on Fifth Avenue. The décor is all high ceilings and walls paneled with dark mahogany, shiny black floors, and various bars set into pockets of the room. Men and women sip fancy drinks, the men in smart suits with crisp shirts and ties, the women in tailored dresses that expose their arms and legs, pointy shoes that surely crush their toes.

Klartino stays a few paces behind me as I approach the hostess, a girl in her early twenties with the Foster five-point star tattooed on the inside of her left wrist. She shows me to a table where Thomas is already seated.

Thomas stands as I approach. He looks smart in a white dress shirt and dark slacks, the outfit completed by a paisley tie and navy-blue blazer. His hair is more like it was at the engagement party than at his apartment—gelled and parted on the side. I see flashes of light—paparazzi—and I realize this is a carefully orchestrated photo op. We're the ideal couple—groomed to perfection, encouraging people in the Depths to vote for Garland Foster in the election instead of the mystic candidate Violet Brooks.

Diners bow their heads and whisper about the soon-to-be-married couple with the potential to unite the East and West sides of Manhattan against the mystic threat.

I smile—like my mother instructed—to hide how sour that makes me feel.

Now more than ever, I feel a lot of weight on my (bare) shoulders.

"Aria, you look beautiful," Thomas says, kissing my cheek. I close my eyes, wondering how strong I will have to be to endure this "till death do us part."

"For a Rose, anything," I whisper, repeating my grandmother's old adage of familial devotion.

"Hmmm?" Thomas says.

Suddenly, something stirs within me—a memory, an emotion, I'm not sure. It's almost as if a voice in my head is whispering,

You love Thomas Foster. Even though I don't *feel* the truth of it in my bones, if it weren't true, why would I be thinking it? My mind and my body feel completely out of sync.

The shots this morning, the machine . . . maybe they *did* work, and my memories are coming back. I glance again at Thomas—I'm so confused that I wind up curtseying and holding on to the ends of my dress too long, imprinting my palms with marks from the beaded fringe. "No, *you* look beautiful!" I say, and from out of nowhere I get the hiccups.

"Aria?" Thomas says.

"I'm fine," I say. "Really"—*hic!*—"I am."

Klartino offers me a sip of water, and I take it. "Thank"—*hic!*—"you."

Thomas reaches for my shoulder, which startles me—a good thing, actually, because I stop hiccupping. His hand is warm on my skin. I can't deny his sex appeal, how smooth and polished he is. Would marrying him be the worst thing in the world? By now, the entire restaurant is staring; dozens of eyes have zoomed in on me, and a handful of cameras are snapping my picture.

"We should sit down," I say.

Thomas nods. "Good idea."

I wave Klartino close; he hunches his already hunched back and brings his ear to my lips. "You're free to go," I whisper.

He shakes his head. "Your father said I'm supposed to stay with you."

"Can you at least sit at another table?" I pull in my chair and place the napkin on my lap. If my relationship with Thomas has to be watched, it can be watched from a distance.

Klartino calls over the hostess, who seats him at a table in direct sight of ours. "The food better be good," he mutters.

When I turn my attention back to Thomas, he's scrolling through the menu.

"See anything you like?" I ask.

He glances at me and lets out a low whistle. "I certainly do."

Thomas's stare lingers for a few seconds, as though there is something about my face that he finds particularly appealing. I shiver even though I'm not cold. A gorgeous boy—a boy I'm about to *marry*—is complimenting me, coming on to me. I can live with that, right? I'm a Rose. I can make sacrifices for power.

So why does Hunter's face pop into my head?

Thomas orders dinner for us, but I can't seem to focus on what he's telling the waiter. Instead, I hear the strange voice again: *You love Thomas Foster.* It's distant, as though it exists wholly outside my body. I close my eyes, imagining I'm looking down at myself, watching a girl in love with her fiancé.

"Why did you call my parents last night?"

Thomas looks up from his glass, startled. "What?"

"My parents. Last night. You called them—why? Did you want to get me in trouble?"

He shakes his head. "Of course not. Devlin called them, not me. I had no idea what he'd done until they showed up."

I stare at him, his perfectly chiseled features, and wonder if he's telling the truth. If anything, he looks concerned. Upset, even. "Okay," I say. "I believe you." Thomas lets out a deep breath; he seems relieved. "How was your day?" I ask. It's what my mom always asks my dad.

Thomas relaxes into his chair. "Good. My day was good."

"What did you do?"

"I trailed Garland on a few meetings," he says offhandedly. "The mayor wants to raise the number of drainings per mystic from two to four per year, and he wanted to walk Garland through the process."

"More drainings?"

Thomas shrugs. "Why not?"

"Isn't two enough?"

"I have no idea," Thomas answers. Our first appetizer, bacon-wrapped scallops, is set on the table. "But he must think more drainings will keep them down. The last thing we want is for these mystics to regenerate too quickly and overthrow us all with their weirdo magic. Plus, they're thinking of lowering the required draining age from thirteen to ten."

"Ten? Isn't that a bit young?"

Thomas forks one of the scallops into his mouth. "They say that a mystic's powers mature at thirteen, but what if that's a load of crap? There could be a bunch of crazy-powerful little *freaks* running around. We've gotta end that before it begins, don't you think?"

He says this so casually. I can't help but think of all the people at Java River, most of whom were surely mystics. They already looked beaten down by the officially mandated two drainings per year; how much worse will it be if that's doubled? If the age is lowered? Would it make them sick—or even kill them?

"Maybe they *should* be allowed to keep some of their powers."

Hunter comes to mind, the way he pressed his fingers to my wrist and instantly healed my wound. "Would that really be so bad?"

"Are you serious?" Thomas rests his fork on his plate. "The mystics set off a bomb that wiped out much of Lower Manhattan. Or did you already forget the Conflagration? Their power is *deadly*. They want to *kill* us, Aria. And you're proposing that we let them keep their powers?"

I shake my head. "That's not what I meant."

"What did you mean, then?"

"I meant . . . maybe not *all* mystics want to kill us."

Thomas laughs heartily, right from his belly. "Don't be a fool, Aria. The mystics would love nothing more than to see us all die so they can control the city." He leans forward. "Especially you."

Our waiter clears away the empty appetizer plates and sets down a palate cleanser—an apple and calvados sorbet—before our first course.

"Is it hot in here?" I ask. Thomas shakes his head. "Because I feel . . . hot," I say, using my napkin to dab at my forehead. My skin feels itchy, too—no, not itchy, but . . . tingly, as if somebody were poking at my insides with a live wire.

"Did you know," Thomas says, wiping the corners of his mouth with his napkin, "that mystic workers are actually trying to start some kind of union? Mark Goldlit in the Council saw one of their proposals. They want *vacation*—can you believe it? And Violet Brooks is supporting this nonsense. If we let them get a foothold with the voters, soon all the poor will want a voice in the government, and then what? Too bad mystics can't be stripped of their voting rights like they are their powers. Then we wouldn't even have to worry about the election."

I'm about to say something biting when I stop myself, tasting the sorbet instead and letting it slide down my throat, numbing me. Thomas is just like his brother. Who is just like his father. Who is, for the most part, just like *my* father. To support the mystics would be blasphemy. I trusted Thomas once, enough to fall in love with him. What changed?

Oh, right—I OD'd. An immense wave of guilt washes over me. Thomas's odd behavior is probably because of *me*. Because I messed up and forgot him. Forgot *us*. He probably has no clue how to act around me.

Thomas takes another bite of his sorbet. "It's good, right?"

The more he talks, the more tiny snippets of—what? memory?—pop to life: lips brushing my cheek, a strong hand on my waist. Running. Hiding. The salty smell of water from the Depths.

Is this my past resurfacing? What I used to feel for Thomas, what made me want to risk it all—my parents' affection, my brother's concern, my friends' companionship—to be with him?

Whatever happened at the doctor's office today, whatever was in those shots, is working. When I look at Thomas, every inch of my skin buzzes, from my toes all the way up to my scalp. I want to jump across the table and rip off his tie, lick his neck, kiss his chin, his lips—it's strange, to feel such repulsion at his words and attraction to his body at the same time.

"Aria?" Thomas pushes his water toward me. "Drink this. You look like you're burning up. Are you sick?"

I swallow the water quickly. "No, no. I'm fine." I glance to my left and see an older couple staring; the woman cups her hand over her mouth and whispers something to the man. "I'm just going to use the restroom."

A waiter points to the back of the restaurant, and I move as quickly as I possibly can. Sweat is rolling down my back; my pulse is racing. I can barely walk.

Is this what they call love?

I stand at the sink and splash cool water on my face. What's happening to me? I blot my cheeks with a soft towel the bathroom attendee hands me, then open my clutch.

There, staring back at me, is the locket.

Remember.

I slip it on and wonder what Thomas's reaction will be.

We make our way through the rest of the meal with hardly any conversation.

Fine. "Thomas?" I say finally.

"Mmm?"

"What if we ditched Klartino and went to the Depths? Just you and me?"

Thomas nearly chokes on a piece of meat. "Excuse me?"

"You heard me."

Thomas stares at me curiously. "Are you out of your mind? Why would I go to the Depths?"

Because that's where we escaped together to be happy, I'm about to say, *and maybe we could feel like that again.* But his expression is so cross I can't get the words out.

"Never mind," I say, running my finger under the chain around my neck. "You haven't said a word about my locket."

Thomas eyes where the silvery heart rests against my collarbone. "You shouldn't wear junk like that," he tells me. "It looks like the mystic crap they sell to tourists."

My fiancé turns his attention back to his meal. Slowly, I remove the locket. Thomas didn't give it to me. Who did?

· VII ·

After dinner, Thomas promises Klartino a thousand dollars if he lets us kiss in private.

We three are standing directly outside the light-rail station near the northeast bridge of my building. Klartino nods. "I'll wait for you in the lobby," he says to me. "Don't take too long."

Thomas takes my hand and pulls me out of the light, to the edge of the platform. My back is against the station's glass wall. Beyond that is emptiness. We seem to hover over the city.

This is what I am thinking about—the dark drop to the Depths just on the other side of the glass, the long fall Hunter saved me from—when Thomas kisses me.

I wait to see if I feel anything, for our marriage's sake, but the voice telling me I love him is gone. At least for now. It's just lips touching. No spark.

"Is something wrong?" he asks as I pull away. His hands feel hot—too hot—against my shoulders. I shake free. His brown eyes are open with concern, his mouth smudged with traces of my lipstick. A lock of chocolate-colored hair is curled across his forehead.

"No," I say, wiping his lips clean with my thumb. Pushing back his hair. The nighttime shadows play over his face; he looks even more handsome than he did in the restaurant. "It's just that . . . I should be getting inside. I'm exhausted."

Part of me expects Thomas to insist that I stay outside in the blazing heat with him, to tell me that he can't bear to live a single second without me, even though I suspect that isn't true.

But he only nods and touches two fingers to my forehead. "Go to sleep, Aria. You've had a long day." He pivots and disappears back inside the station.

I slowly cross the platform and step onto the bridge that leads toward my family's apartment. In the distance I see a figure slip out the back entrance of my building, the same entrance I used last night. I recognize the person's cloak immediately—Davida.

What is she doing?

Davida appears to be heading downtown. Even though Klartino is waiting for me in the lobby of my building, I decide to follow her. I'm a few feet behind, on a separate bridge that runs parallel to hers, but I do my best to keep up.

The shadows from the buildings make it difficult to see her as she weaves in and out of the light, from bridge to bridge. My feet are killing me, and the arcs of the bridges make it harder to run than if I were simply on flat pavement. Damn these heels.

I pass four or five apartment buildings, then reach Seventy-Second Street and cross at the intersection, heading east. Davida's stride is relentless, and she increases the distance between us with each step. The only way I'll be able to catch her is to flat-out run.

Just as I am deciding to do that, I am jolted by a blast of yellow-green light and an intense noise: a power station on my left.

Four men are working, their grimy hands occupied with tools. The power station is a prismlike building with iridescent sides, one of the various triangular skyscrapers spaced around the city to give energy to the power grid. A hatch is open and a tangle of tubes is exposed—thick, snaking glass piping full of bright green mystic energy. The energy pulses and swirls like it's alive.

One of the men, with sandy-colored hair and a spotty beard, stops and notices me. I take a step back. He powers off his drill and the others follow suit.

Eight eyes refuse to blink as they stare at me.

They recognize me, and the pale, sunken skin of their faces chills me. Drained mystics. They're everywhere.

I look across the bridges around me and see no one. There is no one here but these sad-looking men and me. I've lost Davida.

I turn around immediately and head home.

"How was dinner?" asks my mother, seated on the black leather sofa of our living area. Her face is freshly scrubbed, hair still wet from the shower. She is wearing a thick pink robe and sipping from a glass tumbler. All the curtains are drawn, and the overhead lights are dimmed.

Was she waiting up for me?

Klartino has left—after chastising me in the lobby for making him wait so long—and I wasn't expecting a conversation with my mother. "Fine," I lie.

She arches an eyebrow. "Just fine?"

"Nice," I say, correcting myself. "It was very nice."

"Good." She crosses her legs. "You should get to sleep, Aria.

Don't forget that you're filming an ad for the campaign in the morning."

"What?"

"Didn't Thomas tell you about it?"

"No." I squeeze my clutch, thinking of the locket inside. "He didn't."

"There was an explosion earlier tonight on the Lower East Side. A . . . *demonstration* arranged by those damned rebels."

"There was an explosion?" I ask in shock.

She swirls the liquid in her glass. "Yes. We need to take advantage of the timing. We're going to run ads of you and Thomas down at the wreckage, and also one of Garland working with some of the firemen. The poor fools in the Depths may think they're doing themselves a favor by supporting that . . . *mystic* . . . but they couldn't be more wrong. And we won't let her win."

"How many people died?"

My mother takes a swallow of her drink. "Does it matter? Those idiots think they're rallying the poor, but they're only reminding the public how very dangerous mystics are. The rebels will never stop. They need to be exterminated."

I'm speechless, numb. She could at least *pretend* to be sad that innocent people lost their lives. I start to head up the stairs and into my room.

"Aren't you forgetting something?" my mother asks.

I tilt my head, confused.

She bats her eyelids. "Kiss goodnight?"

I force myself to peck her on the cheek. Her skin is ice cold. "Good night."

"Oh, Aria, send Davida down, would you? I have a few things I need her to do."

I can't do this, of course, because Davida is not here. The last thing I want to do is get her in trouble. "Um, I sent her out."

My mother looks genuinely shocked. "You did?"

"Yes, I wanted her to . . . fix the clasp on one of my bracelets." I press my lips together. "It broke."

She glances at her watch. "You sent her out this late? It's past ten."

It's implausible, I know, but all I can do is nod and hope she believes me.

Surprisingly, she does. "I'm glad to see you're finally *using* our servants properly. It's about time. Soon you'll be running a household of your own." She finishes her drink in one large gulp. "Send Magdalena down instead. And be quiet—your father is already asleep."

Kyle is waiting for me at the top of the stairs with his arms crossed.

"Hey," I say. "What are you doing?"

"Heading over to Bennie's," he says.

I try to move past him, but he's like a barricade in a navy-blue T-shirt and jeans. His hair is perfectly messy, as though he's spent a great deal of effort in front of the mirror trying to make it seem like he didn't try at all. Personally, I think it's nice that after all this time dating, he still wants to impress Bennie.

"*You* sent *Davida* out on an errand?" he asks. "I don't believe you. That would be like Kiki buying something on sale."

"I don't care if you believe me or not," I tell him. "Now move."

He doesn't. "You never ask Davida to do anything for you. You hardly even bother Magdalena. Why now?"

"I ask her to do tons of stuff."

"No," he says. "You don't. Now where is she really?"

"Like I told Mom, getting my bracelet fixed."

Kyle takes a step closer. "Which bracelet?"

I take too long before answering, and he laughs. "I'm onto you," Kyle whispers before stepping aside. I don't look back as I pass him.

Instead of changing out of my clothes, I wait for Kyle to leave. Then I sneak into Davida's room.

Davida lives in the servants' wing of our penthouse, on the opposite end of the second floor from where my bedroom is.

I haven't been in Davida's room in months—maybe even years—but her neatness doesn't surprise me. The furnishings are simple and the décor is practically nonexistent: white walls, gray carpet, a narrow bed, and a tall dresser. A small closet and one window that overlooks the Hudson. The only thing that seems personalized is the stitching on her curtains. I walk over to take a closer look: tiny stars fashioned from silver thread, moons and planets intricately designed in red and blue.

Where would Davida keep something private, like a journal?

I sift through the outfits in her closet. Most are versions of her uniform, plus a few bland tops she's allowed to wear out on her days off.

It's not that I don't trust Davida. It's just that—well, I'm suspicious. Dirt from the Depths on the fingertips of her gloves, and now this: sneaking off in the night. What is she not telling me?

I feel around in the gloom under her bed and catch my thumb on the pointed edge of a metal box. I grab either side of it and pull until the thing is in full sight. The box is long enough to store a rifle, like the ones my father keeps in a glass case in his library. There are two clasps. I undo them, lift the lid, and peer inside.

Inside are some of the birthday gifts I have given Davida over the years: an aMuseMe with her favorite songs already downloaded, tiny porcelain dolls with beautifully etched faces, a bounty of jeweled rings and necklaces, an electronic reader with some of my favorite books.

And gloves.

Dozens upon dozens of gloves, all black, neatly folded and stacked in pairs. They look as though they've never been worn—impeccably clean and pressed, no lines or creases.

I pick up a pair and study them: they are linked together by a tiny metal clasp, which I unhook. They feel odd, soft yet durable, as though you could drag a knife across the palm and the material wouldn't tear. The oddest thing about them, though, are the fingertips, each of which is decorated with almost imperceptible circular whorls that I've never noticed before.

I slip one on, and it fits perfectly. I flex my hands and the fingertip whorls immediately start to warm, filling my entire body with a subtle, inexplicable kind of heat.

I extend my hand and stare: What *are* these?

I rip off the glove and fix it back to its partner. I might as well keep them for a little while—there are so many pairs, Davida will never know if one is missing.

Then I pack up everything as it was and leave.

Back in my room, I tuck the gloves and my clutch safely in the back of my armoire.

After a hot bath, I dress in a worn flannel nightgown and press off my bedroom lights. Then I press open the curtains and watch as the city slowly comes into view. The mystic spires are alight with flashes of color. I study them, hoping their oscillation will soothe me to sleep: white to yellow to green.

The change of colors is so fast it'd be easy to miss. But I've been looking at these spires for years.

Eventually I slip underneath my covers, close my eyes, and wait for sleep to overtake me.

"Come," he says, taking my hand as we move in the moonlight—away from the noises of the main canal, onto a narrow street barely wide enough for us to walk side by side.

Reflections of the buildings appear on the water. We run over a tiny bridge. He is in front of me, his hair whipping in the wind.

"Wait!"

"There's no time. They're after us."

He turns to me. I expect to see Thomas's face—only I don't. I see nothing more than a dark circle, covered in a veil of fog.

"Thomas? Is that you?"

"I'm here." He reaches out and pulls me to him. "Don't worry."

I frantically try to wipe away the fog. But the more I try to see him, the darker he becomes, until he's barely there at all, until he's nothing more than a shadow.

VIII

"The mystics will ruin us all!" I scream, clinging to Thomas for dear life and pointing at the man with the sallow skin.

"Cut!"

As soon as the cameras stop rolling, a crew of makeup artists rush over to me, blotting the sweat from my cheeks.

Thomas keeps his arm around me, and I survey the scene of the crime.

The rebel demonstration from the previous night has taken out an entire skyscraper. Explosives were detonated from inside—they shot upward, slicing through the building from the Depths to the Aeries. Thankfully, the occupants were mostly commercial; the only folks who lived there were the poor in the Depths, and it seems they'd been given warning and evacuated. Since the damage was done at night, everyone in the Aeries had already gone home. The explosion was mostly for show.

Unfortunately, thirty floors from the top, the walls burst and toppled over onto one of the connective bridges, snapping the wire cables and crushing a family of five who were heading home from dinner.

"Aria," calls the director of the ad. He saunters over to where Thomas and I are standing—on a bridge perpendicular to the damaged one.

"Yes?"

The director, Kevan-Todd, wipes the top of his shaved head and frowns. "I didn't find your fear believable."

I slip off the mask I'm forced to wear to protect me from the still-settling debris. From a distance, my mother and some city officials look on, craning their necks to see if there's a problem. I want to say that this is ridiculous. There's an actor named James pretending to be a mystic, his body lathered in foundation to make him look sickly, and Kevan-Todd is worried that *I'm* not believable. But I know the ad is important to the campaign, so I get ready for another take.

Thomas squeezes my hand, trying to comfort me. "I'm sorry," I say. "I guess I'm just nervous."

"Why don't you pretend the camera is your best friend?" Kevan-Todd suggests. "And you're just having a casual conversation."

I lift an eyebrow. "A casual conversation about an explosion?"

Thomas lets out a sigh. "Aria."

"All right, all right," I say, slipping the mask back on. "I'll try harder."

Kevan-Todd whips his head around to the rest of the crew. "Okay, guys. Take nine. And let's fix the body bags, hmm? We want them to look like real dead bodies, not deflated donuts."

One of the men rushes over to a group of long black duffels, punching them on the sides to make them seem fuller. I'm not sure what's in them, but the people who actually died last night are already in the crematorium. Later today, their ashes will be scattered in the canals, which is where most people dispose of their loved ones.

"Aaannd . . . action!"

The cameras pan over the wreckage of the building and the bridge, then focus on Thomas. "I'm Thomas Foster," he says in a slick voice, "and this is my fiancée, Aria Rose. Last night, a mystic explosion took the lives of an innocent family. This is exactly the sort of wicked terrorist bombing that our two families have joined together to put an end to. If elected mayor, my brother, Garland, will fight to keep the Aeries safe. To keep *you* safe."

He pauses, and I wait for him to continue. Kevan-Todd waves his hands frantically, and I realize that I've nearly missed my cue.

"The *mystics* will ruin us *all*!"

Then I faint into Thomas's arms.

"Cut!" Kevan-Todd hollers. He shoots me a tepid smile. "Well . . . that's a wrap!"

Thomas yanks off his mask. "Nice job, sweetie." He kisses my cheek. "I'm going to get some water. You want any?"

"Sure," I say, distracted by the screams coming from the opposite bridge, where a slew of teenagers have gathered to watch the filming. Thankfully, they've been contained and the area we're in is secure, but I can hear their shouts:

"Aria! We love you!"

"Thomas is so hot!"

"I want to marry you both!"

I have to laugh because I'm so embarrassed. I've always been in the public eye, but I've never felt like a celebrity before. Two girls wave handmade banners that read:

FORBIDDEN LOVE FOREVER!

It flatters *and* worries me that our romance is more important to people in the Aeries than an explosion. Than death.

I motion to Thomas, wanting to know what he makes of all this attention, only he's off chatting with some girls who have VIP passes and are holding out TouchMes for him to sign electronically.

My mother approaches and gives me a pat on the shoulder. "You were . . . good, Aria." She squeezes out the compliment as if saying it were physically painful. "The ad should be ready to run by the end of the week. We're going to play it in the Depths, make sure that as many people down there see it as possible."

Few of the poor can afford their own television sets, so the city has installed jumbo screens in certain high-traffic areas down below for government announcements. I guess those screens will also broadcast the ad.

"I'm going to Olive and Pimentos for a fitting," Mom continues. "My outfit for the rehearsal dinner is done. Or so I've been told." She rolls her eyes. "You never know with these people. Would you like to come with me?"

I glance back at Thomas, who's still signing autographs. He and Garland are heading to an election strategy meeting soon, and I'd prefer not to be stuck alone with my mother.

Especially when I'm planning to sneak back down to the Depths.

"Actually, I promised I'd meet Kiki for lunch."

"I'd rather you not," she says with a toss of her head. "There's no one to chaperone you; Klartino and Stiggson are on business with your father."

"But I don't need a chaperone."

"That was before," my mother says.

"Before what?"

She tilts her head. "Do you really need me to spell it out for you, Aria? Before you *snuck out* after *overdosing*!"

"Mom, I'm sorry. Really." I give her a pleading look. "Besides, Kiki and I are planning the *wedding*!" It's surprising how easy it is to make up stories for my mother. "She's promised to help me figure out who my bridesmaids should be—God knows I can't remember enough to know who should stand with me."

My mother rests her palm against my cheek. "Poor thing. A little wedding planning is probably just what you need." She looks around, as if convincing herself that there are no lurking dangers, then smiles warmly. "Just be sure you're back in time for dinner with the governor. You know how your father hates for his children to be late!"

Apparently, I need to feign excitement for wedding planning more often. I feel bad for lying to her, but not *too* bad. I kiss her cheek, then say a quick goodbye to Thomas and strike off for the light-rail, waving until they're out of sight.

And then I'm off to the Magnificent Block.

The gondolier pulls up to one of the blue-and-white hitching posts that dot the edges of all the canals, and the boat automatically stops. "Here you are, miss," the old man says, looping a rope around the post and dragging the gondola against the elevated sidewalk.

If he recognizes me, he doesn't mention it. I've brushed my hair out to cover my face as much as I can, but I'm still wearing my dress from the filming: yellow jersey studded with Swarovski crystals, a thick turquoise belt with a silver buckle, and high-heeled sandals that tie around my ankles. I am slightly worried that I'm being tracked, but so far I've been lucky. Either no one has cared to check any of the POD transit histories as of late, or I have my very own Grid guardian angel.

I'd put my money on the former.

Everything in the Depths is much different in the daylight: the water is dingier and browner, the stench—like rotting fish—worse than I remember, the people oddly cheerier. The streets and raised walkways are aswarm with men and women hustling to and fro with bundles under their arms and children attached to their hands. I hop out of the boat and onto a set of cracked steps. It's so hot you could fry an egg on my skin.

"Thank you," I say, dropping a few coins into the gondolier's palm.

A few feet ahead, I see the awning of Java River and step inside.

The old-fashioned bell on the door jingles. People turn to look, then go back to their cups of coffee and plates of sweets. I warm at the sight—the large booths and framed pictures on the walls, the glass case filled with baked goods near the register, the waitress with a piercing in her nostril who served me and Hunter the other night.

I sit down in one of the empty booths. "What can I get you?" the waitress asks.

"Water." Before she can walk away, I add, "And I have a question."

"Well?" she says, tapping one shoe on the tile. "I don't got all day."

I clear my throat. "I was here the other night, with a boy." She stares at me blankly. "A boy named Hunter. He has, um, sort of blondish hair. Kinda rough-looking, but very handsome. Not a model, but—you know . . . modelesque?"

After a moment or so, she rolls her eyes and says, "I don't remember any guy like that. And I don't remember you."

Then she walks away.

I get up and follow her. She disappears into the kitchen, however, so I ask the woman at the register the same thing.

"We were here the other night," I repeat, trying to grab the attention of the older woman, the one with the knotted hair whose skin is covered in liver spots.

"No, you weren't," the woman says while using a rag to wipe the counter clean. "If you know what's good fer you, leave right now. And don't come back, you hear?"

"I don't understand," I say. "I'm just looking for some information about the boy I was with. Hunter. Where I can find him."

The woman grits her teeth. "I told you, girl. I never seen you, nor no boy named Hunter. Understand? Now git." She points to the door of the shop. "Git."

Outside, I blot my forehead with an embroidered handkerchief and search for an open gondola.

The raised sidewalk is mere feet from a canal. A few people are sitting and eating sandwiches, dangling their feet over the water. Down the road, at one of the docks, a line of men and women wait for the water taxi, a boat that holds around fifty people and navigates some of the larger canals. It's cheaper than a gondola, but I can't afford to be recognized by so many people. I haven't been here long; I still have a decent amount of time to get home, shower, and be ready for dinner.

For a moment, I feel a sense of calm—the Depths are less scary during the daytime. I notice the colors of the buildings: faded pink and watery blue, gray and brown and white. Some are decorated with columns, now old and crusty, or carvings of cherubs' faces, which are falling apart. They're almost charming.

I walk down the sidewalk, away from the dock, and look at some of the hitching poles jutting out of the water, hoping a gondolier has roped in, but I don't see any. A string of ratty-looking children push past, nearly knocking me to the ground. "Hey, watch where you're going!" I yell, but no one seems to hear me. Or care.

And then I feel a tap on my shoulder.

I whirl around to see a girl about my age standing before me. She has short brown hair cut just above her shoulders, with eyes of the same color, and she's wearing a dress that seems two sizes too big. Her skin is pale, almost white, and she has the telltale sign of mystic drainings: yellow-green circles underneath her eyes.

"You're not crazy." Taking my arm, she pulls me down a

deserted alleyway that's a bit darker and cooler thanks to the shade of the tall buildings.

"I'm Tabitha." She sticks out her hand.

I take it in mine. Her grip is surprisingly light. Frail. "I'm—"

"Aria Rose," she says. "I know. I work in the back at Java River. I'm . . . a friend of Turk's."

My eyes widen at his name. "So you remember me?"

"Look, I can't say much, but I can tell you how to find Hunter." She raises her thin arm and points down the alleyway. In the distance, I can see a mystic spire rising above the rest of the buildings. Even in the daytime, it is extraordinarily bright. "Follow the lights," she says cryptically, in a hushed voice.

I wait for her to explain, but she doesn't.

"What do you mean?" I ask. "The lights are on poles. They don't *lead* anywhere."

Tabitha glances around nervously. "They do if you know how to read them," she says. "They're not steady. The way they pulse? All the colors? It means something."

I think back to last night, when I was watching the lights flicker from my bedroom window. "So you're saying there's a pattern? How the lights work . . . it's not random?"

Tabitha nods fervently. "The spires hold mystic energy, which is *alive*—it can speak to those who know how to listen."

"No offense, but I don't understand what this has to do with me. Or Hunter."

"Our energy is part of how we communicate," Tabitha says. "How we tell people things that can't be spoken aloud." She cranes her neck to see if we've been noticed. "Normally, two mystics can communicate without talking through a simple touch. I no longer have that ability—that's what happens when we're drained. They use some of the energy to fuel the city and store the extra in the spires."

"Why do they drain more energy than they need?"

She shrugs her bony shoulders. "Power. And money. What else is there?"

"Money . . . what do you mean?"

Tabitha tilts her head. "Stic, obviously. Manhattan has one of the biggest mystic populations in the States. Stic is made from drained mystic energy, then sold illegally all over the world." She looks at me as if I should know better. "Think about it, Aria."

But I don't want to. Who cares if people sell Stic? I've been taught that mystics are dangerous, the mortal enemies of non-mystics, and that their deepest desire is to kill me and everyone else in the Aeries. I was taught that the mystics were responsible for the Mother's Day Conflagration.

How much of that is true?

"Look," Tabitha says, glancing nervously down the alleyway. "Forget all that for now. If you can understand the energy, it will show you how to find Hunter."

"But I'm not a mystic. I don't know *how* to read the energy from the spires. Can't you just tell me where he is?"

Tabitha shakes her head rapidly. "No," she says. "The rebels would kill me if I led you to them."

"They'd *kill* you? Then why are you even telling me any of this?"

"Because," she says, her voice softening. "I can tell you love him."

Now it's my turn to shake my head. "Hunter? I don't love him," I say. "I barely know him. I'm engaged—to someone else."

"Then why are you trying to find him?"

"It's complicated." I look away, wondering how much I should reveal. "I had an accident. And now I'm supposed to be married in a month and I can't remember my fiancé. I've been having strange dreams. I thought maybe Hunter could help me."

Tabitha listens quietly as I speak. Then she leans in and says, "You don't need Hunter to help you with that."

"I don't?"

"No. You need Lyrica."

"I'm sorry—who?"

"Lyrica." Tabitha spews out an address. "If anyone can help you, she can." She turns and says, "They'll have noticed that I left by now. I've got to go." A cough racks her skinny frame. "Wait until dark, then follow the lights. Trust me. You'll find your answers."

At dinner that night, I eat like a proper lady, as always, the way I have been taught.

Kyle rolls his eyes at me across the table, and even then I do not laugh. I am on my best behavior. I listen quietly as my parents discuss politics with the governor.

"Johnny, do you really think this mystic Violet Brooks has a chance?" the governor asks.

My father is silent, then says, "Yes."

The word sounds deadly coming from his mouth. What would happen if Violet did win the election, if some of my father's stronghold over the city was diminished? Would my parents still want me to marry Thomas?

After our main course—rack of lamb, fresh asparagus, and wasabi mashed potatoes—Governor Boch asks why I've been so quiet. "You've always been quite the chatterbox," he says.

I fake a yawn. "Excuse me. I'm just tired."

"Aria filmed a campaign spot this morning," my mother chimes in. "She was *very* effective." Is this her way of trying to be nice? "How was your lunch with Kiki?" she asks, playing with one of her rings, a ruby set in yellow gold. Nothing about my mother is subtle—the blouse she's wearing tonight has fur trim on the sleeves. Only someone like my mother would wear fur in one of the hottest cities in the world.

"It was fun. We picked the bridesmaids for the wedding. Five of them." I'll have to ask Kiki to cover for me. And help me come up with names for bridesmaids.

"That's wonderful, dear."

Kyle is busy texting someone, his phone hidden in his lap. My father just stares at me, his dark eyes fixed on mine.

"Do you have any questions about the election I can help answer?" Governor Boch asks, sipping from his wineglass. He's finished nearly an entire bottle by himself—his lips have taken on a dark purple stain. "I'd be happy to."

"Actually, I do have one," I say. My father raises his thick eyebrows. "Why are more mystics drained than are needed to fuel the city?"

The governor sputters as he's swallowing his wine, making a choking sound.

Kyle leans over and smacks him on the back. "All clear," Kyle says loudly.

"Aria!" my mother says. "What kind of question is that for the governor?"

"A legitimate one," I say. "Isn't it?"

My father raises his knife and points it directly at me. "*That's enough,* Aria." He waits a moment, then slams the knife back down on the table. "What are you going to do before the wedding? Mope around here all summer and ask ridiculous questions? You have an entire year before you enter university. What's your plan?"

I choose not to answer him. The silence is deafening.

"Well?" he says.

"I could get a job," I hear myself saying.

"Aria, be serious." My mother lets out a laugh.

"I *am* serious!" I say. I've never worked before, of course, but it suddenly feels like the perfect way to escape my parents. If I had a job, I'd have a reason to leave the apartment every day.

Kyle stops texting long enough to chime in. "The only thing Aria is qualified to do is shop and hang out with Kiki. And the last time I checked, neither of those are *jobs*."

"Like *you've* ever been employed?" I retort. "*Please.*"

"Surprise, surprise, Aria—you're wrong. As usual," Kyle says. "I worked for Dad two summers ago. I was Eggs's assistant."

Dad chuckles, but my mother *tsk-tsk*s. "Kyle, I told you not to call him that." She turns to the governor, who looks confused. "When Kyle was young, he loved to have eggs Benedict for breakfast. He's since taken to referring to Patrick Benedict as Eggs." She dabs the corners of her lips with a napkin. "It's highly disrespectful," Mom says to Kyle. "You're far too much of a gentleman for that."

I start to object about Kyle being a gentleman, then decide to appeal to my father instead. "If Kyle has had work experience, why can't I? I'd do anything—sort mail, answer phones, whatever."

I don't know much about Benedict, only that he's a reformed mystic who is now a stalwart Rose supporter and does something associated with regulating mystic energy. He's the only mystic I've ever seen my father speak to, let alone trust.

"But Aria," my mother protests. "What would people say? Besides, you have the wedding to think about—there's so much to do!"

"That's why we have a wedding planner," I say. "Actually, that's why we have *three* wedding planners—you should know, you chose them yourself."

"I so wanted *four,* but Johnny put his foot down," my mother says to the governor. "Weddings can be so tiring, and I do hate odd numbers."

"I don't know much about weddings, Melinda," the governor says, holding up his ringless hand. "I've been a bachelor all my life."

My mother takes a quick sip of her wine. "How tragic."

"Maybe if I had a job," I continue, looking down, pretending to be suddenly sad, "I wouldn't worry so much about the wedding. And my memory problems."

It's a dirty move, I know, but at this point I'm sure my parents will do anything if they think it'll make me go along with the marriage.

Dad's bottom lip quivers, which means he's actually considering my proposition. "Fine," he says after what feels like a lifetime. "I'll call Patrick in the morning. Having to be answerable to somebody else for a change might actually do you some good."

Mom frowns, but I don't care. For the first time in what feels like forever, I give my father a real smile.

And much to my surprise, he smiles back.

Before I go to sleep, I stare once again out my bedroom windows, this time with new knowledge of the mystic spires.

They're still enigmas. Energy shoots through them like an electric current. Bright yellow. Hot white. Electric green. The colors flow together so smoothly they seem like one continuous stream.

I glance at my clock, then back out the window, focusing on one spire. There is a flash of yellow—four seconds. A burst of white—six seconds. The ripple of green is the shortest—two seconds.

What does that mean?

I look to the right, where a different spire is nestled between two skyscrapers along the Hudson. I time this one as well. The pulse here changes at a slower rate—yellow radiates for ten seconds, then white for ten seconds. No hint of green.

Tabitha told me to listen. But what in the Aeries am I listening for?

PART TWO

Love will not be spurred to what it loathes.

—Shakespeare

Making Love, Not War

These days, getting cozy with your sworn enemy is all the rage.

By now, everyone knows the story of Aria Rose and Thomas Foster's secret romance—how they defied their parents and fell in love. But unlike Romeo and Juliet, this pair of New York City lovers is getting their happy ending: a wedding at the end of the summer, just after the August 21 mayoral election in which Thomas's older brother, Garland Foster, is running against registered mystic Violet Brooks.

The teen lovebirds have been mum on any details, leading us all to wonder: How did they meet? How did they convince their parents—whose political rivalry dates back to the early twentieth century—to let them be together?

"Forbidden love has been around since the beginning of time," says Professor Jinner of West University. "It's a theme we've seen in the earliest plays and books."

Then why is everyone so obsessed with Aria and Thomas?

"I'm fourteen years old and I've never even been to

the East Side," says Talia St. John, whose family supports the Roses. "But now my mom says we can go. There are probably so many cute boys over there, and now I get to meet them! Everything is changing, and I like it."

Well put, Talia.

But seriously—the union of Aria Rose and Thomas Foster will erase the invisible dividing line that has marked our city for years. And most people see this as a good thing.

Aria and Thomas, no strangers to the flashes of paparazzi cameras, have frequently been photographed on both Manhattan's East and West sides.

"They're showing that two people really can make a difference," says Talia.

And let's face the truth: it doesn't hurt that they're both gorgeous.

Thomas, with his movie star looks, has been making girls all over the city swoon for years. And Aria has the classic features of a storybook princess.

Plus, they really do seem to be *in love*. Even a simple touch of his hand on her back shows how taken Manhattan's no-longer-so-eligible bachelor is with his bride-to-be.

Perhaps even more remarkable is the number of Aeries couples who have admitted to having their very own star-crossed romances—former Rose and Foster supporters who have joined together, putting aside their past differences to unite against the mystic threat.

"I never thought we'd be able to marry," says Franklin Viofre, a Rose supporter who's been having a secret affair with Melissa Taylor, a Foster supporter. "But now that Thomas and Aria are showing everyone that this is okay, I proposed. And she said yes!"

Not everyone is happy with the changes, of course. There have been small protests from those on both sides who seek to keep things the way they've always been: separate. "No good will come from this union," says an anonymous source close to the Fosters. "Mark my words."

Only time will tell. But for now, let's celebrate.

—from the *Manhattan View,* an Aeries society e-column

IX

"Earth to Aria? Hello?"

I look up from my TouchMe. Kiki and Bennie are staring at me like I'm a creature from another planet.

"Can't you actually *break* during your lunch break?" Kiki motions to her half-eaten chopped salad, then to the dining area of Paolo's, the restaurant in the government building where I've been working for the past two weeks. "What's so important that you can't focus on us for an hour?"

"A *half* hour," I say. "Sorry. Work is just a lot more . . . work than I expected."

Filing, getting coffee, and basically being Benedict's unpaid assistant is far from glamorous. And while it does get me out of the house every day and away from my mother's hawk eyes, I am totally and completely bored.

"Well, tell us about it!" Bennie says. Today she reminds me of a child—her dark hair is pulled back into a ponytail, and she's wearing a pastel blue-and-green day dress. "You basically fell off the Aeries—I have no idea what you've been up to, other than the pics I've seen of you and Thomas online. Somebody's been getting some action! And by action I mean *tongue* action."

"Seriously," Kiki says. "Haven't you ever heard of getting a room?"

I roll my eyes. "It's all for show, guys."

The girls exchange a confused look.

"I mean . . . it's important for us to look like we're in love," I clarify. "Important for the election."

I think back to the other night, when Thomas and I went out to dinner on the Lower East Side and had our picture taken outside the restaurant; how his arm fit snugly around my waist as he pulled me close to him, how his breath smelled like the cinnamon gum he was chewing as he leaned down to kiss my cheek. How I felt like, for a split second, maybe this was meant to be—until one of the paps yelled, "On the lips, guys!"

"So does that mean you *are* in love?" Kiki takes another bite of her salad, then stares at me cryptically. "That you remember?"

Her question makes me tense—and upset. The only possible memories I have are weird dreams where I can't see Thomas's face. I know Kiki wants me to confide in her. But I have nothing to say about Thomas, and with Hunter, well . . . I don't think even *she* would understand that. "Can we talk about something else?"

"Sure," Bennie says, sensing that I'm uncomfortable. "What's your schedule like—from start to finish. Go!"

"Well . . . I get up every morning—"

"Duh!" Kiki interjects.

"—and brush my teeth and shower—"

"Aria! Get to the good stuff!"

"Fine, fine," I say, chuckling. "My dad and I ride the rail together—"

"How's that?"

"We don't talk much. Light stuff—the weather, the wedding. His office is in the same building on the top floor but I rarely see him during the day. Mostly I'm just the office bitch. I get water and coffee for people when they want it, organize some of the older filing systems, and process the mystic draining reports. It's pretty boring, actually."

Bennie takes a sip of her Diet Coke. "Have you made any friends?"

I think about the people who work on the floor with me. They're all much older, and while everyone is pretty nice, it's fake nice—I know it's only because of who I am. "Not really. I miss you guys."

"We miss you, too!" Kiki cries. "Why don't you just quit? Wouldn't it be more fun to hang out with us?"

"I *am* hanging out with you," I reply, motioning to the table.

Kiki waves her hand. "You should be hanging out with us *all the time*. Yesterday we got mani-pedis at that spa downtown that we love, and while the woman was painting my nails I just started crying, because all I could think was *Aria* loves *to get her nails painted*." She sniffles. "This is our last summer before you get married, Aria, and then everything will be different."

I start to say that nothing will change when I'm married, but in my heart I know that isn't true. "I can't quit. But I'll definitely make more time for us to hang out."

"Good," Bennie says, smiling at me. "You can start this weekend."

"What's this weekend?" I ask, knowing that Thomas will likely want to spend time with me.

Kiki stares me down. "You can spend *one* night away from Thomas." There's an edge to her voice that surprises me, and I wonder if she's still upset about the affair and the overdose. Not necessarily that they happened, but that she wasn't privy to them before anyone else was.

"What's that supposed to mean?"

"I miss you," she says. "You see him, like, practically every night. What happened to girls' night? Gossiping, watching crappy TV, trying on each other's bras. . . ."

"We never tried on each other's bras," I say. "That's weird."

"I don't mean *literally,*" Kiki says. "It's an expression. I think. Regardless, we used to do everything together, Aria. Now . . . it's like I barely know you."

"Fine," I say. "Let's have a girls' night."

"No!" Bennie shouts. Kiki and I look at her, confused. "I mean . . . I'm having a little soiree. My parents are vacationing in Brazil. It's the perfect excuse to do something fun." Bennie immediately begins texting. "Don't mind me. I'm just setting reminders to hire a caterer, and maybe a DJ . . . oh and we'll need a few bartenders, too—"

"Whoa there," I say. "Why don't we just have a small get-together? Us girls?"

"Stop being so selfish!" Kiki's face is getting flushed; she unbuttons one of the buttons on her blue Oxford shirt and fans herself with her napkin. "I want some action! Some romance! You're both in relationships, and I've got no one," she says, pouting. "I just want a boy to kiss me. Is that too much to ask? Kiss me with some tongue."

Bennie thinks for a moment. "Don't worry, Kiks. I'll ask Kyle to bring along some of his friends. There was this boy in his literature course last semester I always thought was sexy in a, you know, collegiate kind of way. Brown hair, brown eyes—"

"Oh, I just *love* the color brown," Kiki chimes in.

"—and I think his name is Don Marco," Bennie says. "Or maybe it's Paul. I can't remember. Anyway, this will be so much fun!" She stops texting and looks up at me. "I'm going to invite a few people from the Foster side. Is that all right?"

I think of Gretchen Monasty, how she told me at the plummet that some things should just remain separate. Well, screw Gretchen. "Sure, Bennie. Whatever you like."

She grins. "It'll be, like, the first time kids from both sides are hanging out together. The blending has got to start *somehow,* and a party is as good an event as any, right? Just make sure you, like, grind up on Thomas in front of everyone. Show people that true love is what it's all about!" She glances back down. "Ugh. My to-do list is already huge. I need some major assistance."

"I'll do whatever I can to help," Kiki says, looking to me as if to say, *Will you?*

Before I can respond, my TouchMe buzzes. There's a text on the screen from Patrick Benedict:

YOU'RE LATE

"Girls, I gotta go." I motion for the waiter and ask him to put the bill on my tab.

"Will you be there this weekend?" Bennie asks. There's a hopefulness in her voice that I don't want to squash, and I find myself saying yes.

"I guess that'll have to do . . ." Kiki says. It feels like her green eyes see right through me. "For *now.* Don't think I'm not planning you a kick-ass bridal shower, fool."

The office itself is on the two hundredth floor of the Rivington building, just above Fortieth Street on the West Side, about thirty blocks from our apartment. This part of the city used to be called Hell's Kitchen, before the Conflagration. Now it's Rose headquarters.

I say goodbye to Kiki and Bennie, then walk through the body scanner in the lobby and am granted access. It's two p.m., which means that it's time for my afternoon coffee round.

After I take the elevator, I walk down the hallway, passing Benedict's office and those of some of the other executives, and a stainless steel door without a keyhole or a touchpad. I'm not sure what it's for, and nobody else seems to know, either. Then the hallway opens into a maze of cubicles, which is where I work.

I slip off my cardigan and hang it over the side of the cube I've been assigned. Near me are twenty other desks, spread out evenly. The stack of manila envelopes on my desk has piled so high I fear it will topple over. *Mental note: Get on those.* They're copies of the draining reports from over ten years ago, before everything was streamlined electronically. I have to transfer all the data onto the TouchMe system, but it's taking longer than I expected.

I hope Benedict doesn't yell at me.

"Eleanor, would you like any coffee?" I ask the woman at the cube next to me. She's in her midthirties, with straight blond hair that is so glossy it hurts my eyes.

"A mocha," she replies, *"nonfat."* She speaks to me as though I'm hard of hearing. "As in, without any fat."

"Right. Anything else?"

"It's just that yesterday my mocha had fat in it. As in the milk was at least two percent."

Despite her actual words, I'm pretty sure what she means is *You're dumb and I hate you.*

I just nod and repeat, "Nonfat."

"Steve," I say, heading south, where a man with a yellow-and-pink striped tie is perched at his desk, pecking at his TouchMe and occasionally letting out a high-pitched giggle. "Coffee?"

"Hazelnut. Iced." His voice is monotone, almost robotic. "Large. Sugar," he says without even looking at me.

"Okaaay," I say, backing up and continuing to make the rounds. I even write the requests down on a notepad to make sure I don't forget any.

Marlene four desks down orders an Americano, no sugar.

Robert at the far end of the floor asks for a tea, not coffee. "My stomach can't handle the acid," he says.

I take the rest of the inner office's orders, then head back into the hallway where the private offices are. I'll save Benedict for last, since he tends to yell rather than speak. He's the only person here who doesn't seem intimidated by my last name—likely because he works so closely with my father and already knows he's on Dad's good side.

I jot down a few more orders—two regular coffees, one pistachio muffin, and an iced cappuccino—before I knock tentatively on Elissa Genevieve's door.

"Elissa?" I say.

"Come in!"

The door retracts and I walk into Elissa's office, which is painted a sunny yellow. The room is free of clutter, containing only her oblong desk and a narrow bookshelf.

"Aria," she says, seeming genuinely happy to see me. "How are you?" She points to one of the empty chairs by her desk.

"Thanks," I say, taking a seat.

I like Elissa. She's the only person in the office who seems real to me. She works with Benedict, monitoring the city's mystic energy, but I don't hold that against her. They're nothing at all alike: Benedict is short-tempered and harsh, barking out orders around the office like a drill sergeant, while Elissa speaks in soothing, even tones and stops by my cubicle at least once or twice a day to see how I'm doing.

"Good afternoon?"

"It's okay," I say. "How about you?"

Elissa shrugs. She's wearing a smart-looking navy suit with a cream-colored blouse and strappy sandals. Her blond hair is twisted into an elegant chignon, and while her skin is as pale as any drained mystic's, she's somehow able to carry the look well. Looking closely, I can see concealer hiding the bruises underneath her eyes, the blush giving her cheeks a bit more life, but mostly she looks like a striking, beautiful woman—certainly one of the best-looking forty-year-olds I've ever seen.

"Just monitoring the Grid." Elissa swivels her TouchMe so that I can see it. "I'm keeping a close watch for anything strange around the old subway entrances." She points to a few places on the screen where the subways used to be—Ninety-Sixth Street, then Seventy-Second, Forty-Second, Thirty-Fourth, and Fourteenth. "It's rumored that the rebels are living in the old subway tunnels, but we're still looking for a working entrance."

"Well, that sounds a whole lot more interesting than what I've been up to!" I flash my notepad. "Coffee?"

"Everybody's got to start somewhere, Aria." She grins. "No thanks. I saw your friends drop you off after lunch. Did you have fun?"

"Oh. Yeah, we did. Thanks for asking."

"Did you hear about the demonstration this morning?" Elissa asks.

"No! Another one?" The ad I filmed with Thomas started airing last week. I've already seen it more than a dozen times on TV. It was supposed to help *stop* these incidents, not encourage more of them.

"Rebels detonated more explosives, in an office building on the Lower East Side this time. Luckily, the company that used it was in the process of moving, so most of the employees were at the new location. There were only a handful of casualties. But still."

I gulp, immediately thinking of Hunter. Would he ever be part of such a violent act? Would Turk?

"That's why it's so important we find their hideout before they can do any more harm," Elissa says. "I admire their desire for change, but violence is never the way."

"I agree." I think of how my father shot an innocent man simply to prove a point. What would Elissa say about him if she knew that? " 'I object to violence because when it appears to do good, the good is only temporary; the evil it does is permanent.' " I feel a little silly to be quoting from my textbooks. "I think Gandhi said that."

Elissa stares right at me. "Interesting." I cringe; something about Elissa makes me feel dumb. In her smart-looking suit, with her perfectly styled hair and flawless skin, she seems like the kind of woman who always knows just what to say.

"You know I'm a reformed mystic, don't you? Both Patrick and I are."

I nod. "You seem . . . healthier than most registered mystics, though."

She laughs. "Well, thank you. I suppose that's one of the pluses of working for your father. Patrick and I are only drained once a year, so we're able to keep up some of our powers and a semblance of regular life. Otherwise, we'd never function at the office." She pauses, looking thoughtful. "That stays between us, though. Okay? Don't go texting it or tweeting or whatever it is you kids do."

"Okay." Elissa is the only one here who pays me any attention. I'm not going to rat her out. "So is that why you're working for my father?"

"That's just a perk. I believe in rules, Aria," Elissa says. "There must be an *order* to things. It's what keeps anarchy at bay. Your father believes that, too. He's a great man. I promise you—Manhattan would be chaotic without men like your father and George Foster. And someday soon, women like you."

"Do you live in the Block?" I ask.

Elissa chuckles. "Heavens, no. I live up here, on the West Side—with all the other Rose supporters."

It's nice how devoted Elissa is to my family, but doesn't she feel conflicted, knowing most of her kind are housed in ghettos in the Depths while the rest of us—including her—float free in the Aeries?

Maybe when I get to know her better, I'll ask her more about her choices. But for now I have to remain Johnny Rose's naive daughter, so as not to raise suspicion.

"What about women like Violet Brooks? She wants rules and order, too—that's what she says, anyway."

Elissa takes in a sharp breath. "Violet Brooks," she says—and I prepare for the condemnation I know is coming—"is a smart woman with good ideas."

"You think so?" That isn't what I was expecting.

"Your father wouldn't like my saying so, but it's true. Unfortunately, she is also a sadly deluded woman who doesn't understand the system. The only thing a mystic mayor can promise Manhattan is misery and death. She's a threat to the safety of the entire city." Elissa leans forward. "That's why we're all so happy about you and Thomas! Once you're married, no mystic will ever have a shot at public office."

"Aria!"

I whip around and see Patrick Benedict charging right toward me. He's a small man, as thin and pliable as a sheet of metal, his expression always sneeringly intelligent. Today he's wearing his typical outfit—a dark suit with a light-colored tie. His thinning black hair is combed back, his thick eyebrows are raised, and the centers of his cheeks are bright red. Like Elissa, he has the pale skin of a drained mystic, only without the circles underneath his eyes or the gaunt, sickly appearance.

"What are you doing? You're supposed to be working, not fraternizing." He narrows his eyes at Elissa. "You should know better, Genevieve."

"Calm down, Patrick," Elissa says. "Aria is doing a good job."

"A good job?" His intonation lets me know he disagrees. "There's a stack of files on her desk that was supposed to have been cleared already. Meanwhile, she's going off to lunch with her friends and chatting with you." Benedict zeroes in on me. "I've told your father about your work ethic, and he's not happy, Aria. He wants to see you. Upstairs."

I want to stand up and smack the smug expression right off Benedict's face. But I know that won't win me any points—with anybody.

"Now," Benedict says.

I wait outside the double doors to my father's office, which occupies the entire top floor of the building. They're made of shiny brass and adorned with metal roses whose edges look sharp enough to draw blood. Two hulking bodyguards with Rose tattoos up their cheeks stand in front of them, arms crossed firmly over their chests. Catherine, my father's secretary, is seated at her desk.

"Aria, he will see you now," Catherine tells me. The bodyguards step aside, pulling the doors open. I give a small curtsey and then stroll past them. The doors close behind me with a soft click.

The air-conditioning sends gooseflesh up and down my arms the moment I cross the threshold—it's even colder in here than in the rest of the building. The far wall is made up entirely of windows looking out on the Hudson. It's the only touch of modernity in the place. Otherwise, it's all mahogany walls and floors, brown leather couches, and overstuffed bookshelves—throwbacks to the nineteenth-century robber baron style.

"Aria," my father says, motioning to a chair across from his desk. "Sit."

He's in a dark suit today, and a navy-blue tie with orange polka dots. He's clean-shaven and his dark eyes have a sparkle in them, nearly as bright as the jewel in the center of the Rose family crest on the ring he wears on his right index finger.

Behind him is a large oil painting in a gilt frame. Impressionist, from the look of it: a golden-orange sunset over the Hudson River. I don't remember seeing it before. I realize it is mystic enhanced, like the paintings in the Fosters' apartment, when the colors turn and begin to glow pink and red, and the thin blue waves of the river rock back and forth.

"Thanks," I say, glancing at the screen of his TouchMe. Dad sees me looking and presses a button; the entire thing goes blank. "You wanted to see me?"

"Why don't you start by telling me why I'm getting complaints about you from Patrick. He says that you're a slow worker, that you're not taking this job seriously."

"I *am* taking it seriously—"

"You *asked* for this opportunity, Aria. You should be doing everything that is requested of you and more. Instead, you're dallying, doing the bare minimum—if that."

"It's not like that, Dad. Benedict has it in for me!"

"No one *has it in* for you," he replies sternly. "If I get another complaint, I'll send you right back home and we'll forget all about this *job* experiment. Do you understand?"

"Yes," I say, because . . . what else is there to say?

Dad stands and motions for me to follow him to the far wall of windows.

"Look out," he tells me. "What do you see?"

I peer out at the other skyscrapers. From here Manhattan looks cold and intimidating, a metropolis of broken-up islands and naked steel, of stone and glass behemoths.

"I see a city," I tell him.

He clucks his tongue. "That is exactly your problem. This is not just a city, Aria. It is *your* city.

"There's a reason why we aren't as close as we once were," he says. "We're so alike, you and I. Your mother and brother are different . . . softer. I remember once, years ago, you were playing with Kiki and fell down and scraped your knees. You didn't cry or call for help. You just wiped the blood off with your hands and continued playing." He smiles at me, a rare genuine smile. "I knew then that you were meant for great things. That underneath your beauty, you were tough. That you would carry on the traditions of our family."

"But we're ending the traditions," I say. "By marrying Thomas, I'll be helping to end them, our feud—all of it."

"Yes."

Suddenly, from somewhere deep inside me, a question bursts forth. "What if I don't want to marry Thomas?" I ask, thinking of the boy in my dreams—whoever he is.

I wait for my father to yell. Or to slap me. He does neither.

Instead, he presses his hands to the glass, spreading his fingers open. "I was young once, Aria, and I had dreams . . . dreams that didn't necessarily coincide with what *my* father wanted for me." Dad's face softens for a moment. "I put my family before myself, and that is how I built my life. There is not a choice when your family is involved." He pauses. "If you do not choose your family, Aria, then we do not choose you. You will be stricken from the record, as if you've never existed."

My lips begin to tremble, and I worry that I might start to cry—and the last thing I want is to show how weak I am.

"Now go," he says, and I don't hesitate. I immediately start walking across the hardwood floor, toward the door.

"Oh, and Aria?" he calls out. I glance at him over my shoulder; he's standing by his desk, resting one hand on his TouchMe.

"Yes?"

"I love you," he says.

X

That evening, when I get home from work, I go straight to my room.

The stink of roses overwhelms me. My bedroom is full of them—Thomas has sent a bouquet to me for every day that I've worked at the office. The cards that accompany them are full of bland professions of love—*I'll be thinking of you with each passing minute,* one says, and another reads *I love you more and more each day.* They're probably written by his assistant.

I've seen him most every night, as well. He comes to the apartment for dinner with us; he talks about politics and the upcoming election with my father while my mother shows me dress swatches and menus for the wedding.

He's taken me to the movies. We've had ice cream together. He's been sweet.

Does it matter if I can't remember how much I love him? Sometimes I look at him and think, *It's a handsome face. It* could *be the missing face from my dreams—right?*

But my feelings for Thomas are like melting ice. When I try to recall our past, I get nothing more than distorted visions—

half-memories that only leave me more confused. *Remember,* I tell myself, like the note instructed. Like the boy in my dreams has told me. *Remember. Remember. Remember.*

I finish dressing for dinner. My hair has grown longer than I usually keep it, but I don't mind—when it's tied back, in a ribbon, I like how it leaves my face exposed, how the waves fall below my shoulders.

I pull open one of my dresser drawers to root for an Alice band. I move aside a few loose bracelets and some of my tortoiseshell combs, and I see a tear in the drawer lining.

I run a finger over the blue-and-white striped paper. The tear follows one of the blue lines, a cut so minor you can hardly see it. I try to smooth it out with my nail, but when I run my hand over it, I can feel something underneath.

Gently, I grab onto the tear and pull; the paper lifts easily, revealing loose papers. I gather them up and see that they are letters. The one on the top is dated more than six months back.

What are they doing here? I organize them by date and begin reading the oldest one.

It has been three days since we met in the Depths. Three days and all I've been thinking of is you.

I don't even know if this note will reach you, and I don't want to say anything more personal in case it ends up in the wrong hands.

Meet me in the Circle tomorrow night. Please. I just want to look into those starry eyes of yours one more time, and maybe, just maybe, you will want to look into mine, too. (Too corny?)

My breath comes quickly, and I feel a tightening in my chest. I've found a stash of love letters—from Thomas to me!—that I must have hidden away for safety. I pick up the next.

I waited and waited, but you didn't come. This entire week has been miserable. I can't sleep, I can't eat, I drive myself crazy thinking about you. Please, do a guy a favor and just meet me, simply to put me out of my misery?

Tomorrow night, same place? I'll wait until the Circle closes.

I flip to the next one.

You came! I knew you would! I have nothing to say tonight but thank you.

And the next.

It's ridiculous how one encounter can truly change your life. It's been what—a week?—since we met, and you're all I think about. In the morning, when I wake up, I think about your beautiful face, your dark eyes, your skin, your lips . . . and during the day all I hear is the sound of your voice, all I feel is the touch of your hand on my shoulder . . . and at night, I toss and turn, willing myself to fall asleep as quickly as possible so I can dream of you . . . and of us . . . together.

Meet me again? I'll send you directions. And keep checking your balcony for these notes. I don't dare sign my name or give my location outright . . . but we'll come up with a code that works for us, won't we?

Until then.

I clutch the letters to my chest. A relationship is unfolding before my very eyes. Even if I can't remember this happening, all is not lost.

A buzzer sounds.

"Aria!" Magdalena calls over the intercom. "Your mother is waiting for you and your brother to begin dinner!"

"Be right there!" I say into the monitor.

One more, I tell myself.

J—

It's an awesome idea to address each other as Romeo and Juliet, star-crossed lovers that we are. I'm so happy I didn't frighten you. I thought telling you the truth—my last name, and who I am—would make you run . . . but you're much stronger than I imagined, and this secret between us will only make us stronger, surer, as sturdy as the Damascus steel that supports our city. There is so much to know, so much to learn. Where do we even begin? I must see you again. Tomorrow? The night after?

R

Romeo and Juliet! This is crazy! It can't be Thomas who was so sensitive, so artful, so—

The buzzer sounds again. "Aria!" Magdalena repeats.

"Coming!" I say, stuffing the letters back inside my drawer. They'll be safe for now. I leave my bedroom, the carpet beneath my feet plush and soft as clouds. I feel happy for the first time in . . . well, a long time, anyway.

Dinner goes by quickly. Kyle never comes down, and my mother natters on about the wedding plans while Bartholomew serves us—caprese salad to start, and a main course of stewed rabbit over fennel, with new potatoes and other things, but I can't seem to focus on any of it, and I eat without seeing what I'm eating. Thomas and my father are off with Garland, doing something election-related that we're not privy to. I can hear Magdalena puttering about in the kitchen. I don't know where Davida is.

Not that any of it matters. All I can think about is the letters. They're my only real clue to the romantic life I had before my overdose.

After an appropriate amount of time, I feign a headache. "May I be excused?"

"Fine," my mother says, distracted by pictures of centerpiece options for the wedding reception. "Make sure your brother knows that he's going to bed without any dinner. This isn't a free-for-all, it's a household."

I leave the table calmly. As soon as I'm out of sight, however, I run upstairs and into my bedroom. I retrieve the letters from my drawer and lie down on my bed, picking up where I left off.

J—

You didn't come last night. I waited and waited. Is there somebody else? If there is . . . my life will be over. Everything was dark before I met you and now there is so much light—I couldn't tolerate being shut back into the darkness. Or maybe you couldn't escape last night—something to do with your father, your brother? Let me know so I won't worry.

Forever yours,

R

I wish I had my responses! I must ask Thomas if he's saved them. Surely he must have.

J—

Thank you for calming me down. I know I can get a little crazy when it comes to seeing you. You're like the antidote to a poison—calming, soothing. You make me feel safe in a world full of chaos.

It's not fair to us, this unnecessary hatred our families have toward each other. And for what? But never mind that for now. Seeing you in the Depths last night, holding your hand, kissing your neck . . . my God, you were on fire. There is nothing mystic light has that you don't have. You burn brighter than anything or anyone else in the entire world.

I'm yours for as long as you will have me.

R

J—

I don't know how much longer I can keep going like this. Are you ready to be honest? I know it frightens you, what might happen if we admit our love, but what's the worst that can happen—our families disown us, and we live a life of poverty, but a life full of love? Or we leave New York entirely and go somewhere else? Sure, we'll have no money, but nothing is as terrible as not being able to love you for the rest of my life. Why wait? Are you unsure of me—of us? Say the word and I'll scream my love for you from the highest points in the Aeries, all the way down to the lowest canals.

I love you.

R

J—

Did my last letter frighten you? Your windows are shut tight . . . have you changed your mind? We can slow down . . . wait to tell our parents . . . I'll do anything for you. Just let me know what's wrong so I can fix it.

R

J—

Your silence is unbearable. I don't know what to think, other than you don't want me anymore . . . or something terrible has happened to you . . . and if either is true, I can't live for one more day. . . . I will come to you tomorrow night . . . please be there.

R

Now that I've read Thomas's words, I can't believe I ever doubted our love. Any superficial connection I might have shared with Hunter pales in comparison. I slip the letters I have back underneath the paper lining for safekeeping.

I want to *feel* what I must have felt for Thomas when he wrote these letters. No wonder he's been so odd since my overdose. How must it be to feel such burning passion for someone, to have shared such a love, only to have the other person forget you completely?

Suddenly, I remember Lyrica, the woman who Tabitha, the drained mystic from the coffee shop, told me about. Maybe if I sneak into the Depths and find her, she can help restore my memories to me. I have to at least *try.* I owe it to myself, and to Thomas. *Romeo.*

I change my clothes, throw on a pair of dark running shoes and a cap to cover my face, and, on a whim, stuff Davida's gloves into my back pocket. Maybe, if I can find her, Lyrica can explain what's so special about them.

A few pillows under my sheets and anyone who casually looks in will think it's me asleep in the dark.

I tiptoe to my door, pressing it open. Before I take another step, an image pops into my head: myself, in the Depths—

"You came," he says.

"Of course I did."

From his neck down I can see everything—the stiff collar of his shirt, the tanned skin of his forearms—but everything above that is shrouded in mystery, blurry and indistinct, as if he's a partly erased figure in a drawing.

I place my hand on his shoulder. "Look at me." He doesn't answer. "Please."

"Do you remember?" he asks softly.

I shake my head. "But maybe if I can just see you—"

He lifts his head to the light and I cry out: he has no face, only a sheet of white. His mouth is a thin red line. There are deep holes where his eyes should be.

"Remember," the ghost face says. "Remember me, Aria."

I snap out of the memory.

I'm trying, I think, clenching my fists. *I'm trying.*

· XI ·

The motorized gondola moves quickly through the rippling water, down the Broadway Canal. This, I notice, is one of the wider canals I've seen in the Depths—plenty of gondolas can travel back and forth without fear of collision, as well as a handful of the larger water taxis.

We turn down a waterway that is significantly narrower and darker. If there are street numbers etched onto the walls of these older buildings, I can't make them out on the broken brick and peeling paint. There are no light posts here, only mystic-lit sconces and those are far and few between. Most entryways at the water level are covered with locked gates that are crumbling and brown with age. Greenish-yellow algae clings to the bottom of these buildings, tangled like knotty hair after a shower, floating on the water in large clumps.

Eventually, my gondolier pulls up to a rickety wooden dock and lassos one of the posts. He gives the rope a yank and pulls us in. I pay him and in a moment am on the dock. Before I can even thank him, he has removed the rope and set off.

A few apartments give off hints of light above me, and I can see lines of laundry crossing the narrow canal, undershirts flapping in the hot breeze. In the spaces between the tall buildings, the brightness of the spires around the Magnificent Block pulses like a heartbeat in a language I don't understand.

I think of Tabitha—*follow the lights*—and wonder how I'm supposed to do that when I can't even find the address she gave me for Lyrica: 481 Columbus Avenue.

There are campaign posters on the brick walls. They are mixed with hateful graffiti: the words FOSTER and ROSE crossed out or covered with profanity. I lower my cap, determined not to be identified this time around.

Homeless people seem as much a part of the streets as the buildings—young children, grandparents, and every age in between—all with the same weathered faces, tired eyes, dirt-caked skin. They're not mystics, so why aren't we taking care of them?

"You lost, miss?" one woman asks me.

I nod. "Do you know where Columbus Avenue is? Four eighty-one?"

The woman points. I thank her and I head off.

I know I must be getting closer to the Block when I notice the election posters have changed. *These* posters haven't been vandalized. A woman with blond hair stares out at me, smiling. She looks about my mother's age, dressed in a navy-blue blazer and a crisp white blouse. Her face radiates intelligence and warmth. VOTE FOR CHANGE, the poster reads. VOTE FOR VIOLET.

So this is Violet Brooks. The mystic who's running against Garland. Something about her is familiar to me, though I have no idea why.

Finally, the narrow street opens out onto a major road where a series of bridges crosses the wide canal, leading into what must be the Magnificent Block. The canal circles the Block like a moat around a castle, flimsy-looking tenements peeking out from behind a massive stone wall.

Now I can see the numbers on the buildings. I pick up my pace, wiping the sweat from my forehead. Number 477. Bricks that might have once been red are brown with filth. Number 479 is a building with a ratty blue-and-white awning. And the next building should be 481—

Only, the number reads *483*. What's going on here?

I step up to the wooden door—it looks two or three knocks from falling apart—and peer through the window next to it. I can't see anything at first, so I wipe a tiny circle with my hand—dirt immediately greases my fingertips. The inside is completely empty, flooded ankle-deep with water. No one home here.

I go back to 479. The door is hidden behind an iron gate. On the gate is a buzzer with one bronze button. I push it. Maybe there *was* a 481 once upon a time, but it's certainly not around anymore. Did Tabitha give me the wrong address?

I feel utterly defeated. I've come all this way and risked so much in the hope that Lyrica can help me. And now it's as though she and her home don't even exist.

I pace in front of the buildings one last time and press my fingers to the space where 481 should be. The brick is rough beneath my hands. With my index finger, I draw an imaginary line and sigh.

And then the buildings begin to part.

There's no noise, really, only a gentle groan as the bricks start to separate smoothly, slowly, until another much shorter, warmer-looking building appears. No one, not even the homeless people nearby, is paying any attention. I wonder if they can even see what's happening.

The tiny building has orange stucco walls and two large windows that face the street. They're lit with red candles that flicker against the glass. A metal door swings open, and a woman who can only be Lyrica is standing inside.

She opens her mouth and I can see that she is missing a few teeth, her gums more black than pink. "You rang?" she asks.

The house smells wonderfully of cinnamon.

I follow Lyrica past a large wooden staircase, down a zigzagging hallway, into a sitting room on the left. Oriental tapestries adorn the walls, and yellow and green Chinese paper lanterns hang from the ceiling. What look like hieroglyphics are etched in charcoal onto the painted walls.

Lyrica, in her embroidered silk robe, motions for me to sit on a low sofa. "I have not met you before," she says, taking a seat opposite me. There is a strange beauty about her: her gray hair is in thin braids woven with colored beads and gold threads. Her skin is toffee-colored and mostly smooth; her only wrinkles are crow's-feet that spread from the corners of her eyes and a few laugh lines around her mouth.

I am still in shock from the magic I witnessed. "How did you—"

"This place is protected," Lyrica tells me. "From those who

have hunted me before. Not just anyone can seek my help." She stares deeply into my eyes. "Only those who are truly in need."

"I am truly in need."

She nods in agreement. "But of course! You're here! What is your name?"

"Beth," I say. I feel uncomfortable being dishonest, but I want her help—and I doubt that anyone who lives in the Depths wants to help the daughter of Johnny Rose. I take off my cap and place it beside me.

"Beth," Lyrica says slowly, as though she has never heard the name before. "Why have you sought my aid?"

"My memories," I say. "I seem to have . . . lost them."

Lyrica raises her thick eyebrows. "How does one lose one's memories, child?"

I tell Lyrica about my overdose, waking up with no memory of my affair with Thomas. About my trip to the doctor and the strange sensations that followed, feeling suddenly in love with Thomas, then out of love just as easily. I tell her about the dream I've been having, the boy whose face I cannot see. About the love letters. "I just want to remember that I love him before we marry," I find myself saying. "And I have nowhere else to go."

Lyrica, whose eyes have been trained on me the entire time I've been speaking, glances at a glass orb that hangs from the ceiling. After a moment, her eyes seem to brighten—and the orb suddenly swirls with light.

"May I touch you?" She scoots closer, so that we are only inches from each other. "That is how I work best."

"Yes, if it will help."

She stretches out her fingers and leans forward. As soon as she touches my temples, a jolt of energy passes through my body. It shoots down my legs and up my arms, kicking me backward.

"Whoa!" I jump from the sofa. Lyrica looks startled and gathers her hands in her lap. "You haven't been drained."

Lyrica looks at me as though my statement is the most obvious thing in the world. "And?"

I sit back down, pressing my knees together. *The touch of a mystic has the potential to kill a human,* I remind myself. "Be gentle. Please."

Lyrica instructs me to close my eyes. Again she presses her hands to my temples; I feel the same initial jolt; then it fades to a dull warmth that flows through my limbs.

As her energy washes through me, flashes of memory fracture and spin in my mind: images of friends and family, of Thomas, of my parents, of Hunter and Turk and the drained mystics in the Depths, and of my dream of the mysterious boy.

"Open," Lyrica commands, and I raise my eyelids.

Her hands are out in front of her—a green glow emanates from each of her fingertips. It reminds me of Hunter, when he fought off the boys who were trying to hurt me, when he healed my wound with his touch. The light seems solid enough to reach out and touch, only I'm afraid of what might happen if I do.

Just when I grow used to seeing this strange vision before me, Lyrica snaps her fingers. The glow disappears, and a calm washes over her face.

"Would you like a cup of tea?" she asks suddenly.

"Um, sure," I say.

She walks to the back of the room, through a doorway covered by champagne-colored curtains that drape down from the ceiling, and returns with two ceramic mugs. She hands me one—bits of tea leaves and tiny twigs are clumped together at the bottom of the mug, swirling in the water.

"Here," she says, dipping her finger into my tea. I watch as the water begins to heat and bubble. Then she does the same for her mug. "Don't worry," she says. "I washed my hands."

"You can heat water with your finger?" I ask. Not that I'm surprised, really—it's clear that she can perform magic.

Lyrica chuckles. "You are thinking this is not so useful, eh? This same finger, child, can burn a hole right through your skin, into your skull, and singe your brain within a matter of seconds." She takes in my shocked expression. "I can also grill a panini by pressing it between my hands. You'd be surprised how useful that is." She sips her tea and I sip mine. It tastes good, like oranges and mint.

"So," I say. "Did you see anything, erm, interesting? In my head?"

Lyrica sets down her mug. "I will be direct with you. That is the best way." She inhales dramatically, and a few of the candles in the hallway flicker. "Someone has tampered with your memories. But whoever did it has performed an incomplete job."

Tampered with my memories? "What do you mean?" I ask.

"You went to the doctor and had an operation. Is that correct?"

"Not an operation, exactly." I think back to my visit with Dr. May. "But I went through a machine and was given a series of shots. I did remember a little bit afterward, but the memories I had were . . . strange."

I think of that dinner out with Thomas, the strange voice inside my head, the intense feeling of being in love with him, wanting him. Then I think of how that feeling vanished. I think of being in Thomas's bedroom, of the story he told me about us being together in the gondola. Of how I began to see a picture in my mind—but his image was distorted. The colors were all wrong, and nothing felt natural.

"But that happened recently," I say. "I'm still missing memories as a result of my overdose. I don't understand the connection between the two."

"Maybe you only *think* you've been to the doctor once, or had one operation," Lyrica says, pursing her cracked lips. "Down here we call that tampering magic. Tell me more about this overdose."

"I don't remember," I admit. "I OD'd on Stic. I've been told that I nearly died, but that the doctors managed to save me—"

She cuts me off with a vigorous head shake.

"You have never ingested Stic," she says. "I can tell that from the way your body works. Everything inside you speaks, you see, and I just spoke to your body. I read your organs and your blood, and there is no trace of mystic energy there."

"Are you sure? I was told—"

"Whoever has told you this is deceiving you," Lyrica says. "I suppose you had at least two procedures—the first to wipe away the old memories, and a second to put in the new ones."

My breath feels caught in my throat. I *didn't* overdose on Stic. A medical procedure was responsible for removing my memories.

Thomas. This explains why I can't remember anything about our relationship.

"The elimination of these targeted memories was successful, but the planting of the new memories—that was not. That is why the second procedure was performed," Lyrica says. "Only, seeing you now, I do not believe that worked properly, either."

What was it my mother said to Dr. May? *The last time was such a failure.*

Why would anyone want to remove memories simply to implant the same ones a few weeks later? And why would my parents lie to me about my overdosing?

"Is it possible for me to regain those memories? The ones that were removed?"

Lyrica purses her lips sadly. "Not unless they were saved when they were removed. There are ways to contain memories, to fold them up and tuck them away in case they are needed in the future. But that is not medicine—it is magic. And complicated magic, at that." She picks up her tea and takes another sip. I glance down and realize that I've finished mine. "But it is possible. If you were to find the container for those memories, you might be able to release them. But even that is a delicate procedure. And quite a dangerous one."

My heart sinks. I was hoping there would be some easy way, some quick fix.

"But here is the question I have," Lyrica says, her dark irises glittering with something otherworldly. "What kind of memories did you have that were so important someone would want to risk your life to make them go away? And who would do this to you?"

A silence seems to strangle the room. I know the answer to her question, but I don't want to speak it aloud: *My family is risking my life to make me forget.*

I hold out my empty mug. How long have I been here? Minutes or hours? I have no idea.

"Thank you for your help." I dig into my pockets for something to pay her with, and set the gloves beside me on the couch. "I don't know what you charge, but—"

"Where did you get those?" Lyrica snaps. Before I can stop her, she reaches over and grabs Davida's gloves. "You're using these to travel the rail undetected? Is that how you got here, child? Who gave these to you?"

"I have no idea what you mean," I say, snatching them back from her.

"These gloves," Lyrica says, "are enchanted."

Why would Davida have enchanted gloves—and where did she get them?

"See the fingertips?" Lyrica points to the curious whorls I noticed when I first saw the gloves. "The tips are layered with fingerprints, thousands of them—fictional people, people who have died years ago, whoever. Their prints are there, stitched into the very fabric, and they cannot be scratched away. Anyone who wears these gloves can use the rail or the PODs and go unrecognized by the scanners. You'll register as someone other than yourself, and your identity changes every time you use them.

"Be careful with those, child." She turns her head. "It is time for you to go."

At her front door, she touches my shoulder. "Goodbye, Aria, and good luck."

I leave 481 and don't look back. It's only once I'm gone that I realize Lyrica knew me all along.

· XII ·

I should be getting home.

There's so much to process. Thomas, my parents, Dr. May. But I'm distracted: sounds are coming from up ahead, inside the Block. I lift my cap and strain to see over the brick wall that encloses the area—sparks of colored light are shooting into the air like fireworks. What's going on?

Fragments of blue and red and pink light cut through the misty clouds, crisscrossing in a dazzling display. The colors make the area seem more welcoming; I feel drawn to it. The roar of a crowd fills my ears, a mixture of laughter and yelling and applause. Something incredibly festive is going on.

But what?

I wipe the moisture from my palms onto my pants. A few quick, purposeful strides and I'm on one of the bridges. The wall around the Block is massive and imposing, but there's a man-made break I pass through, and just like that, I am inside. No scans, no fingertouch. I guess people down here aren't so concerned with folks trying to break into the Block when so many are dying to get out.

Unlike the rest of the Depths, where at least some of the city pavement is walkable, the inside of the Block is mostly water. In order to cross it and still allow gondola access, mazelike steel walkways have been erected. The railings are slick and grimy, but I hold on to them anyway, scared I might topple over.

The walkway is wide enough for three or four people. I move slowly away from the Block entrance, toward . . . I don't know. There are other walkways parallel to the one I'm crossing; they seem to lead to the very center of the Block, though I have no idea what's *at* the center. From what I can tell, though, that's where the celebration is occurring, where the light is coming from.

I gaze up into the windows of the tenements as I walk past, but they seem to be deserted. The buildings in the Block are constructed on stilts, high enough to clear the water, and they continue far into the distance. A few people shuffle by me, paying me no heed. Then someone grips my upper arm and a surge of energy passes through me, like I'm being electrocuted.

"Whoa," I say, leaping backward and wrenching myself free. I turn to run but the hand grabs me again. *Oh God. I'm about to die.*

The figure wears a hood that covers his or her face. All I can see is sparks in the eyes as the figure leans close to me and says, "You shouldn't be out here." Then he shakes back his hood and I see that it's Hunter.

I sigh with relief. He looks even better than I remember. His sun-streaked hair is messy and he brushes it back with his hands. Under his cloak are a tight navy V-neck and a torn pair of jeans. His blue eyes glisten in the darkness.

"Why do you care where I go?" The question comes out more harshly than I intend.

"I don't. Not really." He bites his bottom lip and looks away. I can tell he's lying. Instead of making me mad, however, it sort of . . . flatters me. I remember Turk telling me how cryptic Hunter is, how difficult he can be to understand.

I glance ahead, into the Block. "Where are you going?"

He raises an eyebrow. "Where are *you* going?"

"Home."

"Through the Block?" I can tell he doesn't think this is a good idea. "Let me help. You look like you could use a tour guide."

"I can make it on my own."

Hunter shakes his head. "I'm not taking any chances with you. Come on, let's go." He pulls his hood back up, takes my hand—I feel a delicious tingle—and we're off.

At first, I'm surprised by Hunter's stealth—how he moves like a cat, how with his hood covering his face and his hands in his pockets, he practically blends into the night—but he *is* a rebel, after all. Used to hiding, disappearing. No wonder he hasn't been caught and imprisoned.

We're mostly silent as we move farther into the Block. I look up; on either side are ramshackle mystic homes with roofs that look like they might cave in at any second. The green-black water below gives off a salty, overwhelming smell. I can tell we're on a slight incline. We must have trekked a mile by now, though I don't know where we're heading.

The shouts up ahead seem to be getting louder. "Come on," Hunter says, glancing over his shoulder. "Slowpoke."

"I'm not slow!"

"You're like a snail. If we were in France, they'd cook you up."

"Oh, please."

Just when I least expect it, the walkway ends. Suddenly, my feet are on something soft—a mass of land has risen out of the water. I'm guessing we're at one of the highest points in the Block. "What's this?"

Hunter looks down. "Grass."

Oh! I've read about this in school—we don't have it in the Aeries. I stop and reach down, running my hands over the flecks of green and brown.

"Aria."

I jerk my attention back to Hunter. "Yes?"

"If you like the grass, you'll *love* the trees."

I flick my eyes up—as far as I can see there is land, more land than I have ever seen, sprinkled with real, live trees. Trees! They are thin and sickly and nothing like the plush plants in the Aeries greenhouses, but here they are. I'm surprised that no one in the Aeries seems to know this all exists.

"You know, it wasn't always like this," Hunter says. Walking next to him makes me feel protected. I can't help but notice the muscles in his arms, bulging against the cotton sleeves of his shirt.

"Like what?" I ask.

"So run-down and tired. The Block used to be beautiful—the hub of the city."

I look around and scrunch up my nose. "What happened?"

"You've heard of Ezra Brooks, obviously," Hunter says.

"Who?"

Hunter's jaw goes slack. "Well, you know about the Conflagration, don't you?"

I think back to what I learned at Florence Academy. "Of course. It was an attack on the city. Now it is a day of mourning, when we remember the hundreds of lives that were lost because of the mystic bomb."

"Ezra Brooks died in the Conflagration. He was the representative the mystics had chosen to run in the election against your family and the Fosters' man. Ezra tried to convince the city to pay for renovations to restore the Block to its former glory. When he died, the government abandoned that plan and made it the only place mystics were legally allowed to live—the most undesirable part of all Manhattan."

"Undesirable? But there's solid ground here," I say. "There's nothing like this in the Aeries."

"True. But think how much hotter it is down here than all the way up there. Nobody who doesn't have to would want to live in the Depths. Besides, there isn't *that* much land."

I look around. It seems sad that all this is hidden, but I suppose it does make sense. "And this Ezra Brooks . . . he was a mystic?"

"Yes. He was a great man, actually," Hunter tells me as we walk past a grouping of shacks, their windows open and bare, their roofs missing shingles and patches of paint.

I think of the campaign posters I saw on the way to Lyrica's house. "Was he related to Violet Brooks?"

"Sure was," Hunter says. "She's his daughter."

I stop. There's a window up ahead with light streaming out; I can see a family—a young man and woman and a child—sitting at a table, eating dinner.

"Nonmystics weren't the only people who died during the explosion, you know," Hunter says. "We lost a lot of people ourselves—innocents who did nothing wrong.

"After the Conflagration the city started the mystic drainings and forced us all to live in the Block." Hunter stops, seeing me staring at the family. "That's the Terradills, Elly and Nic. They have a baby around five months old. Nic owns a gondola with a few other men, and that's how he makes a living."

"Are you friends with them?" I ask.

Hunter considers this. "Friends? Not really. But everyone in the Block knows everyone else. It's a pretty tight-knit community."

As we walk, Hunter points out the homes of other mystic families, most of whom either own gondolas and make their money independently or work in the Depths for the government, operating water taxis, disposing of garbage, performing building maintenance, and doing other mundane jobs. The way he talks about them makes it seem like he knows them all intimately.

"The farther in the house is—closer to the Great Lawn—the more money a family has." He eyes my clutch and my shoes. "Of course, that's relative. It's not even close to, you know, how much money people have in the Aeries."

I try to smile—Hunter is skirting the issue that my family is one of the reasons why all these people suffer, why they all live in such horrid conditions without enough money or food. I suddenly feel sick to my stomach.

"And where do you live?" I ask to change the subject. "Up ahead, where the noise is?" The sounds—music, and commotion, and children screaming playfully—have grown louder as we've worked our way deeper into the Block.

Hunter doesn't answer. "Come on," he says. "There's a POD only a few hundred yards that way, just outside the Block."

"Wait," I say at the same time that he goes to grab my hand. Our fingers touch and my hand buzzes with energy.

He pulls away. "Sorry. I forget how dangerous my touch can be to you—I'm not used to dealing with . . ."

"Nonmystics?"

Hunter cracks a grin. "I was going to say girls. But yeah, sure. Nonmystics."

I feel myself blush—thank God it's dark and he can't see. "Well, don't be sorry. Be careful." For the first time in a long while, I feel relaxed, despite being in this strange, dangerous part of the city. It might have something to do with what Lyrica told me, but I also know it has a lot to do with Hunter, with how he puts me at ease. "I'm not ready to go home just yet."

Hunter's face brightens. "Really?"

Just then, we hear what sounds like a miniature rocket blast in the sky. "Where is all that noise coming from?"

"The carnival," Hunter says. "It doesn't happen often, but it's a great time. Everybody lets their hair down and forgets their worries. For a night, anyway."

"What's a carnival?"

Hunter looks shocked. "Seriously? Well, come on. We can't let you leave the Block without having a bit of fun."

The carnival is the liveliest thing I've ever seen. It's sort of like a plummet party, only instead of celebrating destruction, everyone here seems to be celebrating *life*.

Hunter leads me through a labyrinth of booths with mystics inside them selling their wares—tiny trinkets and dolls and wooden shoes, rows of buns and muffins and candies and chocolates, dresses made of thin material that waves in the wind, and hats, gloves, belts, and more.

Mystics pass me with plates of fried dough, their hands covered in powdered sugar. "Look!" I point to a tank full of water, where a young mystic is sitting, waiting to be dunked. He's soaking wet, which makes me think he's already been submerged. A few feet away, a group of kids are lined up, throwing tiny balls at the lever on the tank and hoping they'll sink him again.

"Looks cold," Hunter says, rubbing his arms. "Want one?" He motions to a booth full of stuffed animals, the kind my mother would never allow me to have when I was younger: teddy bears with bows around their necks, plush giraffes and monkeys and other exotic animals you'd find in a zoo.

"Sure," I say. "Only I don't have any credit here, and I'm almost out of coins—"

Hunter scoffs. "Aria, you can't just *buy* one of these."

"You can't?"

"Nope." He motions to the woman behind the booth, who nods and hands over five plastic rings, all in different colors. They look like cheap, oversized bracelets. Light from the carnival brightens his face. "You gotta win 'em."

"Is that so?"

"Yup." Hunter flexes his biceps. "Here, hold these." He hands me four of the rings and keeps one for himself. "Now stand back and watch a master at work."

Hunter eyes the row of empty soda bottles. Each one is worth a certain number of points—the more points you get by tossing a ring over the bottle, the nicer a stuffed animal you win.

He rolls his neck, then flicks his wrist: the ring soars out of his hand and hits the soda bottle in the middle with a clink, failing to land around its neck, then tumbling to the ground.

"Oh no!" Hunter looks at me sheepishly. "That wasn't my fault, you know. It was a bad ring."

The mystic behind the booth laughs. "Of course," I say. "Factory defect." I slide a blue ring off my wrist. "Here, try this one."

"Thanks." Hunter eyes the center bottle, worth a thousand points—the top prize. "I'm coming for you." He reaches back, tosses the ring. There's too much strength behind his throw—the ring smacks the bottle, then lands next to the previous one on the ground.

"I swear I'm good at this!" Hunter cries. I start to giggle, and he does, too. "Really."

"I believe you. But how about you let me give it a try."

Hunter cocks his head. "Oh?"

I take a green ring off my wrist. "Watch and learn."

I eye that same central bottle and rotate my wrist back and forth, practicing. Not too heavy a throw, but not too light, either. I swing my arm back, then release—the ring sails into the air and drops directly onto the bottle.

"Oh my gosh! I won!" I jump up and down, and Hunter wraps his arms around me. Immediately, I freeze, stiff as a board, and Hunter pulls away, embarrassed.

"Sorry."

"That's okay," I say. "Um, don't worry about it."

Hunter picks the fallen rings up off the ground, and I hand back the two we didn't use. The mystic behind the booth blinks at me. "Which one, miss?"

I'm studying the selection of stuffed animals when, out of the corner of my eye, I see a little girl—no more than seven or eight—standing a few feet away, staring longingly at an orange giraffe. Her face and hands are dirty, and the beige material of her dress is worn.

"That one," I say, pointing to the giraffe. The mystic hands it to me.

Hunter gives the giraffe a pat. "Good choice, Aria. He looks very healthy."

The little girl is staring at me, and I walk over to her. "What's your name?"

She's silent.

"It's okay," Hunter says, as if he knows the girl—which, actually, he probably does. "You can tell Aria. She's my friend."

"Julia," the girl says in a small voice.

I hold out the giraffe. "Well, Julia, I won this for you."

She gives the hint of a smile. "Really?"

"Absolutely." I watch as she reaches tentatively for the stuffed animal. "Will you give him a good home?"

Julia nods emphatically. "Yes. I promise."

Hunter wipes some of the dirt from Julia's face. "You should probably get back to your mom now, right? I bet she's looking for you."

Julia looks from Hunter to me. "Thank you." She runs off into the crowd, the stuffed animal cradled in her arms.

"That was really nice of you," Hunter says. The way he's looking at me is so intense that I can feel myself blushing.

"It was no big deal." I look away. "What's that?" I point to a large, whirring machine that seems to be producing batches of pink fluff.

"Cotton candy," Hunter says, elbowing me playfully. "Want some?"

"No, it looks horrible!"

"Are you kidding? It's delicious!" he yells, and takes my hand again. The jolt is less surprising this time, more manageable. I wonder if he is doing anything with his body to make it this way or if I'm getting used to him.

Everywhere I turn there are more giddy people. It's the first time I've seen drained mystics looking happy. They still look weak, with the pallor I've come to realize results from the drainings—even the children have dark circles underneath their eyes, their skin a pale, chalky color. But no one seems to care. They're all smiling and laughing and chasing each other. There are games set up everywhere, and lights! There are so many lights—it's like something from a movie, the way blues and greens and purples and reds are captured inside paper lanterns that line the booths, tiny bulbs strung across the trees like at Christmastime.

"This is the only part of the Block that wasn't flooded," Hunter says, "which is why there's still grass and trees."

The grass is mostly green with dried patches of yellow and brown; still, it's so soft to walk on that I want to slip off my shoes and run across the lawn in my bare feet. "This is nothing like walking in the Aeries," I shout over the carnival noise.

The trees here are long and tall, with curving, knotted branches and leaves that spread into a canopy over the Great Lawn. In the distance, water has actually pooled in the middle of some of the lower portions of ground, creating tiny blue-green ponds scattered with lily pads. A long iron bridge covered with moss and tangled ivy covers a grander canal that runs along the far side of the lawn.

On the horizon are both the city—the foundation of the towering skyscrapers—and clusters of rocks where couples are resting, leaning back and staring at the sky.

Hunter laughs. "Having fun?" He looks stunning in the light, and for a moment I forget to breathe.

"Aria? Are you all right?"

"I'm fine," I say, waving him off.

We're walking through an aisle of makeshift booths, and then we turn the corner. To his credit, Hunter does a good job of steering me away from the crowds.

"I think I need to rest for a minute," I say.

"Wait." Hunter takes my hand again. "I know just the place."

He leads me away from the carnival, through a cluster of trees and toward what appears to be a miniature mountain. "What is this place?" I ask.

He grins. "Belvedere Castle. It was built a while ago, in the late nineteenth century. It's something, isn't it?"

The structure before me is practically out of a history book: the façade is made of stones of various shades of gray, and there's a corner tower with a conical cap. The castle is enormous, rising over the Great Lawn, where the carnival is set up. It is almost hidden in a quarry of rock, with Gothic arched windows and parapet walls that glimmer like watchful eyes. There is something both spooky and majestic about it—a throwback to another time, another century, situated in the heart of the Block; a hidden jewel amid so much despair.

"It's falling apart," Hunter tells me. "Crazy unsafe. But sometimes I like to come here to sit and think." He glances back at me. "Probably sounds silly to you."

"Not at all," I say.

We stand still, next to each other, studying the castle for a few moments. "Hunter, there's something I want to ask you. I'd like to know . . ."

"Just spit it out, Aria." Hunter roughs up his hair and stares at me with his powerful blue eyes. "What is it?"

"What's it like to have mystic powers?" I ask.

"*That's* what you want to know?" He looks a bit relieved.

I think about Lyrica, and Turk, and whoever must have erased the memories from my mind. "Yes," I say. "I know it's illegal and all, but I'm curious."

Hunter leans back against a tree and shoves his hands into his pockets. "For me . . . it's normal, I guess. I've never known any other life."

"But what's it *like*?" I move closer. We're only a few inches away from one another. "When you healed me, and when you touch me—I *feel* something. Do you feel it, too?"

He nods. "Every mystic has a different kind of power. They're like personalities, I guess. No two are the same. They reach maturity around the age of thirteen."

"What's yours?" I ask. "Healing?"

"Most mystics can heal," he says, "that's just part of our blood. My powers are pretty useless, I guess. I got them when I was twelve—a year earlier than most of my friends. For example, I can walk through walls."

"You can walk through walls? Show me!"

"Oh, so now I'm some sort of freak you can order around for your amusement?"

His words make me feel awful. "No, that's not what I meant at all. I'm sorry—"

"Aria, I'm kidding!" He takes his hands out of his pockets, rubs them together. "Relax. Wanna see me walk through something? No problemo."

The tree that Hunter has been leaning on is thick and gray, with scaly bark and branches like claws. The trunk is six feet across, easily three times his size.

He strolls forward, a fine green glow around his figure. Then, as though there's no tree there at all, he passes right through it. For a second he goes translucent, almost invisible, and I hear a slight whoosh: and then he's on the other side, the green glow fading away like the afterimage when you look into and then away from the sun. Magic.

"That was incredible!"

"Thank you, thank you," he says, taking a bow. "I'm here all night."

Then he walks right through the same tree again. It happens so quickly I can't really see what happens or how his particles rearrange themselves. They just do.

"Remarkable," I find myself saying. "It's hard to believe."

"Aw, shucks," Hunter says. "You're making me blush."

"What other kinds of powers are there?"

"You're not really interested in this, are you?" he asks skeptically, tilting his head. "You're just being polite."

"No, don't be silly," I say. "This is fascinating."

He begins walking toward the castle. I follow, stepping over leaves and roots and fallen branches.

"Some mystics can take on the glamour of someone else," Hunter says, navigating a flight of stone steps. "So you can look like a different person. But eventually it wears off. Other mystics can use their energy to affect the weather, or even the air surrounding them." He waits for me to catch up. "I know a girl who can spin a tornado out of thin air," he says, "and someone who can start a fire"—he snaps his fingers—"like that."

"Can you fly?" I ask. "I've heard mystics can."

Hunter shakes his head. "Myth. The only things that can fly are birds. Well, and Superman."

"What about breathing underwater?"

"I can't," he says, "but my friend Marty can. Only for a few hours, though."

"Hours?"

Hunter chuckles. "Yup."

"What else?"

"All kinds of stuff," Hunter says casually, counting off on his fingers. "Mystics can heal wounds—which you already know. Create light. Manipulate water. Some mystics are able to create illusions or change a solid to a liquid. Some have superhuman strength and speed. Others can use their powers to make magical barriers, which we call shields, to protect areas so that nonmystics can't enter them."

I'm amazed at how different all the mystic powers are from one another.

"Mystic energy can act as an enhancer," Hunter tells me as we walk, climbing the rocks toward the castle, "which basically means that if a metal is coated in mystic energy, it can't be broken by anything other than another piece of mystic-coated metal." He stops for a minute. "A mystic-made weapon is beyond dangerous."

"Is there anything mystics *can't* do? I mean, besides fly."

Hunter thinks for a moment and scratches his chin. "No mystic can bring someone back from the dead."

"I'd hope not. That would be . . . scary."

"I'm probably making it sound more glorious than it is." Hunter steadies himself on a jagged rock, then jumps to another one. I follow his lead. "Plenty of us have really lame powers. I know this girl Nelly whose hand acts like a steam iron. Great against wrinkles but not much else. Or this dude Enrico who can juggle egg-sized balls of light. Whoop-di-doo." Hunter rolls his eyes, and I laugh.

"Why are all the powers so different?"

Hunter shrugs. "But no matter what the power is, it doesn't mean a mystic has more or less energy inside. Every mystic burns as hot as a furnace." He tugs on the bottom of his shirt. "Until they're drained, anyway."

Before I know it, we're standing at the foot of the castle, underneath an enormous stone arch. From here I can see the entire carnival, the colors and the lights, the Magnificent Block ignited with festivities.

"This is gorgeous," I find myself saying.

I think I hear Hunter say *You're gorgeous* under his breath, but his eyes are elsewhere, looking up at the tower. "You know, all those things I just told you about—mystics can't do them anymore. Because of the drainings. We used to be great people who helped build this city. Now look at us—reduced and powerless. This carnival, this bit of excitement . . . it's the happiest I've seen anyone all year."

It's not fair, I find myself thinking. I don't want to be a part of this problem—I want to help fix it. "But how can we know that if mystics kept their powers, they wouldn't revolt against the Aeries and kill everyone? I mean, look at the Conflagration: mystics bombed a building and hundreds of people died."

Hunter looks at me quizzically. "Aria, is that what you think happened?"

"Of course that's what happened." My tone is so certain that I can't help but second-guess myself. "Isn't it?"

"The bomb *was* made of mystic energy," Hunter admits, "but it was made by mystics who betrayed their own kind, who were working for the government. It was the excuse the Aeries needed to crack down on mystics everywhere. They're the ones to blame—those few individuals. Not the entire mystic population."

I feel like I've been hit in the head. "What kind of people would be so awful?"

I think of my own parents. Of what Lyrica told me. If they're responsible for tampering with my memories . . . are they any worse than the mystics who betrayed their own kind?

My cheeks feel wet, and I realize I'm crying.

"Aria, don't cry." Hunter takes my hand to comfort me, and a jolt of energy rushes through me. I pull away.

"I'm sorry. Let me try again," he says. "I need to figure out how to do this without hurting you."

Slowly, he turns his palm upward. He's waiting for me to place my hand in his, but I'm scared. Then I look into his eyes and I *feel* it: Hunter's not going to cause me any pain. I hold my hand parallel to his, letting him know it's okay. A gust of wind sweeps around us, making the tiny blond hairs on my arms stand up.

Carefully, he touches me again—first just with one finger, tracing the outline of my hand. The initial jolt subsides to a warm sensation, making me feel like a batch of cookies that have just been pulled from the oven. Hunter's eyes are focused, his lips pulled together tightly as he presses the tips of his fingers against mine, one by one, until our hands are pressed together.

I study the lines of his face, the curve of his neck, and realize

I've never felt this intimate with anyone in my entire life. I feel as if I'm completely naked.

Hunter gently cups my cheek with his free hand. I can feel his breath warming my neck. "This is better, right?"

I try to speak but no words come out. I am flustered, boiling up inside.

He pulls his hand away and steps back. "Tell me about your family."

"My family? What about them?"

"Your parents. What are they like?" Hunter leads me around the castle, past its crumbling columns. We sit, leaning against one of the walls, and stare out at the night. The light from the carnival and from the nearby spires reflects off one of the ponds below the castle, making the entire area glimmer.

"There's not much to say," I tell him. "All they care about right now is the election. They're so scared Violet Brooks is going to win that they're making my life a living hell. I can barely leave my room without an interrogation. And Thomas—"

I choke on his name. At first, I was mad at myself for overdosing and losing my memories of our relationship. Yes, there were things that didn't make sense—the confusing flashes of remembering, the locket, which he didn't give me—but they were never enough to make me truly doubt I ever loved him. But now that I know I didn't overdose, that I've never used Stic, how do I know that anything I've been told about Thomas is true?

And yet: those letters. The passion there was real. How do those fit in with what I've learned from Lyrica?

"What about Thomas?" Hunter's voice is rough, as though he's holding back emotion.

"We're engaged. There's nothing more to say."

The silence between us stretches on, and I wonder if he heard me.

"Do you love him?" Hunter asks at last.

"What kind of question is that? That's none of your business."

"You're marrying him." Hunter scoots closer, so that our legs are almost touching. "It should be an easy one. Do you love him or not?"

I sigh. "It's . . . complicated."

"Then help me understand."

I try to think of something to say, but all I can focus on is the sight of Hunter's knee next to mine. "I can't. I don't understand it myself." I stare out at the Great Lawn. I feel so at home here with Hunter, even though the Block, the Depths, are as different from the Aeries as anything I can imagine. "What about your family?"

Hunter slumps against the wall of the castle. "What about them?"

"You know a lot about mine, but I know nothing about yours," I say. "Why all the secrets?"

Hunter opens his mouth to speak, when the snap of a branch echoes in the air. He straightens up and looks around cautiously. "Come on." He holds out his hand. "Let's go."

We walk back through the castle and are about to descend the stone stairs, when we look up, and there is a figure looming ahead of us, backlit by light from the carnival.

"Hunter, what are you doing here?" The voice is feminine yet strong. "I thought I saw you at the carnival, and then I watched you go up this way. If someone sees you—"

The woman stops in her tracks. I recognize her face immediately: Violet Brooks, the mystic running for office.

She takes one look and clearly recognizes me.

Hunter turns to me and gulps. "Aria Rose," he says. "Meet my mother."

XIII

A voice in my head screams, *Run!*

"I have to go," I call to Hunter.

"Aria, wait!"

But I ignore him and take off, back through the carnival, over the Great Lawn, outside the Block. To the POD Hunter was going to send me to before. I don't even glance back at Hunter and his mother to see the shocked expressions on their faces.

Not only is Hunter an illegal, unregistered mystic, but his mother is Violet Brooks. She's running for office and attacking my family.

What am I doing?

If I tell my parents that Violet has a rebel son—a fact she's managed to keep secret from the media so far—they'll use it to smear her and ensure that Garland wins the election. But is that what I want? For the Roses and the Fosters to continue ruling the city, for the mystics to continue being enslaved and mistreated?

I don't think my family is right. Or fair. But they're still my family.

I'm not sure I can keep a secret this big from them.

Back home, I enter the passcode and take the back elevator all the way up to the penthouse, then exit into my family's kitchen. The apartment is dark, everything turned off. There's a tiny ding when the elevator doors close, and I wait a few seconds to make sure it didn't wake anyone.

When I'm satisfied, I slink up the stairs, quiet as can be, careful not to disturb Kyle or any of the servants. I'm guessing my parents are asleep in bed by now, too.

Even though she's probably sleeping, I head straight to Davida's room. I need to talk to her now, and I can't risk my mother's sending her out on errands tomorrow before I have a chance to question her. I rap gently on the door. A moment passes and it slides open.

"Aria?" she whispers. Davida is in a nightgown of simple white cotton, her black hair loose around her shoulders.

I step into the room and wait until the door closes behind me. My back is slick with perspiration, my knees weak from running out of the Block. My body is tired from the trip back to the Aeries, but I am somehow wide awake.

"What's wrong?" Davida says, wiping sleep from her eyes.

I cross over to her bed and perch on the edge. Then I pull out the pair of gloves. Davida's deep brown eyes widen. I lay the black gloves on the bone-white quilt and stare at her expectantly.

"Well, now you know everything, I suppose," Davida says.

I throw up my hands. "I don't know anything!"

"Shhh," Davida says, rushing forward and sitting down next to me. "You'll wake Magdalena and the others."

"I want the *truth,* Davida. All of it. Why are you keeping these magical things?" I point to the gloves on the bedspread. "Who *are* you?"

Davida cringes, turning so I can't see her face. The last thing I want to do is upset her, but I want answers—no, I *need* answers.

"Okay," she says, her back still to me. I move to rest a hand on her shoulder, but she flinches away before I can touch her. "I'm a mystic," she says to the wall.

"What?"

"You heard me," she says. "I'm a mystic."

It can't be true. "Davida, I've known you since you were a little girl. You were found in an orphanage in the Depths. You're poor, yes, but you're not a mystic. Your parents died when you—"

"My parents aren't dead, Aria. They're alive." Davida stands and begins pacing. "No one knows. Mystics—even registered ones—are second-class citizens. My parents wanted me to grow up and have a better life. So they placed me in an orphanage and lied. There was another mystic there, a woman named Shelly, who taught me how to conceal my powers so I wouldn't have to register. The gloves help with that—when I touch people, they can't feel my energy. Better that people think I'm a horribly scarred orphan than a mystic freak.

"When your parents took me in, I was so happy to have a home that I vowed to keep my real identity private. And you and I got along so well, I never wanted to disappoint you. I haven't had much contact with my family over the years, but I got a letter a few weeks ago saying that my mother is on her deathbed. She can't afford to see a doctor, so I've been taking her food and medicine."

My heart nearly stops beating from shock. "I'm so sorry."

"Aria, I'm still *me,*" she says, batting her dark lashes. "I didn't tell you because I thought you would hate me. I'm sorry for lying to you, but you and your brother and your parents are the closest thing I have to a family. I was worried if you all learned the truth, they would throw me out."

I immediately want to tell her that my family loves her and there is nothing she could do that would make us feel differently. But I know it isn't true—as soon as my parents find out, they'll feel taken advantage of and Davida will be without a job, her powers drained.

They might even have her imprisoned.

Davida kneels down in front of me. "Do you hate me? Please say you'll forgive me." Her voice breaks and she begins to cry. I reach over to her nightstand for a tissue and pass it to her.

"Of course I don't hate you," I say. "I'm sorry you felt like you had to keep your past hidden from me. I don't want there to be any more secrets between us. Let's promise to tell each other everything, okay? And I'll help you however I can."

Davida wipes her eyes. "I love you, Aria, you know that, right? It's improper for me to say, I'm sure, but—"

"I don't care about being proper, Davida. I love you, too," I tell her, and she places her gloved arms around me and gives me a hug. "I won't say anything to my parents."

Back in my room, I strip off my sweaty clothes and cap and take a shower. I comb my wet hair with my fingers and tie it back with a ribbon. I slip on a nightgown my mother brought me last year from Paris, blue silk with white lace trim.

I'm about to roll back my comforter when I hear a knock on one of my windows. *The wind,* I think, but the knocking repeats, more persistent.

I pull back the curtains. There, outlined against the night sky, is Hunter.

I blink. Am I dreaming?

But when I open my eyes he's still there, smiling at me and pointing to the latch on the window. I flick it open and slide the panes apart. Warm air immediately fills my room.

"What are you doing here?" I ask in a harsh whisper. "Are you crazy?"

"I'm here to see you," he says, his hands gripping either side of the windowsill for balance. "And yeah, I'm a little bit crazy. But nothing you can't handle. Why'd you run off before?"

I glance toward my bedroom door. "You might wake everyone up if you stay. I doubt they'll be too happy about a mystic sneaking in my window."

Hunter holds up his hands. "I'm not sneaking. You opened the window. That counts as an invitation, doesn't it?"

"No," I say. "It does not."

"Look," Hunter says, "I need to explain. Just let me talk to you for a few minutes and then I'll go. I promise."

I stare at him and am surprised by how familiar his face seems. Something about him—his easy attitude, perhaps, or the way he looks at me—makes me feel I can trust him.

"Fine." I roll up the sleeves of my nightgown. "A few minutes, that's all."

"Thanks," Hunter says, fanning himself with his T-shirt.

"Damn, it's hot." For a second, I can see the tight muscles of his stomach, his golden tanned skin. Then he holds out his hand—I let him grasp my fingers, and he pulls me out onto the balcony.

"Your time starts now."

"I don't want to talk here," he tells me. "We could be overheard."

I look out at the city—the view from up here is spectacular. The network of high-wire bridges and covered arcades that connects the buildings is swathed in yellow-white light from the spires; the sky is a murky blue, with gray clouds that look like the wisps of cotton candy at the carnival.

"Where do you want to go?" I ask. "The moon?"

"Nah," Hunter says, letting go of my hand. "I have a better idea."

Carefully, Hunter raises one hand into the air, and his fingertips begin to radiate the same bright green color I saw when he saved me in the Depths. The glow quickly turns into rays of light jetting out from each fingertip, so electric they are nearly blinding.

At first there are five, each like a stretched-out saber. Then Hunter flexes his fingers and the rays coalesce into one thick mass that pierces the sky. He throws back his arm like he did earlier at the carnival, only this time he's harnessing his energy and blasting it toward the roof of my building.

The green light from his hand is resplendent. Hunter lassos it around one of the pillars at the top of the roof like he's some kind of otherworldly cowboy, the lines and muscles of his face pulled taut as he concentrates, his skin tinged from the glow.

Then he extends his free hand to me. "Are you ready?"

"Ready for what?"

He winks and curls his fingers, beckoning me. "Come on, Aria," he says. "Have a little faith."

"Are you crazy? I'm not going to . . . swing onto my roof with you, or whatever you plan on doing."

"Why not?"

The ray seems securely wrapped around the roof post. But really, how could it hold the two of us? Everything about Hunter is improbable. Still, he hasn't failed me yet.

"Okay," I say.

As soon as our fingers touch, something shocks me, making my blood simmer and rushing through my limbs as though I've been struck by lightning. "Hunter!" I cry out, but his eyes are barely more than slits, and he's focusing on my hand. Quickly, the jolt of electricity subsides; I'm left with a warm sort of buzz that makes my skin feel prickly.

"I'm trying," he says. "I want you to be safe with me. Always." He pulls me into his arms; our chests fit together like puzzle pieces. I wrap my arms around his neck, clinging to his shoulders.

"Hold on," he says.

"Oh, I will. Don't worry."

And then I can feel us *moving.*

With one swift jump, Hunter is off the balcony. For a second, we seem to freeze midair, as though time has stopped.

And then we drop.

My stomach feels like it might fall right into the Depths. I suck in some air, but that only makes me cough. I squeeze my eyes shut—if I'm going to die, I don't want to see it happening.

But then I feel us shooting upward, swooping around the sky

as though we're riding on the clouds. I open my eyes. My heart races—it could catapult out of my rib cage at any moment.

"Aria," Hunter whispers. *"Look."*

I stare out into the Aeries—we are suspended midair, wind moving all around us. "Wow," I manage to say. We're surrounded in midnight blue. The glass façades of the skyscrapers glitter like gems. The spires swirl majestically, and the silvery grid of Aeries bridges is like a web of light laid on the city.

And then the top of my apartment building is so close that Hunter yells, "Jump!" and I do, letting go of him and hopping onto the roof. My knees buckle but I don't fall. I straighten and wish I weren't in a flimsy nightgown.

Immediately, the light dissipates, and Hunter tumbles onto the roof, as well.

It takes a minute for him to regain his strength. He leans over and breathes deeply.

"That was incredible," I say, barely able to speak.

"That?" Hunter says casually, wiping his hands on his jeans. "Nah, just a parlor trick, really." He gives a tiny shrug. "But I'm glad you liked it."

"I loved it." The roof deck is mostly barren. I see a few misters to cool the air and panels of smoked glass to protect the patio area. Some garden furniture is set up for those who can withstand the heat, and there's a tiny glass solarium near the far end, where my mother grows her own roses.

"Well then," Hunter says. For a moment he looks deep in thought. I like how the nighttime shadows further define his face and sculpt his jaw; how the blue of his shirt brings out the blue of his eyes, which blaze with excitement; how his nose and lips and teeth all work together in perfect harmony.

Then his arms are suddenly around me, pulling me to his chest. Even over the material of my nightgown, his touch makes my skin tingle. Being with Thomas feels nothing like this—whatever *this* is.

Then I remember the gorgeous letters Thomas wrote me, and I'm racked with guilt.

"Why did you come here?" I glance down, and there it is: Hunter's tattoo. A starburst. Outlined in black ink. The way it's shaded makes the center look like a glowing ball with thin shards bursting outward.

I pull away slightly so I can peer into his eyes. "You *were* on my balcony the night of my engagement party, weren't you?"

He doesn't answer.

"Are you spying on me?"

"*Spying* has such a dirty connotation," Hunter says, running one of his hands up my back. "How about *keeping watch*?"

We're so close I can feel the beating of his heart. The way I feel with his arms around me—so safe, so secure—is like nothing I've ever known.

"Why didn't you tell me about your mom—who she is? Is that why you were *keeping watch* over me? To monitor the competition?"

"No. Maybe." Hunter averts his eyes. "I thought you wouldn't talk to me if you knew."

"Your mother stands against everything my parents believe in," I say. "But I'm not my parents."

"Aria," Hunter whispers into my ear.

"Yes?"

"Just kiss me."

We press our lips together gently, and it's like I am alive, on fire, like I can do anything in the world. I know this is because he's a mystic, but there's something more than that. Something welcoming and familiar, something safe and sexy and irresistible about the way his lips feel, his tongue brushing lightly against mine. Our passion is like what's described in my love letters: it's like coming home, finally, when I never even knew I'd been away.

He loosens the ribbon in my hair, lets it fall to the ground, and runs his fingers through my hair, still damp from my shower. Something about him is so familiar . . . it could be our first kiss or our hundredth. It's all too much, and I pull away to catch my breath.

"Wow," Hunter says, inhaling deeply. "Just . . . wow."

I step toward the edge of the roof, looking at the drop below. There are a trillion butterflies in my stomach. I steady myself and notice the balcony to my bedroom. "Question," I say to Hunter. "How did you get onto my balcony in the first place? There's no entrance from the Aeries."

"There's a loophole," Hunter says. His voice is soft but steady, as though he's worried all this talk of magic and energy and loopholes will scare me half to death—which it sort of has. "From where I live to where you live—to your balcony."

"What's a loophole?"

Hunter makes a face. "It's like . . . a shortcut. You know how your TouchMe screen has easy access to programs you use a lot? This is like that, but for traveling from one place to another. Places you couldn't normally go without . . . trouble."

"Is that how you got to the balcony during my engagement party?"

He winces at the word *engagement* but nods.

"Can anyone use this . . . this *loophole*?"

"No," Hunter says, wiping his forehead with the back of his hand. "It's guarded by a mystic shield. No one knows about it but me. And Turk."

I am about to ask him *why* there would be a loophole from where he lives to my balcony when Davida appears on the roof. She is standing by the solarium when she spots me, and makes a beeline right to where I'm standing.

"Aria," she says, "I've been looking everywhere for you. Your parents just got home from a party that ran late. They're asking after you."

"Oh," I say, not knowing how to respond. I thought they were asleep in bed. I watch as Davida locks eyes with Hunter—a definite change comes over her, some confusing mix of emotions on her face.

They know each other.

Hunter again extends his hand—the familiar green light appears, and he knits together a platform, moving his hands in tight, fast circular motions. The glow of the rays makes Davida look green and sickly.

Hunter leaps onto the platform and it swings downward, moving from the roof back to my balcony. Once there, he raises one arm, and a bright green circle forms, the size of a person's body. It comes out of nowhere, from invisible folds in the sky.

This must be the loophole.

Hunter gives me a brief intense look with desperate eyes. I am about to say something, anything—to call out for him not to leave—when he leaps into the circle. With a pop it contracts into a dot and vanishes.

· XIV ·

"Do you think I should wear this necklace?" Kiki asks the next day, holding out a delicate strand of freshwater pearls. "Or this one?" The necklace draped over her other hand features a Burmese ruby surrounded by pink and white diamonds.

"Whichever," I say. "I like them both."

"Well, they're *yours,* so that makes sense." Kiki gives a quick little laugh and then chooses the pearls. "Aren't you excited?"

Excited? Not really. I feel too guilty to be excited.

I'm engaged to Thomas and yet I let another boy kiss me. And I kissed him back. The worst part? He's not even a regular boy—he's a rebel mystic! If Davida tells anyone, I will surely be dead. I can't even imagine what my father would do, or what it would mean for the election. I betrayed my family, and I betrayed Thomas, and worst of all . . . it felt *amazing.* I wasn't worrying about my memories or politics or what anyone expected me to do.

"I'm *sort of* excited," I say. Bennie's party is tonight; I almost wish I hadn't agreed to go. The last thing I want right now is to hang out with a bunch of Aeries kids.

And Thomas.

"Oh, you're just nervous because there will be photographers there," Kiki says. "Don't worry—if you're feeling camera shy, just send 'em my way. What are best friends for?"

Kiki does a twirl in the middle of my bedroom. Her dress is tight at the waist and flares at the bottom, and it sparkles from all the sequins and crystals sewn onto the bodice. "I wanted to wear something that has a real wow factor," she says. "Which is why I went with yellow. When I walk into the party it'll be like, *Bam! Here I am.*"

I laugh. "You always have to make a wild entrance. Remember my birthday party two years ago—"

"When I dressed up *like a baby*?" Kiki shrieks. "People nearly died. Or should have. No one else could have pulled off a high-fashion diaper."

"You're ridiculous." I motion for her to do the clasp of my dress. Tonight I've chosen to wear a lavender halter dress with a thin bow that ties around the waist and a long, pleated skirt.

"Hey, Aria, what's this?" Kiki asks.

She's holding up the locket I *thought* I'd hidden at the bottom of my jewelry box.

"Careful!" I grab it out of her hand. I stare at the silver heart, then make a fist around it. "It's, um . . . my grandmother's."

"Ooh," Kiki coos. "Why don't you wear it? It's pretty. What's inside?"

"Nothing. And I'm not wearing it." I hate lying to Kiki more than I already have, but I can't imagine telling her *I found it mysteriously but have no idea how to open it.*

Kiki wags her eyebrows. "Can I borrow it, then? It's so mag."

I can't let her wear it—what if she senses something magical? I'd never be able to explain myself. "You know, I am going to wear it." I fix the clasp around my neck and tuck the heart inside my dress.

"All right," Kiki says, fixing her mascara in the mirror. "Whatever."

There's a knock on my door. I press the wall panel and the door slides open. Outside, Davida is standing with her hands on her hips. We haven't spoken all day, and I wonder what she thinks of me. "I wanted to make sure you're aware of the time, Aria."

I glance at the clock. The party technically started ten minutes ago.

"That's fine, Davida," Kiki says, waving her hand. "We'll arrive fashionably late. It's what all the celebrities do."

"Kiki," Davida says with a slight curtsey.

"Okay," I say, trying to avoid any awkwardness. "We'll be ready in a minute."

Davida nods, then walks away, down the hall.

"God, but that girl is frigid and strange." Kiki takes a compact from her purse and blots her forehead. "I know you like her and all, but she has about as much personality as a mannequin. And mannequins aren't alive."

"All right, that's enough," I say, shooing Kiki out of my room. "You've never liked her, not even when we were younger."

Kiki harrumphs. "For good reason."

"And what reason is that?"

"She acts above her station. She's too familiar with you, thinks she's your friend—"

"She *is* my friend."

Kiki looks shocked. "No, Aria. She's not. She's your servant." Her voice is steady and sure. "And you should understand the difference."

She exits my room. I think about what she just said, then grab my clutch, shut the lights, and let the door close behind me.

We step out of the light-rail, and I'm immediately blinded by photographers' flashes.

"Aria! This way!"

"Over here, Ms. Rose!"

"Who are you wearing?"

"Where's Thomas?"

The sounds of cameras clicking and people screaming my name are overwhelming. Thankfully, Kiki is next to me, drinking it all in. "Charmed!" Kiki says, and *"Enchantée!"* She grabs my hand and leads me to the red carpet—it begins on the bridge adjacent to the rail station and continues all the way into Bennie's apartment building.

"This is a *lot* of red carpet," Kiki observes. "There are probably whole countries going uncarpeted just so our feet don't have to touch the floor."

"Bennie really outdid herself," I say. "I thought this was going to be a . . . *small* event."

"Small is for Depthshods," Kiki says, pausing to pull me close and pose for a photographer. "Go big or go *big*—really, there's no other choice. That's what I say."

I suppose I should have known that this party would be a

huge deal. This is the first major event in eighty years that all the young Manhattan elite are attending *together*. Everyone will be here, regardless of allegiance—Foster or Rose, kids from both sides of the island. The plummet party at the American pales in comparison.

"Come on," I say, shoving through a crowd of paparazzi.

"Aria, show me that smile!" one of them hollers. "You're gorgeous!"

"What am I, chopped liver?" Kiki hollers back. "Some people are so *rude*," she says to me. "I'm ready to go inside now."

We strut straight toward the bouncers and head inside, where Thomas told me to meet him.

Bennie's apartment is decorated outrageously, as if it were a nightclub. Long strands of tiny lights hang from the ceiling, stretching across the entire first floor in different colors—red, blue, green, and white—and casting their glow on the white walls.

Kiki and I pass through the foyer and into the living room, which is packed with kids—girls in fancy dresses, boys in dark suits and skinny ties, some dressed down slightly in blazers with eye-catching graphic T-shirts underneath.

"Wow," Kiki says. The ornate curtains are pulled back and draped with crystals, showing off views of the city. Overhead, the expensive chandelier has been removed, a glittering disco ball installed in its place. As it moves, the light hits the crystals and reflects in a hundred different directions.

Servers dressed in funky outfits—red and black jumpsuits with random circles of material missing, exposing their skin underneath—hold out trays of drinks and finger food. Even though the air-conditioning is on full blast, I begin to feel flushed. The music seems to come from everywhere. The bass makes the floor thump as though it has its own heartbeat, so loudly I can feel it in my bones.

I recognize a few of the boys from Layton Academy, the all-boys prep school where Kyle went. There are a lot of kids I don't recognize, though—Foster supporters or university students I haven't met.

"Aria!" A few girls from Florence Academy rush over and give me kisses on the cheek, and I say hello but don't stick around to talk. Thomas said he was coming with a few of his friends from school. Where are they?

"Come on," Kiki says. She grabs two drinks from one of the servers and hands me one. I take a whiff and wrinkle my nose.

Kiki doesn't seem fazed by how much alcohol is in her glass. She takes a big gulp. "Let's see who else is here."

Bennie's living area opens up into a rectangular dining room, where the DJ has set up. The table is covered with so much stereo equipment you can barely see it; the wall with all of her family's portraits is nearly masked by speakers.

"Rock on," Kiki says to the DJ as we pass.

The farther into the apartment we go, the more it begins to smell like sweat and booze. There are so many kids, it's nearly impossible to walk. "Come on, people!" Kiki says, swatting someone's back with her hand and pulling me deeper into the crowd. I feel completely sandwiched in, people pressing against me on either side, laughing and singing along to the music.

The staircase to the second floor is a few feet ahead. There's a large bouncer guarding it—hopefully, that means it's less packed upstairs.

Past the stairs, I see Kyle, holding a drink in his hand and talking to his friend Danny. They look like they're having a serious discussion.

"Where's Bennie?" Kiki yells over the music.

"I dunno," I say, wondering why she's not with Kyle. "Where's Thomas?"

Slowly, we move away from the thick of the dance floor. I take out my phone and send Thomas a text:

Where are you?

"That's the problem," Kiki says. She points to a cluster of boys who are jamming the hall. They're not trying to get anywhere, just standing in a circle, drinking and laughing. Two of them are tossing one of Bennie's mom's Egyptian vases back and forth.

"Hey, come on!" Kiki is loud, but her voice mixes with the heavy music and seems to diffuse into thin air. I use my free hand to plug one of my ears—they're already ringing.

"Can you guys move?" I call out. A few girls standing next to me try to push forward, but there's nowhere to go. "Guys! Move!"

"The lady said move your asses!" Kiki screams, sloshing her drink on them.

Either the shower of gin or the sound of her voice does the trick. The sea of people begins to part. Kids on either side of me speed past the stairs and into Bennie's den and some of the back guest rooms. People from the den trying to get to the dance floor pass us, too.

Kiki and I head toward the stairs. I can't help but notice that the group of boys don't look well. They're sweaty and slack-jawed, and their skin is ashen, almost green. They're so feverish they almost look like they're glowing. One of them leans into the vase he's been tossing and pukes.

"Does anything seem weird to you?"

"Weird? No. Sad?" Kiki stares into the bottom of her plastic cup. "Absolutely. I can't believe I wasted my drink on those fools. I need another. Want one?"

I shake my head. "I'm good, thanks. I'm gonna go upstairs."

"Okay then." Kiki glances back toward the dance floor. "I'll meet you in Bennie's room. Assuming I can get another drink before I'm, oh, I don't know . . . sixty-five?" She flips her hair and heads off.

At the foot of the staircase, I give my name to the bouncer—he checks me off his list and lets me up. At the top is a hallway full of doors. Bennie's room is the last one on the left, but the first door is open a crack, and I hear voices. I peek in and see a bunch of kids sitting around in a circle.

Then someone notices me. "Who's there?"

A girl with purple hair and freaky red contact lenses yanks the door wide. "Hey," she says coolly. She's dressed all in black—even black sneakers.

I give a tiny wave. "Hi. Is Bennie here?"

"Stacy, who is it?" a boy's voice calls out.

Stacy steps aside, and most everyone in the circle gapes at me.

"Aria Rose," says the boy, who I now see has blond hair parted on the side and bright green eyes. "Come on in!" he says. "What's up?"

The group is small. I don't recognize any of them and wonder why they would be on Bennie's VIP list. They're a strange mix of preppy and alternative. The boy who knows my name is wearing a pink shirt with a popped collar and a pair of tight slacks. But Stacy is dressed sort of goth, and a few other kids have several piercings and tattoos. These kids have the same sickly look as the boys downstairs, I realize. What is it with everyone?

"I'm just looking for Bennie," I say. "Do you know where she is?"

The boy takes a swig from a metal flask. "Nah," he says, grimacing as he swallows. "Haven't seen her. I'm Frank." He makes room for me on the rug. "Take a seat." A white-haired boy next to him is smoking a cigarette; he shoots me a bored stare and moves over, as well.

"We know how you love to *party*," another guy says, this one with so many piercings in his face that he clicks and rattles when he talks.

Party? What is he talking about?

The kids laugh. Someone's aMuseMe is playing a psychedelic rock song I don't recognize. A bunch of electric-green pills are clumped together on the floor in the middle of the circle, beside a tiny mirror with a pile of fine white powder resting on it.

A red-haired girl with a spiked necklace leans forward and snorts some powder off the mirror. Behind me, a boy and a girl outside the circle are sitting on a plush leather couch, making out and ignoring the rest of us. The flat-screen TV is on and muted, and a few other kids are chatting at high speed—they sound like actors in a movie that's locked on fast-forward.

"No, man, it's not like that at all," one of the boys is saying, shaking his head. "I love her. I *love* love her. She just doesn't realize it."

"That's because you never call her," one of the other guys says, taking some of the white powder and rubbing it on his gums.

Frank is breaking up one of the green pills into powder and fixing the powder into thin lines. And then I realize the obvious: everyone here is doing Stic.

"Where did you get that?" I ask Frank. One of the girls stares at me like I'm a cop about to arrest her.

Frank chuckles and continues grinding up the pill with his fingers. "Why you asking? Thomas holding out on you?"

He drops the rest of the pill onto a triangular mirror in front of me. Then he looks at me oddly. "Ooh, pretty," he says, reaching out and grabbing my locket, which has fallen out of my dress. He closes his fist around the silver heart.

I push his hand away—as soon as we touch, I scream out in pain. His skin burns like when you jam your finger into an outlet. My muscles contract; I flinch, my body going as stiff as a board, my jaw snapping shut. All the kids laugh at me.

It only lasts a moment, though. Then I feel my muscles relaxing back to normal.

Still laughing, Frank is doing a line of Stic. "Powerful shit." He passes the mirror back to Stacy, who pushes all the powder together into a fat line before dropping her nose over the mirror and snorting.

Wild, Frank stands up and grabs hold of a metal lamp a few inches away. He raises it in the air, then bends it in half as though it were a thin piece of copper. The lamp is now in two pieces, and he throws them to the floor. Some of the other kids applaud. Snot is running from his nose; I can't help but think how powerful Stic is.

"What did you mean by 'Thomas holding out on you'?" I ask.

Frank wipes his nose. "Shouldn't you be asking *him* that?"

"Are you telling me that Thomas is a Stic—"

My question is cut short by the sound of Stacy dropping to the floor. Her head smacks the wood with a sickening thump, and she starts convulsing.

"Babe?" Frank says cautiously.

Beads of sweat have popped out on Stacy's forehead; she seems instantly wet and shiny. And her skin is turning a bright, bright red. Something bad is happening.

Stacy doesn't say a word, just moans. Her limbs twitch, and within seconds her entire body is shaking, her back arching up off the ground while her heels drum against the carpet. She's having a seizure, foaming at the mouth, spit running down her chin.

Frank is on his feet, shoving the other kids away. "Everybody stand back!"

Everyone seems to be screaming now. The couple who were making out on Bennie's couch are now holding each other tightly, and a few of the girls have left the room and are shrieking away down the hall. Stacy's skin gets redder and redder with every second, so red it's painful to look at, like the worst sunburn I've ever seen, as if she's being boiled alive.

There is the stink of scorched *something*. I glance around to see if someone's stray cigarette has accidentally lit the carpet on fire—and then I realize the smoke is coming from Stacy herself. She is literally burning up.

She moves like a fish out of water, flopping a few feet in each direction, rising from the floor and falling back down again. The smoke grows stronger, thicker, and then—

Stacy bursts into flames.

"Shit!" Frank looks around frantically. "Somebody do something! Help!"

Without thinking, I dump my glass onto Stacy's body.

Then the kid next to me takes *his* drink and dumps the liquid on Stacy. The water briefy quells the flames, but then they rise up again. Another girl pours her drink on Stacy, as well—a cosmo, from the looks of it—but the flames only grow stronger.

I rush over to the cabinet in the corner and rifle through the drawers until I find a pea-green blanket. I unfold it and cover Stacy's body, smothering the flames as Frank helps hold her down.

"Oh my God," the girl with the spiked necklace is saying next to me, fanning herself with her hands. "Oh my God oh my God oh my God!"

I back away from the smoke. My eyes are tearing up, and it's hard to see. Suddenly, a bunch of EMTs burst into the room. I don't think anyone called them, but no one in the Aeries ever has to: I'm sure there's a fire alert on the Grid. One of the benefits of so much of the city being monitored electronically.

We all back into the hallway while the EMTs do their work.

They are quietly efficient. While two strap Stacy onto a gurney, a fireman sprays down the room with an extinguisher. When they leave, Frank follows the gurney, and I wonder what will become of Stacy.

"That was wicked awesome," one of the boys beside me says.

I shove him against the wall. "Shut your stupid mouth," I say. He's too shocked to respond.

Downstairs, the party is still raging, the kids completely oblivious to what happened upstairs. I feel so much hatred for these people—my people—that I'm choking on it. Kiki's not in the kitchen, so I just start opening every door in Bennie's apartment to find her. At this point, I've completely given up on locating my missing fiancé.

First is an office of some sort; a couple is sleeping something off with their heads under a desk. Then I find Bennie's father's library, empty save for his collection of books and three guys smoking pot out of a tiny glass bowl. Next is a long exercise room—tons of machines that probably never get used. I open the door, press on the lights.

And there is my fiancé, kissing a girl who is not me.

Thomas is standing in the middle of the room in a pale blue dress shirt that is open at the neck. His belt is unbuckled, and Gretchen Monasty has one of her hands down his pants. The top of her dress is rolled down, exposing her pink lace bra.

Thomas looks over, lipstick on his chin. His dark hair is cow-licked, as if Gretchen has been running her fingers through it for the past hour. His expression is priceless: a mixture of surprise, fear, embarrassment, and lust.

He pushes Gretchen away so quickly that she almost falls to the ground.

"Aria! It's not what it looks like," he calls out, but I'm already gone—out the door, down the hall, running as fast as my heels will carry me.

· XV ·

There is only one person I can talk to, one person I *want* to talk to.

Hunter.

The nose of the gondola breaks the waters of the canal, moving swiftly down Broadway, tiny waves rippling on either side of us. It's sweltering hot, and my head is still spinning from the chaos at Bennie's party. Remarkable that Thomas managed to take my focus away from a girl who literally ignited before my very eyes—but he did.

I want to feel hurt, to feel devastated beyond belief by his actions—sneaking around with Gretchen Monasty behind my back. How long has this been going on? But really, how can I be mad at Thomas for kissing someone else when I did the exact same thing?

I'm surprised by how easy my escape was, and confused that no one has detected my movement on the Grid so far, but I'm not complaining. I have no destination—I came to the Depths to find Hunter, but I have no way of contacting him. So I've instructed the gondolier to take me to the Block, and I'll figure it out from there.

We sail past high, dark buildings, underneath arched bridges, and past other gondolas and water taxis. I don't know how long we've been motoring along when I notice the spires along the main canal. I've never seen the energy within them act like this, pulsing on and off, surging and diminishing to the beat of some invisible music. I glance at the gondolier to see if he notices anything strange, but his eyes are focused ahead, his hand on the steering wheel.

Suddenly, I feel the heart-shaped chunk of metal around my neck heat up against my skin. I yank it out from underneath the fabric of my dress—and it's *glowing.*

A golden light radiates from it. I cup the locket in my palms and try to open it, but I still can find no seam or latch. I drop it back inside my dress before the gondolier notices; it's hot against my skin.

What *is* this thing? And why is it reacting like this now? When Frank grabbed it, he had just taken a dose of Stic. I wonder if the overload of energy coursing through his system activated it somehow.

Some spires brighten as we draw near, while others dim almost to darkness, and the locket throbs as if there is a human heart trapped inside. I think back to when I timed the rush of color in the spires from my window. I noticed that the pattern of light—white, yellow, and green—was different in each spire, but it didn't mean anything to me then. I couldn't figure out the pattern.

Only now, with the way the locket is reacting . . .

Follow the lights, Tabitha told me.

Okay, Tabitha. I'm listening.

"Excuse me?" I call out to the gondolier.

He raises his head.

"Can we stay straight, please?"

He points left. "But the Block's that way, miss."

"I know," I tell him, "but I've changed my mind. Straight ahead, please."

He obeys, and we stay on track. Up ahead, the canal is about to fork: on the right, the spires seem to churn a bright green light that flashes on and off. The locket warms and the beat inside it seems to quicken. To the left, the spires seem to dull, the light fading to a soft white.

"Turn right up here," I say.

He obeys without another word.

We pass a series of ramshackle buildings with ratty awnings and even rattier docks. A cluster of gondoliers idle with their boats tied to the pilings, waiting for passengers and smoking cigarettes. They watch us and talk among themselves.

Up ahead, a particular spire pulses dramatically, and the locket around my neck begins to purr.

"This way," I tell the gondolier. "I mean, left, please."

He turns onto a narrow side canal. Here, the waters brush dangerously close to the doors and windows on the first floors of the buildings, showing just how much the water level has risen over the years. Higher up, mystic sconces line the buildings.

I watch as the sconces blink in ways I cannot understand but am driven to follow. I give a few quick directions—left, then right, then left again—and our waterway opens up onto a larger canal. The gondola picks up speed, and soon we're moving very fast. Wind whips my hair every which way, and the locket thrums against my chest.

The spires lead us farther and farther south, until finally the locket calms and a sense of relief washes over me.

"We're here," I say, not knowing where here is. I hand the gondolier a few coins from my clutch.

He pulls alongside the nearest dock and I am out and on my way.

I have no idea where I'm going. I walk on cracked pavement and over a tiny bridge—this part of the city is more run-down than near the Block, if that's even possible. Store windows are boarded up, and there don't seem to be as many apartment buildings. Gaps mark the skyline—places where buildings must have plummeted and crumbled into nothingness. And then I realize that the water I see up ahead is not a canal, but the ocean.

The misty outlines of the Manhattan and Brooklyn Bridges come into view.

I must be at the very southern tip of the city, in the area that used to be called the South Street Seaport. I look for a spire and spot one a half-block away. Its tip glistens in the night, the light swirling with a silvery-white glow.

As I walk toward it, the locket seems to awaken.

I must be heading in the right direction.

Few people are out on the streets, and no one is dressed like I am—for a party in the Aeries—so I try to blend into the shadows by the closed storefronts along the street. I stride down the sidewalk as though I belong here. I pass a couple walking arm in arm; a few homeless men sleeping on the ground beside overturned hats, hoping for spare change; a teen not much older than me who whispers "Stic?" as I sweep by.

Then a figure catches my attention.

Someone in a dark hooded cloak is walking a hundred feet ahead, heading swiftly in the same direction I am. The figure glances around mysteriously, passing underneath the post that I noticed swirling only moments before.

When the light hits her face, I gasp.

It's Davida.

She must be here, I reason, to bring food to her mother. But no—if that were the case, she wouldn't be here at all. Her mother must live with the other registered mystics in the Block.

So what is Davida doing all the way down south?

I'm tempted to call out her name, but I worry that she'll run away. Instead, I follow her down the street to a cast-iron subway entrance. Green globes are mounted on poles on either side, the paint mostly chipped off. At one time there must have been a stairway descending into the subway, but when the system was flooded, the city sealed off the tunnels, making them impossible to enter.

Only . . . Elissa Genevieve told me how her team was searching for a way into the underground subway tunnels to flush out the rebels. How all the entrances are blocked with mystic shields. They can't *really* be impossible to enter, can they?

Davida moves from shadow to shadow until she is right in front of the entrance. She positions herself directly underneath one of the globes and bows her head. Covered in black, she's practically invisible. She reaches out and touches one of the posts, and the globe on top blazes green for a moment, then returns to normal.

And then she starts to sink.

It happens so quickly—I watch as her legs disappear, then her torso, and finally her face vanishes into the cement, as if the ground itself isn't solid and giant hands are lurking underneath the pavement, pulling her down.

I wait for a second, checking to see if anyone witnessed this intense bit of magic. But I seem to be alone. The street is quiet, almost too quiet.

I sneak over to the entrance and examine the sidewalk. Rock solid. I stamp on the place where Davida was swallowed up. Nothing happens. I grab the same post she did, but the globe doesn't light up.

The entryway itself is plugged with cement and sealed off with a metal cover. I kick it with my foot and immediately regret doing so. The cover is completely solid, and now my toes hurt. *Nice going, Aria. Those shoes were expensive.*

I think for a moment. I saw Davida light up the globe with her touch. Why didn't that happen for me? *She's a mystic,* I think. *I'm not.*

I wipe sweat from my neck with the back of my hand. I may not be a mystic, but this locket certainly has some kind of power. What if . . .

A few steps and I plant my feet right where Davida stood, underneath the far globe of the entryway. I unclasp the locket. My stomach fills with a nervous, tingly feeling, but I touch the silver heart to the post anyway: as soon as the two pieces of metal meet, the globe on top ignites with color.

And then the cement and the metal covering beneath my feet liquefy.

The drop is quick. My legs feel like they're being squeezed in vises; my chest deflates; my arms ache like they're being pricked with dozens of needles. My entire body is *hot*. I look up as the Depths disappear from view. What if I fall into nothingness—or get stuck? My neck is almost at the pavement now, and I breathe as deeply as I can and shut my eyes.

I pass through.

I hit the ground and open my eyes. I've fallen onto a flight of stairs. Above me, the cement ceiling ripples, like a pool of water after you've thrown a stone into it. I reach up and touch it. At first it's solid, but then it flows away from my touch.

I stumble down the stairs, which end on a platform at the mouth of a darkened tunnel. The walls around me are covered with tiny colored tiles, and there are sconces afire with mystic light on either side of me. This isn't an abandoned station; it's clear this place is an active hideaway for people who don't want to be found.

Not people, I think. *Rebel mystics.*

The thought makes me shudder. I recall the ad I filmed in the wreckage of one of their explosions. I'm naive if I think they're all as nice as Hunter. If Hunter is even nice. Who knows what he wants from me?

What have I gotten myself into? There's no going back, though—only forward. I'll find Davida, and she'll explain everything.

I glance around at what must have been a waiting area for people to board the subway. The ground is slick with grime and eroded from where, at one point, it must have been completely flooded. I walk to the edge of the platform. The subway tracks are full of muddied brown water. The tunnels seem to run in a continuous long line, but the only way to get down them is to swim.

Then I see a strip of concrete a few inches above the water level. I can't see far enough to know how long it is, but there's nowhere else to go. So I start down the tunnel, into the inky dark.

I can't see Davida, but I hear footsteps ahead of me and assume they're hers.

With a soft splash, I step into warm, shallow water. The ground angles downward, and the water gets deeper and deeper. Another step, and I sink to my calves into the water. If I continue along this route, I'll have to breast-stroke my way through.

No thanks. I feel along the wall and look up: there's just enough light to make out rungs set into the concrete—a metal ladder. I slosh toward them, climb up, and soon find myself on a ledge above the tunnel. My shoes are ruined now; I'd kick them off completely, but who knows what I'd step in.

I advance, and a lightbulb embedded in the wall blinks on. The ledge connects to what I can now see is a network of metallic catwalks. These are not the flooded, abandoned subway tunnels we were taught about in school. Someone has put a lot of work into this place—a lot of mystic work. No one else could have done this.

I take another step. Another light blinks on, and the one behind me goes off. There must be a series of lights, all on sensors. Which means that every step I take can potentially alert someone to my presence.

Way up ahead, I see lights blink on and off—those must be from Davida.

I quicken my pace and follow the catwalk along the flooded tunnels, and eventually I reach an archway. On the other side, everything is awash with light. There are many sconces here, many more than in the tunnels, and they burn a bright green, but the color seems somehow soft, not overwhelming.

It seems like I've stumbled upon some type of intersection. Below me is a flat square of earth, higher than the water level but lower than the catwalks.

The tunnels continue to run past this place in parallel lines—but to my left and right, parts of the earth have been hollowed out, making it possible to travel from tunnel to tunnel without having to go aboveground. It's likely that some of the rebels make their homes in these makeshift tunnels. Which means they could be anywhere, watching me. Ready to attack.

I need to get out of sight.

I swing my leg over the railing, figuring I can drop to the ground, where it's a bit darker, but my dress gets caught, and I'm stuck. The fabric is snagged on a tiny tooth of metal—I tug at it, wrenching it back and forth, climbing back onto the catwalk and trying to free myself without ripping the dress, but I fail utterly.

With a loud noise, the skirt rips hem to hip, and I end up slicing my leg in the process.

"Ow!" I cry out, then cover my mouth with my hand, praying no one heard me. Blood immediately seeps out of the cut, a long line of red up my calf.

This night just gets worse and worse.

Suddenly, there's a pounding on the catwalk from the shadows straight ahead. It sounds like a herd of elephants.

Someone heard me.

The lights blink on and off so quickly that it's impossible to tell who or *what* is coming at me. That is, until the light bounces off a familiar head of golden-blond hair.

Hunter.

"Aria?" He's dressed in a black T-shirt that shows off his muscles, and a slim pair of gray jeans. "What the hell are you doing here?"

"Nice to see you, too."

He blinks. "Sorry. I mean . . . hi."

"Hi."

He smiles hesitantly. "Seriously, though: what are you doing here?"

"I was looking for you," I say, the words rushing out.

He places his hands on my shoulders and draws me into a hug. "It's not safe for you here," he whispers. "Come on."

Hunter stands back and takes my hand. This time, his touch doesn't elicit anything more than a tiny spark inside me. It's a thrilling spark, sure, but it's not the wild, humming thrill I felt the first time we touched. It's more like a soft sense of warmth—of comfort. He must've learned how to better control his energy.

He leads me along the catwalk. We turn right, down another tunnel. "What is this place?" I ask.

"After the Conflagration," Hunter says, "all the mystics were forced to register with the government and have their powers drained. But some refused and burrowed into these old tunnels, which were flooded and unsafe." Hunter smiles and I feel a different kind of warmth. "I say *were* because the mystics cleared most of the abandoned tunnels. It was the work of decades, and it cost lives. But thanks to their work, the tunnels are here for those of us who want to escape the drainings. Us 'rebels' have been hiding out down here ever since."

It's grown brighter as Hunter talks, and all of a sudden the tunnel opens up into another subway station. It's like the station I first saw when I dropped through the seal, only this one is preserved. Lived in. Mosaics cover the walls. I see platforms with benches where passengers used to wait for the subways, polished turnstiles—and an actual *train* with cars.

"Oh wow," I say, letting Hunter help me off the catwalk and onto the platform.

I run my hands along the side of a silver subway car. The metal is cool to the touch. Its windows have been blacked out, and even though the subway is old and unattractive, especially compared to a light-rail car, I can't help but be impressed. It makes me long for a simpler time, a time without mystics and Fosters and Roses.

"This is what people used to get around." There's a wide smile across Hunter's face; he seems happy to be able to share this piece of history with me.

"Where are the fingerscans?"

Hunter laughs and points to one of the turnstiles. "No scans. People used to buy tokens that they would drop into a slot, and the turnstile arm would turn."

I laugh, too. "It cost money to ride the subway? That's ridiculous."

"It's true," he tells me, resting one of his hands on my back. I nearly melt at his touch and the power from his fingertips seems to soothe me.

It hardly feels dangerous at all.

"Remember when you asked me at the carnival where I lived? Welcome to my humble abode, Ms. Rose," he says, bowing like an actor at the end of a play.

"Why, thank you," I say, curtseying. I giggle, which makes Hunter laugh, too, harder this time. He's so handsome when he laughs I can hardly stand it. He presses his hand to one of the subway cars, and the door opens. "Want to come inside for a spot of tea?" he says, affecting a British accent.

"I'd love to," I say.

Hunter extends his arm and I enter the subway car. I nearly faint from shock.

I'm not sure what I was expecting, but it certainly wasn't this: the subway car is an actual *home*. I'd pictured rebels living in rough-and-tumble circumstances, sleeping in tents on the ground or huddled next to trash can fires, dirty and desperate.

But the inside of this subway car has been converted into an apartment. Not my parents' apartment, granted, but a comfortable one nonetheless. There's a kitchen with a breakfast nook, a stove, and cabinets. A long sofa is pushed up against one of the walls, piled with soft-looking pillows, and there are metal bookshelves full of books—plays and novels and collections of histories of Manhattan. A turquoise guitar is resting on a stand next to the sofa; I remember that Hunter told me he loved music that first night at Java River.

"My very own bachelor pad," Hunter says.

"It's wonderful," I tell him. I walk over to a picture of him and his mother. Hunter looks about ten years old; they're both smiling, seemingly without a care in the world. This is what I love about pictures—the ability to capture a moment in time that you can never get back.

"Aria, you're bleeding," Hunter says.

I glance down at my leg—he's right. The cut looks deeper and more serious than it did before, and a trail of blood has stained my skirt and my skin.

"Stand still," Hunter says, and presses his hand to my leg. I watch the green glow surround his hand—it feels like a heat lamp has been placed over the cut. My skin seems to sizzle and blaze, and it hurts sharply for a moment, and then the glow is gone and everything is back to normal. No more cut.

Hunter walks over to his sink and dampens a washcloth. He wrings it out, then kneels on the floor and gently wipes the blood off my leg. His touch is delicate as he moves from my ankle to my calf, rubbing in tiny circles, leaving me nearly breathless.

He lifts the washcloth and lightly kisses the spot where the cut was. His eyes are trained on mine, ocean-blue and sparkling with delight. "All better," he says, standing up and dropping the cloth in the sink.

I'm still standing in the middle of the subway car when he asks, "How did you get down here, Aria? All the entrances are blocked with mystic foils."

"I followed someone," I tell him, which is . . . *sort of* the truth.

"That person opened up something, and I was able to get through. I was desperate to talk to you."

He raises an eyebrow. "Is everything okay?"

I sit on the edge of his sofa. Where to start—the girl OD'ing on Stic at the party? Thomas OD'ing on Gretchen? Davida skulking around South Street Seaport like a spy?

Instead, I turn the tables on him. "Why don't you just register? Wouldn't it be . . . easier?"

Hunter goes rigid. "Easier? Look, Aria, if I register, then I have to get drained." He pauses. "Do you have any idea how much that hurts?"

I think of Tabitha, who told me about the lights, and Hunter's mom—both registered mystics. "Not really. I mean, a little bit."

He stands. "They hook you up to this horrible machine and stick you everywhere with wires. Then they suck the life out of you—or just about. All your power, everything that makes you who you are—and capture it in some glass tubes. I've heard the pain is like knives slicing open every inch of your skin."

"I never knew," I say, suddenly feeling a crushing guilt. My family does this.

"The drainings leave you weak for *months,* so weak you can barely walk at first." He stares at me with an intensity that makes me nervous. "But it's not about the pain. It's the whole *point.* Our powers are like our souls. What your parents—what your government—make us do is killing us slowly and surely. I'll never register, Aria. Never."

"I understand," I say quickly. "Really, I do."

Hunter walks over to one of the blacked-out windows. "Besides, I have to save my powers in case I need them."

"Need them for what?"

"Healing a cut on your leg, for one," he says. "Or in case my mother loses the election." He comes to where I'm sitting and places a hand on my knee. His touch is like nothing I've ever known; each time his skin meets mine, all I want is more, more, more.

"You're probably wondering why we don't live together," Hunter says. "Me and my mom."

"Well, yes, but—"

"Mystics didn't always live in the open," he says. "My grandfather was one of the first to come out."

"They didn't?"

Hunter shakes his head. "My ancestors have been persecuted from the beginning of time. We've been called everything—witches, warlocks, demons—and killed for who we are. Burned at the stake."

"So what happened? What changed?"

"Before the First World War, when so many people emigrated to the United States for a better chance, a new life . . . mystics fled by the hundreds. Ellis Island welcomed us with open arms. We hid at first, establishing ourselves here, but eventually, nobody wanted to hide anymore." Hunter clenches his fists. "Pretending to be something you're not sucks the life out of you. Even worse than the drainings." He relaxes his hands, stretching out his fingers. "There were a few . . . *demonstrations* of our power here in the States, and word got to President Truman. He spoke out, welcoming mystics in exchange for our help building up the cities. Once global warming set in, well, we were indispensable."

"Until the Conflagration," I say. It happened before I was alive, but this event—the explosion—was when people realized exactly how powerful mystics were, and what could happen if that power was used for evil instead of good.

Hunter nods. "My grandfather was killed in the explosion. My mom has followed in his footsteps, living openly, registering, trying to change the system—but I refused to be drained. I didn't want to screw things up for her politically, though, and so I ran away, right before I was scheduled to be drained, as my power was cresting. If anyone from the Aeries asked, my mom told them she didn't know where I was. Eventually people just forgot I existed."

"And she's okay with that?"

"She worries about me," Hunter says. "Wishes we could live together. But some things are more important."

"Like an election?"

Hunter frowns. "You don't get it, Aria. This election is the first time we're being taken seriously. The lower classes, the poor nonmystics, believe in my mother and are actually supporting us. No one has dared to even challenge anyone in the Aeries since the Conflagration, and now . . . we could *win*. You see what life is like around here—don't you think it should change?"

"I—I . . ." I look away. How can I possibly tell Hunter that I believe in his cause, when it will mean the downfall of my family?

"Look, never mind. I shouldn't have asked you that." Hunter softens his voice. "I know why you came here, Aria."

"You do?"

"You want to know about the loophole to your balcony."

"Oh," I say, weirdly relieved. He doesn't know that my feelings for him are like a drug I shouldn't have—feelings that I can barely admit to myself, let alone to him.

"But I can't tell you that," Hunter says. "There are things that will endanger you if you know them, and I want you to be safe. You have to trust me."

"I barely know you," I say.

"That doesn't mean you can't trust me." Even though we're alone, he lowers his voice. "The rebels are as split as your stupid Roses and Fosters are above. Sorry, I don't mean you. No offense."

"None taken," I whisper.

"My mom leads a peaceful coalition, but there are other rebels who are preparing for a war. You probably already know about the demonstrations—that building that exploded, the family that was killed—but those are nothing compared to what will happen if my mother loses the election. There will be a revolt. And I will be fighting with them."

I'm speechless. A war? And Hunter will be fighting against my parents?

"If anyone sees you down here, there will be trouble," Hunter says. "Which is why, as much as I would like you to, you really can't stay." He leans in and I think he's going to kiss me on the lips. I close my eyes, waiting, but all I feel is a gentle peck on my forehead. "You're an incredibly special girl, Aria, but it's too dangerous for us to be together. You have a fiancé and a life that doesn't belong with mine. Go back to the Aeries," he says, pulling away. "Where you'll be safe."

His words stab my soul—how can one person go from being so kind to so cold within seconds? "You didn't seem to mind hanging out with me when you were kissing me on my roof," I say, trying not to let my voice falter. "What could have possibly happened since then? Did you change your mind because it's complicated?"

Hunter stares at me silently.

I stand up. "Boys are so . . . stupid. I thought you were different, but you're just like Thomas. And my father."

"What's that supposed to mean?"

"It means," I say, "that you only look out for yourself."

Hunter moves in front of me, barely an inch away from my face. "You have no idea what you're talking about, Aria. You're so far off from the truth, it's crazy."

"Then prove it."

For a second, I think Hunter is going to take me in his arms and kiss me. But then his expression turns melancholic. "You really have to go," he says.

He steps back and holds his hand up in the air. He concentrates for a moment; then a green circle of energy, like the one he disappeared into the other night, opens up in the middle of the subway car. The opening of the circle pulses, the energy swirling and growing like flames in a fire.

The loophole back to the Aeries, back home.

If he wants me gone, I tell myself, *I'll go. But not without saying goodbye.*

I race forward and plant my lips on his. I kiss him feverishly, as though the end of the world is upon us and there is nothing left but us, together, and this final fiery expression of desire.

The locket comes to life against my chest, searing my skin. I step closer to the fiery loophole and thrust one of my hands inside. My skin prickles and stings; I feel something pulling me inside, away. I look back, over my shoulder, at Hunter.

"Come to my balcony on Monday night," I say. "I'll be waiting for you."

· XVI ·

"The girl literally blew up!" Kiki says.

We're at my kitchen table, eating breakfast on Monday morning. Sunday passed in a blur. Thankfully, I made it back safely via the loophole on Saturday night. I had to kick open my windows and accidentally broke the lock, but otherwise? Not even a scratch.

Davida kept to herself all of Sunday; every time I went to her room or tried to find her to ask why she'd disappeared underground, she was nowhere to be seen. My mother and I discussed table settings for the wedding and decided on a floral arrangement for the centerpieces (roses, no surprise there). Garland and his wife, Francesca, came over for dinner and we discussed the election, which is just over a month away. Thomas didn't come—no doubt he was too embarrassed about what happened the night before.

The tone of the meal was somber. My parents are worried that Violet Brooks actually could win the election—and then what? Garland and Francesca were both nice, but I wish there were something more to them. "I'm incredibly excited about your wedding, Aria," Garland told me, flashing a bright white smile and grabbing his wife's hand. "The day I married Franny was the happiest day of my life."

"Oh, Garland, that's so sweet," Franny replied. They reminded me of a young Jack and Jackie Kennedy, only less interesting. And less Catholic.

This morning—Monday, July 18—Kiki showed up unexpectedly, just after my father left early for a meeting downtown. I'm already dressed for work, in a navy-blue pencil skirt and a white blouse with pearl buttons. The locket is still around my neck; now that I know it has powers of some sort, I'm too nervous to take it off. In the other room, Kyle is eating an egg white and broccoli omelet, watching TV alone.

"Really?" I ask. "She *literally* blew up?"

"Okay, well, she didn't 'blow up' as much as . . . fizzle." Kiki bites into an apple. "I was there, of course. Saw it all firsthand. I cannot believe I watched someone OD right before my very eyes. I am *so* traumatized," Kiki says, pressing her hand to her forehead.

I'm not sure why Kiki is lying about witnessing the overdose, but she *does* love being the center of attention. There's no need to call her bluff. She's not hurting anyone.

The image of the girl on fire is hard to forget: her body shaking uncontrollably as the drugs overtook her, her crimson skin spontaneously combusting.

"Anyway, the point is that she's dead and *I saw it*. I wonder if I have to go into therapy now," Kiki says.

I shoot her a sideways glance.

"Well, *more* therapy than I'm already in," she says. "I ran into

Thomas, too." Kiki raises an eyebrow. "He said you left early because you weren't feeling well. Are you okay now?"

Hmm. Makes sense that Thomas didn't tell her about Gretchen. *I* certainly want to tell her, but I haven't decided what to do about it just yet. Inform my parents and call off the wedding? Pretend it never happened?

Until I decide, best to keep it to myself. "Yeah, I'm fine. What time is it?" I put down my spoon without finishing my oatmeal, no longer hungry. "I don't want to be late."

"It's eight-thirty," says a voice from the hallway. Davida is walking toward me with a stern expression on her face. Her hair is up; she's wearing her black uniform and, of course, her gloves. "Aria, may I have a word with you?"

Before I can respond, Kiki answers, "No, Davida, you may not."

I'd laugh if Kiki's tone weren't so serious. "What's your deal, Kiki?" I ask.

Kiki tugs on the hem of her striped cotton day dress. "I promised your father on my way in that I'd escort you to work and make sure you got there on time," she says, "and I won't disappoint him."

Kiki takes one final bite of her apple, then drags me into the foyer. My purse is in my hand, and before I know it I'm out the door.

"I hate how she orders you around," Kiki says, tapping her foot impatiently as we wait for the elevator. "You should get rid of her once and for all."

For some reason, Kiki's dislike of Davida really bugs me this morning—more than usual. Also, I'm annoyed that she's basically made it impossible for me to speak with Davida when I *need* to ask her about the other night. "You know, how I interact with my servants is really none of your business."

Kiki flinches as though I just slapped her. The elevator dings and the doors retract. "Come on," she says. "Some of us have places to be."

At work, I can't seem to do anything right.

I accidentally spill coffee on my blouse and have to rush to the bathroom to try to scrub it out before it leaves a stain. I'm left with a white collared shirt that has a huge wet spot just underneath my right breast. So embarrassing.

Then, because I'm so upset about the spill, I do something to the TouchMe at my desk—I must've touched a wrong button on the screen—and the monitor goes blank. I'm forced to wait for someone from technical services to come and reboot the entire system.

"Don't worry," the young man—Robert—says. He looks about my age, maybe a few years older. "We'll get you back to work in no time, Ms. Rose."

My phone buzzes as I wait for Robert to finish. It's Thomas calling. This is the fifth or sixth time he's called me since Saturday night. I let the call go straight to voice mail. I'm not in the mood to speak to him, not after the party.

Gretchen Monasty.

I think back to the plummet party, when she was so rude.

Was Thomas hooking up with her then, or is this a more recent development?

My phone beeps: Thomas has left me a message.

The sound of his voice makes me bristle.

Aria, it's me. We need to talk. I care about you so much, and I don't want you to have the wrong impression. Please call me back. I miss you.

The message ends. I play it back. *I don't want you to have the wrong impression.* What other impression could I have?

I press Delete and stare at the phone, incredulous. I caught my fiancé cheating on me. Shouldn't I be breaking down and crying, unable to get out of bed or move a muscle?

Oddly enough, all I feel is . . . relieved.

Who is this boy I'm supposed to marry—did I ever even know him at all? Or has our entire relationship been a sham? And yet . . . The locket. The letters. Who are they from, if not from him?

"Ms. Rose," says a voice, bringing me back to the present. It's Robert, standing before me with a timid smile.

"Yes?"

"All fixed," he says. "Have a nice day, now."

I watch as he walks to the elevator, undergoes a body scan, and then steps inside. The door zips closed behind him, and I think, *Great. Back to work.*

I've barely sat back down when I'm accosted by Patrick Benedict, who slams his fist down on my desk. His brown eyes seem darker than usual today, his bony face a collection of sharp angles and nearly translucent skin, so thin I can see the blue veins that run across his forehead. He's hunched over, and his eyes are bloodshot, as though he's been up all night. His hair is slicked back and parted on the side, his lips drawn back like those of a dog about to fight, exposing his stark white teeth.

"Did you have a nice weekend?" he asks.

I can tell by his tone that he doesn't actually care to know. I look away for a second and realize that most of the floor is paying attention to us, their heads poking up over the cubicles.

"What do you mean?"

Benedict waits for a moment, then he reaches over me and logs into his email account on my TouchMe. Within seconds, he's able to bring up a series of pictures from when Stacy overdosed Saturday night—someone in the room must've taken photos on their phone. They're mostly of me, a mirror with crisp lines of Stic in the background, my body leaning over the girl as she's OD'ing.

"A very concerned citizen sent me these this morning," Benedict tells me. "Do you have any idea what this could do to the election if they get out? Your stupidity is risking everything your family has worked *years* for."

"But I didn't do anything *wrong,*" I say.

Benedict shakes his head. "A picture says a thousand words. Don't you know by now that some people will do anything to get ahead?"

People like you? I want to say, but I hold back.

"Your family is a prime target, Aria. We were able to keep you out of the public eye during your first overdose." He smacks his lips together. "I doubt we'll be able to do the same if you suffer a second one."

I curl my hands into fists and hide them behind my back. I

know I never ingested Stic—Lyrica confirmed that much. Something else is going on; I just don't know what it is.

Yet.

"What do we do now?" I ask, motioning to the screen. "Maybe we can explain to the press that I tried to save her, I wasn't doing any drugs myself."

Benedict closes out his email. "It's already taken care of. We traced the email to a teenager on the East Side. We found the digital shots and erased them before they were sent to any tabloids."

I'm immediately relieved. "Oh, well . . . thank you."

"I did not do this for you, Aria." Benedict squints, looking meaner than before. "I did it for your father. I'm not even going to tell him about this, this incident, because he's busy focusing on the election." He leans in closer. "Which is what you should be focusing on, too." He straightens up. "This is precisely what I *shouldn't* be doing—wasting my time on snotty little kids when there's important work to be done, when there's—"

"That's enough, Patrick," says a woman's voice, cutting him off.

I look up, and there's Elissa Genevieve. Her silky blond hair flows past her shoulders, and she's dressed in a smart pair of gray pants, black heels, and a lavender blouse open at the neck.

"Aria gets your point. Don't you?" she asks me.

I nod.

"Honestly, Patrick. You don't need to harass the poor girl."

Benedict is clearly shocked that Elissa has come to my defense. He stares at her, then at me, and rubs his eyes. "Fine," he says. Then he walks away.

Once he's disappeared into his office, Elissa turns to me.

"Thank you," I manage to say.

"Any time," says Elissa, giving my shoulder a squeeze. "He's right, though, Aria. People look up to you in this city. I know that can be a lot of pressure sometimes, but that's your lot in life."

I can tell Elissa is trying to help, but she doesn't know what I'm going through right now. So I just say, "I understand," and get back to work.

That night, I wait for Hunter.

I don't want him to think I dressed up *too much* to see him, so I select a sleeveless orange dress from my closet and step into a simple pair of tan flats. I brush my hair and pull it away from my face, dab some moisturizer on my cheeks, and run a light coat of lip gloss across my lips.

I've been poised on the edge of my bed for what seems like hours when I hear a light tap on my window.

Eagerly, I press the touchpad on my wall. The curtains part, and I can see a shadow on my balcony. I easily pull the windows open, feel the hot air against my face, and stare up into the eyes of—

Turk?

The outside light glints off his Mohawk. His eyes are dark and metallic-looking, and a grin plays across his angular face. He's wearing a sleeveless yellow T-shirt, the lines of his tattoos accenting his defined muscles, coiling around his arms like snakes.

"Miss me?" he asks.

I shake my head and take a step back. "What—what are you doing here?"

He hops inside and closes the windows behind him. "Hot out there," he says, wiping his forehead. "Thanks for inviting me in."

"I didn't."

Turk collapses into the chair in front of my desk. He looks around my room and whistles. "Sweet pad," he says.

"Seriously," I say, crossing my arms. "Where's Hunter?"

"Story of my life," Turk mutters. "Hunter, Hunter, Hunter. You know, I'm a pretty skilled guy myself."

"Apparently," I say, gesturing to my window. "Did you use the loophole to get here? How does it work? How did you get past all the security measures in the Aeries?" I ask, thinking about all the people on the night shift monitoring the Grid. "Can't the loophole be detected? Or is it . . . invisible?"

Turk scratches his chin. "You ask a lotta questions."

"I'm serious," I tell him.

"Who do you think *designed* these so-called security measures?" Turk scoffs, standing up from the chair and pacing around my room. "Who do you think designed the entire Aeries? Mystics. We built up this entire city." He points out my window, to the surrounding buildings. "Security measures? The Grid? They're nothing. If need be, we can take down the entire Grid."

"So why haven't you?" I ask.

"We're not looking for a war, Aria. We want to win the election fairly."

"Who's *we*? You and Hunter?"

Turk shakes his head. "Everyone. All the drained mystics in the Block and the rebels underground. We don't want anything more than what you have, Aria. We just want to be treated equally, like human beings."

But *are* they human beings? The magic they can do, the powers they have, they're not natural. After watching Stacy OD, what Stic did to her body, knowing that Turk's or Hunter's touch has the potential to kill in a mere instant . . .

"What are you thinking?" Turk asks softly.

No, I tell myself. *That's an awful way to think. I'm not my parents.* I think of Davida, of Hunter. I want everyone to be treated fairly.

"I'm confused," I say. "I don't know what to think anymore."

"You don't have to figure it all out right this second," Turk says, widening his eyes, "but one day soon, you'll have to choose a side. I hope you choose the right one."

"I hope so, too," I say.

Turk stuffs his hands into the pockets of his jeans. "Hunter couldn't make it. Obviously. So he sent me—he didn't want you to think he was standing you up."

"Oh. Thanks." I'm disappointed. I didn't realize how much I want—*need*—to see Hunter until now.

"No problem," Turk says.

"Why couldn't Hunter make it?" I hear my voice falter, nervous that Turk will tell me what I don't want to hear—that Hunter thinks I'm annoying, a nuisance. A child.

Turk is about to speak when my door opens. "Aria? Who are you talking to?"

Turk and I freeze immediately.

Kyle stops in the middle of the room when he sees Turk. His

entire body goes rigid; the veins in his neck and forehead bulge, and his cheeks flash tomato-red. He looks like he's just seen a ghost. I've never seen Kyle so angry.

"What the hell?" Kyle turns to me, then back to Turk. "Who are you? And what are you doing in my little sister's bedroom?"

Turk doesn't wait around to answer. He hops out onto the balcony and opens the loophole—the green circle blazes wide. Turk looks back over his shoulder, winks, then plunges through. With a snap like a rubber band, the loophole shrinks and fades to nothingness, as though it were never there in the first place.

Kyle bolts through my room and onto the balcony. He swipes the air with his hands, as if there is anything there to grasp on to, but the air is just air—hot and thick and heavy with moisture.

He screams, a scary, primal roar. "I'll find you!"

I'm frightened. Kyle has always been laid-back. Why is he reacting like this, like it's the end of the world?

"Explain yourself," he demands, coming back into my room and shutting the windows behind him. "What do you think you're doing, Aria?"

"Nothing," I say, realizing how ridiculous that must sound. My brother walked into my bedroom and saw a dangerous-looking boy standing there—a boy who disappeared into a mystic loophole. As an answer, *nothing* doesn't really cut it.

"You've been seeing a mystic behind everyone's back?" Kyle asks, spitting out the words as if they're poisonous. "Behind your *fiancé's* back? How could you?"

"No, Kyle." My entire body is shaking. "It's not like that—"

"What's it like, then? Do you have any idea what Mom and Dad would do? Are you insane, Aria? You're playing with fire."

"He was nobody." How can I explain that Turk means nothing to me? That *Hunter* is the one . . . the one I love? The thought nearly makes me laugh. I barely know Hunter. Maybe Kyle is right. I am insane.

"Kyle," I say, "you don't—"

"Understand?" he asks, glaring at me. "These people aren't like us, Aria. They're barely human. They're *using* you, and you're too foolish to see that. What you're doing is dangerous, and more than that—it's disgusting. I can't believe you'd stoop to that level. Just like before."

Is he referring to my overdose? I can't tell whether Kyle is about to scream again or cry, his face is so twisted up. I'm about to tell him that he doesn't know what he's talking about, that I never took Stic in the first place, when he continues yelling. "Don't you have any respect for Thomas? For me, for your family?" He nearly chokes on his words. "For *yourself*? A mystic like that—someone undrained—could *kill* you."

"How dare you throw words like *family* at me," I snap. "My family doesn't care about me—forcing me to marry someone I can't even remember!"

"And whose fault is that?" Kyle yells back. "No one forced you to be an addict."

"That's *not* what I am."

"Prove it," Kyle says, raising his eyebrows. "Oh, right—you can't."

I don't know why, but at that moment, I think about my brother as a little boy. How we'd play together when our parents were away, how we'd sometimes stay up late and sneak into the kitchen, eating colored ice pops from the freezer. How after my father would yell at him, I would sneak into his bedroom and comfort him while he cried, even though *he's* the older one.

But I haven't known that Kyle for a very long time. "You're just like Dad," I say. "You care more about money and politics than you do about me. You're too busy kissing ass to see past yourself."

In a split second, Kyle's anger morphs into an intense sort of sadness. He doesn't answer me—instead, he looks away and walks out.

My bedroom door shuts behind him.

All those things he said to me, those awful insults—did he truly mean them, or was he just upset to discover a part of my life that he wasn't privy to?

And what exactly did he mean, *Just like before?*

· XVII ·

When I awake the next morning, I expect to be under total lockdown.

Magdalena enters my room early to help me prepare for the day. Usually, she assists my mother, but since the weekend, she's been helping me in the mornings; I wonder if this is something my mother requested or if Davida has purposefully made herself scarce. I'm not sure why she would do this, since we need to talk.

I study Magdalena's face for any sign of strangeness—a quirk of the eyebrow, a judgmental glint in her eye—but she seems unaware of what happened last night.

Downstairs, my mother is eating apple slices and reading. She looks up as I enter the kitchen. "Did you sleep well, dear?"

I nod. "Where's Kyle?"

"He went off early with Danny to get fitted for a new tuxedo," she says. "Speaking of which, we have an appointment this coming weekend for a gown fitting." My stomach knots. The last thing I want to do is try on my wedding dress and imagine myself walking down the aisle.

To meet lying, cheating Thomas.

"I know," I say, still not ready to reveal what I've learned about Thomas's infidelity. It's too big a secret to drop at the moment; who knows exactly what it might be worth. Plus, if I *do* tell, I'm worried it will somehow backfire on me: my parents might think I'm hesitant about the wedding and keep a closer watch on me, maybe even assign me a bodyguard. And I certainly don't want that.

Even early in the morning, my mother's makeup is perfect—a light shimmer of blue on her eyelids, a dusting of blush on her cheeks—and her hair is wrapped into an exquisite French twist. "Good, then. Maybe I'll add a spa appointment on top of that, and we can make a girls' day of it!"

I realize that she has no clue about last night. Which means Kyle must have kept his mouth shut. I'm relieved but also frightened—if he didn't tell my parents about Turk, he's planning on handling the situation himself.

"Is Davida here?" I ask.

"She's out running errands." Mom looks at her old-fashioned wristwatch. "You should be running along to the office, Aria. A Rose never blooms late."

At work, I try not to call attention to myself.

Most of the day, I lie low in my cubicle, doing my best to stay out of Benedict's way. Thomas calls me twice, and I ignore him both times. He texts *Answer me, please* to my TouchMe. I want to keep ignoring him, but I know how important this wedding is to our families, so I reply, *I'm fine, just busy, talk to you later* and hope he leaves me alone for the rest of the day.

Then I search the Internet on my TouchMe for information on Violet Brooks.

Forty-nine years old, daughter of the now-deceased Ezra Brooks, Violet seems like the perfect mystic representative. She's been fighting to increase mystic rights for years and has served on several government-sponsored committees, both in New York and in Washington, D.C.

But most of America is frightened of mystics—they only populate the major cities, so few people in the Midwest have ever even *seen* a mystic. After the Conflagration happened and the mystics were blamed, they were seen as terrorists within their own country.

Violet Brooks is trying desperately to change that image. Interestingly enough, none of the articles profiling her mention that she has a son.

After I run out of Violet Brooks articles, I read up on the drainings themselves. But no one writes any details about what the process is actually like. The only one that refers to it paints it as "euphoric" for the mystics, "who long only to cede their powers for the betterment of people everywhere—mystics and nonmystics alike." I don't believe that for a minute.

I usually break for lunch in the cafeteria on one of the lower floors, but today I stay and eat a sandwich Magdalena made for me. Most of the other cubes are empty—the floor is silent, almost creepily deserted.

I'm heading to the bathroom when I see Benedict leave his office with my father. I duck behind one of the cubicles, poking my head out just a bit. The two of them walk over to the stainless steel door and it opens. A high-pitched beep sounds for a second. Then they slip into the room, and the door closes with a click.

I've never seen anyone use that door. I wasn't even sure anything was behind it.

I go to the bathroom and then finish my sandwich. About half an hour later, I see that Benedict is safely back in his office, surrounded by a group of assistants. I figure my father must be, too, so I tread softly down the hallway, making sure nobody's looking, and approach the door.

There's no scanner, no place to insert a key card. How did they get in?

I stare at the shiny metal door for a few moments longer, trying to understand how it works, until I hear someone approaching, and I scurry back to my desk.

Only, I can't seem to get much *work* done. All I do is think about Hunter.

At first, I thought he sent Turk to visit me last night because he didn't want to see me. But what if that isn't the case—what if something was stopping him from making the trip himself? What if he got in trouble with his own kind for visiting me?

After work, I take the light-rail back toward my apartment building. Instead of going home, though, I take one of the bridges to the closest POD and pray that no one is tracking me. I wait in the shadows until the rush hour traveling subsides; then I approach the scanner, ready to descend.

Only, when I submit my hand, the sign over the POD terminal blinks red instead of green.

flashes across the tiny screen adjacent to the scanner. This has never happened before. Immediately, there's a sinking feeling in my stomach. I've been locked out of the Grid.

Has my father done this? Or Benedict, because of what happened with the pictures? Or some Grid monitor who has noticed my frequent trips to the Depths? Whoever the culprit is, it's even more imperative now that I find Hunter. I have to warn him: if someone knows where I've been going, they'll know who I've been going to see.

I hurry back home, keeping my head down. I'm about to enter my building when I realize that Davida's gloves are still in my clutch. If they do what Lyrica said, I should be able to use them to travel the rail undetected. I'll head downtown toward the Seaport and find Hunter. My parents have tickets to the opera tonight, so they won't be home for dinner, and no one will be expecting me.

I yank out the gloves and slip my hands inside. Immediately, I feel the fingertips warm and come alive. I double back to the light-rail station.

Inside, a rush of cool air meets my skin. The entire waiting area can't be more than the size of a city block in the Depths, and I cross it quickly, getting on the line of people waiting to head downtown.

I'm at the terminals in mere seconds. I'm about to submit my hand to the scanner when my stomach lurches. This has got to be illegal. What if I get caught? *Oh well,* I think, *here goes.*

I press my hand to the scanner and watch the laser read the prints on my gloves. A name pops up on the overhead screen—

—and I am directed ahead to Terminal Three. The doors slide open, inviting me to enter.

I almost yelp in relief. The gloves worked!

I slip nervously into the light-rail car. Just as the doors close, however, I see two hulking men dressed in black suits rush through the crowd, pointing at me. They must have been sent to trail me once I was denied access to the POD. They have badges of some sort, which they flash as they push their way to the scanner.

They are approved and slide into a rail car directly following mine.

"Please state your destination," the overhead electronic voice tells me. If I say "South Street Seaport," the men will surely follow me. I have to lose them.

"Seventy-Second Street," I say, and my car speeds away into the night.

The city buildings whir by, blurring, then flickering into existence at each transit point. There, gone; there, gone. The car stops at Seventy-Second and the doors open. As I exit into the station, another car blinks in right behind mine. The doors open, and the men in black step out.

This confirms my fear. They've been assigned to tail me.

Before the doors have a chance to close, I dart back inside the car I just left. "Hey!" screeches an overweight woman with a few grocery bags. "I've been waiting here—that's my car!"

"Sorry! Not anymore!"

"Correction," I say. "Forty-Second Street." The goons try to enter my car—the doors close just as one of them sticks his hand inside. I hear the cracking of bone; then the doors open again. I can see the men's faces clearly through the glass: two of my father's lower assistants, Franklin and Montgomery.

Franklin is cursing at me; he yanks back his hand and the doors close again. The car surges through a few more stops and I'm there.

I step out at Forty-Second Street, knowing that the men are likely right behind me. I run through the waiting area, pushing past people, maybe knocking an elderly woman to the ground. I'm moving so fast, there's no time to look back. I hear "Watch it!" "Hey!" "Look where you're going!"

I cut the entire line of people heading uptown and rush over to a car going in the opposite direction. "The line starts back there, sweetheart!" someone says, but I ignore him and submit my fingerprints; this time, the scanner reads the gloves and the name

STEPHANIE MONTELL

lights up overhead.

My car's doors have just opened when I hear a man shout, "There she is! Stop her!"

It's Montgomery, rushing toward me. Franklin is only a few steps behind him.

They leap over children and hurdle benches, but they're still too slow: I rush into the open rail car and press the Close Doors button, announcing "Ninety-Sixth Street."

Montgomery is still in the terminal, pounding his fist against the wall as I blink away.

My heart is pounding. Where do I go? What do I do?

I get off at the Ninety-Sixth Street stop, then reverse my steps, rushing across the waiting area to snatch a car heading back downtown, again pushing through the line of people until I get to the scanner. Then I hop into another car. Thank God for Davida's gloves.

I watch as another car blinks in on the opposite side of the station with Franklin and Montgomery on it. Franklin runs at me as though he wants to wring my neck.

I punch the doors closed and head downtown.

I have to curl my hands into fists to stop them from shaking.

At the next station, I again dash out of the rail car and over the station platform and press my hand to another touchpad. This time I am *Gustav Larsson.* My new car whispers uptown as another downtown train blinks in across the way. Are my father's stooges aboard? I can't tell.

I switch cars again around Canal Street, this time as *Terri-Lynn Postlewait.* Once I'm inside, I crouch down out of sight until the car rushes away. Maybe they won't stop to question why an empty car has taken off for Battery Park. Maybe they'll think I've ditched the light-rail altogether and headed toward a POD. Maybe they'll just be too tired to chase me, as tired as I feel.

Finally, I reach the Battery platform. Mine is the only car, and after the doors open, I say, "Union Square!" and leap across the threshold before they can close me in. Then I make a mad dash for the platform stairs thirty feet away.

If my father's men are following, I need to be out of sight before they arrive.

I've always thought I run quickly, but it seems to take hours for me to close the distance to the stairs. When I'm ten feet away, I hear the sharp whine of another car about to arrive.

Desperate, I fall to my belly and slide headfirst into the stairwell just as another car shoots into the station with a whump of displaced air.

Maybe they'll be looking up, looking high, and won't have seen me. Surely they're onto the gloves by now.

I go slowly down the stairs, so as not to make noise, but not too slowly, and I'm out of sight below the top step within a few seconds.

I hear a high-pitched trill—the preacceleration whine of the car I was on—then the soft pop as it blinks away uptown. It's followed by two pairs of pounding feet crossing the platform, a shouted, "Damn her!" and then the hiss of a car's doors opening, its engines warming, and the pop as it quickens away toward Union Square.

I let loose a ragged sigh of relief. I'd like to curl up on the stairs and catch my breath, but I can't afford to risk it: if Franklin and Montgomery figure out I've ditched them, they might retrace their steps. I need to get home. Fast. Warning Hunter will have to wait.

At home, I strip off my clothes, hop into a warm shower, and scrub my skin until it's red. I squeeze the locket between my fingers and wonder at its powers. How am I going to find Hunter?

I dry off, slip into my white terry cloth bathrobe, and wrap a towel around my hair.

That's when my father bursts into my room.

He's still in his tuxedo, even though the opera isn't over for another hour and I didn't expect him and my mother home until after midnight. His hair is slicked back, his cheeks are smoothly shaven, and he looks incredibly handsome tonight, save for his eyes, which are red with anger.

Directly behind him is Franklin, whose shirt is soaked with sweat. He's breathing heavily, and pointing a crooked finger directly at me.

"She sent us on a wild-goose chase!" he says. "We had to follow her all over the city as she jumped from light-rail to light-rail. Montgomery and I had no idea how she was doing it, her name wasn't showing up anywhere. She must've been using some kind of . . . magic."

Franklin exaggerates the chase—in his version, I jumped a dozen trains, went all over the city, and endangered myself by running across the platform bridges. I can't help but smile a little bit, and that sets my father off.

"I give you a bit of freedom, and you use it to play games?" he says.

"Games?" I'm surprised at how angry I feel. "*You're* the one playing games!"

My father slaps me. It stings, but not nearly as much as the knowledge that he'd strike me at all. "Fess up and tell me where you were going. Do you have some sort of mystic-enhanced goods?"

I work my jaw for a few seconds, then pull the ties of my robe tighter around my waist. The gloves are hidden under my bed; I hope he doesn't check for them. "I have absolutely no idea what your dog is talking about. I've been here all night. And I have no such *goods*."

"Bull," Franklin says. "I saw you! And so did Montgomery!"

Be confident, I tell myself. "You must have mistaken someone else for me," I say, pointing to the towel around my head. "I just got out of the shower."

Dad peers sidelong at Franklin; I can tell that a speck of doubt about his assistant's story has entered his mind.

"Look at him, Dad"—I motion to Franklin—"he's all red and sweaty and disoriented. He's probably on Stic. *He's* the one with the goods, not me."

My father clearly doesn't know what to say.

We hear a knock and look up to see Davida standing in the doorway, wearing her uniform. "If I may, Mr. Rose," she says, "Aria has been here all night. Mrs. Rose asked me to keep an eye on her, and I did."

A flush of relief fills my body. Davida isn't mad at me about the roof incident with Hunter. She's covering for me.

My father seems more confused than anything. He shakes his head and says, "You better hope you're telling the truth. Good night, Aria."

Then he drags Franklin out of my bedroom by the neck.

· XVIII ·

My bedroom door zips closed behind my father and Franklin.

Davida leans against the wall, looking concerned. "Aria, we need to talk. Now."

I sit down on the edge of my bed, and Davida sits next to me. I remove the towel from my head and toss it on the floor.

We sit and stare at each other for a few moments, not saying anything. Then we both burst into tears and envelop each other in a hug.

Davida blurts out, "Do you love him?"

"Thomas?" I say. "I don't know . . . I don't think so."

Davida's dark brown eyes are brimming with tears. "No, not Thomas. *Hunter.*"

I think back to that night on the roof. What must Davida have thought of me—cheating on my fiancé? Of course, she doesn't know about Thomas and Gretchen, but that doesn't make what I did right.

"There is so much I can't explain," I say, trying to decipher my feelings. "I don't even know Hunter, not really—and yet there's something between us, something that makes me feel as if I've known him forever." I hiccup, then smile. "That probably sounds ridiculous, but . . . my feelings for Hunter are real. That much I know." I wipe some tears from my eyes. "Is it love? I don't know. Maybe. I'd like for it to be."

I'm shocked by my outburst, and a little embarrassed. I look at Davida, waiting for her to reassure me that I'm not crazy. Or maybe tell me that I *am* crazy, and to stop seeing Hunter, to figure out things with Thomas, to—

"Then I will protect you both," Davida says. "For as long as I can." She has stopped crying, but her eyes are filled with something even sadder—an indelible grief or some other dark emotion. She seems on the verge of saying something else, but then she blinks and brushes some of her black curls behind her ears, looking away.

"Are you okay?" I take her shoulder.

Davida swallows. "I am. I will be. As long as you're safe, and happy."

She takes my hand from her shoulder and pulls it into her lap, holding it tight. Her gloves are soft and smooth, and they remind me of what happened tonight, and how I followed her in the Depths the other day.

"I have to ask you something," I say, clenching her hands, "and I need you to tell me the truth: What were you doing by the Seaport? Were you visiting your parents?"

Davida averts her eyes, studies the carpet on my floor. Eventually, she nods.

"But why aren't your parents living in the Block?" Davida's lower lip begins to tremble. "You can tell me anything," I say to her. "You know that, right?"

Davida takes a shuddery breath, and suddenly she seems so young—like the girl I've known forever. I see again the full-of-life eleven-year-old I used to chase around the apartment, who braided my hair with roses and baby's breath and read me stories at night when my mother was too busy.

"You have my back," I say, "and I have yours. Always and forever."

And with that, Davida takes her hands from mine and removes her gloves.

Slowly, she peels back the black satin fabric, rolling the glove on her right arm down until it's off completely and she turns her attention to her left arm.

I gasp.

There are no scars anywhere. The skin up to her elbows is peachy and smooth, just like the rest of her.

She looks up with a tight-lipped grin and shrugs. "No one in the Aeries has ever seen me without my gloves," she says. I can tell by the way her voice falters that she's nervous. "Like I told you, the material blocks the transmission of my powers, so I can go undetected. But I am not the only one who is unregistered. My parents are, too. They don't live in the Block, Aria. They live underground."

It was one thing to think of Davida as an orphan, or a mystic with sick parents. But to know that her family is actively against mine is incredibly disturbing. I walk over to my window, pull back the curtains, and stare out blindly at the night. I think back to Hunter at the carnival, about him describing the various powers mystics have.

"What are your powers like?" I ask. "What is it that you can do?"

Davida stands. "It's better if you don't know."

"You owe me at least that much," I say, pleading.

Davida lowers her head. "Hold out your hands," she says, "and close your eyes."

I step toward her and extend my arms, palms up. Then I shut my eyes. Davida's fingertips brush mine and my skin begins to buzz. I feel a pull, as if something inside me—my blood, my organs, my soul—is being yanked out through my pores.

The pull subsides and settles into a warm throbbing that isn't entirely unpleasant. Just strange. Every strand of hair on my body feels alive, and there is a crackle of energy in the air around me.

"Open your eyes," Davida says.

When I do, I am staring at myself: at my wavy brown hair, still wet from the shower, at my hazel eyes, irises alert with green flecks, at the turn of my nose and the sharp cut of my cheekbones, at my jaw and my lips and my white, white teeth.

Davida looks just like me.

"I can borrow someone's appearance," Davida says. The only thing about her that isn't me is her voice. "Cast a disguising glamour on myself and others. That's my talent."

Tentatively, I reach out and touch her, running a finger from her temples to her chin, softly, slowly, and down her neck to her collarbone. This is my body. How strange!

There is a rustling outside, from the balcony. In a blur of color, Davida is herself again; the change happens so quickly it's remarkable. She rushes over to my bed and puts her gloves back on.

I go over to the windows and open them, stepping out onto the balcony in my bare feet. No one is here.

"False alarm," I say. "Too many mystics coming to visit lately. Puts me on edge, I guess."

Davida climbs out behind me and scans the balcony. She points to a tiny green pill lodged between two paving stones. "A mystic wouldn't be taking Stic." Davida holds the pill up to the light, then shoves it in her pocket. "Only someone who needed a power boost to get to this balcony in the first place. Somebody is spying on you. Or trying to, at least."

She pulls me back inside, shutting the windows behind us. "Don't open these again," she instructs, fixing the latch. "I mean it."

The next morning, Thomas shows up uninvited to escort me to work.

"You really don't have to come with me," I say as we leave my apartment building. It's the first time I've seen him since Bennie's party. My father's man Stiggson trails a few feet behind us. Klartino and my father left a few minutes before us.

"Don't be silly. I've been waiting for a moment alone with you." Thomas takes a bouquet of white roses from behind his back. "Pretty, huh?"

I study them. "Did you know that in the War of the Roses, giving someone a white rose was a sign of betrayal, like a warning that soon after, that person would be killed? Are you trying to tell me something?"

"Geez, of course not, Aria," Thomas says. His grin falters as he tosses the flowers to the ground. "What's with you?"

"What's with *me*?"

He reaches for my hand, but I pull away, walking a few steps ahead of him over one of the silvery bridges glinting in the light of the morning sun. The air is sticky-hot. We're silent for a few moments, and then he stops me outside the rail station.

He pulls a tiny velvet box out of his pocket. "Here. Maybe this'll cheer you up."

I take the box from him and open it. Inside is the most gorgeous engagement ring I've ever seen. The central gem, an oval-cut pink diamond, is surrounded by a cluster of tiny rubies and white diamonds.

It stares out at me from the plush box, mocking me.

"It took longer than I expected, but the jeweler finally finished the engraving." He takes out the ring, and shows me the inside: *Aria & Thomas* is etched lightly into the band. Then he slips it onto my finger. I want to protest, but Stiggson is watching. "I'm so sorry about the party," he says. "It's not what you think. I hope you didn't tell anyone."

I laugh. "What is it, then?" I ask, keeping my voice down. "And no, I didn't. But not because of you—I don't care *what* you do, Thomas."

"*She* came on to *me*," Thomas says. "You have to believe me, Aria. I would never cheat on you. I love you—"

"Don't," I say, holding up one of my hands. "Don't say that. You don't mean it."

"But I do," he says urgently. "I love you, Aria."

"You wouldn't have cheated on me if you loved me. That's not how love works."

Thomas rolls back his shoulders in defeat. "What do I have to do to convince you that I'm telling the truth?"

I think for a moment. "My letters."

"Huh?" Thomas says, confused.

"Bring me the love letters I wrote you. I want to see them."

Thomas rubs his forehead. "Aria, what are you talking about?"

"Love letters—I found them in my bedroom."

I wait for his response. Does he know about the letters? If he's able to produce them, well . . . that changes things. But if he's not, it only confirms my suspicion that our relationship was completely fabricated by our parents. That we probably never even met before the night of our engagement party.

Thomas looks up at me, frowning. "I—I don't have them. I didn't save them."

"Oh." I decide to give him one more chance. "What did you call me in the letters? What was your name for me?"

Thomas raises a hand to my forehead. "Are you sick? Do you have a fever?"

"No," I say, shaking his arm away. Even if he didn't save the letters, if he'd written them, he'd know to call me Juliet. "Are you a drug dealer?" I'm surprised I even asked—but there you have it.

"What?" he asks, his eyes widening in shock. "What are you talking about?"

"Are you a drug dealer?" I repeat. "Do you deal Stic or anything else?"

He shakes his head violently. "Of course not."

"Then why did someone at Bennie's party tell me you do?"

Thomas opens his mouth, but no words come out. "I don't know," he says eventually. "But whoever it was . . . they were lying."

I clench my hand into a fist. "Why would someone lie about that to me?"

We stand together in silence. Thomas hooks his thumbs in his belt and stands incredibly still, looking like a lost boy. I shake my head, pushing past him and into the station, Stiggson on our heels. "Don't call me until you have an answer," I tell him.

When Stiggson isn't looking, I slip off the ring and hide it in my clutch.

Later that night, after work, dinner, and a session with a dress designer who draped me in fabric swatches and took all my measurements, when I *still* haven't heard from Hunter and I am beginning to go crazy with worry, I sneak into the Depths.

Kyle is out with Bennie, my parents are at a political strategy session with the Fosters, and I'm home alone. I haven't heard a peep from Thomas. Tonight, Violet Brooks is speaking at a massive rally in the Magnificent Block. I saw news coverage at work with the details; everyone was buzzing about it. Attending will be dangerous, but surely Hunter will be there. And going is my best shot at finding him.

I dress in dark, loose-fitting clothes and wear my hooded cloak despite the heat. I brush my hair forward so that it covers most of my face, and hope I won't be recognized. I'm about to sneak down the back elevator when I feel a tap on my shoulder.

I spin around. It's Davida. She's wearing her uniform, plus a thin cloak—much like the one she made me, the one I lost the first time I went into the Depths.

"Where are you going?" I ask.

"I'm coming with you."

"What? No. It's too dangerous."

"I know where you're going, Aria. And it will be safer if I'm there with you." She pauses. "No secrets, remember?"

I nod. Davida knows the truth about Hunter and me, and I know the truth about her. "Fine," I say. "Besides"—I give her a tiny grin—"I could use help with directions."

We each use a pair of gloves to fool a POD scanner, then hire a gondola to the Magnificent Block. We disembark near where Lyrica lives and head over a series of bridges, over the alleyways of water, and into the Block itself.

"This way," Davida says. It's so much easier to navigate these streets with her by my side. She makes sure to keep us out of the light, hidden in shadows—safe. If anyone recognizes me, tonight of all nights, well . . . who knows what could happen.

We enter the Block and I'm startled by its beauty: dozens and dozens of men and women are ahead of us on the walkways, carrying bits of mystic light ensconced in tubular holders.

"Here," Davida says, passing me a tube from a man standing behind us, who's carrying extras. She holds it in front of her face; the tube emits a soft white glow that plays across her features. I glance ahead, at all the lights and the people moving toward the Great Lawn. The glow from the tubes trickles into the night sky, reflects off the creaking metal walkways, and glints off the surface of the oily water beneath.

We move at a slow pace as the crowd grows. At last, we reach the open space where the carnival was held—only now a stage has been set up, and there are thousands of people crowded around it.

"It's not just mystics here tonight." Davida leads me to a spot on the lawn where we'll have a good view of Violet. "The poor, too, who live elsewhere in the Depths—actually, the crowd is mostly made of nonmystics, which is a pretty good thing. We need all the support we can get."

I glance around for Hunter or Turk, but don't see them. I wonder if Davida's family is here. I pull my cloak tighter, making sure to hide my face, and tip my hood back slightly so that I have a better view of the stage.

Violet Brooks's amplified voice rings out through the night. "It is time that we are free people," she is saying, "that we are treated like equals."

There is a roar from the crowd.

"We should not be drained of our life force. We should be revered for it! We mystics were the ones who helped build Manhattan and its sister cities, Los Angeles, Chicago, and Austin, and made it possible for society to thrive despite the rising water levels and the dire effects of global warming. We built the Aeries. We healed the sick. We made the Damascus iron and steel, the metals that support the weight of the elite.

"And what is our reward? Required drainings—which will be increased if Garland Foster is elected. Those in the Aeries look at us like batteries: things to charge their city. They look at us and see a cheap energy source. But we are not batteries! We are people!"

Davida raises the light in her hands; a few others raise their lights, too. "She's trying to motivate registered mystics to actually vote," Davida says. "Technically, if you're registered with the government, you have the right to. If she can win over the poor *and* get the mystics to actually place their votes, we'll outnumber the people in the Aeries. But usually no one votes, because the only options are, well . . ."

I shrug. "Don't worry. I get it."

Violet continues, "But now you have a real choice: elect another of those evil leeches who have sucked this city dry? Or a mystic, who understands your suffering and sacrifice?"

Violet Brooks raises her hands over her head and the crowd erupts in applause. In her simple black blazer and pants and her white shirt, she looks like a tiny speck of a person from where we sit. What can she possibly hope to do to stop the Roses and the Fosters? But the deafening roar of approval makes clear her power: she may be tiny, but behind her stand thousands.

"When I am elected, I will stop the drainings! There's already enough energy on reserve to last a century—they drain us now to keep us weak. Because they fear us.

"Manhattan, it is time for a change. When I am elected," Violet continues, "no longer will mystics be segregated. No more will the rich live high above and the poor down below. We will be one city—united by our love for New York and for each other."

The crowd hoots and hollers in response. Some boys around our age stand on each other's shoulders and wave their lights in the sky. Next to me, a woman and her husband are clutching each other, smiling.

It's here, in this moment, surrounded by people I have never met and listening to Violet speak about a future Manhattan with equal rights for every citizen, that I realize I want Violet to defeat Garland and win the election—no matter what that means for my family. I hear myself cheering with everyone else.

"She has a way with words, don't you think?" Davida says.

"Definitely." I inch closer to her, our arms touching. "I'm glad you came with me. It means more, listening to this with you here."

Davida smiles—her lips curl up and her face radiates happiness. As soon as she does, I realize how distant we've become over the last few years. How much I'd like for us to be friends again.

"I'm glad I came, too," she says.

At the podium, Violet stands proudly, pumping her fists high in the air.

And then she drops to the ground.

The noise of the crowd is so loud that it's difficult to tell what's happened at first, but then I hear it distinctly: the sound of gunshots ripping through the sky.

"Get down!" people start shouting, and then there's a suffocating commotion as the people around me try to evacuate the lawn. People who were cheering only moments before have gone wild, almost feral. The crowd surges around us, squeezing my chest and lifting me off my feet. "Davida!" I scream. "Davida!"

Violet Brooks is hustled offstage, likely to safety. It's the last thing I see before the hood of my cloak falls forward, over my eyes. Bloodcurdling screams pierce the air; it sounds like people being trampled underfoot.

I fall to the ground and begin to crawl, yanking back my hood so I can see. I look around frantically, searching for Davida. Where is she?

The rush of people fighting to pass me is too intense—men and women are getting elbowed in the stomach, punched in the face, shoved aside. Instead of trying to leave the lawn, I step back onto a thick patch of grass, toward a cluster of trees.

"Davida!" I spot her a few feet away—she's okay, and seems to have the same idea I do. A man knocks her to the side as he runs past her. She stumbles toward me, reaching out for my hand. I grab it and pull her back, into the trees.

The crowd surges forward like a stampede of animals. It's strange to watch from outside, how the faces and bodies seem to blur together until they look like one solid mass.

We catch our breath for a few minutes, and eventually the crowd thins. People pick themselves up off the ground and begin to walk. There's no more yelling or screaming. Fallen tubes are everywhere, cracked glass scattered across the lawn.

"Are you all right?" Davida asks me, wiping her gloves on her pant legs and whisking off her cloak.

My wrists and elbows are sore, but otherwise, I'm fine. "Yeah, are you?"

She nods. "Did you see what happened to Violet? Is she—"

"I don't know," I say. "I hope she's safe."

I could have lost my life tonight. And Violet Brooks most

certainly could have lost hers, if she hasn't already. The only people who'd want to assassinate her are my parents and the Fosters.

The realization sickens me. Is there no end to what my parents will do to get their way? Will they stop at nothing, leaving a trail of dead bodies in their wake?

I am racked with guilt. With anger. If my parents tried to kill Violet Brooks tonight, then surely Hunter will be in danger if they find out who he is. They already did . . . *something* to me, their own daughter. My father will not hesitate to murder Hunter.

Hunter is good at covering his tracks, at living as a rebel without being caught, even when he's in the Aeries. At basically disappearing off the Grid. But what if that's not enough? I *will* protect him. And I'll protect the people in the Depths if I can, poor people who want a better life, mystics who want equality.

And most of all, I think as Davida clings to my arm and we exit the Great Lawn, I will protect myself.

· XIX ·

At work the next day, I sit back and watch the higher-ups—two dozen men and women—trickle past my cubicle and upstairs to my father's conference room for an emergency meeting. Most likely to discuss the failed assassination attempt. Patrick Benedict hustles out of the room with the stainless steel door, and we lock eyes as he passes.

I wait for a familiar sound without even realizing it: the click of the door latch locking behind him. It never comes.

The attempt on Violet Brooks has been all over the newsfeeds: it was confirmed early this morning that one of her bodyguards lost his life; she and the rest of her team escaped unharmed.

I stand up from my cubicle just as my TouchMe buzzes: Kiki. I let it go straight to voice mail. I already owe her a half-dozen phone calls. What's one more?

The few people who don't have their noses pressed up against their TouchMes are busy upstairs. A better opportunity may never come.

As casually as possible, I walk over to the water fountain and take a drink. Then, after a moment, I stroll to the keyless door—it is ajar a quarter inch. I have my hand against it and am about to push it open when—

I feel a tap on my shoulder.

I whirl around and see Elissa Genevieve staring down at me. "Here," she says calmly. "Allow me." Then she reaches past, pushes open the door, and we're inside.

I really don't know what I was expecting.

A secret office where Patrick hid important files on me, on Hunter, or even on Violet Brooks and her father, Ezra Brooks? Assassination plans mapped out and tacked to the walls? An armory full of mystic-powered long-range weapons? Video feeds from every camera in the Aeries and the Depths, tracking every citizen through every step of the day?

What's inside is nothing like any of that.

I follow Elissa down a long hallway. Our heels clop loudly against the tiled floor, and my breathing is so labored I can hear it. At the end of the hallway is a white door that opens onto a flight of stairs. We descend one floor, and there's another doorway, this time with a retina scan; Elissa submits her eye; the door unlocks, and she hurries me through before it closes.

Inside, the overhead lights are so bright I have to squint. Three of the walls are covered with long white curtains. The fourth is blue-black metal. A door much like the one we came through stands smack in the middle of it.

Elissa walks over to the far wall, yanking the curtains aside. I whistle: behind them, the wall is mounted with dozens of glass tubes. They're about as thick as my wrist, covering the entire length of the wall and disappearing into the floor and ceiling, so it's impossible to see where they begin or end. Are they fifty feet long or five hundred?

I go over to the opposite wall and pull the curtains aside: more tubes. The floor is white marble, and in the center of the room is a large metal throne that resembles nothing so much as an old-fashioned electric chair, the kind used for executing criminals. Straps dangle from the body, armrests, and legs of the chair. I don't even want to think about why people have to be strapped into the thing.

"What *is* this place?"

"This"—Elissa motions around the room with her arms—"is one of the rooms in which Patrick, under the instruction of your father and George Foster, drains the power of the mystics who live in the Magnificent Block."

"Oh." Suddenly the beautiful glass tubes take on a sinister, cruel look. I walk closer and run my fingers down one of the tubes; I can see they're lined with a thin coating of something silver and glittery.

"Quicksilver." Elissa points to the silvery substance. "It's another word for mercury. The only element strong enough to contain mystic energy."

The quicksilver sparkles under the bright lights. "It's beautiful."

"Beautiful, yes, but also volatile," Elissa says. "It's quite dangerous to handle."

"Where do all the tubes go?"

"Different places." Elissa motions to a row of tubes. "Some go to transformer stations, where the raw power is stepped down and filtered directly into the city's power grid. The spires you see everywhere—those are where the waste energy from that process is burned off into the air."

I notice the swirling green liquid inside the tubes—the same as what's inside the city's spires. Drained mystic energy.

"But that's only a small percentage of the drainings. Most of it is captured and sent elsewhere."

I think about Violet Brooks's speech, how she said that the city already has enough mystic energy to run for years and years and years, yet they're still draining mystics every day.

I already know that the real purpose of the draining is to control the mystics. But another reason pops into my head: the mystic energy is being used to create—and sell—Stic.

Tabitha's words come rushing back to me—Manhattan has one of the largest mystic populations in the world, and Stic is being sold here illegally. How much money do my parents and the Fosters make selling it? Is *this* really why they will stop at nothing to maintain their control of the city—the source of their profits? To control the farm where they raise mystics to harvest?

It's sickening. This room disgusts me. It's nothing more than a torture chamber.

"Why did you bring me in here?" I ask Elissa. "Why didn't you report me?"

"I won't sugarcoat it for you, Aria. You're a smart girl. You would have figured it out eventually." She strolls to the center of the room and places her hands on the back of that grim chair. "You already know that I'm a reformed mystic. What you don't know is that I'm a double agent. I'm working with the rebels. If Violet

Brooks loses the election, I'm going to help overthrow your parents and do what I can to destroy these places. They're evil."

Elissa? Double agent? "Is that why you've been so nice to me?"

She sighs. "You're not like your family, Aria. You're not greedy or cruel. You want what's best for this city—I can tell. And I need your help."

"My help? What can I possibly do?"

"I know you've been in touch with some of the rebels," she says. "I have my sources. I haven't reported you—in fact, I've helped you, deleting red alerts from the computer system that have popped up when you've accessed PODs in the Aeries. I've kept your secret, Aria."

It makes sense now—why I haven't been reported for sneaking into the Depths. I *do* have a Grid guardian angel: Elissa.

"But recently," she continues, "Patrick has gotten suspicious. He assigned someone else—a worker named Micah—to monitor the Grid without me knowing, and your access to the POD was denied. Micah is the one who sent your father's men after you the other day, the ones you sent on a wild-goose chase." I'm shocked that she knows about that, but I don't interrupt her. "Since then, Patrick has been watching you himself, trying to discover whether you're able to access the rebels' underground warrens."

"He knows about the underground?"

She casually sits down in the chair. "Of course. Your father and the Fosters have known about the rebel hideouts for years, but they've been unable to find an entry point. It takes mystic power to get through the wards and barriers the rebels have erected, and all the legal mystics aboveground have been drained."

"Even you? Even Patrick? Don't you still have *some* of your powers?"

She sighs. "But I still don't have access to the subways. Not just *any* charged mystic can get through—most need a passkey of some sort. So the rebel mystics are safe from Patrick and your father . . . and from me. Without all my powers, I have no way to warn them of what's coming." She pauses. "Your father is planning something that could wipe out the entire underground. They'll be slaughtered, and everything Violet Brooks has struggled for will end."

I want to believe Elissa, but is *anyone* who they say they are? Davida, Hunter, Thomas—now this? "Why should I trust you?"

Elissa glances down at her watch. "Come. You'll see."

She stands and goes to close the curtains. Then she motions for me to hide behind the set of curtains opposite the chair. We disappear just as Benedict enters the room. A high-pitched beep sounds as he opens the door, the latch clicking behind him. He must have just left my father's emergency meeting. I peer through one of the slits, watching him take a white lab coat off a hook on the wall and slip it over his suit.

Seconds later, the other door opens. Through it walks Stiggson in his typical all-black attire. He's dragging a woman whose hands are cuffed.

"What's happening?" I whisper to Elissa. She doesn't answer, but holds a finger to her lips and motions for me to keep watching.

Benedict flicks on a few switches as Stiggson pushes the woman into the chair. Her blond hair is lifeless; her eyes are the color of dishwater.

"No," she says weakly, her lips turned down.

Stiggson ignores her and straps her in. He slips a bite guard into her mouth and immobilizes her head with a series of belts that go underneath her chin and across her forehead. Then he undoes the cuffs and gently places them in a container.

Benedict opens the curtains nearest him. He scans the wall and adjusts a series of tubes and levers. At last, he presses a circular green button. The sound of some kind of vast machine coming to life fills the room. It doesn't seem possible, but the lights in the room burn even brighter.

Benedict places a pair of goggles over his eyes, then hands another pair to Stiggson, who dons them and steps back against the wall.

Two large black discs emerge from the floor on either side of the chair. Benedict presses another button, and then it begins.

The woman seems to brighten and glow, as though she is burning up from within. Thin filaments of green light—like the ones I've seen flow from Hunter's fingertips—writhe out of the woman's chest. They coil and snap and move so sinuously that they're almost pretty. The tendrils of light layer themselves one upon another, always moving, until they form a tight sphere around the woman, a bright woven cage of light.

It would be beautiful, if not for her cries of pain. She moans and whimpers around the mouth guard. I cover my ears with my hands, but the sound gets in anyway. It's the sound of someone being slowly murdered.

Bright washes of color fill the room. The sphere of light begins to unravel, rays like bright spaghetti coming loose and spooling onto the black discs, from which they are funneled into two massive glass tubes filled with quicksilver.

Stiggson is smiling as though he's enjoying the view. Benedict's expression is much harder to read. Terrified, I grab on to Elissa's arm so that I won't make a noise.

After what seems like forever, Benedict presses a sequence of buttons and quiets the machine.

The woman goes limp.

Stiggson picks her up, slinging her over his shoulder like she's a sack of potatoes. He lays her onto a nearby gurney and covers her body with a black cloth, then wheels the table through the far door, out of the room. This must be why I've never seen mystics coming and going before—there's a secret entry to this room I don't know about.

Benedict glances around, dusts off his hands, and follows. Once he's gone, we emerge from behind the curtain.

I'm shaking so badly I can barely walk, and I have to remind myself to breathe. "Who do we tell about this? It needs to stop—right now!"

Elissa rests her hand on my shoulder. "There's no one to tell, Aria. The procedure you just saw? It's legal, and it happens every day."

"But it can't be. It's horrible!"

"I know. Believe me, I know."

I feel stupid then—of course she knows. She's been drained. "I'm so sorry, Elissa. For what my family has done to you. To every mystic."

"It's not your fault, Aria," she tells me. "What's important is what happens next—what we do to right these wrongs."

"But what can I do?" I ask, my voice trembling, not with fear, but with anger.

"Help us," Elissa says. "Help our cause. When the time comes, I will give you a message to carry for me. And that time will be soon, Aria. Meanwhile, I'm trusting you. Keep my secret."

"I won't tell a soul, I promise," I say, looking at the metal chair. "I won't betray you."

• XX •

J—

My love, my life. Every second I'm away from you is a second more that I live in the deepest, darkest agony. I only just saw you, but now I'm home, and your phantom kisses still live on my lips, on my cheeks, and in my heart. When will we run away together? Find a place we don't have to sneak around and lie? We've spoken of this before, but I need it now, like air—the moment for us to get out of this damn city is near. I can taste it. I'll see you in three nights, my love, as we've planned. Until then—

R

I place the letter on my bed, next to all the others. I'm rereading them to see if there's anything—any clues—I've missed.

Downstairs, my parents and the Fosters have assembled for a meeting; I excused myself to "go over plans for the wedding." Thankfully, everyone is distracted—even Thomas—because Garland is practicing his speech for a broadcast he's giving tomorrow morning.

I ruffle through my clutch, where the ring Thomas gave me

is still buried. It's gorgeous, that much is undeniable. But could Thomas, who gave it to me, truly be the author of these love letters, the star of my forgotten memories, the owner of my heart?

Not a chance in hell.

There's a noise at the window. I thrust the ring back into my clutch and hide the letters. Then I rush over to the window and part the curtains.

There on the balcony is Hunter—separated from me by a mere pane of glass.

It's been nearly a week since I've seen him. I open the latch and let him inside, drinking in the sight of him. Why does he affect me so? The strong, sure way his body moves, how his black T-shirt clings to his chest. The slight arch of his eyebrows, the teal-blue of his eyes, the gentle way his mouth curls up when he smiles. I'm alert to every bit of him. Could he have written the letters? No—surely he would have mentioned them to me if he had.

Without any words, he pulls me to him, sliding his arms down my back, wrapping them around my waist. He smells like cinnamon and smoke. I nuzzle my head into his shoulder, lightly kissing the soft skin of his neck.

"I didn't know if I would ever see you again," I whisper. "Were you at the rally? You disappeared, and I had no way of contacting you, and—"

"Shhh," he says. Something about our embrace feels so perfect that I can't help but wonder if our bodies were made for each other. "It's okay. I'm here."

I let myself enjoy the moment for as long as I can. Then, slowly, I pull away. "You're here *now,*" I say. "But where have you been? I asked you to meet me, and you send Turk instead, and my brother saw him. Did he tell you that? Then you drop off the face of the earth!"

Hunter raises his hands in surrender. "I give up. I tried to stay away from you, because I thought it was the right thing—the *safe* thing—to do. But I can't stop thinking about you. And I can't have you wandering the Depths looking for me. It's *dangerous,* Aria. More dangerous than you can imagine."

Even though I heard him, I want him to say it again. "You . . . think about me?"

He pulls me back into him and kisses my forehead. "Every minute of every day." He gives my left cheek a kiss. "I know things are complicated"—he kisses my right cheek—"but I think . . . well, I think that—"

"Not here," I say, taking his hand and pulling him toward the open window, onto the balcony. "It's too risky." I think about the draining and what my parents would do to Hunter if they barged in and caught him. "Take me to the roof."

Hunter lets go of my hand and closes his eyes. I watch as the rays of light shoot from his fingertips, knitting together the way they did before. He swings back his arm and throws—the ray extends like a lariat, then catches onto my roof. He takes me in his arms.

And we jump.

I cling tightly as we move, feel the hard muscles beneath his shirt. I feel . . . alive.

On the roof, the hot wind moves around us, and I glance up. The final pink rays of dusk are melting away, blending into night.

Hunter's heart is beating steadily, pumping blood and mystic energy through his body—energy that could easily kill me.

But Hunter would never hurt me.

Not like my father.

Together we stare out at the plate-glass windows of the chiseled skyscrapers. It feels like we are in our very own world together in the sky. A dreamlike city of towers.

"Why do you do this to me?" I ask finally, breathing in his scent.

He laughs. "What do you mean?"

"I mean, my life, it was all figured out. Sort of, at least." I pivot so my back is against his chest, his arms snug around me, our eyes fixed on the darkening sky. "And then you came along."

"And then I came along," he repeats softly.

"And you changed everything." I turn to face him. "The way I feel about you—it seems like I'll die if I don't see you . . . and then, when I *do* see you, like I'll die if you leave. It's—it's got to be—well, it feels like—"

"Love?" Hunter asks, his eyes wide. "Could the things you're feeling be love?"

I gulp and nod at the same time. "I think so," I say. "I hope so."

"Me too," he says. "More than anything in the world."

Then he leans in and kisses me. Not on my forehead or cheek, but on my lips. A real kiss. A kiss that feels like it can change the world.

His soft lips press against mine, and then they part. I can feel his teeth and his tongue, and then I lose myself in him—how he tastes, how he smells, how he feels. He grabs the hem of my denim skirt and bunches it in his fists. Almost in response, the locket around my neck begins to pulse, warming my skin. Hunter is everything I have ever wanted, everything I never knew I wanted until I met him. Nothing matters except us, together.

"This is insane," I whisper into his ear. "I barely know you, but the things I feel . . . it's like I've been waiting my entire life for you."

"Ow," he says, pulling away and rubbing his chest. "What's that?" He motions to my neck, where the locket must have pinched the skin under his shirt.

"Oh," I say nervously, "nothing. I mean . . . it's a locket."

I tug the locket from the top of my blouse, holding it out for him to see. Faint golden light seeps from the edges; it pulses in my palm, throbbing as though it's alive.

He peers at it strangely. "Why haven't you shown me this before?"

"I don't know," I say, admitting that I found it in my clutch. "I wanted to keep it a secret until I knew how to open it."

"You can't open it?" Hunter asks, sticking out one of his fingers to touch the locket. It practically hops in my hand and gets warmer than it already is, like an egg about to hatch. I won't be able to hold it for much longer.

I shake my head. "I tried everything, but I can't figure out how." The closer the locket is to Hunter, the more it vibrates. "It's never done anything like this before, though. Maybe it has something to do with you—with your energy? Look how it responds to your touch."

I take off the locket and drop it into Hunter's hand. It blazes like a miniature sun. "Wow. What do you think it does?" I ask.

Hunter takes a deep breath. "Well—"

Before he can continue, he's interrupted by footsteps and my father's voice shouting into the night.

"Stop right there!" my father cries out. Hunter turns around, and there he is—Dad, dressed in a navy suit, hair blowing in the wind. Stiggson is right behind him, his gun pointed straight at Hunter. Next to Stiggson is Klartino.

"Step away, Aria," Stiggson tells me in his gravelly voice, and Klartino gives a sharp nod. Two even larger men are standing behind them, one dressed in white, the other in black, their skin covered in tattoos.

"It's not you we want," Klartino says. "It's the mystic. Give him to us and no one will get hurt."

I hear another set of footsteps as Patrick Benedict emerges on the roof. He looks upset and genuinely shaken, glancing between my father and me, gasping slightly when he sees Hunter. Kyle follows, running onto the roof with a metal pipe in one of his hands, as though he's about to strike someone.

"I'm not going anywhere," I say, louder than I intended. I step between Hunter and my father's men. It feels almost natural, like I've done it before.

"Aria, step aside," Hunter whispers into my ear. He stuffs the locket into the back pocket of his jeans. "They want me, not you."

"I'm not leaving you," I say.

"Everyone is here, Aria," my father says, evening out his voice.

"The Fosters, Thomas—they're all downstairs. Don't make a fool of yourself."

"You think I'm acting like a fool?" Stiggson has his gun aimed at my head. Surely he'll kill Hunter if I step away. "You don't know anything," I say, ignoring the gun and looking right at my father.

"I know more than you think," he says. "You believe yourself to be in love with this . . . mystic. This *thing*. But you don't know the truth about him, Aria. About what he's capable of."

"I trust him more than I trust you!" I say.

"Don't be an idiot, Aria!" Kyle yells. He takes the pipe and snaps it in half with barely any effort—a move that should be impossible for any human, no matter how strong. I think back to Frank at Bennie's party with the lamp. Kyle must be on Stic. Then I remember the Stic I found on my balcony. Kyle's been spying on me.

"Aria, it's too dangerous," Hunter says. "Let them have me—I can fight them."

"No," I say softly. "I can't risk losing you."

"What's it going to be, Aria?" Stiggson says. "I don't want to shoot you. I'd rather settle this peacefully." But then I hear him release the gun's safety with a click.

"Aria, hold on tight," Hunter whispers. My arms are spread wide, as if I'm a bird in flight, protecting him.

"Yes," I say.

"Oh, enough of this crap," my father says, taking the pistol from Stiggson's hand and aiming it straight at us.

Then he shoots me.

Well, he shoots *at* me. Before he manages to pull the trigger, Hunter has blazed bright and grabbed me, making my skin feel as though it's been set on fire, and with his arms wrapped completely around me, Hunter and I drop through the roof.

• XXI •

Hunter can walk through walls.

And drop through ceilings.

This is what I'm thinking as we plunge through the roof of my building.

It's nothing more than a whoosh, like when I found myself on the other side of the subway entrance down at the Seaport. There's a tingling sensation and a slight change in air pressure, but it doesn't *feel* like I'm doing something that should be physically impossible—penetrating a solid layer of metal and plaster and cement.

And yet I am. Magic.

We drop lightly and seem to resolidify in midair.

When my feet touch the floor, I open my eyes: we are standing in the middle of my family's living room, Hunter clinging to me as if for his life.

My mother is sitting on the love seat, legs crossed, mouth wide open in shock. Erica Foster is perched beside her, and Thomas is standing by the liquor cabinet, drinking what looks like bourbon over ice. Garland is chatting with his wife, his hand on her shoulder; he pauses midsentence, staring at Hunter and me.

"Aria!" My mother spills her martini all over herself. "What in the Aeries?"

Before she can say anything further, my father, Klartino, and Stiggson burst into the room. Benedict follows a few seconds behind them.

"Get him!" my father cries, and one of his goons takes a shot at Hunter.

It only takes a second for Hunter to react and we're plummeting again, sinking through to the floor beneath our penthouse.

This floor also belongs to my father. "There are men with guns in the next room," I tell Hunter, motioning across the sparse living room to one of the bedrooms, where I know his bodyguards sometimes sleep.

"Where's the exit?" he asks.

"Upstairs," I say. "This is part of our apartment, too. My dad owns all of this."

We hear pounding footsteps above—it sounds like an army is running through the halls. "Come on," Hunter says, grabbing my hand. "They'll have to take the elevator. We can outrun them."

"This is crazy!"

We hear the ding of the elevator. Hunter kisses me fiercely. "We can stop anytime, Aria. I'll surrender. Just say when."

"Never," I say, squeezing his hand even tighter. "Let's go."

In a flare of energy, Hunter pulls me through the wall. For an instant, I feel like I'm being crushed in a vise. Then I pop through and I'm free, in the hallway, stumbling toward another apartment, following Hunter.

His hand is sweaty, but I don't dare think about letting go.

At the end of the hall, he grabs me again and we drop through the floor as though we're a building during a plummet party—*bam!*

And through another, and another, into a deserted apartment.

We always land lightly on our feet; somehow Hunter is able to control our density.

The wall closest to us is painted a dark green and adorned with gold-framed paintings, while the far wall is all glass, with metallic silver curtains seeming to frame the sky.

"Come on," Hunter says, pulling me along one of the corridors, opening the front door and looking left, then right.

At the elevator bank, we see the lighted numbers counting down.

"They're coming to this floor," I say. "These elevators only run between my family's floors."

"Where are the express elevators?" Hunter asks.

I point to the other side—a wall with an enormous painting of Manhattan along its length. "In there. They go straight from the penthouse to the lowest floor."

"Good idea," Hunter says. He picks me up and cradles me in his arms.

"Hunter?" I say, watching the lighted numbers over his shoulder. "They're here."

The elevator dings.

"Yeehaw!" he says, sticking his head through the wall. As the doors open, he leaps through the wall—

and into the express elevator.

We slam against the elevator car's far wall, startling the lone passenger inside, one of my father's men, whose name is Bizwick. He struggles to pull a pistol from his belt.

Hunter punches the man. His head snaps back against the wall, and he falls on the carpet, unconscious.

I give Hunter a peck on the cheek. "Good job."

We reach the first floor; the elevator dings, and we emerge. No one is expecting us to come out of the express elevator bank. Instead, twenty men with guns have their sights trained on the stairwell.

Before anyone can even shout, Hunter has yanked me through the wall of the building. We're in some sort of cement-walled access hallway beside the elevators. He leans through the next wall, then grabs me and pulls me with him, and we're outside on the walkway that encircles my building.

We're alone.

"Run," Hunter says, urging me toward the silvery bridge that links this building to the one across the street. He catches my hand and we sprint across the span, turn, and pass the light-rail station.

We stop in the shadows on the other side to catch our breath.

"I can't keep running," I say, my breath ragged. My shirt is soaked with sweat, and my eyes are stinging.

From here I can see my father's men flooding out of the building, hurrying toward us, guns cradled in their arms. Inside the terminal, a cluster of onlookers stare, no doubt wondering what the fuss is all about. There's no way we'll be able to catch a car.

"Stop!" a few gunmen shout. "Or we'll shoot!"

"What now?" I ask. There's nowhere to go.

"We're gonna get a little wet," says Hunter. He leaps onto one of the platform railings, pulls me up with him, and wraps his arms around me.

We jump.

I've heard of people who go skydiving. They jump out of a moving plane wearing a harness. They fall a few hundred feet; then a parachute opens up, and they glide through the air until they land safely on the ground.

I'm told it's fun. But I can't imagine doing it myself. I'm too terrified.

Falling with Hunter is what I imagine skydiving would be like, only without the parachute.

I scream all the way down.

The wind takes my breath and my scream away, blows my skirt up around my waist and my hair across my face. Hunter's fingers dig into my shoulders; he's holding me close, it feels like we're one person plunging to our death. It happens so quickly I don't even have time to say *I love you.*

And then, as when he took me through the floors, we seem to grow lighter, less dense, and the air seems to be passing through us.

By the time we reach the canal below, we're falling about as fast as a balloon that's lost most of its helium.

We splash down so slowly that we barely make a ripple.

The water is colder than I imagined. And we sink deeper than I expected. It takes me a moment to remember that I don't know how to swim. Water rushes up my nose, murky liquid fills my mouth, and there's no air anywhere.

Then Hunter heaves me up, and we break through the surface of the canal. He swims us over to a dock and lifts me as though I'm light as a feather, then climbs up beside me.

"Aria?" Hunter says.

"You said a *little* wet," I sputter. "I'm . . . soaked."

"I lied." He starts to laugh. "We don't have much time. Your father and his men are likely taking a POD even as we speak."

I nod and get to my feet. My throat feels raw, my eyes are blurry, but I'm all right. A few gondoliers are chatting idly at a nearby deli, smoking and paying us no attention.

Hunter eyes one of their empty gondolas, then helps me step in. I don't question him. He hops in behind me, unties the boat from the dock, and guns the motor, and we speed off. We get a few feet before the gondoliers realize what has happened. "Hey!" one shouts, running over and waving his fists in the air. "Come back here!"

"Sorry!" I yell behind me. "I'll buy you a new one once this is all over!"

Then I give a little wave and look at Hunter. We burst into laughter—we can't help it. Dropping through walls, jumping hundreds of stories into the Depths.

"This is insane!" I tell him as I wring out my skirt.

It's dark now. I don't see or hear my father, but he and his men are surely close behind.

We travel south, losing ourselves among some of the smaller canals off Broadway, taking as many turns as possible.

Just when I'm sure we've lost them, I hear motorboats.

"They're using police watercraft." Hunter motions to the gondola's engine. "This thing can't compete. They'll be on us in minutes."

I point at a dock up ahead. "I'm slowing you down. Get off there and make a run for it. You'll be faster without me."

"I already lost you once." Hunter shakes his head. "I won't lose you again."

"What? What are you saying?"

Hunter pulls up to the dock and hitches the gondola's rope around a post. He lifts me onto the raised sidewalk and clambers up beside me. Then he yanks the locket out of his jeans pocket.

Just then, the gray storm clouds overhead rumble. Lightning fractures the sky, and before I know it, raindrops are falling on my already wet clothing.

Hunter pulls me off the street into a darkened alleyway. The police boats have put on their sirens, which cry into the night, growing louder and closer.

The sirens are nearly deafening by now.

"I recognized it as soon as you showed it to me. It's a capture locket," Hunter says. "These things are extremely rare and powerful. Use it carefully, and only when you're alone."

"But how?" I search for an explanation in his face—only, I can't see it. His features are hidden by a mask of darkness. I try to push him into the light, under a streetlamp, but my feet are plastered to the broken cobblestone beneath me.

"I don't know," he tells me. "Each one opens differently depending on what's inside."

So little time is left.

"Take this." He folds the locket into my hand. It throbs as if it has a pulse, giving off a faint white glow. "I'm sorry for putting you in danger."

"I would do it all again," I tell him. "A thousand times."

He kisses me, softly at first, and then so fiercely I can hardly breathe. Rain falls everywhere, soaking us, splashing into the canals that twist through the hot, dark city. His chest heaves against mine. The sound of sirens—and gunshots—reverberates between the crumbling, waterlogged buildings.

My family is drawing closer.

"Go, Aria," he pleads. "Before they get here."

But footsteps are behind me now. Voices fill my ears. Fingers dig into my arms, tearing me away.

"I love you," he says gently.

And then they take him. I scream in defiance, but it is too late.

Out of nowhere, a circle of gunmen surrounds us. Someone grabs my arms, twisting them forcefully behind my back. I kick and scream, trying to free myself, but the hold on me is too strong.

"Hunter!" I scream.

"Aria!" he calls back, but then his voice is muffled. A gag has been shoved into his mouth, and I see Stiggson and Klartino saying something to him. In the distance, I think I see Davida at the edge of the street, hovering near one of the gondolas. I wonder if anyone else can see her—but the hulking figures are much closer to me, focused only on Hunter.

One of the men pulls a bag over Hunter's head and clamps his hands behind his back with a silvery pair of handcuffs. He is carried aboard one of the superior police gondolas that followed us, then tossed belowdecks like a piece of cargo.

"Hunter!" I cry out.

But my call isn't answered.

Someone shuts the hatch, and the boat pulls away from the dock, heading off to deeper water. There's a crunch behind me, as if someone has just stepped on a branch or broken a piece of pavement.

I turn my head.

My father emerges from the shadows. He aims the wicked barrel of his pistol at my head.

Inside me, something bursts.

"I hate you," I say to him.

He steps forward. "You're going to watch this. As a lesson."

I shake my head no and close my eyes.

"Open your eyes, Aria."

Grudgingly, I do.

The boat slows. My father calls out a few orders; the men get Hunter from the hold and wrestle him into a standing position. The bag is yanked off his head, and I see his face—that gorgeous, beautiful face—look for me in vain. One of the men presses his gun to the back of Hunter's head.

"You've led us on quite a chase," my father says, "but this is the final stop. You *will* marry Thomas, our family *will* unite with the Fosters, and Garland *will* win the election. That is how this story ends."

He raises his hand into the air—a signal.

There is a flare of light and the sharp report of a gunshot.

Hunter's body falls forward, hits the side of the gondola, then folds over and drops into the water with a sickening splash.

I try to shriek but my voice has shriveled up. I feel my eyes roll back into my head, and then I slip through my captor's hands, falling again, this time into black oblivion.

PART THREE

The heart has reasons
of which reason is ignorant.

—Blaise Pascal

· XXII ·

I wake up in my bedroom with a throbbing headache.

It's a searing, wrenching pain, as though someone is beating at my skull with iron fists. And the pain is not just in my head; it shoots up and down my arms, it slithers along my legs. It scrapes against my skin, making me feel raw and worn and tired.

I glance down: everything *appears* normal. I am wearing my favorite pair of flannel pajamas, and my curtains are open slightly, letting in slivers of light. I try to swallow, but my mouth is dry, so I reach for the glass of water I usually keep on my nightstand.

This is when I realize I am handcuffed to the bed.

And as if that isn't bad enough, my mother is hovering over me.

"Thank goodness," she says, leaning over to press one of the buttons on my wall. "I'll have Magdalena bring you some fresh orange juice."

"How long have I been asleep?" I ask groggily. I try to sit up, but the handcuffs make it impossible. There's a bruise on the inside of my arm where there must have been an IV.

"Not long," my mother says, taking a seat in one of the oversized chairs near my closet. "Just a few days. We had you tranquilized."

I feel my eyes bulge in shock. "You had me *what*?"

My mother adjusts her light pink Chanel jacket. "You're too melodramatic, Aria." She purses her lips. "You've put us through so much. Everything your father and I have worked toward . . . what your grandparents fought for . . . thank goodness they're dead."

There's a knock on the door. Mom presses it open, and Magdalena enters, carrying a tray she sets at the foot of my bed.

"Here you are, ma'am," she says, more to my mother than to me, then leaves.

Mom raises her eyebrows. "Aren't you going to eat? You must be starving."

"How?" I ask, raising my arms. The handcuffs clank against the metal bedpost.

"We'll take those off soon enough." Mom picks up the glass of orange juice, places a straw in it, and brings it to my lips. Reluctantly, I take a sip—the cool, sweet liquid soothes my throat.

"There, there," she says, taking her free hand and running it through my hair. Her wedding ring catches in some of the tangles.

"Ow!" I cry, jerking away.

She loses her grip on the glass; the juice spills all over and soaks the pillow and sheets. "Watch what you're doing!" my mother screams. "Magdalena!"

"I don't want Magdalena," I scream back, "and I don't want you! Leave me alone, you awful, awful woman!" Memories come rushing back, of being forced to watch as my father had Hunter executed. I stare at my mother with the coldest expression I can muster. "You stood by and did *nothing*. You killed him."

"You're delirious," my mother says, but her face reveals she's affected by my words—her jaw is tightly clenched, and the wrinkles she's had so much surgery to hide are showing. "I did no such thing."

I lower my voice and speak as calmly as I possibly can. "You are no longer my mother," I tell her. "And I will sooner bring down this entire family than marry Thomas."

For a second, her lower lip trembles. Then she composes herself and reaches over to my nightstand. She picks up a long silver needle and a vial of clear liquid. She empties the vial into the needle, then grabs hold of my arm.

I try to pull away. "What are you doing?"

"Hold still," she says, locating a vein. Then she stabs me.

I feel a rush of calm throughout my body. My blood grows thick, my eyelids heavy. My mother's face is the last thing I see before falling back asleep, and I think I see her laughing.

I dream.

White. So much white. As though a freshly washed sheet has been draped over the entire city, a bone-colored canvas, waiting to be filled.

My dreams splatter onto the canvas in color, every which way and larger than life, full of garbled images—carousels and cotton candy; thin beams of green mystic power; the chrome latticework of Turk's motorcycle wheels; brown-black seaweed clinging to the side of a gondola; the glint of the quicksilver in the draining room's tubes; the pulsing, liquid movements of the energy in the spires; the disappointed, angry look in my father's eyes; the sound of a gunshot.

Mostly, though, I dream of Hunter.

Dreams of how his arms felt around me, the soft kisses he rained down on my collarbone.

And then I remember that he's dead, and I wake up in agony, screaming into the night.

Two weeks pass. Eventually, my handcuffs are removed and I'm allowed to move around, as long as I stay within the confines of the apartment. My friends—Kiki, Bennie, and my other bridesmaids—have been told I'm incredibly ill, and that I will contact them as soon as I'm better. Kyle mostly ignores me, keeping to his room with his door locked or staying over at Bennie's.

My TouchMe has been confiscated. The only visitors I'm allowed are wedding planners. They ask me questions that I refuse to answer, hoping my lack of response will delay the inevitable. Instead, my mother answers for me. She chooses the cake (a three-tiered yellow cake with chocolate ganache, decorated with sugary red roses), and I have final measurements taken for my gown. My mother provides a list of her favorite songs to a musical director, who will rehearse with the band.

There will be no bridal shower—part of my punishment, I suppose, though really I couldn't care less. The wedding is set to take place Labor Day weekend, almost two weeks after the mayoral election on the twentieth.

Thomas doesn't visit—which I appreciate. He calls occasionally, but I always pretend to be sleeping to avoid speaking to him. His ring sits on my nightstand, collecting dust.

"I can't believe she's just gone," I overhear my mother say to

Magdalena one day when she thinks I'm not listening. She's talking about Davida, missing since the night of Hunter's murder. "We practically raised the girl and then she just vanishes into thin air?" Mom rubs her temples. "People are so ungrateful."

Secretly, I wonder where Davida is, if she's informed the rebels about what happened to Hunter. I hope she has, and that they can seek justice on his behalf.

One night, Kyle sits down next to me on the living room sofa. I have a bowl of fruit that I'm picking through with a fork. The television is on, but I'm not paying any attention to it.

He sits down and clasps his hands together. I study him out of the corner of my eye: he's wearing a navy-blue T-shirt and plaid shorts. I don't say a word to him.

We sit this way, in silence, until he speaks. "I'm sorry, you know."

I don't respond.

"Aria? I said I was sorry."

I shake my head. "I can't hear you. I don't converse with assholes."

"Look," he says, unclasping his hands and resting them on his knees. "About that mystic—"

"Hunter," I say, feeling an ache in my chest. "His name was Hunter."

Kyle ignores this. "I'm your brother, I want what's best for you. Even though you don't think so now, in time you'll see that I did the right thing."

"The only thing I'll see in time is how much more of a traitor you are," I find myself saying, "and I already think you're a huge one, so that's saying something." I turn and look at him. Despite what he's saying, he looks sheepish, ashamed. "You take Stic," I say, getting up from the sofa. "You used it to jump from your balcony to mine and eavesdrop on me. That's how Dad knew we were on the roof." I look him dead in the eyes. "Hunter's blood is on your hands. I don't want to talk you. Ever again."

Kyle looks at me, stunned. "Aria—" he starts, but I don't wait for him to finish.

I scramble up the stairs and into my room, where I flop down on my bed and stare at the tin ceiling.

There's a knock on my door. "Go away, Kyle," I mutter.

Another knock.

"I said, *go away*."

The knocking continues, though. I heave myself out of bed and press the touchpad on my wall. The door slides open. "Kyle, just leave me—"

"It's not Kyle," Thomas answers, standing before me with a bouquet of roses. He's wearing a red dress shirt and a pair of linen pants, the collar open slightly at the neck. His hair is gelled and pushed back from his forehead; I can see a tiny mole near his temple that I've never noticed before. "May I come in?"

"No," I say, crossing my arms. Even though I hate Thomas, I wish I'd washed my hair in the past few days. Oh well.

Thomas smiles. "But I'm here to apologize. Again." He steps inside anyway, walking past me and resting the bouquet on my desk. "These are for you."

"Very original," I say, perching on the edge of my bed. "So?

You might as well get it out—the sooner you're done talking, the sooner you'll leave."

"Aria," Thomas says, sitting down next to me. "You're thinking about this the wrong way. I'm not the enemy here."

"You lied to me. *And* you cheated on me with Gretchen Monasty."

Thomas shakes his head. "Gretchen is nobody to me."

"But you still— You know what? It doesn't matter," I tell him. "I don't love you, Thomas. I don't remember anything, and you used that to your advantage. I've never taken Stic. *You* have. The only reason we're getting married is because of some political scheme our parents cooked up."

Thomas leans back. "And?"

"What do you mean, 'And'?" I say, raising my eyebrows.

"I mean," Thomas says, "who cares *why* we're getting married. So maybe we didn't fall in love the way you thought we did. Are you happy here"—he motions around the room—"locked up like some kind of prisoner? You keep fighting against your parents, but there's a reason why they run this city, Aria. They're smart."

"What's your point?" I ask.

"My point," Thomas says, "is that we can be smarter. So maybe you wanted that mystic. Did you ever stop to think that *I* might have wanted something else, some*one* else?"

An image of Gretchen comes to mind, Thomas's lips pressed to hers.

"Our first kiss, how we met—nothing you've told me is true, is it? I don't even care about Gretchen. You're a *liar,* Thomas."

He raises his eyebrows. "There are worse things than lying, Aria. Especially when you're lying to protect someone."

"And who exactly were you trying to protect?"

He shakes his head. "You really don't get it, do you? I was trying to protect *you*."

"Me? Try *yourself*, Thomas."

"Both of us," he clarifies. "You're not the only one who's expected to do what your parents tell you to do. So why fight it? Marry me, and then do whatever you want. I'm no warden like your father. Wanna sneak around with a mystic on the side? Go for it. I don't care. Think of our union as a business transaction. A way for us to remain wealthy and powerful, to get what we want. Soon Garland will run the city, and after that, I will. Don't you want that—to be the wife of the most powerful man in Manhattan?"

I look away. How did I ever imagine that those heartfelt letters, those professions of love, could have come from someone like *him*? Thomas cares about wealth and prestige and image. Only someone who truly *loved* me could have written those letters—not someone resigned to a marriage of convenience. Or were the letters just another part of this whole fabrication, planted to make me believe Thomas wrote them?

Were those memories I had of us together in the Depths, of falling in love . . . were they ever truly of Thomas? Or did I just convince myself they were? Is this all part of what Lyrica suggested, that my memories have been tampered with?

"I want to get married when I'm in love," I say eventually. "I want to spend the rest of my life with someone because I *want* to, not because I *have* to."

"We can't always get what we want, Aria." Thomas shrugs. "Hunter certainly didn't."

I slap him. "I don't choose you."

Thomas brings his hand to his cheek and snarls at me. "It's not a choice. Your parents haven't told you? The wedding has been moved up. We're now to be married *before* the election. Be smart and go along with it—otherwise, you might get us both killed."

· XXIII ·

The next day, Kiki and Bennie come over to cheer me up.

I'm unsure why my mother has broken her No Visitors rule, but I don't complain. Apparently I've made a "miraculous recovery" and am no longer sick. Go figure.

My family has managed to keep the Hunter incident out of the papers. They've announced the new wedding date, and Thomas wasn't lying. We're now to be married on August 11, two Saturdays before the Tuesday election on the twenty-first. I can't believe I was one of the last ones to find out about the change.

"We just came from our dress fittings," Kiki says, blotting her forehead with a handkerchief. "The design your mother picked out is *gor*geous."

"Divine," Bennie chimes in, motioning to her chest. "Tight around the top, with a cinched waist and then"—she lets her hands fall downward—"va-va-voom, all the way to the floor!"

Kiki giggles. "But don't worry. We won't upstage you. We promise."

I manage to roll my eyes. "Believe me, I'm not worried."

"You know, just because you were sick doesn't mean you

couldn't text us," Kiki says, yanking open the curtains. "Or allow your room to look like something besides a mausoleum. Seriously, Aria."

I shield my eyes from the light. The past few days, my mood has been so dark that I wanted my room to match.

I can't believe Hunter is gone. I feel hollow to my core, emptied out by a sadness that refuses to let go. My body is ragged, my nose and eyes raw from crying. In a way, it doesn't even seem real . . . and yet I know he's dead. I saw them shoot him.

The only thing that will make his death *mean* something is to warn his family—to sneak underground and alert Violet Brooks and the rebels that my parents are coming after them. But the way I've been monitored lately, I can't even do that.

"So, out with it," Kiki says, plopping down next to me on the bed. "Why did you have the wedding moved up—especially since you've been ill. What's wrong with you, anyway? Are you *so in love* with Thomas you just can't wait to be married?" She laughs. "Aria the *lovesick* Rose."

Bennie laughs along with her, and I wonder how they could possibly be so naive. I wish I'd told them everything from the beginning; now it's too late. I think about what Thomas said, how one wrong move could get us both killed.

Would my parents actually murder me if I disobeyed them? No matter what, I'm still their daughter. But with the election at risk, well . . . I don't know *what* they'd do.

And that scares me.

"Aria, you don't have to tell us if you don't want to!" Bennie says. She looks like a sailor today, in a cute white dress with blue trim. "But if you do want to tell us"—she skips forward and takes a seat next to Kiki—"we won't complain."

I wonder if Bennie suspects what might be in store for her if she stays with Kyle—a lifetime of servitude to the Rose political cause.

"The new date was my mother's idea," I say. "She thinks it'll be better for the election."

The girls nod as if they understand. "That makes sense," Kiki says. "Meanwhile, I still don't have a friggin' date to the wedding! I want some cute guy to dance with during the slow songs and make out with in the bathroom."

"Time is tick-tick-ticking away!" Bennie says, clapping her hands together.

"Oh, blah," says Kiki, standing up and looking at herself in the mirror. "No guys ever notice me anyway, not when I'm sandwiched between the two of you. You have bodies like celery sticks, except with boobs and butts. Mine's more like . . . an eggplant. Maybe even eggplant Parmesan." She sighs. "Holy Depths, I'm jealous."

Bennie turns to me, rests her hand on my wrist. "So, Kiki and I were thinking—why don't we come over on Wednesday night with some girls from Florence? We'll watch movies and eat popcorn and gossip. It'll be fun. A low-key bachelorette party, since your mom said you weren't feeling up to having a real one."

She said that? I'm not surprised.

"I'll have to ask my mom," I say, "and I doubt—"

"We already got her okay!" Bennie says with a little jump. "Oh, this is going to be so upper! And don't worry, Aria—we're planning everything."

"You just have to show up," Kiki says, giving my shoulder a squeeze.

Even though a party is the absolute last thing I want to have—besides a wedding—I nod. Kiki and Bennie squeal with excitement.

Well, I think, *at least some people in the world are happy.*

A few hours after they're gone, I begin to hear a lot of noise—what sounds like four or five women chattering and walking back and forth past my bedroom.

A vacuum begins to whir, and at the same time, my mother raps on my door. She opens it and speaks to me from the door-frame. I'm resting in bed, on top of the covers.

"Aria," she says, "just so you know, I'm heading downtown with Erica Foster."

"Okay. What's with all the noise?"

She glances down the hallway. "Oh, we've hired a cleaning service to go through and dispose of Davida's things." She straightens the diamond pendant around her neck. "Anyway, I'll be back by four. They should be finished by then."

I watch her leave my room, then lean my head back against the pillow. I wonder what happened to Davida. She was probably so traumatized by what my family's done that she's gone off to be with her mother. I'm about to close my eyes when I think of something and sit back up.

Davida's stash of gloves. I can't let them be thrown away.

I hop out of bed and sneak down the hallway, past Kyle's bedroom and into the servants' corridor.

Davida's door is wide open. I poke my head inside and see

dozens upon dozens of garbage bags, halfway stuffed. Three women in all-white uniforms are sifting through the mess. The sight makes me incredibly upset. Not only have I lost Hunter, but I am losing Davida, too.

"Excuse me?"

The women stop what they're doing and look up at me.

"I just need a moment in here alone—can you come back in five minutes?"

They look at each other and shrug, then leave the room. I shut the door and go straight to where I last saw the gloves—underneath Davida's bed. I drop to the floor, reaching out my hand and feeling for the sharp corners of the metal box.

It's not there.

I pull back my hand and glance around the room. There must be at least twenty bags filled with the clothes and books and trinkets Davida has collected since childhood. Thankfully, the bags are open, so I don't have to undo any knots. I quickly sift through it all—two bags are filled with uniforms of different sizes, some so small they must have been from her girlhood. Did Davida never throw anything away? Another bag is packed with toiletries and underwear; none of the bags holds a metal box. Or the gloves. Where in the Aeries could they be?

I stand and wipe the sweat from my forehead with my pajama sleeve. What's left?

Her closet.

It has been left open, mostly empty. I scroll through what little remains—a few casual sweaters and dresses my parents gave

Davida for special occasions, the clothes she only wore once. She was always in her uniform. These garments are all practically new.

I pull out a pink gown with rhinestones on the collar and begin to tear up. This is the dress I gave Davida for her sixteenth birthday.

I press the soft material to my face and breathe in. Traces of rose-scented detergent fill my nostrils. I picture Davida on the night of Hunter's death, looking between us and sobbing.

I put back the dress and remove a sweater that used to be mine. I suppose I'll take it back until she turns up again. But instead of it feeling soft, it feels . . . crunchy.

What?

I hold the sweater up to the light. It looks normal, but then I slip my hands inside and feel something stiff lining the material. Slowly, I turn the sweater inside out. I gasp at what I see: the entire inside is lined with paper, the paper covered with Davida's handwriting, stitched into the cotton.

I place the sweater on Davida's bed, then remove another piece of clothing—a thin white nightshirt. I slip my hands inside and feel the same stiffness, then roll up the bottom: there is another set of notes sewn inside.

I go through the rest of Davida's closet: a red knit dress she wore once to temple, a white jersey dress with black trim, a stark black blazer, a pleated navy skirt, a soft green cardigan. There are at least a dozen pieces here that are filled with writing. Without hesitating, I grab the items off the hangers, bundle them into my arms, and take them back to my bedroom.

My parents have turned off my door lock, so I must work

quickly. From one of my drawers, I take a jeweled letter opener and use it on one of the garments—the sweater. Carefully, I cut through the stitches and watch as the notes fall to the floor like playing cards.

Once they're all out, I wad up the clothes, take them back to Davida's room, and stuff them in the first open sack. Then I go back to my room, close the door, gather the notes together, and begin to read. The first one I grab is dated over a year ago.

> *There are no safe places to record my thoughts. My TouchMe is compromised and monitored; my email is read by Mr. R's crew. Maybe the old ways are best—they're too full of themselves to look for old-fashioned evidence of who I am—ink and paper, words written in heart's blood.*
>
> *I can't say what they suspect and what they don't. My eyes and ears are open, alert for any information I can relay back to the team—anything we can use to help stop this travesty.*

Seems I've come across a diary of sorts—notes Davida thought would stay hidden if her room was searched. I place the cards on my bedspread. I sift through the piles; there are notes here that date back over six years, from when Davida first came to live with us. I search out the more recent ones, then continue reading:

> *5/14*
>
> *Snuck home today. How good to see everyone. I wanted to stay, but they tell me I'm more important where I am, that I must be patient . . . but how long do I have to wait?*

6/24

Today was a dry day. Aria isn't feeling well; her head is still hurting from the operation. I don't know exactly what they've told her—only the lie that she overdosed on Stic. I wonder if she'll believe what she's been told. She's too smart to be fooled by such simple lies. I pray that she recovers.

So Davida knew that my parents lied to me about the overdose—and she didn't tell me?

The next note was written the night of my engagement party:

6/28

Garland Foster will be a candidate in the upcoming election. Aria is to marry Thomas Foster, who will then move to the West Side of Manhattan and live under the Rose family's watch. The news is epic, and so unexpected. I have sent word to the others, who must prepare immediately.

6/29

My heart hurts today. It's been weeks since I've seen my family. Sometimes the hours pass like days up here, and the days pass like years. When can I go home for good? When will I see him again?

7/8

Sometimes I think she knows me better than I know myself. It's so hard to keep my true feelings hidden. Especially when I want to be honest with her . . . only I can't. Not yet. But when I saw them together, I nearly cried out in pain. I felt as though the air around me was a noose, suffocating me, choking the very life out of me. It's not fair.

7/9

Last night I dreamed about my own wedding, the white dress I'll surely wear, the vows I'll read, which I wrote over a year ago. . . . It's hard to believe I've been engaged for nearly as long as I've been alive, but the day is getting closer. . . . I'll be eighteen in just a few months, and then I'll be going home. To him.

The more I read, the more I begin to form a picture of who Davida really is. She was placed in my household as a child with the intention of getting into my parents' good graces and eventually, when she was old enough, reporting back to the rebels with information that would help them overthrow the Roses. The orphanage? A lie. No woman named Shelly taught her to conceal her powers. The gloves were supplied by her family, the story about her scars concocted by her parents. All the times she's gone missing recently, she was traveling into the Depths, to the rebels. Not only that: she's been betrothed to a rebel mystic practically since birth.

7/10

Today I baked a cinnamon coffee cake with Magdalena. She asked to see my scars, but I refused—

I continue flipping through the papers. Davida's notes seem to run the gamut from entries about my family and me, to her general musings on life, to politics. Then I stop on this one:

7/15

Sometimes I fear he doesn't love me as I love him. I can still remember the way we played together when we were children. But it's been so long. So very long that I've been hidden away up here . . . Can he even recall my face?

Tonight I saw him. But his heart belongs to another. My soul, I fear, has been irreparably shattered. I can never tell her the truth. It is not her fault but his. And mine, I suppose, for believing in fairy-tale endings.

How could Davida never have told me any of this? How could I not have known, never have suspected? I've lived under the same roof as the girl for practically my entire life.

I feel betrayed. By Davida *and* by my parents, who've manipulated me to no end.

When I get to the most recent note, I feel my heart stop.

I'll do my best to forget him. To focus on the task at hand. . . . I've heard whispers about retaliation against Violet. . . . I've sent warning already, but hope I'm not too late.

The name of my betrothed will no longer pass my lips. He is not mine to have; he loves another.

This is the last time I will write it—now let me rid myself of him forever:

Hunter Brooks

XXIV

Dr. May flashes me a scary look. "Honestly, Aria, I'm just trying to help you."

The room is as white as I remember, and it smells like a combination of fresh lemons and antiseptic. His old assistant, Patricia, is nowhere to be seen.

"I don't believe you," I say, cocking my head toward the metal tray full of needles. "This isn't exactly a music hall."

I was told we were leaving the apartment to hear the orchestra for the wedding ceremony perform. I thought it was odd, as my father was with us, and this seemed like something he'd leave up to my mother. As soon as we got into the light-rail, I knew where I was really being taken: Dr. May's office.

I don't have all the answers yet, but here's the only thing that makes sense: Dr. May is involved in altering my memories. Before, I thought he was trying to bring them back, but now I know he's responsible for removing them. He'll erase my memories of Hunter and replace them with fake feelings for Thomas. Probably at my parents' request.

Hunter. Davida. Even though I'm about to be operated on, all

I can think about is the fact that they were . . . well, what were they? Davida was in love with him—that much I gathered from her writings—but I have no idea how Hunter felt. And it's not like I can ask him.

Dr. May grabs for my arm. I throw myself toward the end of the table.

All he does is laugh. "You're fighting the inevitable," he says, nodding toward the door that my parents are waiting behind. Dr. May rolls up the sleeves of his white lab coat, then picks up a fresh syringe. "You can either agree to the operation now, or we can sedate you and *then* operate."

Dr. May reaches for me again. This time, I raise one of my legs and kick him in the stomach. "Oof!" he grunts, doubling over. He staggers to the wall and hits a red button.

An assistant enters. "Get me a sedative," Dr. May tells the young woman. "Now."

The woman is turning to comply when Patrick Benedict walks into the room. I recoil—he's just about the last person I want to see here.

"Perhaps I can be of some help," Benedict says to Dr. May. They shake hands; of course they're friends.

"She's impossible, this one," Dr. May says, pointing to me with the needle. "I would've used a sedative from the start, but it interferes with the procedure. I suppose it's a risk I'll have to take."

"Why don't you give me a few moments alone with her?" Benedict suggests. "Aria and I have always had a certain *understanding*."

Dr. May gives Benedict a firm nod, then strides out the door, motioning for his assistant to follow. I watch as he pulls my parents into a tight huddle in the hallway.

The door zips closed.

"Alone at last," I say in jest. Benedict has never liked me—his being here is a terrible sign.

He ignores my comment, keeping his eyes on my parents and Dr. May through the window. He waits a few seconds, then roughly grips my shoulders.

"Ow!" I say.

"Shhh!" He lowers his lips to my ear, and whispers urgently. "We only have a minute, so listen carefully, Aria. I am going to give you a pill that you must swallow immediately. Then allow them to submit you to the machine. The memory alteration procedure will be a failure; however, when you emerge from the machine, you must pretend it was a success. You will be asked a series of questions. Watch for me before you answer. If I blink once, answer in the affirmative. If I blink twice, answer negatively. Do you understand?"

He pulls away and slips a tiny white pill into my hand. I curl my fingers around it and stare at him. I'm incredibly confused.

"Why are you doing this?"

"There's no time for explanations," Benedict says, peering sideways at the laboratory door. "You must trust me, Aria. For Hunter's sake."

Hunter.

The door slides back open, and Dr. May waltzes back in. Me, trust Benedict? He's practically an ogre, always rude to me. And on top of that, he's devoted to my father. Why on earth should I trust him?

But Hunter's name rings in my ear. Davida is missing. There is no one else who wants to help me. I glance down at my fist, the tiny pill hidden inside. At this point, what do I have to lose? I bring it to my mouth, faking a cough.

I swallow the pill just in time.

"Well?" Dr. May asks quizzically, standing before me with the needle.

I breathe deeply. "I'm ready."

When I emerge from the machine, I feel about the same, only hazier. The inside of my arm is sore from the series of injections Dr. May administered, but other than that, I remain me. I gulp down a glass of water.

"How are you feeling?" my mother asks. Her arm is linked with my father's, and they both look concerned, but I know it's for the wrong reasons: they don't care how I'm feeling, they just want to know whether the operation was successful.

Benedict stands a few feet behind my parents with his arms crossed. He gives me a slight nod. I should respond positively. "I feel . . . fine."

"Aria, do you know why you're here?" my father asks. His dark eyebrows are raised, his forehead creased with lines.

Benedict blinks twice. "No," I say.

Dad offers Benedict a quick smile—the kind I'd miss if I weren't watching for it.

But I am.

"Aria," Dr. May says, stepping toward me, "you had another Stic relapse. Your mother found you convulsing on your bedroom floor, and—well, you almost didn't make it."

My gut reaction is to laugh, but instead I bite my tongue. From the corner of my eye I see Benedict's entire body tense, like a live wire. Suddenly, I realize this is one of the most important moments of my life. I need to convince Dr. May and my parents that the operation was successful. There's no way Benedict will be able to protect me again. If I'm not persuasive, I might actually lose my memories—this time, for good.

But what exactly am I supposed to remember this time around? How can I tell what they tried to erase?

I take a shuddery breath. "I—I—I did?"

My mother nods solemnly. "Perhaps you were nervous about the wedding? I don't know why . . . you love Thomas *so much,* and Thomas loves you. . . ."

She trails off and stares at me, barely blinking. I know she and my father are waiting to see if I object. I don't need to look at Benedict to know how to respond.

"I do love Thomas," I say, keeping my voice steady. My mother grasps my father's hand; they radiate relief. "I'm not nervous about the wedding. I . . . don't remember what happened." I take another breath. "I'm sorry."

"I'm going to ask you a series of questions, Aria, to determine the extent of your memory loss." Dr. May picks up a portable TouchMe and keys something into the pad.

"Actually," my father says, "why doesn't Benedict ask the questions." The tone of Dad's voice makes it clear this is not a question; it's a demand. He must think that Benedict will be tougher on me. "No offense, Salvador."

"Yes, yes, of course," Dr. May says, a bit flustered. "I'll record her answers."

Benedict straightens his tie and steps forward, stopping a few inches from the examination table I'm seated on. The air-conditioning is on full blast, and my skin is covered in goose pimples. I draw the hospital gown tighter around my waist.

"What is your full name?" Benedict asks.

"Aria Marie Rose," I reply.

"When were you born?"

"October fourteenth."

"Who are your parents?"

I point to my father and mother. "John and Melinda Rose."

"What is your fiancé's name?"

"Thomas Foster," I answer.

Benedict glances at my father, then back at me. He widens his eyes just a bit, and I can tell this is when the important questions are about to begin.

"Do you know a boy named Hunter Brooks?" Benedict asks. He gives two deliberate blinks.

"No," I respond. My mother breathes an audible sigh of relief.

"Do you know where Davida, your servant, has disappeared to?" Again, he blinks twice.

"No," I say. "I didn't even know she was gone." Dr. May grins, and I know I am doing well.

"Are you in love with Thomas Foster?" One blink from Benedict.

"Yes," I say.

"Do you have any concerns about your upcoming wedding?" Two blinks.

"No," I say, and then grin big. "I just hope I look good in my dress."

Benedict turns to my parents, who beckon—he steps away and speaks with them in hushed tones. Dr. May joins them for a moment, and I am left with my own thoughts:

My parents tried to wash Hunter Brooks from my mind. They failed.

They want me to believe I am in love with Thomas and marry him. I'm not.

And Benedict wanted to put a stop to this procedure. He is my father's right-hand man, his biggest supporter. What could his betrayal possibly mean?

Dr. May clears his throat. "Aria, you're going to be fine. Your parents want you to see a therapist, someone I'll recommend, so that we can get to the root of your Stic addiction." He pauses. "I'm worried that if you continue using this drug, your memory won't be the only thing at risk—your life will be, too."

"I want to get better," I say, trying to sound sincere. On the outside, my parents look the same—my mother and father, the only family I have besides Kyle. But I know what they truly are: Liars. Murderers. In my mind's eye I see Hunter's knees buckle and his body tumble overboard, see him disappear into the murky water. I feel a pain deep in my chest.

He is gone. I'm still here.

The best way to honor his memory is to put a stop to whatever plan my parents have set in motion. "I'll do whatever I have to do," I say, "to make things right."

My idiot parents beam at me.

A few hours later and I am home.

Dr. May gave me a slew of painkillers, but unlike the first few times I had the procedure, this time I feel perfectly fine. It must have something to do with whatever inhibitor Benedict gave me.

Kiki calls, and we chat for a few minutes until dinnertime. I pull the locket out of my clutch and turn it over in my hands. Thankfully, my parents hadn't suspected it was anything other than normal and didn't throw it away. Hunter said he didn't know how to open it—and if he didn't, who will? The only person I can think of is Lyrica, but there's no way I'll be able to escape to the Depths to see her. Not now.

I place the locket around my neck and tuck it under my blouse. It's risky, but I want to feel close to Hunter. This is the only thing I have that he touched. I glance at the clock; it's important for everyone to think I'm normal, so it's off to dinner I go.

Downstairs, the whole Foster clan is seated at our dining room table, along with the whole parade of evil stuffed shirts: Mayor Greenlorn, Police Chief Bayer, Governor Boch. Stiggson, Klartino, and a gaggle of bodyguards, all in their black suits, hover quietly in the next room, attempting to blend in with the intricate pattern of the wallpaper.

I take a seat next to Thomas, who looks blandly dashing in a light blue button-down shirt, open at the neck, his hair parted at the side and combed back.

"How *are* you?" he asks, kissing me. He puts on a good show, that's for sure. If I blacked out all of the lies, the deception, the cheating . . . I suppose I could convince myself that he actually loved me.

Unfortunately, I know who he is. He might not be responsible for anything that's happened to me, but he's certainly happy enough to go along with it.

All eyes are on me, though, so I chirp, "Great!" making sure to rest my hand on the table to show off the new engagement ring, which sparkles even brighter than the chandelier above the table.

Across the table is Benedict, who is wearing the same clothes from this afternoon. I catch his eye but he looks away.

We are served the soup first, a light summer bisque. I push around tiny globs of corn with my spoon. I can't imagine eating—my stomach is churning with nervous energy. I keep wondering how I'm going to be able to steal a moment alone with Benedict. Why did he help me? Does he know Elissa is a double agent, working secretly for the rebels? Are they working together? I want to ask him, but I promised Elissa I wouldn't blow her cover.

"Aria?" I hear Erica Foster say as though she's repeating herself.

I give a quick smile. "I'm sorry."

"That's all right, dear. I was just telling your mother how beautiful the engagement ring looks."

"Oh yes," I say, staring down at the big hunk of diamonds resting on my finger. The silver band feels tight, as if it's squeezing the very life out of me. "It's quite something."

The meal passes slowly, as if every minute is an hour. The talk, of course, is all politics and poll numbers, when it's not about the details of the wedding—which, to be honest, is the same thing.

"The seated dinner will be delicious," my mother tells Erica Foster. "Filet mignon with a peppercorn sauce, broccoli florets, and bronzed new potatoes—"

"Excuse me," I say. "I have to powder my nose."

"Everything okay?" Thomas asks.

"Absolutely," I say.

"Aria?" My mother raises a brow. "Do you need me to accompany you?"

All heads turn my way. "I just have to pee!" Kyle rolls his eyes. "I mean . . . I don't need any help! Thank you."

I stand, placing my napkin on the table in front of me. Benedict isn't looking at me—he's talking to the police chief.

I walk out of the dining room and down the hall, where our guest bathroom is located. Then I stroll right past it and into the tiny room where we keep guests' coats, purses, and briefcases.

I do a quick scan for Benedict's brown leather briefcase and recognize the gold clasp immediately. I've seen him carry it at work and always thought, why carry a briefcase at all? Most everything in the office is computerized, so it's not like he has to carry around many papers.

It's mostly empty. Inside is a half-drunk bottle of water and a slim manila envelope containing a single sheet of paper. Scribbled across the top is an address and the words *Fred M. Rose family.*

The handwriting is familiar.

Where's the top-secret information? Where's the reason he's helping me? I sigh, slipping the paper back into the envelope and the envelope back into the briefcase.

I return to the dinner table and place my napkin on my lap.

"Everything all right?" Thomas asks me.

I fake a smile. "Sure. Why wouldn't it be?"

Once everyone is gone, I get ready for bed. Magdalena runs a brush through my hair and helps me wash my face. She gives me a pill from Dr. May; I pretend to swallow it, then spit it into the garbage once she's gone.

I try to fall asleep, but I'm restless. Images of Hunter flash through my head—of his face, his lips. I remember the way his arms felt around me. It's not fair. We knew each other so briefly. And now he's dead because of me.

I wonder what Violet Brooks is doing. Is she thinking of her son? Does she suspect she'll never see him again? And Turk! Poor Turk. He deserves to know what happened to his friend.

I slip out of bed and to my windows, opening the curtains and looking out into the night. Where is the loophole? How can I access it?

A shadow flickers across the balcony.

I blink and it's gone. I press my face up against the window. Kyle? Davida?

No. That's ridiculous. Nobody's there.

I close the curtains and am about to get back into bed when I feel the weight of the locket against my chest. I take it out from underneath my nightgown and stare at it, rubbing my fingers over the polished silver, searching for a clasp that I know isn't there. A capture locket. What does that mean?

Maybe there's an answer in the note I found with it.

I go over to my armoire, where I've hidden the note. I know it only says one word—*Remember*—but maybe there's something I didn't see.

My fingers shake as I hold the piece of paper up to the light. I flip it over, but the back is blank. There is nothing new here. What was I thinking, that suddenly I'd look at the note and the answers I'm searching for would magically appear?

I'm about to hide it back in the drawer when something clicks, like a latch snapping into place inside my head.

Remember

I stare at the word, the clean lines of the letters, the swoop of the *R*, the curve of the *m*'s.

The handwriting is familiar. I saw it earlier this evening.

In Patrick Benedict's briefcase.

· XXV ·

"Isn't it lovely?" my mother asks.

Tentatively, I step into the apartment. Thomas is by my side; he reaches to take my hand, and I let him, even though my instinct is to shrug him off. Or slap him. But it's important that everyone think what Dr. May did was a success. That I've forgotten about Hunter. That I love Thomas.

"Gorgeous," Thomas says, pulling me into the living room.

We are standing in what is soon to be our new apartment. It's two floors down from where I live now, in my family's building. Part of the arrangement with the Fosters is that Thomas will live on the West Side, with us, as long as Garland is in office—a sort of collateral to make sure the Fosters include our family in every political decision they make.

I glance up at the white ceiling, then out the far wall of windows that overlook the Hudson River. Are there cameras in places I can't see? I'd hardly be surprised.

"From Paris," my mother says, motioning to a stark black couch. The room is sparse, modern, with eggshell and rose walls.

Across from the living room is the kitchen, which has the

atmosphere of a formal bar, with wineglasses, porcelain plates, and jewel-encrusted goblets on display. There's a silvery brick pattern on the kitchen walls that appears to have been stamped into galvanized metal.

It feels like someone else's home. Someone I wouldn't like.

"What do you think, Aria?" Thomas asks, giving my hand a squeeze.

I take in the carpet, the television, the paintings—everything selected by my mother. "It's all so gorgeous," I say, trying to sound enthusiastic.

My mother bursts into a wide, open smile. "There's still a lot to do, of course—we need linens for the bedroom and towels for the bathroom. Oh, and . . ."

I tune her out. All I can think of, all I've been thinking of since last night, is Benedict's handwriting. Did he write the note that accompanied my locket? Or was the note I found in his briefcase written by someone on his staff? Either way, he'll be able to identify the author, who must be the same person who left me the locket.

The only problem is getting to him. I'm not allowed back to my job in the office anymore, unless . . .

"Mom?" I say.

She stops midsentence. "Yes?"

"Would it be possible for us to drop by Dad's office today?"

She blinks as though she's never seen me before. "Whatever for?"

"I just remembered," I say, coming up with something on the fly, "that I left a pair of earrings Kiki lent me in my desk."

"I'll have someone pick them up," she says.

"But there's a security code on the drawer."

"So give me the code." She shoots Thomas a suspicious look.

"It's a fingertouch," I say, bluffing. I don't think my mother has any idea that the desks at the office aren't even locked—at least, I hope she doesn't. "I really want to wear the earrings to our rehearsal dinner in a few days," I say. "They'd be so lovely with the dress I picked out. You know, the emerald one with the crushed velvet hem?"

My mother makes a tiny noise with her tongue. "That dress *is* lovely. . . ." She takes a moment to think, then sizes me up. "The earrings are that important?"

"Yes," I say, nodding emphatically. "They're so chic."

My mother is nothing if not a sucker for fashion. "Fine," she says, relenting, and I can feel my entire body relax. "I'll come with you."

I can't hide the sigh that escapes. How will I ever be able to steal a few moments alone with Benedict when she'll be monitoring my every step? And what will she say when she realizes the desk drawers aren't even locked?

"Let's go now," she says, pecking Thomas on the cheek. "We'll see you later, dear." She turns to me. "Aria, we have a final fitting for your dress at noon. And we don't want to be late."

At my father's office building, we step out of the elevator onto the floor where I used to work. Everything is how I left it: the cubicles, the people, the water fountains, and the restrooms. I see the stainless steel door that I snuck through with Elissa, the one that leads down a long hallway and into a blinding room where I once watched a mystic have her powers drained. Just remembering it makes me shiver.

Across the hall is Patrick Benedict's office. I'm sure he's inside, working.

"Which one was yours?" my mother asks, fixing the strand of pearls around her neck.

"Oh, it's right over there." I point to my empty cubicle. "Do you have to use the bathroom?"

"No," Mom says, tilting her head to stare at me. "Why do you ask?"

"No reason," I say. *Other than I need a few minutes alone.* "Just, you know . . . that *I* have to go."

Mom puts her hands on her hips. "Then go."

"Uh, right. Sure." I don't move.

"Well, what are you waiting for?"

Then, out of nowhere, Elissa Genevieve appears and saves me. "Aria!" she says with a bright smile. Then, "Melinda, so nice to see you again."

I see Mom take in the cut of Elissa's navy-blue skirt, her crisp blouse and sapphire necklace. She's impressed.

"It's been such a long time since we've spoken," Elissa says.

"Yes indeed," Mom says. "How have you been?"

Elissa and I lock eyes; even though we are completely silent, I shoot her a pleading look that she immediately recognizes.

"I was just going to the bathroom," I say.

"Of course," she says, pointing toward no bathroom that I know of. Then she steers my mother away from me and into a conversation, complimenting her necklace and asking where she gets her hair done. My mother dives in, and I figure I have five minutes—ten, tops—before she comes looking for me.

First stop, Benedict's office.

I give a quick knock on the door. "Who's there?" says a voice from behind it.

"Aria," I say in a hushed voice.

The door whispers open. I step inside and the door closes behind me. Benedict is there at his desk, staring up at me with his hands resting on the mahogany.

"Hello," he says. His tone is warm—the nicest he's ever sounded.

Without saying anything, I open my clutch, take out the note and the locket, and slide them in front of him.

I'm not sure what I expect. Maybe for him to seem surprised, or completely confused. Instead, he studies the locket for a moment, glances at the note, then looks up at me with a blank expression on his face.

"I've been waiting for you to come to me with this."

My heart skips a beat. "You have?"

"Indeed," he says without taking his eyes off me. "We don't have much time. I assume someone has accompanied you?"

"My mother," I say. "She's chatting with Elissa."

"First things first," Benedict says, getting up from his desk and walking around it until we are almost touching. "You mustn't let on what I did for you yesterday, or that the procedure did not work. It is of the utmost importance that you keep up the pretense."

"Until when?" I shake my head. "I can't marry Thomas. I just can't."

Benedict clears his throat. "We don't have time for female hysterics right now, Aria. Listen: I am not who you think I am. Although it appears that I work for your family, in reality I work for the rebels."

"Why?" I ask, my voice cracking. "If you secretly work for the rebels . . . why would you help erase my memory in the first place?"

Benedict's eyes go dark. "I had no choice. To keep my true alliance a secret, I had to obey orders. Before the procedure, however, I extracted the pieces of memory that your parents were attempting to erase."

"You did?" I ask, shocked. I wasn't expecting that.

"I hid your memory inside a capture locket." He picks it up gently. "They are very rare—only a handful exist in the world. They are crafted from pure Damascus silver and enhanced with mystic energies."

"But why?" I ask. "Why did you do that?"

Benedict's sigh seems to come from his soul. "I have not always worked against your father. For many years I stood by him, a turncoat to my own people. Your father *saved* me from a mob during the troubled times after the Conflagration, and, well, blood debts run deep. It was only recently, within the past two years, when the possibility of Violet Brooks's running for election and winning became a reality, that I switched sides." He flips his hand. "A turncoat who turned again. Since then, I have done what I can. I even faked Violet's draining: though she's a registered mystic, she retains her powers." He stares at me desperately. "No one can know any of this, Aria."

"But . . . she *looks* drained."

"It's fake," Benedict says. "Makeup to help her appear sick. People see what they want to see, Aria. You of all people should know that."

"Why didn't you tell me any of this before? Why did you wait for me to come to you with the locket?"

"You wouldn't have trusted me. You barely do now," he says, and I can't help but appreciate the truth in his statement. "There is a time for everything, Aria. Now is your time."

I stare at him and realize that there is much more to Patrick Benedict than meets the eye. Even though he doesn't believe in the drainings, he's lying low, hiding in plain sight, obeying my father and dreaming of the day he won't have to. He's looking to the upcoming election to make that come true. To bring change. He's like Elissa in that way. Outwardly, they are so different: she is personable, while Benedict is an introvert. But deep down, they're both working for a better tomorrow.

"I owe you an apology," I say, "I thought you were . . . different."

"No matter," Benedict says, shrugging off my words. "Now we both know the truth." He extends his hand and drops the locket into my palm. "You should go. Your mother will start to wonder."

"How do I open the locket, though?" I ask. "I tried to find a clasp, but it's stuck."

Benedict shakes his head emphatically. "No, no, it's not meant to be opened."

"It's not? Then how—"

"It is meant to be *eaten,*" Benedict says.

Which is so strange that I don't know what to say.

"The time has come," Benedict says cryptically. "Tonight, in private, swallow the locket. The memories trapped inside will be released and absorbed into your body. But remember, Aria—once you do this, there's no going back. You will remember all you have lost."

I am about to ask him to explain further when there's a knock on the door. Benedict presses a button on his desk and it slides open—in the doorframe stands my mother, with Elissa beside her.

"Aria!" my mother exclaims. "Why are you annoying Patrick when he's working?" She approaches me and links her arm with mine. "Elissa just suggested that you and Thomas go to Bali for your honeymoon! I've never been."

"It's gorgeous," Elissa chimes in.

My mother sucks in her cheeks. "I do love an island. I'm sorry if Aria was bothering you, Patrick. We just came for a pair of earrings. Did you find them, dear?"

"No," I say apologetically. "I looked, but . . . they must be in my room."

My mother rolls her eyes. "Honestly, Aria." She smiles at Benedict. "She'd lose her head if it weren't for her neck. Come, let's go." Mom gives me a tiny pull. "Goodbye, all."

"Goodbye," I echo. Benedict is back at his desk, but Elissa is looking at me strangely.

She keeps staring until my mother and I enter the elevator and the doors close behind us.

The rest of the afternoon is a whirlwind.

I have the final fitting for my gown. The white bodice, studded with crystals and diamonds imported from Africa, is tight around my rib cage, almost like a corset, with padding that makes it seem as though I actually have breasts. The back is made of silk strands crisscrossed in a basket-weave effect that is simply gorgeous. The skirt flows down to the floor and into a train that trails behind me in white waves.

"Magnifique!" my mother says to the seamstress.

I stare at myself in the mirror. I see a girl—no, a woman—who is about to embark on the biggest journey of her entire life: marriage. From the neck down, I look completely ready. But from the neck up, all I see are worry lines etched across my forehead, purple shadows underneath my eyes.

What's going to become of me? Even if I manage to swallow the locket, what good will my lost memories do me now? Hunter is dead, and unless a miracle happens, Garland—a complete figurehead to my parents and the Fosters—will win the election. I will marry Thomas, who doesn't love me, and I will live in the same building as my parents, who treat me like property to be bought and sold. And scrubbed clean, if need be.

"What do you think, Aria?" My mother smiles, and all I want to do is punch her for what she did to Hunter, for what she has done to me.

"It's beautiful," I say.

By the time we run a few errands and return home, it's past four o'clock in the afternoon.

"Mrs. Rose!" the doorman, Henri, says to my mother as soon as we enter the building. "We tried calling your TouchMe but you did not answer."

"What is it?" my mother asks, her voice frantic. "Is everything all right?"

Henri motions to the elevator bank. "Your runaway servant, Davida, has been found. She is restrained, and waiting for you upstairs."

· XXVI ·

When Davida sees me, she flinches.

She's cuffed to a high metal chair that's been pushed against the living room wall.

"She isn't saying a word," my father says.

"Who found her?" my mother asks.

"Magdalena," Dad replies.

"I was leaving the building to run some errands," Magdalena says softly, as though her voice is caught in her throat. "And I saw her lurking on the bridge outside. I came and reported her immediately."

I glare at Magdalena. How could she?

Stiggson stands behind Davida, the sleeves of his shirt rolled up, exposing his multicolored tattoos. A silver knife is in one hand, the blade glistening. Klartino is next to him, holding a sleek black pistol.

My mother removes a tiny blue sticker from her purse, places it on the inside of her wrist, and sighs. I recognize it immediately: a mystic-infused antianxiety drug. She must be incredibly upset.

"She won't say a word," my father laments, shaking his head. "What are you hiding, Davida? Where did you disappear to? Eh?" I watch him clench, then unclench his fingers. "Talk, goddammit!"

"I know what'll make her talk," Stiggson says, raising his hand to show off the knife. He lays the sharp edge against Davida's cheek. I watch her tremble when the metal touches her skin. She looks thinner than I remember, haggard. She's still wearing her all-black uniform, gloves to the elbows.

"Tell us where you went," Stiggson says, "or get a new scar that no glove will cover up." Klartino grins in approval.

Davida remains silent. Stiggson presses the knife into her cheek; it pierces the skin, and a thin stream of blood begins to pour down her face, her neck, into her blouse.

I can't take it any longer. "Stop!"

Stiggson looks up at me, as do my parents.

"You'll never get her to talk that way," I say. "I grew up with her. No one knows her as well as I do." All I need is a few minutes alone with Davida, to figure out what happened to her. "Let me talk to her in private."

"Absolutely not," my mother says.

"Please." I look at my father. "I'm sure I can convince her to open up. But you've scared her. Let me just chat with her alone. Ten minutes, tops." I hide my hands behind my back so my parents won't see that they're shaking.

My father is contemplative for a few seconds. "Ten minutes," he acquiesces. "But no more."

My mother frowns, but I've already moved toward Davida. Klartino unlocks her cuffs; then I drag her down the hall and into my room before Dad has time to change his mind.

"Are you insane?" I ask her once we're safely behind my bedroom door. I reach for a tissue from my desk and use it to wipe the blood from her face.

Stiggson stands guard outside, and I try to speak as quietly as possible while still getting my point across. "Sit," I tell her, pointing to the edge of the bed. She does.

"Why did you come back? It's like you have a death wish, Davida!" I pace back and forth, trying to expend some of my pent-up energy. Davida remains quiet, motionless. "Are you just going to sit there silently?"

"I—I don't know what to say." Davida's voice is lower than usual, huskier. "I'm sorry."

"You're going to have to tell them something." I cock my head toward the door. "You know my parents—they won't rest until they know every single place you've been since—"

I'm about to say *that night* when I feel my throat close up. The dark water. The gunshot. The sound he made as he fell . . .

"Aria?"

I blink and take a few breaths, in and out, steadying myself. "Why did you run away?" I ask her. Davida stares at me with intense pain in her eyes. "When were you going to tell me that you were a spy? That you were . . . promised to Hunter?"

No answers. Davida merely squeezes her eyes shut to hold back tears.

"We said we would tell each other the truth," I say, sitting next to her on the bed. The locket thumps against my breastbone. "The *whole* truth. You didn't."

We're so close that our legs are touching, my bare arm rustling against the cotton sleeve of her uniform. She stinks of the Depths—of fog and smoke and old dirt, of salt and sweat and desperation. Davida leans her head back, exposing the curve of her neck, and takes a ragged breath.

Then I catch her eyes; they seem bluer than I remember. Blue? Aren't they brown? Have I truly forgotten so much?

But there's something more: the longer I stare at her, the more I see something beyond the sadness, a layer of yearning, of longing. I look at her, at the pain in her face, and remember what it is to be in love, to have that flutter in my chest, to feel *alive,* as though every pore in my skin were a portal to my soul.

Slowly, I move my palm from her hand. I slide a finger inside the top of her glove, pulling it down. As soon as my bare skin touches hers, I feel a jolt—the locket seems to leap from around my neck. There is a white-yellow glow emanating from inside my blouse. I dip my free hand inside, pull out the locket, and gasp.

The heart-shaped silver is glowing, as if it were a tiny ball of magic. It pulses steadily, throbbing in the center of my palm. The only time it's ever *glowed* before is when Hunter touched it on my roof. Before he was—

"Oh," Davida says, staring at it in awe. Then she looks up at me, catching my eyes. And then the strangest thing happens: she leans forward, letting her nose graze mine, and kisses me.

Instinctively, I start to pull away, but even though I'm not attracted to Davida, her lips are soft, familiar somehow. Has she ever kissed Hunter? She must have. I think back to my parents ripping him away from me, snuffing out his life. I miss him more than I can bear.

I close my eyes, and imagine that it's him—Hunter—giving me one final kiss. Pressing one of my hands around to the back of Davida's neck, I pretend it's Hunter's neck, that he's still here with me. That we still have a chance.

Maybe it's because my grief is so fresh, my pain so strong, but in my head, he is there; we are together, we are one. His mouth against mine is wet and warm and incredibly soft, like velvet.

The blood rushes to my head, and I suddenly feel sharply dizzy. My heart feels like it has taken wing in my chest, begging me to carry it far, far away from this place.

And then I begin to cry—my chest constricts, and fresh tears mingle with the sweat on my cheeks and lips. What am I doing? I am not with Hunter. He is dead.

Our time together was so fleeting, and yet . . . Hunter was the real thing: sexy and funny and moody and secretive and strong and tender. So many people never find true love. I used to think that was a tragedy, but maybe the real tragedy is finding it—knowing it exists, knowing that another person can make you weak with a touch, make you laugh with a word. He can look at you and understand who you are. And then having it ripped away.

I pull back and open my eyes. When I do, I nearly faint.

It *is* Hunter before me.

He looks at me like a frightened deer, eyes wild and bright, his blond hair disheveled, his skin slightly stubbled and as perfect as I remember it.

"Damn you, Davida! You can't be him!" I remember her talent: she can take on another's face and body.

"You don't understand—"

"I understand enough," I snap. "And soon I'll understand everything."

Leaping off the bed, I back up against the windows, yanking the locket from around my neck and holding it in my hands. It is so hot it sizzles, vaporizing the sweat on my skin and sending tiny wisps of steam into the air.

Benedict's voice echoes in my mind: *Tonight, in private, swallow the locket. The memories trapped inside will be released and absorbed into your body. But remember, Aria—once you do this, there's no going back. You will remember all you have lost.*

Now that I'm about to swallow it, the thing looks huge.

I glare again at Davida-as-Hunter, who doesn't try to stop me. She only nods encouragement.

Here goes, I think, tilting my neck and dropping the locket into my mouth.

· XXVII ·

The locket touches my tongue, and I burn. I open my mouth to scream, but all I exhale is steam as the locket seems to come to life on its own and burrows its way down my throat.

And then there is an explosion, and everything around me disappears.

The roar of the Depths fills my ears.

This is so stupid. I place my hand on the POD scanner for the tenth time. But just like the nine times before, nothing happens. I never should have taken this bet with Kiki—that I could last fifteen minutes by myself in the Depths. Now the freaking POD doesn't work. What if I get stuck down here and my parents find out?

I give up and turn around. "Move it!" someone shouts, rushing past me—a young man with two loaves of stale-looking bread in his arms. What's the hurry? We're in the Depths—it's not like there's anywhere good to go.

I hear the calls of the gondoliers as I follow one of the canals, hoping it'll take me to another POD. A heavyset gondolier flashes me a semi-toothless grin. I walk over and ask for directions.

"You don't need a POD, sweetheart." Even from where I am on the dock, I can smell the sourness of his breath. "You just need me."

I lean back. "I'm really just trying to get home."

"Come home with me," he says, smirking. "I'll show you a good time." Then he grabs my wrist. The boards of the dock creak as he tries to pull me into his boat. No one around me seems to notice—or care.

"Stop!" I yell. "Help!"

His fingers are around me like a clamp, dragging me forward. Then I see a figure whiz in front of me. I hear a loud snap and the pressure around my wrist releases. I fall into a strong pair of arms that pull me back to the sidewalk, toward safety.

The figure, I realize, is a boy. A *gorgeous* boy. Locks of dirty-blond hair cover his eyes, but even so, I can tell they're blue. They're practically hypnotizing.

"Asshole!" the gondolier yells. "You broke my wrist!"

"You're lucky that's all I broke," the boy calls back. "Creep." He softens his voice. "Are you okay?"

I nod.

"Where are you heading?"

"Home. The POD was broken, I was trying to find a new one."

He breaks into a grin. "I can help you."

"You've already done enough—"

"I won't take no for an answer." He motions ahead. "Ladies first."

We pass a street with a few tiny storefronts. "You're very kind," I say.

"Thanks. It's not every day you find a beautiful, semi-stranded girl in need of help." He flexes his biceps jokingly. "Lets me show off my superhero skills."

I laugh. "Superhero, eh?"

"Something like that. I'm Hunter, by the way."

"Aria," I say.

"Yeah, I know—I mean, I recognize you."

I'm not surprised. Most people in Manhattan recognize my face. "Well, it's nice to meet you, Hunter. Thank you for saving me."

"No problem. That's what superheroes do."

He presses his hand to the small of my back, steering me forward. Despite the intense heat, his touch gives me chills.

"So what are you doing down here?"

I glance at my clothes and frown. "I guess I stick out like a sore thumb."

"Not in a bad way," he says. "But . . . yeah, you sorta do."

I sigh. "My friend dared me to come down here. It was stupid of me."

He's silent for a moment. "Why?"

"Why was it stupid? I was almost abducted by a gondolier, for one. I'm not sure what the point of the dare was. There's nothing special down here anyway."

Up ahead, I see a line for a POD. I'm immediately relieved, and begin to walk a little faster.

"Well, you met me."

"Hmmm?" I say, a bit distracted. "What do you mean?"

"You said there was nothing special down here. And then I

said, 'Well, you met me.' " He blushes, then stares at the ground. Is he hitting on me?

Slowly, he looks up, meeting my eyes. The way he studies me makes me tremble—with nervousness, with excitement.

"Maybe I can see you sometime. You know, in the Aeries."

He *is* hitting on me!

"Look, Hunter, that's really sweet, and you're . . . *really* cute, but—"

"Never mind," he says. A bit of the light in his eyes seems to dull. "I'm just being stupid. I've never met anyone so beautiful in my entire life and it went to my head." He flashes me a grin; his teeth are perfectly white. "Anyway, here's the POD. Goodbye, Aria."

Whoa. Was I rude to dismiss him so easily? Who knows what would've happened if he hadn't stepped in with that gondolier. He seems funny, and he didn't have to walk me all the way here. He didn't even seem to care who I am. And he called me beautiful. No one has ever called me that before.

"Hunter," I say—

But then the memory burns away in a wash of fire that seems to ignite the world and me with it—as though every particle in my body is separating. I imagine electricity lighting up my spine like a neon tube, searing away my skin in bursts of color and heat—the angriest reds, the most unbearable blues, yellows hotter than the surface of the sun—and the colors blend together into a white-hot nothingness.

And I realize I am looking up at a sky burned bright white from summer heat.

I am in a boat, leaning back on the seat, and Hunter is rowing, singing a silly song about the *Flying Dachshund*.

"It's the *Flying Dutchman,*" I say. "It's a boat filled with ghosts."

"Maybe in the Aeries," he says, easily steering the boat under some branches, where cool shadow dapples the water. "But here in the Magnificent Block, it's a flying weiner dog, and he only appears to couples who are truly in love."

"You're so corny," I tell him. Hunter stops rowing. His face is flushed from the heat, his cheeks rosy and warm. He settles the oar on his thighs.

"Oh yeah?"

"Yeah," I say, smiling.

I see his hand shoot out and skim along the water. We're in one of the smaller, lazier canals that runs through the Great Lawn. I shouldn't be here—it's a Saturday, and I told my parents I was seeing Kiki. Instead, I followed instructions in a note he left on my balcony and came to the Depths. It's our third date. I just hope I wasn't tracked. If my parents knew I was hanging out down here, they'd ground me. If they knew I was hanging out with an unregistered rebel mystic, they'd ground me for life.

Hunter raises his hand, flicking the water at me. "Hunter, gross!" I yell, wiping the water from my arms.

He just laughs and starts rowing again. *"And the doggy with the tail in the skyyyyy!"*

"You may be good at a lot of things, but singing isn't one of them." I lean back in the boat and stare at the sky. "Hunter—look!"

Up ahead, there's a burst of color shooting from behind a cluster of trees. "Are those fireworks?"

Hunter turns his head and steadies the boat. The sparks—red and purple—fly up with a series of pops and then land a few feet away from us in the water.

I gasp. "I *love* fireworks."

"Good," Hunter says, "because these are just for you."

As he's talking, I notice that the ashy remains of the fireworks have begun to glow bright orange, turning the surface of the canal into a sort of canvas. The ashes become more dazzling until I realize they're in the shape of something . . . a dachshund?

Hunter starts to laugh hysterically.

"What's going on?"

"Just watch," he says. Within seconds, the outline of the dog—its stubby legs, floppy ears, and long back—starts to *move*.

"Oh wow," I say. The dachshund leans on its hind legs and jumps, skidding across the water in a loop-de-loop, then another one, all the while wagging its tail. This is more than just fireworks. I look at Hunter, trying to figure out how he's making this magic happen.

"What—"

Then the dog jumps again and curls into a ball, licking and nibbling at itself. A few seconds later, it trots over to the edge of the canal and lifts its leg to pee.

"Turk!" Hunter cries out. "It wasn't supposed to be like that!"

I hear a loud chuckling coming from off in the trees—and then a shiny Mohawk appears. "Gotcha!" the other boy, Turk, calls back. He must be one of Hunter's friends.

"Oh, now I see." I lean over and swat Hunter's arm. "You're a big faker."

Hunter is still laughing. The rich, hearty sound is infectious, and I find myself laughing, too, doubling over and clutching my stomach in pain.

Then his laugh softens. We both catch our breath, and he laces his fingers in mine, pulling me to him. His touch dizzies me, leaves me weak. "Hunter, be careful—the boat—"

"I may be a faker about the dachshund," he whispers, "but not about my feelings for you."

He presses his lips to mine, sealing us together. I'm sweaty from the heat and my clothes are practically glued to my skin, but none of that matters as soon as Hunter runs his hands down my back. My body responds to his caress like I've been waiting for it—for him—my entire life. All I want is more, more, more. . . .

"No, no, *no,*" Turk says. "This is a bad idea."

"How is it any different from my other bad ideas?" Hunter asks.

The three of us are in the middle of Hunter's subway car apartment. Turk is pacing, shaking his head like a crazy person. "Because this is illegal."

Hunter flashes him a look.

"I mean, *really* illegal. It goes against all our rules, Hunter." He looks at me. "Aria, I want you guys to be happy—but if Hunter's caught, even the other rebels won't take pity on him. He'll be cast out." Turk leans one very buff arm against the wall. "And don't even get me started on your mother—"

"Then don't get started," Hunter says. "Turk, you're here

because I trust you. You know how much in love we are." He slips an arm around my waist. "But if this is too much for you, then leave. I won't take offense. You've already done so much."

Turk sinks onto the sofa. "Leave? How am I supposed to *leave,* Hunter? You're my best friend. I love you both, but this is going too far."

Hunter shrugs, then goes over and claps Turk on the shoulder. "It's gonna be okay. I promise." Then he turns to me. "Here's what'll happen, Aria. I'm going to create a portal between my apartment and your balcony."

"A portal?"

"Yeah, like . . . a secret tunnel. Only it's going to be invisible and magical and—well, the details aren't important. What's important is that it'll allow me to come right to your balcony. No more sneaking around through the Depths or risking getting caught."

"Will I be able to use it to come here?"

"You can travel it with me," Hunter says, "but it can only be activated by mystic energy—you won't be able to use it on your own."

"And how do you make this . . . portal? Is it dangerous?"

Hunter considers this. "A little. But don't worry. Just watch."

I step away as Hunter lifts his right arm and stretches out his fingers. At first, nothing happens—all I see is how hard he is concentrating, his lips pressed together tightly, his brow furrowed. But then his hand begins to glow green: electric rays shoot from his fingertips with a soft hum.

The rays look like they're about to hit the wall. Then they stop. Hunter lets his hand pulse steadily for a moment; then he curls his fingers and the rays begin to bleed together, shrinking. They're not long and thin like jousting swords anymore. Now they're so small they don't look like rays at all—instead, his hand is like a glowing green ball. Bands of energy start moving around the hand like rings around a planet, faster and faster. All I can hear is a loud whizzing. All I can see is this pulsating magical fist.

The whizzing grows so loud it's nearly deafening. Then there's a loud zap as Hunter punches the empty space in front of him. The air reacts as if it were solid, cleaving open into what looks like a miniature black hole, the edges of which are ablaze with green light.

The sounds in the apartment return to normal. I glance back at Hunter. The rays have completely disappeared. Turk's jaw has gone slack, as though he's in shock.

"Now," Hunter says, slightly out of breath. He points to the loophole and grins. "Who's first?"

I hurt with such an intense pain that I can barely see. There is nothing to focus on save the agony. It feels like I am burning up, ripping apart. All I can see are dots of color that grow brighter as the pain increases. The dots begin to move, weaving in circles of blue and pink and yellow. There is fire and there is heat. Then something cool rushes over me. The dots begin to form a picture. Another memory . . .

"Aria, there's something else you should know." Hunter takes my hands in his; we're standing in the middle of my bedroom, about to say goodnight.

"What is it?"

He frowns. "I hate to be the one to tell you this. But the Conflagration—the terrorist explosion that killed all those innocent people and sent the mystics underground twenty years ago? That was orchestrated by *your* family. By your father. He bribed a group of mercenary mystics to create a weapon. A defensive weapon, he claimed. But then he turned it against them and detonated it in a public place so no one would ever trust mystics again."

I always knew my father was a bad guy, but this . . . "So my entire life—the lives of everyone in this city—has been based on a lie."

"I'm so sorry, Aria."

Before I can respond, I hear my father's voice. "Aria! Open up." His fists pound savagely on my bedroom door. "I know you're in there with him. It's all over, Aria. Open up the door."

"Hunter," I say frantically, "you need to go. Now." I rush over to my windows and open them; immediately, hot wind blows into my room.

Hunter's lips are trembling. "Come with me."

"That will only make things worse." My bedroom door sounds like it's about to crack. We have seconds, at most. "I'll be fine." I kiss him passionately. *"Go."*

Hunter activates the loophole on my balcony at the same time my father breaks through my door. Kyle rushes past, reaching for Hunter as he disappears into the loophole and it seals behind him.

"Where did he go?" My father grabs my shirt, twisting it and lifting me off the ground. I can hear the material start to tear.

"I don't know."

"This isn't a game, Aria. Tell me where."

"I told you . . . I don't know!"

He drops me and my knees hit the floor. A piercing pain shoots up my thighs. The man before me barely resembles my father anymore. His skin is blotchy, his eyes bulging out of their sockets like an angry animal's.

Then he raises his hand and smacks me—my teeth clamp down and slice open my tongue. Tangy blood fills my mouth.

"Johnny, stop!" my mother cries from the doorway.

"You're a traitor!" My father stares at me with a look of pure disgust. Something silver glints in his other hand—he's holding a pistol. "This ends now, Aria."

"Aria," Kyle says from the corner, "don't be an idiot. Tell him where the mystic is hiding."

"Kill me if you want," I say. "I won't be some puppet for you."

My father unlocks the safety of his gun. Points it directly at my head.

"No, Johnny!" My mother rushes into the room. "Don't!" She comes up to my father, who pushes her away.

I close my eyes. This is it. I'm about to die.

Then I hear another voice. "Johnny. Wait." I open my eyes. Benedict is in the room, looking concerned, a syringe in one of his hands. "There's a better way."

My father turns to him. "Speak, Patrick."

"We can flush her memories of this mystic boy and build new memories in their place." Benedict uncaps the needle. "It's experimental, but she doesn't have to die, Johnny."

My father looks at us all—my brother, my mother, Benedict,

and me—and nods. "All right." His eyes find me again. "Maybe this time around you'll be a better daughter."

"Maybe you'll be a better father," I say, spitting blood.

I can tell he wants to hit me again, but he doesn't. Benedict approaches—I try to back away, but Kyle comes from behind me and grabs my arms, twisting them behind me. "No!" I scream.

"You're going to sleep now, Aria," Benedict says.

Slowly, sketches of memories begin to find their places, like birds coming home to roost. Pictures of my parents flash before me; my feelings for Hunter return and take root. The secrets and lies and betrayals. Davida. Thomas. Everything that was cast out of me is returning, only clearer. And it hurts. There is a fine white net of pain covering me, like I'm being stabbed all over, every pore ravaged. But there's an undeniable comfort in the pain—I own it. It is the price of knowing.

I am in Dr. May's office. My entire body is immobilized. I am on a table, hands at my sides, about to be slid inside a large machine.

Benedict leans over me. "Aria, can you hear me?"

I try to answer but find I can't speak.

"Listen closely. Hunter is not gone to you forever. A mystic's heart is not like a human's. They take different forms to the naked eye—some are different colors, some are fractal boxes, some seem to be made of glass."

Benedict disappears for a second, then returns. "The heart is the seat of a mystic's power, and the localized energy there works its magic on the eye of the beholder—to look within it is to see an ever-shifting reality, a quicksilver mirror of ourselves. You have to trust that at some point after this, you will gaze inside his heart and see yourself, and that recognition will unlock everything."

I'm trying to understand what he's telling me—I'll find Hunter again, even though they're wiping out my memories?—but I'm feeling so sleepy.

"Aria, do you trust me?"

I have no energy left. All I can do is nod.

And then I feel whole again, together, my body burning not with pain but with something else—love, maybe.

The love letters, Romeo, the boy in my dreams whose face I've never been able to see, is Hunter.

It's been him all along. Behind everything, Hunter.

And just like that, I am back—back in my room, in this prison cell that I call home, with the boy I love before me, asking me, "Do you love me?"

"I do," I whisper. "But are you *you*?"

He takes me in his arms and whispers, "It's really me. And it's really you, now, Aria. You've come back to me."

I grab Hunter's arm for balance, feel his strength beneath my grip, the lithe muscles of his arms. How is he here? I watched him die . . . didn't I?

Suddenly, my throat closes up, and my skin begins to itch like I'm having an allergic reaction. The joy at being in Hunter's arms vanishes, replaced by anger—at my parents, at my brother, at Thomas: everyone who lied to me.

I can't breathe.

"Aria?" Hunter says, his face frantic. He slips behind me and clasps his hands together just below my breastbone.

Then he yanks his hands hard into my gut.

I cough and the locket goes flying out of my mouth and lands under my armoire with a plink.

My eyes water, and I gasp and fill my lungs with air. Then, without warning, I vomit all over myself.

· XXVIII ·

"Everything okay in there?" Stiggson asks, rapping twice on the closed door.

"Yes!" I yelp as Hunter comes back from the bathroom with a wet towel. I use it to wipe the vomit from my mouth and chin while Hunter vigorously scrubs the carpet. "I only need a few more minutes."

I take a sip of water from a glass on my nightstand. I can't believe I just threw up. More so, I can't believe I threw up *in front of Hunter* and that he's actually cleaning it up right now—which is incredibly sweet but awfully embarrassing.

"Hold on." I motion for Hunter to stop. He looks at me with his beautiful blue eyes, and he's so handsome that I want to cry.

"What?" he says.

I let my jaw go slack. "You're alive!"

He drops the towel, then stands and embraces me. I don't care that my breath is sour—Hunter is here, taking me in his arms. Nothing else matters.

"I thought you were *dead*." The words rush out of me; there's so much I want to say to him, now that *I remember,* now that I know the truth. "I don't understand. . . . I watched you get—I saw you—"

"I know," Hunter says, kissing my neck just below my ear. "It's complicated, but I'm here."

"It's really you?" I whisper.

"Heart and soul." I can feel his chest against mine, rising and falling, his warm breath on my cheek.

"How were you able to look like Davida?"

"It's complicated," Hunter says. "But basically, that was her doing. I kept the glamour she cast on me so that people would truly think I was dead. But tonight, I couldn't stand it any longer and came looking for you—and I was caught."

I glance back at my bedroom door, where Stiggson's shadow is waiting. "Explain to me what I saw. When you were shot."

We sit back down on the bed, and Hunter takes one of my hands, interlacing his fingers with mine. Davida's uniform is tight on him now that he's in his regular body.

"That night," Hunter says, carefully choosing his words, "when your father's cronies got hold of me, they put quicksilver cuffs around me. It's what they use to immobilize mystics. I couldn't move. Then they threw a bag over my head and tossed me into the hold of the police boat."

I wince. "I remember that."

"There were three men in the boat with me, and they were all up top." Hunter bites his bottom lip. "I only know this because Davida pulled the bag off my head and told me so. She'd stowed away."

I think back—Davida *was* there that night. But then she'd disappeared. "But why was she there?"

He takes a deep breath. "You know Davida's talent?"

"She can take on someone else's appearance," I say, thinking of the day when Davida took on my face, and I stared at a mirror image of myself.

"That kind of power—to take on another person's form—is incredibly rare. Only one in a hundred thousand or so has that talent."

And then I remember what I learned from her secret journal: she and Hunter were betrothed. They'd been promised to marry since birth. "Oh no," I whisper, suddenly realizing.

"I couldn't move," Hunter says, a desperate edge to his voice. "I'd been stunned. I couldn't even speak. I could only watch as Davida sliced off my cuffs, stole my face, and took my form. Then she gave me hers. She rolled me behind some crates where no one would see me, and . . ."

"She took your place," I finish for him. I place my free hand on his cheek—he's hot, burning up.

"I didn't have a choice, Aria. I had to lie there and listen as they dragged her up top, made her stand in the stern, and then . . . shot her."

Hunter sobs quietly, and I wipe his tears away with my thumb. "Shhh. It's not your fault."

"Of course it is!" Hunter says in a harsh whisper. "If I hadn't taken you to the Depths, if I hadn't—"

"You can't think like that," I say. "She sacrificed herself for you. The least you can do is make sure her sacrifice wasn't in vain."

He says nothing for a moment, just stares at me before nodding. The hurt in his eyes nearly breaks my heart. It's clear that he felt deeply for her. "Right. The next morning, once the boat had been docked and the stun worn off, I snuck back underground. Alone."

Suddenly, I hear her voice in my ear: *Do you love him? Then I will protect you both . . . for as long as I can.*

Davida didn't sacrifice herself only for Hunter. She sacrificed herself for me. For both of us, and for what we mean together. My father is right about one thing: a marriage between feuding families can be powerful. Instead of the Roses and the Fosters coming together, what would a union between a Rose and a *Brooks* do for Manhattan?

Hunter's cheeks are glistening with tears. He wipes his nose on his sleeve, then uses his hand to brush back his hair. I want to enjoy this moment with him, but it's nearly impossible. People are waiting for me outside my door. Expecting to see Davida.

"Did you love her?" I'm not sure why I need to know, but I do.

Hunter nods. "Yes."

"Oh." I feel my pulse quicken. That wasn't the answer I expected.

"As a friend," he clarifies. "I was supposed to marry her, but that was before I met you. I'm in love with *you,* Aria. Davida knew that." For the first time tonight, Hunter smiles. "I loved you the first time I saw you. I loved you even more the first time I kissed you that day in the Block."

"You're the one I want to be with, Hunter," I say, trying to convey all the things I feel. "And I love you, too." I can't help but relish in this one moment of happiness amid so much sadness.

"Davida loved you, Aria," Hunter says, gripping my shoulders. He stares right into my eyes, as if he can see directly inside me. "That's why she did what she did."

I feel tears well up. "Even though there was so much I didn't know about her. I . . . I loved her, too. And you"—I rest my palm against his cheek—"this whole time you've known our history and you never said anything?"

He nods, silent.

"The letters . . . Romeo and Juliet . . . they were from you?"

Another nod.

"That night, when you saved me from those boys and took me to Java River—how did you just sit back and let me think we'd never met?" I ask. "Why didn't you tell me the truth?"

"That we'd had a secret affair and were madly in love, and your parents erased me from your memory?" The way Hunter says this makes me realize that I never would have believed him if he'd told me. I would've thought he was nuts. "I knew you'd lost your memory," he says. "Davida told me. So I didn't expect you would recognize me. Not saying anything was one of the hardest things I've ever done, but I knew it was right." He takes my hands, pulls me close. "And now you remember. We have each other, and that's all that matters."

There's a noise like something falling, and Hunter leaps up and rushes over to the windows. He peeks out the curtains. "We will be together, Aria, but not right now."

"What?" I say, standing. "What do you mean?" I point to my window. "Let's use the loophole, get out of here—"

"It's too dangerous," he says, taking a few steps toward me. "We should wait until things have calmed down, until after the election—"

"They've moved up the wedding, Hunter," I say. "It's in five days."

"They *what*?" Hunter says, louder than he intended to. Someone pounds on the door; then there's the clink of something metallic.

"Aria! Open up *now*!"

"They're looking for ways to get underground," I say, "to kill the rebels."

"They'll never manage," Hunter says with a surprising amount of confidence. "So don't worry about that."

"They're planning something awful," I say, shuddering. "We have to go underground. Warn the rebels, and your mother, and figure out some way for us to get the truth out to the rest of the city. We owe it to ourselves . . . and to the people of Manhattan."

Relief flashes in Hunter's eyes. "I was hoping you'd say that."

"The loophole," I say, but Hunter shakes his head. "It's been disabled," he says. "Turk sealed it off when he thought I was dead. We'll have to enter somewhere else."

"The Seaport entrance?"

"It's being monitored." Hunter scratches his chin. "There's an entrance on Forty-Second Street, on the West Side."

"Perfect."

It's only when I stop to breathe that I realize my bedroom door is open: Stiggson, my brother, my parents, and the Fosters are in the doorway, their mouths wide open.

And behind them are five burly men with guns pointed directly at my head.

· XXIX ·

"*You* again?"

The disbelief in my father's voice is undeniable. He's not even yelling, which is how I know he's really mad, though his cheeks have lost some of their earlier redness. His thick eyebrows are drawn together over his eyes, which are muddied with confusion. A light sheen of sweat covers his forehead.

Dad whips out his pistol. "How many times do I have to kill you?"

Hunter stands still in the middle of the room, hands at his sides. There's an eerie silence; then he shrugs and says, "Nine? Guess I'm more like a cat than I'd like to admit."

No one laughs. The bodyguards simultaneously step forward. Behind them, George and Erica Foster are standing with queer expressions on their faces, while my mother looks as if she's got something caught in her throat. Benedict and Kyle are there, too—Kyle with his arms crossed, Benedict trying to signal something to me that I can't understand—and behind them, I see a glimpse of Garland and Thomas in the hallway.

The gang's all here.

"Where's Davida?" my mother asks. She points a finger at Hunter. "Did you murder her, mystic?"

"Of course I didn't," he says. "*I'm* not violent."

"Don't speak to my wife like that," Dad says, the barrel of his gun still trained on Hunter. "In fact, don't speak at all. How dare you show up in my home, after what you've done to my family—"

"How about what *you've* done to *me*?" Hunter says. He throws his arms up. "Just let me and Aria go and we'll leave you alone forever."

"I don't negotiate with mystics," my father says, snarling.

Hunter glances back toward the balcony, as though he might rush and jump off.

"Don't," I whisper to him. "It's too risky."

"Enough!" my father shouts. "This has gone on long enough. You cover your tracks well, I'll give you that. We searched the entire city for you and never found you the first time. I was sure we finally had you that night in the Depths. I have no idea how you managed to come back from the dead, mystic, but once and for all, it will end. Here." He unlocks the safety of his gun. "Now."

I throw myself in front of Hunter. "No," I say, spreading my arms. Now that I know Hunter is alive, now that I've finally recovered the memories that were stripped from me, I'll do anything to protect him. I can't lose him again.

"Aria, this time I *will* shoot you if you don't move."

"Then shoot me."

I feel Hunter's breath on the back of my neck. "Aria, don't do this," he says. "Step away. Please. I don't want you to get hurt."

I lock eyes with my father. "I love Hunter. I will always love Hunter."

Dad's finger tugs at the trigger of his pistol. "Then I hope you die happy, Aria."

"Johnny, wait." It's Benedict. His eyes look watery, and he fidgets with the cuffs of his sleeves as he pushes past George Foster. At the side of the room, next to my bed, Klartino shifts the aim of his gun from Hunter toward Benedict. "You can't kill them. Especially not Hunter."

Dad scoffs, tilting his head so that a lock of black hair falls over his forehead. "Of course I can."

"No, you don't understand—"

"Perhaps *you* don't understand, Patrick." Dad's eyes blaze with rage. "This happened the last time: you stepping in, trying to help. *We can replace her memories,*" he says in a mocking imitation of Benedict's voice, "only look how that worked out. This boy doesn't get another chance. He dies now."

"The mystic is your key to the underground," Benedict blurts out. This seems to pique everyone's interest.

"What do you mean, Patrick?" George Foster asks.

"He's a rebel. Never been drained. His power will unlock the seals on the hidden entrances. Once he opens them for us, we'll be able to flood the underground. Take them by surprise."

My father seems to consider this information, as does the rest of the group. I know Benedict is trying to buy Hunter and me some time—but I also know that what he's saying is true. Hunter *can* unlock the seals. But if he does, all the rebels are at risk. I don't want that responsibility on my shoulders.

"Just deal with us," I say to my father, but my words are lost on him. The possibility of snuffing out the rebels once and for all is too tempting for him to ignore.

"The mystic has to be alive, though," Benedict says. "Otherwise, he won't be able to open any of the entrances."

George Foster breaks away from his wife and whispers something into Dad's ear. I glance at Hunter, who has a worried look on his face. *I love you,* he mouths to me.

I love you, too, I mouth back.

George Foster pulls away, and Dad motions to Stiggson. "Fine. Cuff the boy." Then he speaks directly to Hunter. "You'll lead us to one of the mystic entrances and allow us to go through. If we find out that you've warned your people of our arrival, Aria will die. If you do as we say . . . she'll remain unharmed."

Hunter nods, as though he's actually considering this ridiculous plan. He can't be, though—can he? "And what happens to me?"

"You'll die, of course. But I promise to make your end as painless as possible."

"No!" I shout. "This is unacceptable, this is—"

"Aria," Hunter says, "there's no point in fighting. It's the best way—the only way."

"You can't honestly believe that," I say to him, as though we're the only ones in the room. We've just gotten each other back; I'm not going to lose him again.

I stare into his eyes and the lovely blue of them washes over me like a wave, soothing my nerves. I think back to the night of my engagement party. *I always thought true love would sear me.* Well, here

I am—on fire, ablaze with love: my chest feels like it's been broken open, my heart about to be ripped out and crushed.

And there's nothing I can do to stop it from happening.

"Cuff him," my father repeats.

Stiggson marches forward, his steps heavy and methodical, the quicksilver cuffs in one hand. Hunter flips his wrists over, submitting. Stiggson looks at him funny—just as he's about to unlock the cuffs, he changes his mind and punches Hunter right in the stomach.

"Stop!" I shout.

Hunter doesn't make a noise. Then Klartino rushes up, takes out his pistol, and smashes it against Hunter's cheek.

"Please, stop!"

Still Hunter is silent. His nose explodes with red, red blood, which drips over his mouth and down his chin, soaking his shirt.

Stiggson moves behind Hunter and yanks back his arms. There's a sickening sound as they pop out of their sockets. Hunter's face remains stoic. He doesn't want to show my father that he's winning.

A flash of silver, then Stiggson clamps the cuffs around Hunter's wrists. Hunter flinches when the metal touches his skin, the first time he's acknowledged any pain. I wonder if it burns.

I start to object again, but my father silences me with a look. Stiggson pushes Hunter in front of him, forcing him out of my room. They move slowly, as if they're in a funeral procession. Hunter glances over his shoulder at me—I connect with him for a moment. *I will come for you,* I think as hard as I can, hoping he can somehow understand me.

And then Klartino's in my face. He pushes me onto the chair at my desk, then slides my arms behind me, binding my wrists with some type of wire coil that digs into my skin.

"What are you doing?" I try to wriggle my hands, but it's impossible.

My mother holds up her hand. "You're staying here, Aria."

"What? Why?"

"You know why," she says. "I'm so disappointed. I thought we'd cured you. That we could be a family again, without that mystic. But nothing's changed. You would rather risk your life on a romantic folly than devote yourself to our family, to this city—"

"I *am* devoted to this city," I say, "much more than you or Dad."

My mother slaps me so quickly I don't even see it coming. The sting on my cheek doesn't hurt, though. It only makes me mad. "Fine, lock me up. It doesn't mean I won't find a way out—I've done it before, and I can do it again. Just try me."

My mother seems surprised by my outburst. Her brown eyes widen, and she flushes. Thomas looks at me sadly, then leaves. The room has emptied; everyone is downstairs but me and my mother.

"I know what you did to me," I continue. "I remember *everything.* And I will never forgive you."

Mom tsks at me—the kind of sound a mother might make if her daughter got a bad grade in school or stayed out past curfew. But we are so far beyond that now. This is life or death.

"Good night, Aria," she says. Then she leaves.

I immediately try to loosen the wiring. If anything, it seems to get even tighter, and something sharp pierces the skin on both arms. I scan the room, trying to see if there's anything I can rub up against that might cut the wire, but I can't see anything—just the edge of my desk.

Then I notice the metal handles on the windows to my balcony—could those slice the restraints?

I use my feet to make tiny hops in the chair over to the balcony. If I can loosen the wire, then I can open the windows and maybe . . . somehow . . . open the loophole?

I sigh and toss my head back. I'm incredibly frustrated. There's no way I can open the loophole—especially now that the only magical thing I have, the locket, has been emptied.

I'm five or six hops away from my windows when they burst open.

They crash loudly against the walls, and my hair is blown back by the gust of wind that hits my face. At first I can barely see anything—the balcony is full of blazing green light. But I squint and then I see it:

Turk.

On his motorcycle.

Hovering outside my balcony.

Bright green jets shoot from the exhaust pipes; the slick chrome wheels are popping against the dark sky. Three super-red LED lights are blinking right below the leather seat.

"Turk!"

Slowly, he lands the bike on the balcony, kills the engine, and hops off. His Mohawk is dyed bright orange tonight. He's wearing a tight wife beater and shorts that show off his calf muscles and his tan skin.

"You okay?" he asks, walking toward me. "Some of the other

rebels, ones who don't like you so much, found out about the loophole, so I had to seal it. But I've been keeping an eye on you regardless. Just caught what's happened. I waited until they left your building to come inside."

"They took him—they're going to—"

"Shhh," Turk says, "all in good time, lady. All in good time." He surveys the situation. "You tied up?"

"Why else would I be here?" I roll my eyes. "Can you help?"

Turk grins. "Ah. The magic words."

"Come on, Turk—there isn't time for any of this. They're going to *kill* him!"

"I thought they already did." Turk laughs nervously. "All right. I'm going to blast away whatever's tying you up." He walks around me. "Hold your hands still—don't move. I don't wanna accidentally disintegrate a finger or something."

"Not funny."

"Just hold still, Aria."

I keep my eyes on Turk's bike. I can't see his energy, but I can hear it—like the buzzing of a hornet's nest directly in my ears. A jolt hits the chair. I'm knocked forward onto my side. I try to move my arms and find that I can. I bring them in front of my face—the metal ties are still around my wrists, like sickening bracelets. I push myself to my feet.

"Thanks," I say to Turk.

"No problem."

I cock my head at his bike. "Let's get out of here."

"To where?" Turk rubs his forehead. "You got a plan?"

"They're going to use Hunter to gain access to the subway systems. We've gotta get down there, warn the rebels—"

"First of all," Turk says, looking defeated, "at the speed of the rails, your family, the Fosters, and whatever backup they have are probably already in the Depths. We'll never catch up with them. And more importantly, we have no idea where they're going, which entrance they're going to try to use. There are dozens. We'll be racing around trying to find them and . . . and we won't be able to save him. To save anyone."

Turk punches the wall. "Damn!" His fist breaks through the plaster with a crunching noise and a cloud of dust poofs into the air.

"That was dumb," I say.

He rubs his knuckles, which have started to bleed. "No, it wasn't."

"Wait—Times Square. Hunter mentioned something about Times Square . . . is there an old entrance there?"

Turk thinks for a second. "Yeah, there is." He smiles. "Come on. I know exactly where to go." He fumbles in his pocket for a second, then takes out a silver ring. "Here."

"A present? How sweet."

"Not just any present—it's a passkey."

"A what?" I ask, looking at the ring. It looks like . . . a ring. I take off my engagement ring and slip Turk's ring on instead. My finger begins to throb lightly.

"The only way to break a mystic seal is with mystic energy. That's how the rebels enter the underground," Turk says. "But since you're not a mystic, you'll need a passkey to get in. I infused some of my energy into the ring—it's in case we get separated, so you can still hide down there."

"Thanks," I say, knowing this will come in handy. The ring reminds me of something else: the locket. I have a sudden urge to find it. "Hold on." I feel for it under the dresser and pull it out. It's cracked and dirty, but I place it around my neck anyway, as a symbol of what my parents did to me. I won't let their actions cripple me. I will turn my past into my future—with Hunter.

I follow Turk onto the balcony, where he picks up his helmet and drops it onto my head. I clutch my skirt in my hands, bunching it up so I can step onto the bike.

"Ready?" Turk asks.

"Just one more thing—do you have your TouchMe?"

He nods, pulling it out of his pocket. "Why?"

I grab it with one hand and begin to type in a number. "Because my mother took mine, and there's someone I have to call."

• XXX •

By the time we descend into the Depths, the sun has disappeared, and the sky has bruised over in shades of purple and blue.

"I still don't understand what *she's* doing here," Turk says over the roar of his bike. Turk's motorcycle powers us over a series of bridges as we ride along the Broadway Canal. Most shops are closed for the night, but there are a few people milling around the streets and walkways who dive out of our way as we pass—this is no time for cautious driving. Who knows what my parents are doing to Hunter, how long he has to live. We've got to save him.

Elissa Genevieve grips me tighter around the waist.

When we first picked her up, Turk practically refused to speak to her. "She works for the enemy."

"No, she doesn't," I told him. "She's working to help you from the inside, just like Benedict."

Elissa nodded. "Yes, he and I work together!" Her long hair was pulled back into a severe ponytail, her face devoid of makeup. I'd texted her to meet us at the Circle in the Aeries, explained what had happened. Invited her to come with us. To help.

"I've never seen you underground before," Turk said skeptically.

"I've been drained," Elissa said. Dressed in all black—Lycra pants and a form-fitting top—she looked ready to fight. "I no longer have access."

"She helped me," I told Turk. "She showed me what happens in the draining room. She's on our side, Turk."

Turk scratched his forehead. "We don't have time to discuss this. If Aria trusts you, then I trust you." He pressed a hidden button under the handlebar of his bike, and the seat extended noiselessly, making room for all of us.

Almost. Now I'm sandwiched between Turk and Elissa; I can practically feel my organs rearranging themselves. The mist coming off the canal waters is thick and heavy, swirling around us in curls of gray, like smoke from an oversized cigar.

When we reach Fiftieth Street, Turk slows down. Times Square is only a few blocks away, and we don't want to give any warning that we're here.

It starts to rain. A smattering at first, then fat droplets that spray my face and soak my clothes. "Shit," Turk says. The white light from the bike's headlights pierces the smog, allowing us to see—but only what the beam touches. Around us, the rain and darkness and heat of the night lick at me like a dog's tongue, making me feel sloppy and tired.

I brush my hair back with my fingers and wipe my cheeks. There's no time for tired. All I can think is: *Hunter.*

We go another block or so; then Turk pulls over in front of a row of derelict buildings and shuts off the engine. "We should walk from here. Less conspicuous."

Elissa slides off the back of the bike, and I can breathe again.

She holds out her hand and helps me down. Turk wheels the motorcycle over to an old fire hydrant. He unwraps a chain from around the body of the bike, then locks the cycle to the hydrant.

When he's done, he searches for us in the dark—practically all I can make out are the whites of his eyes. "There's a spire somewhere around here," he says. "We should be able to get more light if we keep moving."

We walk together silently. I grab Turk's shirt and follow him. I hope he knows where he's going. My feet crunch over bits of broken pavement, an empty soda can. I can't see the Broadway Canal, but I know it's near us—I hear the slap of water hitting concrete and smell the foul, salty stench.

We go another block or two and turn right, over a bridge, and then I see a spire in the distance. Its light blankets the area with an iridescent glow. The familiar energy inside swirls and undulates white-yellow-green, white-yellow-green. I listen for signs of Hunter, of my parents, but all I hear are the muted voices of passersby in the distance, the shuffling of our feet, and the wild beating of my own nervous heart.

The neighborhood looks seedy. The streets are full of trash, the store windows covered with graffiti or smashed in. The buildings here seem crowded, overlapping like crooked teeth. Rats scurry along carrying bits of paper and rotting food. Overhead, faded marquees hang sadly from abandoned theaters, lightbulbs crushed or missing, windows smashed in.

"This used to be the center of the city," Turk says as we pass a wide intersection of avenues. A green sign that says 42ND STREET hangs from a post on one of the bridges. I see the entrance to the old subway station—the biggest I've encountered so far. Circles of different colors, red, yellow, blue, each with a faded number inside, are painted over the entrance.

I glance behind me to make sure Elissa is okay. She's peering around wildly, as if searching for someone. When our eyes meet, she looks guilty for a second; then she relaxes and gives me a tight grin.

"Is that how we get underground?" I point to the subway entrance, which is sealed with blocks of concrete laced with steel girders. It looks all but impenetrable. I search out the green posts, like the ones near the South Street Seaport, but I don't see any. I wonder how we'll get in.

Turk shakes his head. "No. The entrance is up there." He points a few blocks ahead: I don't see anything except a dirty, oversized sign about half the length of a city block. It was probably white at one point, but that was many years ago. Now it's a filthy beige, with large red block letters: TKTS.

"There?"

Turk nods. "Come on. But careful." He steps in front, motioning for us to follow; behind him, we stand pressed up against the wall of one of the buildings. There's a drooping awning overhead that's providing us with some well-needed shadow: the center of Times Square is bright, brighter than I anticipated. We'll have to stay around the edges so as not to be seen.

Turk listens carefully, then signals for us to proceed. I make sure I don't step on anything that might break and give us away. The closer we get to the TKTS sign, the more voices I hear. I look out toward the middle of the square.

And that's when I see him. A block away.

"Come on, boy," someone says. Hunter's head is down, his arms cuffed behind his back. His shoulders slump forward; he shuffles his feet as if it's painful to walk. There's a guard on either side of him, Stiggson and Klartino following directly behind. My father and George Foster walk a few feet ahead, bodyguards flanking them, along with Thomas, Garland, Kyle, and Benedict. None of the women are there.

I cover my mouth so they can't hear me gasp.

I poke Turk in the back and we stop in our tracks. Elissa, too. "What's happening?"

"Shhh," Turk hisses.

We press so close to the building that I can feel the bricks making imprints on my back and the palms of my hands. From this angle, we can see Hunter and my father's crew, but unless they come around the corner and run smack into us, we should remain out of sight.

We watch as the guards pull Hunter toward one of the buildings with a faded gold door. The windows are blackened with grime. "Is it this one?"

Hunter studies the door for a second. He's barely recognizable, his face is so bruised. His forehead is sliced open, his cheeks red and swollen. His hair is streaked with blood and matted to his head with sweat. My stomach feels like it's being wrung out. I might be sick.

"Don't recall," Hunter mutters.

My father strolls over to him, lifts his chin in the air with one finger. The sleeves of Dad's dress shirt are rolled up, exposing his thick forearms and the corded muscle there. Hunter tries to look away, but Dad grabs his jaw. "Look at me," he instructs.

For a second, they stare at each other—then Hunter spits at my father.

As soon as the spit hits his forehead, Dad attacks. He pulls back his arm and punches Hunter in the gut, then on the right side of the face. His fist connects with Hunter's chin with a loud smack.

Hunter doubles over, vomiting blood and bile and whatever else is in his stomach onto the pavement.

"Ready to stop the bullshit and show us where the entrance is?" my father asks.

Hunter doesn't answer. His lip is split—I can see that from here—and his eyes seem snuffed out, lifeless.

"I can't see," Elissa whispers from behind me. She shifts her weight forward and kicks something out from behind her—an empty glass bottle? I don't know, but it makes a sound that alerts everyone to our presence.

My entire body tenses, and I hold my breath. Turk's eyes are wide, alert. Nervous.

The guards raise their noses in the air like trained dogs, and I see my father whip his head around. Kyle, who's standing a few feet away with a pistol trained on Hunter, turns. "Who's there?" he shouts.

Elissa squeezes my hand, and I squeeze Turk's. I'm so scared. Maybe if we're quiet . . . *really* quiet . . . they'll ignore us.

Just then, someone stumbles over a bridge on the far side of the square. A man, from the looks of it, a bottle of booze in one hand. He turns onto the street where my father and the others are and freezes.

Kyle shoots.

The bullet lodges right in the man's forehead. The bottle falls, smashing on the ground, and the man drops to the pavement like an abandoned marionette.

"Just some drunk," Kyle calls out.

Relieved to have found the source of the noise, Dad and his goons shove Hunter to another derelict storefront. But for a split second I see Hunter glancing in our direction—there's a flash of life in his eyes.

He knows we're here.

I hope with all my heart that he'll lead my father away.

And then, as if he can hear my prayers, he opens his bloodied mouth and says, "Okay. I'll show you. It's down this alleyway."

He points in the opposite direction of the sign, and I know he's lying, trying to buy us more time. The goons hold their guns to his back, piloting him forward, their figures diminishing as they move into the distance.

Turk pulls us away from the street corner and into a huddle. Then, finally, he lets go of my hand. "While Hunter is distracting them, we need to go underground and get with reinforcements. We can outnumber them." Turk points to the ratty TKTS sign. "See the gray building just under the sign?" We nod. "That's where the entrance is. We'll rescue Hunter and disappear back into the subways, where we can figure out our next move."

"Sounds like a plan," I say, relieved to have one.

"I've never used that entrance," Elissa says, nodding toward the banded cement blocks. She doesn't apologize for making noise—for almost getting us killed. Shadows and light from Times Square play on her face, making her seem older than she is. "How will I get in?"

Turk rolls his eyes; I can tell he wishes she weren't here. He swipes a hand over his hair. The rain has flattened down his Mohawk, which sweeps over to one side. "Aria has a passkey." I raise my hand, wiggle my finger with the ring on it. It's the only part of my body that feels warm. Elissa's eyes shine with recognition.

"You'll have to grab her hand when she uses it," Turk instructs. "You both should be able to gain entrance that way. I'm going to stay here, make sure they don't hurt him too bad."

"But I don't know where anything is down there," I say. "I'm not sure I could even find Hunter's place by myself. What if I get lost? And besides, who will listen to me? You two go. I'll stay here and watch out for Hunter."

Turk shakes his head. "Absolutely not, Aria. I'm not leaving you up here alone." He sighs. "We'll all go together, then, and hope nothing happens to Hunter in the meantime."

"Then let's go," Elissa says confidently, standing up straight.

We wait for the perfect second to break. As soon as my father's group is out of sight, Turk waves his hand and whispers, "Now!"

We bolt out of the shadows, high-stepping over a pile of broken cobblestones and dashing along a wide, high bridge that crosses the canal. There before us is the entrance, just beneath the faded sign. Like the old subway entrances, this, too, is sealed with steel-reinforced concrete.

Then I notice a spindly post, practically hidden behind the wall of concrete. It's made of metal, and at the top is a small green globe. It must have been decorative at one point, but now it's fused to the steel, bent, so that if you weren't looking for it, you certainly wouldn't find it.

"The globe," I say. "It's a smaller version of the ones at the Seaport."

I'm reaching for it when I hear a gunshot.

I look over my shoulder and Turk is on the ground, grabbing his chest. A plume of blood has blossomed on his T-shirt and is seeping through his fingers. His face is frozen in shock.

"Elissa, watch out!" I say, but then I see the expression on her face: she's grinning, her smile wicked and dark.

And then I notice the gun in her hand.

She shot Turk.

Before I can react, Elissa grabs my hand and twists off the ring Turk gave me: the passkey.

"Elissa, what are you doing? I thought . . ."

"You thought wrong," she sneers, laughing triumphantly. "I work for your parents, and the Fosters, hunting out rebels. That's my real job. No one, not even Patrick, knows the truth." She takes a deep breath.

"How long have you been doing this?" I ask, trying to keep her talking, hoping to think of something, anything, that will allow me to escape.

"The Conflagration?" Elissa says. "The bomb was *my* pet project, made from *my* energy."

It all makes sense now: Elissa was the one who turned against her people for personal gain, who was given a spot in the Aeries and hired by my parents to get the mystics out of the picture. She must have been in her early twenties then, and she's been working for my family ever since.

Elissa runs back out into the street. "I have the passkey!" She holds the ring above her head like a trophy. "And I've found the entrance!"

There's a sinking feeling in my stomach. I've been betrayed. Turk's been shot. And now I am about to die.

· XXXI ·

Suddenly, Times Square is alive with movement.

Armored men creep out of buildings and onto the streets like ants, crawling over bridges, lining up to penetrate and attack. Some of the men I recognize as my father's supporters, or George Foster's; others must be part of the city's police force, which my father and George have in their back pockets.

There's no time to think. I just *do*.

I grab Turk by the armpits and drag him underneath the sign, which hangs diagonally and blocks us from view. My palms are sweaty, and he's heavier than I expected. His eyes are shut in pain.

I hear the sound of commands being hollered into the air, of dozens of feet approaching. It's stopped raining now, and the air is damp and hot. Any second, my father will be back with Hunter. There's only one thing I can do.

I let Turk down to the pavement, then grab the green globe. With my free hand, I reach across Turk's chest, pulling his arm so that his fingers touch the globe, too.

The ground beneath me liquefies.

My body begins to thrum as though drumbeats are reverberating through the ground, throbbing in my bones. There's a weird sensation like being squeezed through an ultrathin tube. I close my eyes.

We fall. . . .

And land on a dirty tiled floor. It used to be white, I think. Huge chunks are missing. Along the ceiling are colored circles like the ones outside the subway entrance. At one time, they must have pointed to specific trains.

Ahead of me is a network of tunnels that branch out in different directions. I seem to be on a platform of some sort: to my left are old stairways that lead down to tunnels full of water, lined with high catwalks like down at the Seaport. To my right is a wall covered in graffiti and old, unrecognizable ads. Ahead is darkness.

I look up and see that a few lights seem to be embedded in the walls. If they're anything like the ones down at the Seaport, they're likely motion sensitive. I need the light, but I don't want to leave Turk, and he's in no position to walk.

I kneel beside him and check his pulse—it's faint but there. Still, I know the wound will be fatal if he bleeds out before I can get him any help.

I bite the end of my sleeve and rip off a piece of my shirt, which I crumple into a ball and hold to Turk's wound, letting it sop up the blood. Overhead, the stomping of feet is heavy, as if there are a thousand men above us.

"Turk? Can you hear me?"

Nothing.

Then, for a second, his eyes flicker open. "Aria?" His voice is weak, but it's enough for me to believe there's a chance he'll make it.

"Turk? Are you okay?"

He tries to speak, but it only sounds like gargling. "There," he manages to get out eventually. He can't lift his arm but raises one of his fingers: up ahead, there's a bright red disc the size of an eyeball on the wall. I would have walked right past it.

What does it do? There's really no time to waste wondering. I rush over to it: a button of some sort. It sticks at first, but I apply some pressure. I hear a click.

And then the wind is knocked out of me by a huge subaural pulse that I can feel in my muscles, in the pit of my stomach. It makes me dizzy and nauseous at the same time, and shakes loose dust from the ceiling and rafters.

After a few seconds, I can breathe again. I have no idea what just happened.

"Come on," I say, doubling back to Turk and lifting him up, careful to avoid his wound. With his back against my chest, I drag him step by step. Tiny amber-colored lights in the walls turn on as we move, and I can see there are six fat pillars in front of me: three on either side, lining the platform. They're each more than twice my size and crumbling with age, but they could provide cover.

"What *was* that?" I ask Turk once I get him behind the first pillar.

From here, I can see that there's a tiny alcove off the platform, and I drag him inside. It smells mustier here, and the ground is caked with dirt. I lean him against a wall, then sit down next to him, checking his wound again and pressing the now-bloodied cloth more firmly against his chest.

His eyes are open, and his breathing seems normal. More normal, at least. "An emergency beacon," he says. It takes him longer than usual to get the words out, but they come. "You can't be a . . . mystic and not f-feel it. Doesn't matter wh-where you are . . . you f-feel it in your v-very soul."

So it was an alarm? Good boy, Turk. Now maybe we have a chance of surviving.

"Shhh." I wipe sweat from his forehead. "Just rest."

I'm blotting his cheeks and neck with another strip of fabric from my shirt when we hear what can only be my father's troops falling through the ceiling and onto the platform. Elissa must have opened the entrance with the ring Turk made for me.

There's a symphony of thuds and metallic sounds: the unlocking of bullet chambers, the funneling in of new ammunition, banging, beating, snapping, ticking, as weapons are drawn and held and battle is prepared.

And then—voices. "Come on, boys!" someone yells. The troops from above begin marching forward, hulking bodies with guns ready in their hands. "Keep your eyes out for these tricky freaks. Shoot anything that moves."

I glance out of the alcove, farther into the tunnels. Where are the mystics? Didn't they hear the alarm? Why isn't anyone coming to fight?

"Stay here, Turk," I say, leaving him shrouded in the darkness of the alcove. He tries to hold me back, but he isn't strong enough.

I creep forward slowly, just a few inches, still shielded by the column, and peer out.

Dozens upon dozens of uniformed men are marching into the tunnels, the tiny wall lights brightening as they advance. Some of them are in uniform, some in civilian clothes, but in one way they're the same: they all carry weapons.

"No mystic leaves alive!" screams a husky voice. It sounds like George Foster's.

I look for my father, for the Fosters, Hunter—anyone I recognize. But all I see is face after nameless face, brainwashed denizens of New York who are devoted to my family.

For a moment, I pity them. Then I think of Hunter. Of Davida. Of what my parents did to me, stole from me.

The pity washes away, leaving something else in its wake: fury.

I breathe evenly, trying to ready myself for what's about to happen. It's only a few seconds before I see the first jolt of green light.

Mystics rush out of the opposite end of the tunnel. They're skinnier than the men from the Aeries, less solid, with the wiry arms and spindly legs that come from being malnourished and living in the Depths. My heart sinks: the rebels are outgunned and outnumbered.

But then they start to glow.

I've only ever seen Turk, Hunter, Davida, and Lyrica use their powers, but that's nothing compared to what I see now. What's taking place in here is like nothing I've ever experienced or even dreamed of.

Mystics flood the platform, every inch of exposed skin turned green.

Rays extend from their hands in all different sizes—thick, thin, short, long—so many that from where I'm standing, the beams look like a patchwork of color, knitted together over the platform in some kind of electric blanket.

The light from the rays is bright, too bright. This must be what it's like to stand on the surface of the sun, the world around you burned away in a smothering glare that you see even with your eyes closed, that you feel scorching your flesh and the bones beneath it and the walls of every cell that makes up your being. And you know that there's no resisting, that you're just going to wither and turn into a pile of ash blown on the wind.

I feel a wave of relief. They heard the alarm. The rebels have come.

"Attack!"

Everything happens quickly, like a movie on fast-forward. I can hear the steady sounds of machine guns being fired, bullets ricocheting off the tunnel walls.

I shield my eyes and squint out: the mystics look like they're on fire. A man rushes past me, his entire body aglow, followed by two women who are swinging lassos of coruscating light from their fingertips.

Almost immediately, the ground is decorated with fallen, decimated human bodies.

Ahead, underneath a faded red circle with the letter *L* in the center, a young female mystic with wild curly hair holds both hands out in front of her like she's surrendering.

Only she's not.

The air around her hands begins to swirl, gathering dust and turning into a miniature tornado that she raises from the ground.

Two of the city policemen look at each other. "What the—"

But the tornado swallows their voices. It grows larger and larger, circling them so violently that I can't even see what's happening. Then there are sickening sounds: a whoop and a whack as body parts fly everywhere.

Hands. Feet. Arms. Legs.

And heads.

All at once, the tornado disappears, having completely blasted the men apart. Someone's finger lands near my feet, the white bone completely fleshless.

I look away so I don't vomit.

That's when I see a mystic with shaggy hair and a well-trimmed beard extend energy from his fingertips. He blends the rays together until he fashions a kind of sword, cutting through the air and slicing one of my father's men in half.

Behind my father's man, another man is raising his rifle to shoot—and I'm unable to shout out, unable to do anything but gasp.

The mystic turns just in time, and he uses the light-sword to slice off the man's hand.

It falls to the floor, fingers still gripping the gun.

The man screams in agony, but then the bearded mystic brings his sword around and slices off the man's head, too.

Farther down the tunnel, two mystics pull each other close, pressing the sides of their chests together, arms behind each other's backs. They each extend their free arm and let loose ten rays of green energy, one from each fingertip, each as bright—and deadly—as lightning.

"Shoot!" one of my father's men shouts to his friend. "Take them both down!"

One of the mystics gets shot in the leg.

I see her knee buckle, but then she nods at the other mystic.

And they begin to spin.

The joined rays of light slice through the men, dicing their bodies. The flesh sizzles as it burns, sending blinding-white smoke into the air. Then smoke and blood are everywhere, and the body pieces cascade to the ground.

Once the mystics have made a complete circle, they stop. Their rays retract into their fingers. The mystic who was shot touches her leg, heals herself, and they're ready to go again.

The acrid smell of burning bodies and cordite from the gunfire is everywhere. The air is thick with the powder of pulverized tiles, and the metallic stench of blood makes it difficult to breathe.

I feel like I'm choking.

I rush back into the alcove. I take a huge gulp of air. Turk is still against the wall, his eyes glassy but open. He's breathing, at least.

Suddenly, I'm thrown back against the wall of the alcove as a mystic emerges through it. He looks at me, surprised. He has a mustache and seems around my father's age.

"Didn't think I'd find a girl standing here," he says, catching his breath.

"I suppose you can walk through walls?"

He nods. "Well, back to it," he says after a moment or two, and hurtles through the tunnel wall before me, disappearing in a cloud of smoke and green light.

The alcove is filling up with noxious air. I don't think we'll be able to breathe in here in a few minutes.

I glance at Turk, who's smiling. "Are you okay to walk?"

"I think so," he says. Color seems to have come back to his cheeks, though sweat is dripping down them onto the ground. "I heal pretty quickly."

"Let's get out of here, then."

I grab his hand and help him up, and together we creep out of the alcove.

The battle on the platform is still raging and spreading into distant tunnels. As far as I can see, the tunnel is filled with zigzags of green light refracting off the walls and the earsplitting sound of machine-gun fire.

Ahead of me to the right is a flight of stairs leading down into the flooded subways. It's the only place I can think of to hide.

Turk and I stumble down the stairs. At first, only our feet are wet.

Then our ankles.

And then the water is up to our thighs.

"Wait," I say, looking at the wall. There must be a ladder to a catwalk here somewhere. It's just too dark to see it.

Somewhere behind us, a mystic wields his energy just long enough for the green light to let us see—there! A steel ladder is only a few sloshes away.

I push Turk ahead of me, making him climb first. Then I pull myself up the rungs, thankful to be out of the water, shaking off my clothes once we're on the catwalk.

"Which way?" I ask Turk.

He points, and we walk. It's silent at first, but after two or three minutes, I begin to hear voices. Shouts, actually. Which means the battle has spread all the way down here.

The catwalk descends and drops us off in an abandoned subway station, like the one Hunter lives in, but there are no subway cars here. An entire dirt wall has been blown out, creating a new tunnel.

Up ahead, I see more flashes of green light—and the screaming is growing louder.

"Maybe you should wait here," I say, grabbing Turk's arm. "You're wounded."

He shrugs me off. "Not too wounded to fight." He exposes his chest so I can see that he's stopped bleeding. "Let's go, Aria."

We step into the tunnel and I realize that it functions as a bridge, connecting to another tunnel that runs parallel to this one.

I scramble forward. On the other side, where I couldn't see before, mystics line the catwalks, shooting off rays of energy, even hanging off the ladders. Policemen yell in agony as the rays strike them, burning them to cinders in tiny bursts of light and heat.

There's much less flooding here. We must be on higher ground: there's only a murky brown layer of water that stops midway up people's legs.

Then I hear breathing—breathing that isn't Turk's or my own. We're not alone.

"Hello?" I say. "Who's there?"

A figure steps out of the shadows. I recognize her immediately: dark hair brushed behind her ears, a stoic, handsome face—and familiar blue eyes.

Violet Brooks.

Turk steps closer to me.

"Aria Rose?" she asks. "Is that you?"

I nod.

"What are you doing here?"

The sight of her nearly makes me cry. Some of the pale, sickly concealer she wears has sweated off and is running in streaks down her cheeks and neck and arms, exposing the healthy skin underneath. She looks so much like Hunter—even her voice has a similar cadence. "I—Hunter—he—"

"It's too dangerous for her here," she says, turning to Turk. "Protect her. Get her out of here alive."

Turk nods. "I will, Violet."

She kisses me on the forehead, letting her lips linger for a moment. Then she turns and rushes off, out of the passageway and into the tunnel.

She immediately obliterates three of my father's men, letting loose beams from her fingertips that grab them in bright embraces. The skin and muscle from their bodies seem to melt right off their bones, leaving exposed skeletons that clatter as they hit the ground.

Once they're gone, I finally see Elissa.

She's standing knee-deep in the tunnel water with a machine

gun, shooting at mystics left and right, her face twisted in concentration. At first she doesn't see Violet, and Violet uses this to her advantage—she takes off running.

As her body gathers speed, her skin begins to glow: light green to dark green to a color so electrifying I can't look directly at her.

I shield my eyes and watch as Violet runs *up* the wall of the tunnel.

She skips over the catwalk and onto the ceiling, flips in midair, then drops like a cannonball directly onto Elissa.

Bam!

Water splashes up as their bodies collide, but Violet wraps her arms around Elissa's neck and hangs on, strangling her as Elissa struggles and stumbles and blindly shoots off bullets from her machine gun. Rounds chatter into the roof and walls and water until Elissa drops the gun and tugs at Violet's arms.

With a scream, Elissa throws Violet off and into the shallow water on the tunnel floor. Before Violet can get up, Elissa swivels around, takes a pistol out of her belt, and shoots Violet right in the chest.

"No!" I hear someone scream. Someone I know. Someone I love.

Hunter catapults himself from off one of the catwalks. How did he get away from my father and George Foster? He extends his arms, then blasts Elissa with a beam of energy that stupefies her.

She topples over.

"Mom!" Hunter says, rushing to Violet. He pulls her out of the water as if she's weightless, searching frantically for somewhere to drag her.

"Hunter!" Turk calls. "Over here!"

Hunter lifts his head, and our eyes meet. His face brightens immediately, even though it is beaten up beyond belief. He begins to pull his mother over to where Turk and I are hiding.

And then Elissa gets up.

It seems to happen in slow motion: the way she raises her arm, her smile a crooked gash in her pale face. The way a green light seems to coalesce around her hand—she must be using whatever energy she has left—the way she swings her arm around behind her like a pitcher winding up.

Hunter is bent over his mother and can't see, doesn't realize what is about to happen.

Before I know what I'm doing, I'm running. I'm only fifteen feet away, but it feels like a huge gulf.

My right foot lands, and I see Elissa's arm begin to come forward, see anger light her face.

My left foot strikes the ground and then I'm in the air, throwing myself at the boy I love.

He lets out an "Oof!" when I plow into him, and we go down in a mess of limbs as a gunshot echoes through the tunnel.

"Hunter," I whisper, running my hands across his chest, making sure he's all right. His eyes are closed, but I don't see any wounds or fresh blood. He must've passed out. I kiss him on the lips, knowing he's okay, and then I stupidly stand up.

And I feel my entire body ignite.

Green energy explodes all around me, blinding me. I am on fire.

A memory: the *real* first time Hunter kissed me. His lips on mine in the Great Lawn. At first it was a sharp buzz that made my tongue taste like metal and my entire body tingle with electricity. Even the tiny hairs on my arms stood up. But then it was something more. It was warmth—not heat, but warmth, flowing through my arteries like lava, calming me. It made every color seem new, as if before then I'd only been seeing the world in sepia tones. My vision was clear, my senses attuned to everything around me: birds chirping in the trees, crickets rubbing their legs together in tiny symphonies, even the way things *smelled*—the salt water, the moss on the trees, the muddied scents of earth. For the first time, I felt alive with promise. And that promise felt like the reason for being alive.

Finally, I knew why I was here, what I was supposed to do: love Hunter. That knowing filled me with so much joy and thankfulness that I'd met someone to love. Someone who wanted to love me, too. Together, we would offer something to the world that was more than just our individual selves. Together we would be stronger; we would make everything around us better.

And that's what life is for: to love, to create, to blend, to harmonize.

And to die.

I fall into a silky, pitch-black nothingness.

XXXII

And then I am awake, and it's like nothing has changed. The battle still rages around me. I can hear it. I don't want to have to see it.

I am facedown on the ground, surrounded by water and earth; I can even taste the sandy, wet dirt in my mouth. People are rushing around me, and I suppose they imagine me dead.

I *should* be dead.

I was hit square in the chest by a bolt of mystic energy. The sensation was like being touched by a mystic, multiplied by infinity:

The bright ray arrowing directly into my chest.

Burrowing inside me.

Flooding me with a galvanizing current.

Lighting me up, the pores of my skin expanding as they were illuminated, burnished with a lethal green glow.

I'm not dead . . . am I?

I hear voices shouting: "Taylor, watch your back!" "Elissa! Elissa!" "Oh God, Derek, can you hear me?" "Pull, pull, pull!" I open my eyes a crack—boots move around me, stepping over me. It smells like barbecue, and I know too well what that charred scent is from.

Slowly, I angle my head so that my mouth is out of the water and take a deep breath. I wait to see if anything hurts. My arms are sore, but otherwise, I'm fine. I open my eyes and recognize the silver buckle on a pair of shoes a foot away.

Thomas. Standing over me.

I tilt my neck and see Thomas fighting. With Hunter.

Hunter has his arm out and is using his energy to create a barrier to deflect the bullets Thomas is shooting at him. Tiny rays jet from his fingertips to form a shield of translucent energy, which he wields like an ancient knight.

"Come on, Foster!" Hunter is shouting. His hair is wild and his cheeks are flushed red. "That all you got?"

Thomas ignores his taunts, watching as his bullets continue to bounce off the shield, ricocheting and hitting people behind me or lodging in the tunnel walls. "Too much of a pansy to fight like a man?" Thomas hollers. "Oh, that's right—you're not *actually* a man, are you?"

Hunter grows angry—I can see his features squeeze together, his forehead tighten. Thankfully, he keeps up his shield. *Come on, Hunter,* I think. *Don't let him get to you.*

Frustrated, Thomas lets loose another series of bullets.

Hunter flexes his fingertips and the shield turns a brighter shade of green. This time, inches before the bullets hit, they turn soft and melt into the water on the ground.

Thomas shakes his head. "What the—"

"Too hot for you, Foster?" Hunter calls, smirking.

They keep at this for a few more minutes, circling, weaving

through other mystics and men—they clearly have eyes only for each other.

"Come on!" Thomas screams.

Hunter leaps over a fallen body, and I watch as his shield begins to flicker.

The green light pulses for a moment, then disappears entirely.

Hunter has a shocked expression on his face. Thomas uses the opportunity to shoot at him, but his gun's magazine is empty. He calmly ejects it and inserts a fresh one.

Hunter closes his eyes and holds out his hands and the shield appears again, surrounding him like a bubble. But then it fades.

He's getting tired. He won't be able to keep this up for long.

"Don't have much left, do you?" Thomas teases, his lips curled in a smirk.

Hunter's shield disappears again; he tries to revive it but can't. Thomas laughs heartily.

In the distance, I can see my brother fighting a female mystic. I can't see my father, but I don't imagine he'd get into the heart of a battle.

I try not to call attention to the fact that I'm still alive until I can figure out my next move.

"Nowhere to run now, mystic," I hear Thomas say to Hunter, whose face is awash with fear. Thomas has him up against a wall, his gun pointed at Hunter's forehead. My beautiful, courageous Hunter—I have to save him. I have to help him.

I glance next to me, where one of my father's men has fallen, eyes closed, dead. In his grasp is a machine gun. If I can do this right, I'll have a moment—one moment—to grab the gun and fire, taking Thomas down. If he sees me first, he'll shoot me. And then he'll shoot Hunter.

I can't fail.

I take a breath, mentally preparing for what I have to do.

One, two, three, I count in my head. Then I'm off.

I grab the neck of the machine gun, prying it from the dead man's hands. The weapon comes to me easily, as though I'm supposed to be holding it.

Then I jump up, pointing the barrel of the gun at Thomas's back. I don't want to kill him, but I have to. He's certainly not going to show any pity—if I wait any longer, I'll lose Hunter.

"Stop!" I scream. Confused, Thomas turns around to see me. He opens his mouth to speak, but before he can, I close my eyes and pull the trigger.

The sound is deafening.

I don't let go until the kickback from the weapon makes me drop it. Water soaks my hair and face, but Thomas has fallen beside me, his eyes open in surprise.

Suddenly, the earth around me begins to shift.

"Aria," Hunter says. His face is covered in dirt and sweat, but he's never looked more beautiful to me. "We've gotta get out of here. They're setting off a bomb."

I spit out murky brown water. "Who?"

"Your father's men—I heard him talking about it. Come on."

Hunter grabs my arm, and I'm able to bring myself to my feet.

My eyes land on Patrick Benedict, who is soaked with blood and gore, a gun strapped to his chest. He is farther down the tunnel, where the ground has yet to be flooded, his feet on the bottom rung of a ladder.

He leans down and places both of his hands on the ground.

Immediately, the dirt goes soft, like quicksand, and begins to boil. His touch causes it to stir and flow, emanating a soft yellow glow.

A dozen or so of my father's men plunge into the liquefied ground up to their waists. They scream in shock. When Benedict withdraws his hands, the ground goes solid again.

Their screams end abruptly.

I realize it's because they're dead.

He looks at me triumphantly. Then I see Elissa come up from behind.

She points her gun.

And shoots.

The bullet hits Benedict in the back of the head, and he falls off the ladder, plummeting to the ground.

Water is spilling out a side tunnel now, washing over the bodies, and Benedict gets swept away and vanishes beneath the cloudy currents.

Then there's an incredible blast.

The ground trembles.

Tunnel walls begin to fold in on themselves.

The catwalks twist and bend, screeching as they snap. Ladders drop into the water. Chunks of the ceiling begin to fall like deadly rain.

Everyone is screaming. Shouting.

"Come on," Hunter says to me. Turk is there, too.

"But Benedict—"

Hunter shakes his head. "We have to go, Aria. Now."

He pulls me back into the passageway and we head toward the platform where we came in. The catwalks are no longer useable, so we slosh through the water, trying to reach safety before the underground fills and collapses completely.

There are no winners here.

I spit water from my mouth, wipe it from my eyes.

Violet Brooks—the mystic hope—is dead.

Hunter grabs my hand, pulls me up the flight of stairs onto the platform.

Patrick Benedict is gone.

The ground is covered with bodies. For a moment I fear I'll be swept away. Hunter and Turk find my arms.

I killed Thomas.

I close my eyes, letting the crowd carry me away.

The streets are full of sirens. Before I can get my bearings, Hunter pulls me onto a side street, out of sight; we stand underneath a dark awning, trying to make sense of everything that's happened, while Turk helps tend to a group of injured mystics.

What's left of my clothing is soaked, and Hunter's skin is cold and clammy. He rests his head against mine, taking me into his arms and trying to warm me.

"The secret tunnels," I manage to say. "They're ruined."

"Shhh," Hunter tells me, "don't worry. Aria, we're alive." He presses his lips to my ears. "You and me. Together. Nothing else matters right now."

I fall silent, listening to the sound of our breathing. The air is hot, but it's still a welcome change from the misery of the tunnels. I feel my locket against my chest and think of everything Hunter and I have been through. He's right—the backlash of what just happened is something we'll have to deal with for the rest of our lives.

I pull Hunter's face to mine. Even though he tastes of blood and tears and sweat, I don't want him to stop kissing me. And then I start crying—because he's here. With me. After all this, even with what we've fought for in jeopardy, we still have each other.

It's raining again, and the falling drops mix with my tears until I can't tell one from the other. I may not have my family, but I have my memories.

And then I feel my knees go weak. "Hunter," I gasp as I feel a shooting pain in my side. He pries his lips from mine, staring at me with a look of pure concern.

"Aria?" he says softly, scared.

"I love you," I tell him.

Hunter sweeps me into his arms just as the world seems to close around me.

· EPILOGUE ·

I wake in a world swathed in white.

But that's just the sunlight on the white walls and the sheets and the bleached tile floor. A plastic bag filled with liquid hangs from a stainless steel hook; a tube runs from it into my arm, secured with a piece of clear tape.

To my right is a set of windows, and below the windows is a chair. In one of them is Hunter.

He's asleep, his head tilted back and sideways. He looks tired and yet still so gorgeous despite his injuries: his bottom lip is swollen, the bruises beneath his eyes green and purple. The slash across his forehead has begun to fade. Otherwise, he seems fine, dressed in a clean T-shirt and jeans.

I lie there for a few minutes, watching him. He must sense that he's being stared at, because his eyes flutter open. He yawns and stretches his arms toward the ceiling.

Then he smiles.

"You're awake." He rises from the chair and comes to my side. Gently, he takes my hand in his.

"Where are we?" I ask.

"We're upstate. Outside the city. Turk and I smuggled you here three days ago."

"Three days?" I repeat. The last thing I remember is coming out of the tunnel, kissing Hunter, then . . . nothing.

"You were hit by a beam of mystic energy," Hunter tells me. "It should have killed you—and would have—if not for this." He reaches over to a table beside the bed. Then he holds out the locket in his palm, tapping the silver heart with one finger. "Lucky for you, it's a capture locket, and it caught the beam and saved your life."

It's tarnished now. Black. But I don't mind. So much has come to be because of this locket. It's so small, and yet in every way that matters, I'm here because of it.

"Having all that energy so close to your heart, well . . . it took a toll on your body," he says. "You're going to be all right, though."

"What about everyone else?" I ask, remembering things I saw. "I thought Benedict—"

"He's dead," Hunter says softly.

"Elissa?"

Hunter shakes his head. "She made it out."

I think about how many others must have died, both mystics and humans. Thomas, who I shot. I don't even realize I'm crying until Hunter rubs my hand. "This is a war for our freedom, Aria. It comes at a high price."

"Your mother . . ." I say tentatively.

Hunter clenches his jaw. "She's dead, too."

"Oh, Hunter," I say, sitting up and pulling him into a hug. "I'm so sorry."

He lets me hug him for a moment, then pulls away. The news of his mother makes me think of my own mother, my own family, and wonder if they are alive. "Now that you're up and I know you're okay, I have to go back."

"To Manhattan?"

He nods. "It's up to me now to carry on the Brooks legacy. I have to take my mother's place. No matter what happens now—whether the election still takes place, whether your family uses the explosion in Times Square to clamp down on the mystics even more—people are counting on me."

"I know," I say. "But why does it have to be you?"

"Aria," Hunter says in a soothing voice. "I don't want to upset you. I love you. But this is my duty. You understand, don't you? It doesn't mean we have to be apart forever." He grasps my hand. "Just for now."

I look away from him, at the IV and its slow *drip, drip, drip.*

"No," I say at last. "You're going to need help. I should come back to Manhattan with you and support you—publicly."

Even though he tries to hide it, a tiny smile breaks out on Hunter's face.

"Not a bad idea."

"I'll expose the sham of my relationship with Thomas," I say, figuring it all out in my head. "I'll go on TV and tell everyone what my parents did, and why we shouldn't let them remain in power." I think of the engagement ring still on my dresser and what it stands for. "I'll expose all their evildoings."

"I appreciate the offer," Hunter tells me, running a finger down my cheek, "but the risks are too great. What if you got hurt? I couldn't live with myself."

"This is what I was meant to do," I say, and for the first time, it seems true. I've never known what I wanted to do with my life—I never really had to decide. But now I know.

With Hunter by my side, I will fix things. Heal the wounds my family has inflicted. Fight for love and truth and freedom.

My father was right about one thing. Manhattan is my city.

•ACKNOWLEDGMENTS•

Thank you:

To everyone at Random House Children's Books, especially Françoise Bui, for her fierce insight and support, Colleen Fellingham, Kenny Holcomb, and the incomparable Beverly Horowitz.

To my parents, Elizabeth and Steven Malawer, my family, and my friends, especially Blair Bodine—who encouraged this novel when it was just an idea on a train to Boston—Kate Berthold, Julia Alexander, Anna Posner, Nic Cory, and my sister, Abby, who has always been my biggest fan. Special thanks to Ruth Katcher, Paul Wright, Dan Kessler, and Bronwen Durocher for their early reads and thoughtful comments. To Stephanie Elliott for seeing a spark in the darkness, and to Christopher Stengel for his design ingenuity.

To Michael Stearns, for being a tireless thinker, a brilliant teacher, and a wonderful friend. Your sense of story and language brought *Mystic City* to life. This book simply would not exist without you.

And lastly to Josh Pultz, who is—above all—a true peach.

About the Author

Theo Lawrence was born in 1984 and is a graduate of Columbia University and the Juilliard School. A Presidential Scholar in the Arts for Voice, he has performed at Carnegie Hall and the Kennedy Center as well as Off-Broadway. He is pursuing a master's degree in literature at Fordham University and lives on Manhattan's Upper West Side. His apartment is full of pictures of dachshunds.

Welcome to the roaring twenties . . .
where anything goes.

'Rich and captivating. The dishiest new series I've read all year.' Lauren Kate, *New York Times* bestselling author of *Fallen*

Available now.

Vixen: 978 0 552 56504 2
Ingenue: 978 0 552 56505 9
Diva: 978 0 552 56506 6

Have you ever FALLEN in love?

978 0 552 56173 0

978 0 552 56180 8

978 0 552 56179 2

978 0 552 56181 5

Discover the series the whole world is talking about.
by LAUREN KATE